The
Green Man's
Challenge

The Green Man's Challenge
Juliet E. McKenna

WIZARD'S TOWER

Wizard's Tower Press

Trowbridge, England

The Green Man's Challenge

First edition, published in the UK September 2021
by Wizard's Tower Press

Paperback ISBN: 978-1-913892-22-7

Cover illustration and design by Ben Baldwin
Editing by Toby Selwyn
Design by Cheryl Morgan

http://wizardstowerpress.com/
http://www.julietemckenna.com/

Contents

Praise for the Green Man Series	8
Author's Note	12
Chapter One	13
Chapter Two	25
Chapter Three	35
Chapter Four	49
Chapter Five	64
Chapter Six	76
Chapter Seven	86
Chapter Eight	97
Chapter Nine	107
Chapter Ten	115
Chapter Eleven	128
Chapter Twelve	143
Chapter Thirteen	154
Chapter Fourteen	169
Chapter Fifteen	180
Chapter Sixteen	193
Chapter Seventeen	206
Chapter Eighteen	221
Chapter Nineteen	231
Chapter Twenty	242
Chapter Twenty-One	255
Chapter Twenty-Two	269
Chapter Twenty-Three	284
Chapter Twenty-Four	296

Chapter Twenty-Five 309
Chapter Twenty-Six 323
Luck Is Where You Find It 332
Acknowledgements 369
About the Author 370

JULIET E. MCKENNA

For Cheryl

Praise for the Green Man Series

Praise for The Green Man's Heir

Finalist for The Robert Holdstock Award for Best Fantasy Novel, the British Fantasy Awards 2019

"... any way you look at it, the book is a delight from start to finish. [...] It's one of my favorite books so far this year." — Charles de Lint in *Fantasy and Science Fiction*

"I read this last night and thoroughly enjoyed it, more please!" — Garth Nix on Twitter

"I really enjoyed this novel!" — Kate Elliott on Twitter

"Juliet McKenna captures the nuances of life as a stranger in a small town in much the same way as Paul Cornell does in his splendid Lychford series, with the local gossips, the hard-pressed police, the rampaging boggarts and rural legends come to disturbing life. Thoroughly enjoyable; a UK fantasy author branching out (oh god, sorry for the inadvertent and terrible pun!) and clearly having a great time doing it. Highly recommended." — Joanne Hall

"So far up my street it could be my house." — K.J. Charles on Goodreads

JULIET E. MCKENNA

"*The Green Man's Heir* is a thoroughly engaging, at times almost impossible to put down, tale which, despite besides its titular character, is peopled with an impressive array of interesting and intriguing women." — *The Monday Review*

"After a stumbling start, I found myself unable to put down *The Green Man's Heir*. If you're looking for a book to read on your summer holiday, then this is it." — Charlotte Bond via The British Fantasy Society

The Green Man's Heir is a straightforward fantasy story, with a lively pace and characters who wonderfully come alive. It starts as *Midsomer Murders* set in the Peak District but with added supernatural element and turns out to be the book you won't put down because you enjoy it too much." — *The Middle Shelf*

"I hope this turns into a series. I'd love to read more about Daniel's adventures." — N.W. Moors in *The Antrim Cycle*

"And she has absolutely nailed it. This is a complete and utter joy." — S.J. Higbee in *Brainfluff*

"I'm certainly on board for reading more such novels." — Paul Weimer in *Skiffy and Fanty*

"Brilliant concept, compellingly told" — Virginia Bergin on Twitter

Praise for The Green Man's Foe

Finalist for Best Novel,
the British Science Fiction Awards 2020

"I loved *The Green Man's Heir*, and while I expected to thoroughly enjoy *The Green Man's Foe*, I did not expect it to be even more satisfying than its forerunner. Which was foolish of me, I admit – I should know by now that McKenna is more capable of outdoing her previous tales in a series." – *The Monday Review*

"If you've read the first book then I'm pretty confident you're going to love this one, and if you haven't read the first one then you need to remedy that straight away." – Naomi Scott

"This is one of my outstanding reads of the year." – S.J. Higbee in *Brainfluff*

"*The Green Man's Foe* is a great addition to what is becoming a great series. I was entirely caught up in it for a couple of days. It is a must read if you have enjoyed the first one, and a great reason to start on this series if you have missed it." – *The Middle Shelf*

"*The Green Man's Foe* is a tasty serve of mystery and myth that has done quite enough to cement this series as one I'll be reading and cheerleading for from now on." – Imyril at *There's Always Room for One More*.

JULIET E. MCKENNA

Praise for The Green Man's Silence

"These Green Man books provide a wonderful blend of British folklore and ordinary people trying their best to make the world — or at least their corner of it — a better place. The characters are likeable, while the mythical creatures are earthy, dangerous, and full of that Sense of Wonder that makes fantasy such a pleasure to read. Recommended." — Charles de Lint, *Fantasy & Science Fiction*

"Highly recommended for fantasy fans who are looking for well-written fae adventures with a difference." — S J Higbee in *Brainfluff*

"This is undoubtedly one of the best books I've read this year and I thoroughly enjoyed it. I can hardly wait for the next book!" — *The Monday Review*

Author's Note

A bonus story follows this novel. As the writer, I had questions about what would happen at Blithehurst when Dan was called away. I soon had the answers, but found no place for them in the story he has to tell. Since I was pretty sure established readers would be wondering the same things as me, I decided to let Eleanor tell this particular tale. I hope you enjoy 'Luck Is Where You Find It'.

Juliet E. McKenna, Oxford 2021

Chapter One

B eing alone isn't the same as being lonely. I've always been a loner and I've never had a problem with that. I've been told that's because I'm an only child. Maybe it's because I grew up in a cottage more than a mile outside the village where I went to primary school. Whenever people have been determined to find reasons, I've nodded as if I agree. It's not as if I could tell them the truth.

Besides, perhaps these things are part of it. It's not as if it mattered, and nodding usually satisfied the secondary school teachers who needed to tick Daniel Mackmain off their careers guidance list. The same went for concerned tutors before I dropped out of university, or girlfriends hoping for something longer term than good sex and casual fun. As far as I was concerned, all anyone needed to know was I'm generally happy enough on my own.

So you'd think I'd have no problem with spending six months as the only resident member of staff at Blithehurst House. This is the privately owned country house where I've lived and worked for the last couple of years. I'm partly the estate carpenter, and partly working to make the woods here into an asset that earns some decent income. I also turn out woodwork from ornaments to tables to put them on. Those sell very nicely in the garden centre and gift shop that used to be the stables.

They used to, anyway. The garden centre might have opened up again over the summer, and the cafe was doing the best it could, but takings were way, way down. There was no point in me adding to the unsold stock while the manor and gardens were still closed to the public on account of the pandemic. I'd been wondering what I was going to do with the time I had on my hands. Doing the bits of maintenance that cropped up and looking after the coppicing I'd started didn't exactly fill my days. Then Eleanor, my boss, asked me to move into the main house instead of staying in the estate cottage I rent in the woods.

Eleanor's the Beauchene – pronounced 'Beechen' – who runs the family business these days. She explained the insurance company were insisting someone was living on the premises. She was desperate to stay in Durham, where she was deep in research for her PhD, as well as juggling crisis budgets, shut-down cash-flow projections and seeing how many jobs she might save at Blithehurst with government furlough money.

I didn't envy her those headaches, and moving into the big house was little enough for me to do to help. I could see the insurance company's point. There are enough small antiques, old silver candlesticks and other valuables in the display cases to make a burglary worthwhile. Blithehurst is pretty isolated, out in the countryside where Staffordshire edges into Derbyshire. At the same time, it's close enough to the motorways to offer a decent chance of escape for thieving bastards coming up from Brum, or down from Manchester.

Crooks will travel a fair distance for the prospect of a decent return. Before I came here, I'd worked on building sites stripped of copper pipe and brand-new boilers by gangs travelling two hours each way. That's what Martin the foreman said anyway, when he told us what the cops had told him, when the gang was caught unexpectedly fast thanks to a tip-off from a vengeful ex-wife.

Moving into the manor wasn't a hardship. I was staying in one of the comfortable guest rooms, with the conveniences of Wi-Fi and central heating as the autumn grew damper and colder. I didn't have either of those in the cottage, so I shouldn't be complaining. I had no reason to be concerned about the cottage itself. I don't own anything worth stealing, even now I have a place to call home. I keep pretty much all my tools in my workshop, in the converted dairy yard. That's close enough to the main house to be on the same alarm system. The garden centre and cafe out by the car park have their own circuit, but I'd get an alert here if anyone broke in, and so would the local police. There hadn't been a hint of any trouble so far, and I wasn't expecting that to change.

So I should be sleeping as soundly as I'd done all my life, wherever I happened to be. Not a chance. Not these days. Those reasons why I was fine on my own were a load of bollocks now. A whole lot of things had changed, and I was getting more and more pissed off.

Now I understood why the best way to make somebody want something is to tell them they can't have it. I had people I wanted to spend time with, and there were a whole load of reasons why I couldn't. Tonight, and not for the first time, I'd gone to bed knackered, to find myself awake and staring at the ceiling well before dawn. The same tedious, pointless thoughts were chasing around in my head like hamsters on a sodding wheel.

I wasn't worried about getting hammered by the virus sweeping the country. I've only just turned thirty and my work keeps me physically fit. What bothered me was the chance of catching it and not realising because I didn't feel ill. If that happened and I went to see my dad, I could pass it on and that could kill him. He's fit and he's active, but he's pushing eighty years old, and we couldn't take any chances. Thankfully, he had friends locally who would get his shopping so he didn't have to risk the supermarket. We could still talk on the phone.

Yes, we could, but it wasn't the same. When you don't have many people in your life, the ones you have are important. Since I'd been based at Blithehurst, I'd got used to seeing my parents every month or so. It's an easy run down the motorways to the exit just past the Warwick services and on through the familiar lanes. I hadn't realised how much I had missed home while I'd been living much further away, in the north and in Scotland.

Then there was Fin: Finele Wicken on her driving licence. I had been starting to think we could have a longer-term future together when the first lockdown was declared. Since then we'd kept in touch by phone, but whatever the ever-changing rules said, we'd been wary of getting together. Fin has a whole load of family and she didn't want to risk getting sick in case one of her parents or sisters or cousins fell ill and she needed to go home to help out. Home as far as she's concerned is the Fens, east of the Wash, right on the other side of the country.

There were practical considerations as well. She lives near Bristol, and that's around three hours' drive away. More when the traffic's not on your side, and it usually isn't around Gloucester. My Land Rover was still off the road and I was currently driving an elderly Fabia that technically belonged to Eleanor Beauchene's mum. That's been fine for local errands, but the gears felt spongy to me and I wasn't particularly happy with the brakes, whatever Jake at the local garage said. I didn't want to take it on the motorway and have something drastic go wrong. That could be the last thing I'd know before some half-asleep lorry driver turned the old car into a roller skate.

Add to that, Fin and her sister Blanche have been working all hours trying to keep their business afloat. Projects that needed to consult a pair of freshwater ecologists had all but dried up. Ha ha, very funny. The puns come easy, but it was no laughing matter. They had rent to pay, and other bills, and it wasn't as if I could help out. I wasn't earning much from selling my woodwork, and who knew when that would change? Things could get worse instead of better if another full lockdown was announced.

I wasn't even sure Fin would accept a loan from me. I was certain she wouldn't take any money without a definite agreement to pay it back. She knew I was saving every spare penny I could to get my Landy running again. I knew I didn't want to put that sort of strain on our relationship.

So we'd agreed it was better to be safe than sorry, and best to stay apart until this weirdness was over. Except there was no way to know when that would be. People were talking about a second spike of virus cases now the winter was approaching. There was supposed to be a vaccine coming, but no one could say when that would be ready.

I hated all this uncertainty. I really hated it. I like to know what's happening. I like precision. I like to be in control of a situation. Measure twice, cut once. Get the job done right, first time, every time. If there's a problem, it's there to be tackled and I'll start looking for solutions. But there was nothing I could do about any of this, and I really fucking hated it. Lying there in the darkness, I'd gone through everything I'd read and heard on the news for the umpteenth time. Yet again, I'd come up with sod all by way of useful conclusions.

If I'd been in my own cottage, at least I could have said 'Oh bugger it' and got out of bed. I keep a few old hand tools there, and there are generally some oddments of wood that I've picked up walking around the estate. So I could do some carving to take my mind off everything. It's a whole lot harder to waste your time on problems you can do nothing about if you're focused on doing something constructive with your hands. Even if I already had a ready supply of ornaments and trinkets in the workshop for whenever the shop needed restocking... whenever that might be... wouldn't I just be wasting my time making any more?

Maybe, but sod it, my time was my own to waste. It wasn't as if I had a whole load of other things to do, besides check on the manor and the other buildings three times a day.

I decided that I'd bring back a couple of chisels and other bits and pieces when I went into the woods to check on the cottage tomorrow – no, later today. As soon as it got light, I'd make my first circuit, then I'd take a walk through the woods. I make sure to vary the time of my walk-rounds, just in case anyone might be keeping track.

I'd just beaten my pillow into a more comfortable shape and was trying to convince myself I would soon doze off when I heard a noise that made me stiffen, alert. A noise in itself wasn't so unusual. Blithehurst was built in the early days of Henry VIII's reign, and any house this old has its creaks and murmurs. This wasn't the sort of sound I was used to hearing here, though, and I didn't know what it was.

I sat up in bed and heard the noise again. It was more of a knock than a creak, or maybe a short rattle. Whatever it might be, it definitely wasn't my imagination. First things first. Where was the sound coming from? Downstairs, I decided. Okay, so it wasn't a bird or a squirrel or something else that had got into the attics. That was good news because stray wildlife can make a hell of a mess, and the last thing I wanted to be doing was repairing some damage to the roof as the autumn weather got worse. On the other hand, it was bad news because a routine problem like that would be quick and easy to deal with.

I got out of bed and dressed in the darkness quickly and quietly. I heard the noise again as I buckled my belt. I couldn't tell if it was coming from outside or if there was someone inside the house.

What was most likely? The windows were wired with sensors, so if one had been forced, or broken by accident, I'd be deafened by the alarm by now. So whoever – or whatever – was sniffing around must still be outside the house. It was my job to make sure they stayed there. I found my trainers and laced them up tight.

Moving to the bedroom window, I eased the curtain aside and peered out. There was nothing to see on the gravel approach at the front of the house. I couldn't hear any movement either. Of course, that didn't mean there wasn't someone or something too close to the front wall to be seen from this narrow window. I hadn't heard a vehicle, but that didn't mean much either. Getting a car this close to the house would mean taking bolt-cutters to several solidly locked gates. Better to do a recce on foot first, before taking the risk of being seen clearly up to no good by someone passing by. That might be unlikely, but taking chances gets crooks arrested.

I thought about switching the light on. If there were some chancers out there, come to see if the house looked easy to rob, that might be enough to put them off. On the other hand, it might get them ready for a fight. I'd read it wasn't only decent, law-abiding people getting more desperate as this crazy year went on. People working from home meant fewer domestic break-ins, and not every burglar could re-train in cybertheft.

I decided to leave the lights off and picked my phone up off my bedside table. I have far better than average night vision and I wanted to keep that advantage for as long as I could. I went out onto the landing that runs the width of the old house from the so-called King Charles bedroom away to my left and to the long gallery on my right.

I made my way through the morning room where long-ago Beauchene ladies did their sewing and headed down the wide carved-oak staircase. Enough light came through the unshuttered upper windows for me to see where I was going. The hard-wearing carpet protecting the polished wood from tourist feet meant I didn't make a sound as I reached the house's south-facing dining room on the ground floor.

Once I knew what I was dealing with, I could flick a light switch. Any burglars looking through a window could see who they'd be facing if they tried to break in. Come on, if you think you're hard enough. I'm six foot four and take XXL in most clothes. I've stuck with a number-one haircut since before I left school, and it's fair to say when I put my mind to it, I can look like an evil bastard ready to rip your arm off and beat you to death with the soggy end.

Not that I'd actually do that, or risk anything that even came close. I've learned the hard way, and more than once, that coppers don't give people who look like me the benefit of any doubt over 'reasonable force'. That's a shame, I thought wryly. Relieving my current frustrations by giving some thieving scum a well-deserved thumping might be therapeutic. Maybe that wasn't entirely a joke. Regardless, dealing with burglars should be as straightforward as evicting stray magpies from the loft. I had the alarm company's number on my phone, and they would send the police.

The thing was, though, there were other possibilities at Blithehurst. There was an equally good chance that whatever was making these noises was something the cops would never believe, even if they could see it. A boggart might be scraping at a window. Perhaps the black shuck I sometimes saw out in the woods had come to prowl around the house. Maybe that had scared the living shit out of a squirrel which was now frantically looking for somewhere to hide.

I didn't only get this job because I'm handy with a hammer and nails. The main reason why my dad lives in an isolated cottage, and why we keep ourselves to ourselves, is my mother is a dryad. She's the last of the centuries-old tree spirits who once tended the oak forests where we live. Those woodlands have long since shrunk to a remnant that was saved to be a local nature reserve. My dad's been a volunteer there for decades. That's how he met my mum. When he took early retirement from the engineering firm where he worked, he took over as the site warden.

My dryad blood means I can see boggarts, sprites, shucks and naiads as well as a whole load of other things that most people think are only found in folk tales. I know better, and so does Eleanor Beauchene, thanks to the local dryad who bore one of her ancestors a son. That was to stop a distant cousin inheriting the estate, which would have seriously inconvenienced the tree spirits who live here.

I'd come to Blithehurst after a naiad I'd done a favour for told me I'd find someone who understood living with a foot in both worlds. I found a hell of a lot more than that. Once we had saved the manor from a murderous threat that only the two of us would believe, Eleanor had asked me to stay on. She had definitely found life lonely, as the only one of her generation who could see dryads and the like. The greenwood blood in her family was running very thin after a couple of centuries.

I stood in the darkness at the bottom of the stairs and wondered what might be out there. I wasn't going to move until I had some idea where it was as well. Even a dryad's son's night sight wasn't much use to me now. These ground-floor windows had tall oak shutters that I closed at dusk every night. As well as giving the house added security, that meant the downstairs rooms were pitch black. They were also full of obstacles. If I tried to stay away from the china-filled display cabinets along the walls, I could walk into a table or chairs. The solid wooden furniture had been shrouded in dust sheets until we could open up for tourists again. I might trip over the trailing edge of some cloth and lose my balance. I didn't want to do that. The bigger we are, the harder we really do fall.

So I stood and waited. I didn't hear the noise again, but gradually I realised I could see a dim green light. It was barely bright enough to outline the archway in the wooden screen that separated the dining room from the half that had been turned into a sitting room, where the original Great Hall had been divided in the seventeenth century.

I'd seen that eerie light before. That wasn't necessarily reassuring. Still, now I was pretty sure I wouldn't be dealing with burglars tonight, or if I was, I wouldn't be doing it alone. Any crooks out there would get a whole lot more than they bargained for, as well as an interesting choice. They could tell the cops what happened and be tested for drugs to explain hallucinations. Or they could keep their mouths shut and hope the nightmares would eventually stop.

I found the torch setting on my phone and made my way safely past the mahogany dining table. When I reached the wooden screen, I saw the green radiance was coming from the corridor that led to the wing of the house to the west of the main entrance. I followed the glimmer, expecting it would take me to the library. That had been going to be the house's chapel until Henry VIII fell out with the pope. The Beauchenes at the time had still used the room for Catholic services, innocently pointing out the clearly pagan carvings and the bookshelves to any suspicious Protestant official checking up on them.

The drifting light slid straight past the library door. It led me along the corridor and past the kitchen towards the house's side entrance. The green radiance briefly outlined the outer door as it passed under and around it like smoke. The barest sheen lingered to tell me I was wanted on the other side.

I made a quick detour into the office that was the house-keeper's sitting room in Blithehurst's Victorian days. I punched in the code to unset the security system. I was pretty sure I knew who was waiting outside. That didn't mean I was necessarily safe, but no one who'd be answering an alarm could help me with that. There's a metal locker fixed to the wall by the control box to hold the estate keys, and I had my key to that on a chain on my belt. I opened the locker, took the key to the side door off its hook and braced myself as I went to open up.

I was right. The Green Man was out there, gazing up at the sky. Shadows hung around him and he wore a dark cloak that looked like woven tree bark wrapped around his broad shoulders. I switched off the torch on my phone and stepped out onto the gravel. It was later – or earlier – than I had realised. The sky was pale with pre-dawn light.

I've seen the Green Man from time to time ever since I was a boy. I hadn't thought very much about it as a kid. Having him around suited me. Since Mum knew someone was watching to see I didn't do anything lethally stupid, I could explore the local woods and fields, roaming as far as I liked. He was just one of those things my family didn't talk about to anyone but ourselves, like the glittering sprites only Mum and I could see. Like the way she could shift her appearance from looking like a goddess in a book of Greek myths to fitting in with the other parents at the school gate.

As I got older, I'd realised there was more to my relationship with this ancient and mysterious being. The Green Man started turning up in my dreams when I had a hard choice to make. I'd wake up knowing what I had to do, even if I didn't necessarily like it. If I needed another prompt, I'd catch sight of that emerald radiance in the eyes of a leafy face in a tree, or in some carving here or there.

A while ago, things changed again. Now he expected me to get involved in clashes between those who live unseen alongside ordinary people who have no idea what's out there in the wild places and the twilight. That's why he had wanted me to come to this part of the country in the first place.

That had only been the start of it. People without a non-human ancestor can still have an inkling of the in-between world. Recently, some of those had tried to turn their half-understanding to their own advantage. They had no idea of the dangers they might let loose. If I didn't stop them, who would? As far as I could tell, the Green Man approved of the things I'd done.

It was still vanishingly rare for me to meet him face to face. The last couple of times, men had died soon after. A shiver ran down my spine as I walked towards him and the gravel crunched under my feet. I stopped as he turned. He took a step and loomed over me. My heart was pounding, and not only because it's so rare for me to be looking up at anyone. I couldn't look away from the vivid emerald light of his eyes, deep-set in the mask of oak leaves that make his face and beard.

Once he was satisfied he had my full attention, he turned to point at the distant horizon.

Look to the south. Ancient menace stirs. Subdue it anew.

I didn't hear him speak as such. His order simply arrived inside my head with a resonance that left me dizzy. The next moment, he was gone. I gasped for a breath that I didn't realise I'd been holding. Seconds after that, the phone in my hand rang with an incoming call.

Chapter Two

I nearly pissed myself. I did drop the sodding phone, and somehow that cancelled the call. Then I couldn't see where the bloody thing had gone in the dim light. Of course the handset had landed screen down. Fuck. I wreck more phones than anyone I know, and I can hardly put down 'fighting monsters' on an insurance claim.

Rather than try looking and risk treading on it, I took a step back into the doorway. I switched on the house's discreetly hidden outside light, and that showed me where the phone was. For a wonder, the screen wasn't cracked, though that didn't make me feel much better. I felt sick with apprehension as I swiped the phone open and checked the call log. No one rings before daybreak to tell anyone good news. Had something awful happened to my dad?

No, the missed call had been from Fin. That wasn't any better. Was her sister Blanche okay? She and I were still getting each other's measure. To be fair, that's mainly because I don't really understand how having brothers or sisters works. Regardless, I'd hate anything to happen to her, or anyone else in their family. I like their mum, Helen, a lot, and their dad, Simon, is a decent bloke.

My wrecked Land Rover was in a barn on his farm, after it had been drowned in a storm surge in the Fens – not that we told Simon anywhere near the whole story. He's as unremarkably human as my dad. Unlike my dad, he has absolutely no clue that there are things he can't see in this world. Then there were the horde of cousins, and Fin's gran was in an old folks' home near King's Lynn...

I could waste time wondering until the sun came up, or I could just find out. I stabbed the screen with a clumsy finger to return Fin's call.

She answered at once. 'Hi, Dan. I'm sorry to wake you.'

I could hear the strain in her voice. 'I was up anyway. Are you okay? What's wrong?'

'I'm fine.' But she fell silent.

I waited for as long as I could stand it, which was probably less than a minute. 'Is it Blanche? Your mum? What's happened?'

'What?' Fin was startled. 'No, everyone's fine. It's nothing like that.'

She paused again. This time, I forced myself to shut up and wait for her to speak.

She sighed. 'This is going to sound completely mad, but I think I've just seen a giant.'

Now I was the one lost for words.

'Dan? Are you still there?'

'Yes, I'm—' I couldn't work out what to say.

'I'm going to come and see you. We can't talk about this on the phone.' Now Fin sounded far more like her usual self. 'I need to get some fuel, and then I'll be with you in about three and a half, maybe four hours.'

'Where are you coming from?'

'Near Swindon.'

'Okay. Drive safe.' I had a whole load of questions, but those could wait until she got here.

'See you soon.' She ended the call.

I looked at the phone and wondered what was going on. The one thing I didn't need to ask myself was whether Fin was mistaken. As far as I was concerned, if she said she'd seen a giant, that's what she had seen.

The reason I'd been thinking about the possibility of a future together is Fin can see the same things as me. Not that she has greenwood blood. If a dryad chooses to give her human lover a mortal child, that baby will only ever be a son. A dryad's daughters will always be tree spirits, the same as her. These days, there are very few of either. I've never found anyone like me, even after years of searching.

No, Fin's a swan maiden. So are her sisters and her mum, so it's hardly surprising her parents ended up divorced, because that's a hell of a secret not to share. A whole lot of her relatives on that side of her family can turn themselves into swans, including the men, though I have no idea what they call themselves instead of 'maidens'. As a talent, it certainly has its uses, as well as its limitations. They can't do it if they're carrying anything more than the odd button or zip that's made of metal. Once they're transformed, they have their human wits about them, but they can only do whatever a swan does, no more and no less. Fin could fly here if she wanted, but she'd do the journey a whole lot faster in a car and she wouldn't be exhausted when she arrived.

I yawned. Taking that breath of the cold, damp autumn air helped wake me up. There was no chance of me going back to sleep anyway. Was what I'd just heard from Fin and from the Green Man connected? That had to be a safe bet. Even without looking on a map, I reckoned Swindon must be roughly due south of here. But seriously, Swindon? History around there goes back about as far as the start of the railways, as far as I was aware.

So what could I usefully do before Fin arrived and told me about whatever the hell she had seen? First things first. A shower, and a decent breakfast with plenty of coffee would help me stay alert. I closed the side door and locked it, and went back upstairs to start the day like a normal person.

I felt better once I was showered and shaved, and after I'd eaten a couple of bacon sandwiches in the modern kitchen. That's tucked away in a room off the historic kitchen, where tourists can marvel at the black-leaded cast-iron range and admire the gleaming copper saucepans. 'Like Downton

Abbey' is something the staff who give the tours hear a lot. They don't explain that Eleanor's mum was still using the big kitchen at Christmas and family gatherings until they opened up the house as a visitor attraction.

Blithehurst is expensive to run. Financial pressures meant setting up a family trust to manage the manor and the other estate properties that the Beauchenes own. Eleanor and her parents, brother and sister are shareholders in the business now, along with a few other relatives. They would never be poor, not by my standards anyway, but like the man said, more money, more problems.

I washed up my mug, plate and the grill pan, and went along the corridor to the room by the side door where the staff leave their coats and change their shoes. I swapped my trainers for boots and grabbed the new weatherproof coat I'd bought online. I usually get my clothes from army surplus or workwear shops, but that hadn't been an option recently. I also have to admit having a coat that sheds rain rather than soaking it up was a definite plus now I was walking this site three times a day. I hadn't planned on buying something so expensive, but it wasn't as if I had a lot else to spend money on. Not until we could start work on restoring my Land Rover anyway.

I headed outside and looked down the slope of the gardens towards the river and the medieval ruins. The Tudor manor wasn't the first house on this site. The Norman knight who William the Conqueror gave these lands to built a fortified residence down in the bottom of the valley. He wanted his walls protected by a moat linked to the shallow river by sluices. I walked down towards the water, but I wasn't heading for the ruins. I took the path that led to the footbridge and headed for the wooded pasture on the other side of the river.

The rare-breed beef cattle that are one of Blithehurst's various sources of income looked at me, mildly curious. As I walked up the long slope, I wondered what they had made of all the peace and quiet over the summer. Not a lot, probably. I kept my distance and the cows lost interest, going back to eating grass.

This path leads up to a Temple of Venus that dates back to 1731. The guidebook tells visitors it was built when landscaping country parks was all the fashion for the gentry. Another hobby at the time had been building neoclassical monuments inspired by rich men's grand tours through Greece and Italy. This fake temple had a modest three-stepped circular plinth, six pillars and a dome sheltering a statue of the goddess. Someone thoughtful had added curved stone benches, so visitors can sit down and catch their breath as well as admire the scenery. The view is well worth the walk. I took a moment to look back across the valley now the sun was up. The trees selected by generations of Beauchenes to ornament their gardens were turning red, orange and gold, and the old fortified manor's broken walls looked as picturesque as the peaceful Tudor house.

So much for that. I turned to look at the temple and the statue. What the guidebook didn't say was this alluring vision of womanhood wasn't some sweaty sculptor's erotic fantasy. The statue's a faithful likeness of the dryad who gave the Beauchene family that son they needed to save their inheritance. Asca had been endlessly sketched by her lover. I'd seen his portfolio in the library, and it was definitely Not Safe For Work. I'd also seen the resemblance for myself, though Asca kept her clothes on around me. My mother's blood makes me immune to the allure that dryads use to get what they want by seducing mortal men.

I sat down on a bench to wait. Hopefully it wouldn't be too long before Asca realised I'd come to talk to her. I wanted to know if the dryads knew anything useful before Fin arrived. Meantime, I enjoyed the birdsong as the local wildlife got on with their day.

'What brings you here?'

Bollocks. I stood up, turned around and managed a cheerful smile. 'Good morning, Frai.'

Blithehurst's oldest dryad didn't bother masquerading as a grey-haired granny when there were no tourists around. She was swathed in what could have been a cloak from any era of history, and no one would mistake her for human once they saw the greenish colour of her wrinkled skin. Her eyes were one solid colour without white or pupil, and unlike the other dryads I'd met, not green. Frai's penetrating gaze was the vivid copper of autumn leaves.

She looked at me. 'Well?'

There are two dryads at Blithehurst these days. There were three when I first arrived, and Frai blamed me for her granddaughter leaving. As if I had any influence over a dryad. It was Sineya's decision to set up home in the Cotswolds woodland where a job for the Green Man had taken me. That happened the spring before last, but that made no difference to Frai. A dryad can really hold a grudge. My mum still hasn't forgiven the Roundheads for the English Civil War. She's not interested in the politics, but she remembers trying to help the dead and dying on the battlefield at Edgehill.

'What did your master want?' Frai snapped.

So she knew the Green Man had woken me up. I didn't ask how. I don't understand the relationship between the Green Man and the dryads, and I don't imagine I ever will. They stay with their trees and the land that sustains them, while he comes and goes from forest to forest for reasons only he will know. That's between him and them, and I'm not about to get nosy.

What was much more important was I realised I had the upper hand here. Frai wanted answers from me. I still needed to watch what I said if I was going to turn this to my advantage. Folk tales with humans making mistakes in conversations with pixies or fairies don't tell the half of it. The one thing those stories do get right is that if you want something from them, you have to be ready to give something back.

'He came to warn me that some ancient menace is stirring in the south.' If I needed to know about something dangerous from the way back when, Frai was the oldest dryad I'd met. I didn't know how old she might be, but according to my mum, her own grandmother remembered the Romans.

'He didn't tell you what this threat was?' She glared at me.

I thought very carefully about what to say next. Frai's response didn't mean she didn't know. Dryads don't lie, but they can be incredibly devious when they don't want to give you a straight answer. Coming straight back with a question of their own is a favourite tactic.

I didn't think she was trying to be evasive. A dryad will always know if someone's telling a lie, and thanks to my mother's blood, I've got a fairly good ear – or nose – for bullshit. I decided to try something else.

'He didn't say, but I've just had a phone call from Finele. She says she's seen a giant.'

Frai looked at me, astonished. Her jaw actually dropped. I was petty enough to enjoy the moment. She had given me a seriously hard time just after Sineya left, making sure every job I turned my hand to went wrong. I stopped gloating a second later as I realised something else. If Frai was lost for words, I wasn't likely to get any help from her or Asca. Bollocks.

Her glittering copper eyes narrowed. 'Is the swan maiden coming here?'

There was no point in denying it. 'Yes. She'll be here later today.'

'I wish to see her.' Frai wasn't asking. That was an order.

'I'll let her know.' And as far as I was concerned, Fin could make up her own mind about that, whatever Frai demanded.

Fin had met the Blithehurst dryads before I did. She'd been just another visitor to the house and gardens, but Sineya had seen what she was, and of course Fin could see the dryads even though they weren't making themselves visible to the ordinary tourists. Sineya had put the two of us in touch when I needed help with that thing in the Cotswolds.

Frai wasn't interested in that. The old dryad's priority was Blithehurst, first and last. As far as she was concerned, the estate needed another generation of humans who could see the dryads and do as they were told. Unfortunately for her, Eleanor Beauchene and I were just good friends who were never going to become lovers. Worse, neither Eleanor nor her brother or sister showed any inclination to start having kids with anyone else.

I didn't particularly like the way Frai was looking at me. She'd tried to insist that I owed her a debt, since I was responsible for Sineya moving away. The old dryad could hint all she wanted. I wasn't going to be bullied into having a kid either. I wasn't anywhere near ready for that, and I could guarantee neither was Fin.

'Bring her to see me as soon as she arrives.' Frai gestured imperiously and disappeared.

Dryads are also very good at having the last word.

I managed to stop myself saying the swear words I was thinking out loud. Just because I couldn't see her didn't mean she wasn't still there. I also reminded myself that what a dryad doesn't say can be as significant as whatever she does share.

Frai had been startled by what I'd just told her, but she hadn't said it was nonsense, or that Fin must be mistaken. Then she'd changed the subject before ending the conversation fast. If she'd known something I would find useful, I reckoned she would have tried to get something from me in exchange.

As I walked back down the slope to the river, I reckoned I could take a couple of things from that. Firstly, giants must be real, though exactly what that meant was anyone's guess. Secondly, dryads don't know much about them. No, that wasn't quite right. These dryads living at Blithehurst didn't know. Was there any chance my mum might remember something she had once heard? It was all very well the Green Man saying giants were a menace, but I needed details if I was going to do anything about that. Subdue it anew, he told me. Okay, tell me how?

Asking Mum about that could wait though. I wasn't going to give Dad the shock of an early-morning phone call. I couldn't ask Mum anything without telling Dad what was going on, and that would be a difficult conversation. Me taking on another challenge from the Green Man was going to worry him. He'd been stressed enough by things I'd already got caught up in, and he only knew what I'd felt I had to tell him. I had to explain why the Land Rover had been flooded by seawater, but I'd seriously downplayed how close I'd come to being drowned myself.

Besides, I needed to wait until I knew exactly what Fin had seen. There was no point in telling Mum half a story. Crossing back over the footbridge, I headed for the old ruins. I checked the gatehouse doors and windows and the entrance to the Great Hall's undercroft. Everything was still secure. I took a look at the moat in case there was something that needed dealing with in the water or in the river. There wasn't. Some of the ducks came surging up to see me. They still seemed to expect any human to have food for them, despite these months with no visitors. I thought about asking Fin if she could explain to them why they were out of luck. That idea made me grin.

I walked around the manor house, looking for any possible cause for concern from the roofline down past the guttering and all the way to the basement's ground-level windows. Everything looked fine. I went on to check the outbuildings around the dairy yard where I had my wood carving workshop. That reminded me I'd planned on getting a few tools and some materials for doing a bit of work if I couldn't sleep.

Once I was satisfied that everything was okay in the yard, I took the path that led out into the woods. It's about a half-hour walk to the old estate cottage that I'd renovated in return for paying next to no rent. Everything was okay, though the cottage felt a bit cold and damp. As I stuck a few bits and pieces in a canvas work bag, I reckoned I had better come down here and light a fire in the wood stove for a couple of hours soon.

After that, I went to take a look at the coppices. I was walking back towards the garden centre and wondering about getting a cup of tea when my phone rang.

It was Fin. 'I'm in the car park.'

'You made good time,' I observed.

'Hardly any traffic on the motorway apart from HGVs. Oh, and tossers in big Audis and BMWs who think they can go as fast as they like.' Fin chuckled. 'I saw a couple of cop cars waiting to catch them and one who'd got pulled over.'

'Good to know.' I grinned. 'I'll be with you as quick as I can.'

Chapter Three

I walked faster and soon reached the parking area where the converted stable block overlooks the road. Janice, the cafe manager, was setting up the outside chairs and tables, so I gave her a wave. She waved back, and I guessed she was smiling though I couldn't see that through her mask.

I walked over to Fin's Toyota as she was getting out. Her white-blonde hair was quite a lot longer than I was expecting. Other than that, she looked the same as always: average height, average build, and as far as I'm concerned, absolutely gorgeous in jeans and a cream sweater. We stood looking at each other for an awkward moment. I wanted to kiss her, but that probably wasn't sensible these days. She was making no move to get closer to me.

'Do you want to get a coffee?' I gestured towards the cafe.

'I'd rather have one at the house.' Fin waved a hello to Janice and then stretched her arms above her head to ease her shoulders.

I could see tension in her expression as well. 'Fine by me.'

Fin got a lightweight backpack and her waterproof jacket out of the car, and we took the path towards the house. Checking to make sure we weren't being watched by anyone arriving in the car park, I moved the solid wooden barrier with an uncompromising red-and-white 'No Entry' sign painted on it.

I'd built a couple of those when the garden centre had opened up again after the first lockdown. Stringing the usual chains between the posts on the paths hadn't been enough, despite the hanging signs clearly saying 'No Admittance Beyond This Point'. A remarkable number of people seemed to think that didn't apply to them. They explained they assumed those notices simply meant the house was shut but they could still go and walk around the gardens. I got tired of having the same conversation.

I was always polite, so no one could complain to Eleanor. I didn't have to get cross. When you're my height and saying 'no' a lot without smiling or offering any explanations, people usually get the message.

Fin watched me manhandle the heavy barrier back into place. 'Have you had a lot of hassle from visitors?'

'Not since I put this up.' I grinned. 'And the shuck's been dealing with the dog walkers.'

Their owners might not be able to see the shadowy beast, but even the biggest, bravest pet refused to go any further once they caught sight of the huge black spectral hound with eyes like blazing coals.

'It's taken to strolling round the park and gardens.' I had no idea why, or how, or even if the shuck had realised the manor was closed to visitors. I'd asked the dryads, but they had just shrugged and changed the subject. When the house did reopen, I really hoped the scary beast would head back to its usual haunts in the woodland. If it didn't, well, that was a problem for another day.

I unlocked the gate to the formal gardens, waited and relocked it behind us as Fin headed for the house. I caught up with her and pointed. 'We can use the side door.'

She followed me inside. 'Loo?'

I took her backpack as she held it out to me so she could take off her jacket. I took that from her as well and hung everything on a hook as I nodded at the toilet door.

'Through there. I'll get the kettle on.'

I left the doors open so she could find me in the modern kitchen. Fin might have met Blithehurst's dryads, but she'd only done the guided tour inside the house.

I got out mugs, the cafetière and the ground coffee I'd bought months ago, when I'd hoped Fin would be visiting me. I'm fine with instant, or I drink tea, but I know what she prefers. It was a sealed supermarket packet, so it should still be okay. She came through the door as I was carefully pouring hot water from the kettle.

'That's better.' She looked around the little kitchen. 'You'd never know this was in here, would you?'

'That's the idea. Are you hungry? I've got eggs and cheese? Something on toast?'

'A cheese omelette would be great,' Fin said fervently.

'Coming right up.' I got out a pan.

'So.' Fin sipped her coffee as I found everything I needed in the fridge. 'A giant.' She shook her head as if she still couldn't quite believe what she was saying.

'Where did you see it?' I broke eggs into a bowl and beat them with a fork.

'I'm doing some work not far from Marlborough. There's an industrial estate on the edge of a village where there's a business that packages up fancy salads. The stuff gets brought in by lorries from places in the UK and Europe, then it's washed and bagged and gets a label that manages not to break any advertising regulations while giving the idea that the leaves are hand-picked by smiling Wiltshire locals.'

'And the real locals aren't keen?' I switched on the hob and put the pan on the heat.

'They'll put up with the lorries in return for the jobs, but it looks like the operation is polluting the local stream with pesticides washed off the lettuces and the rest. That stream flows into the River Kennett, which has a whole lot of sites of special scientific interest, as well as various nature-restoration projects going on.' Fin took another swallow of coffee.

'Anyway, I was flying over the valley, to get a better idea of the lie of the land as the sun came up. It's the best time of day to do that sort of survey. Then I saw... something. It looked like a shadow moving across the downs above the village. Only I couldn't see what was casting it. Then I realised it wasn't a shadow, but a shape, sort of like a shuck. You know how they look solid one moment and then they don't? But this was definitely a human shape, and when I got a bit closer, I realised just how big it was. It was hard to make out much more in the twilight though. Then it disappeared into a cluster of trees.'

I added salt and pepper to the eggs and dropped a knob of butter in the pan. 'How big are we talking?'

Fin frowned. 'That's hard to say. I didn't want to get too close. Fifteen feet tall, maybe a bit bigger?'

More than twice as tall as me then, and massively more than my weight, if the usual laws of maths and physics applied. Well, I'd faced bigger things than that before. On the other hand, I hadn't done that on my own. I poured the eggs into the pan. 'How much cheese do you want?'

'Let me.' Fin came over and cut a couple of slices from the block of cheddar I'd put ready. Then she cut another piece and began eating it. 'You're taking this very calmly.'

'I'd already reached my limit for being freaked out before you rang.' I explained about the Green Man waking me up as I finished cooking the omelette and found Fin a plate, a few tomatoes and some cutlery.

'That's a hell of a start to your day.' She took the food from me. 'So what do we do now?'

'This doesn't necessarily have to be something "we"—' I broke off as I caught the look she was giving me. 'Okay, first we eat, and then we find out whatever we can about giants. I've already tried asking the dryads here,' I added. 'I didn't get very far.'

Those bacon sandwiches were a distant memory by now, so I made myself some peanut butter and jam on toast and joined Fin at the table in the big kitchen. As we ate, I told her about my conversation with Frai.

She grimaced as she finished and put down her cutlery. 'Do you think there'll be anything useful in the books here?'

'We may as well take a look.' I stood up. 'Then there's always the Internet.'

Fin followed me to the library. I switched on the light and walked past the sofas, armchairs and coffee table to open the shutters. The room has two deep bay windows, south-facing, and each one has a substantial writing desk set there to get the best of the daylight.

Fin had picked up her backpack from the hooks in the corridor. She sat down at the right-hand desk and took out a tablet, its charger and a notebook. For the moment, though, she was more interested in looking up at the ceiling.

It's worth the stiffness in your neck. Carved beams going crossways and lengthwise frame the square panels of medieval carving. Beauchene family records say they were salvaged from the old fortified manor by the river. If you look carefully, there are faces here and there among the garlands of flowers and leafy sprays. The guidebook says the woodcarvers were amusing themselves, using their imagination to depict creatures from stories and ballads. As soon as I saw it, I knew at least one of the men who'd been involved had some wildwood blood. I could see sprites and what I now knew was a hob, as well as what was definitely a shuck, not the wolf the guidebook claimed. Most significant of all, there's a Green Man's leafy face in the shadows of each corner.

I realised Fin was looking at each one of those in turn, and remembered what I'd told her about seeing the shimmer of his presence in more than one similar carving's eyes.

'He's not here,' I said. 'Not as far as I can tell, anyway.'

Fin laughed and blushed a bit. 'I'm not sure if that's a good thing or not. Okay, do you want to see what's online or take the books?'

'My laptop's upstairs, so why don't you see what the Net has to say.' I gestured at the desk. 'The Wi-Fi password's on a card in the top left-hand drawer.'

As Fin looked for that, I turned to the shelves. I knew where to find the books on folklore. Spending six months on my own here, I'd had plenty of time to browse. There's only so much Netflix you can binge-watch.

A lot of them dated back to before the Second World War. The bookplates said they'd been bought by Eleanor's Great Uncle Charles. We think he'd been the last Beauchene family member before her who could see the dryads. Eleanor had made her own additions to the library as well, browsing new and second-hand booksellers' websites. If the wyrm we'd driven away from Blithehurst ever came back, we wanted to be prepared.

I soon had a decent stack of books to carry over to the desk in the other bay window. We both worked in silence. Fin made a few notes as she went. I found myself reading different versions of the same stories and theories over and over again, without making any real progress. Eventually I closed the last book. I scowled at the shelves, wondering where to look next.

Fin put her tablet down and looked across to me. 'So what have you found out?'

I sighed. 'Fee fi fo fuck all. There aren't actually that many folk tales, besides Jack the Giant Killer, Jack and the Beanstalk and a few other pantomime stories. It does look useful to be called Jack if you're going up against a giant, and oh, yes, having a magic sword that cuts through anything, as well as a coat that makes you invisible, comes in very handy. They mostly live in the West Country and Wales for some reason.

Also, giants seem really stupid, which is just as well because they're also man-eaters. But none of this goes back very far. The stories only seem to have been circulating since the 1700s, and no one quite knows where they came from. How have you got on?'

'I've found references in what claim to be histories from earlier than that,' Fin said, 'though I'm not sure how much help they'll be. Have you heard of Geoffrey of Monmouth?'

I nodded. When Eleanor and I had realised there was a wyrm's egg about to hatch under Blithehurst, we'd searched for stories about serpent dragons. Ideally, we wanted hints on how to kill the wyrmling before it killed us. Geoffrey had offered the story of the red dragon the Welsh put on their flag, which was interesting but not particularly useful. I hadn't bothered reading his other stuff.

'According to him,' Fin went on, 'Ancient Britain was a land inhabited by twenty-odd giants until a boatload of refugees from the fall of Troy turned up. They were led by a hero called Brutus, who's not to be confused with the one who knifed Caesar. Anyway, the giants attacked, but the humans managed to kill them. The last one to hold out was the leader, Gogmagog, who died after being thrown off a cliff in a wrestling match with one of Brutus's allies, Corineus.'

'How did he manage that?' I vaguely recognised the giant's name, but I couldn't say from where.

Fin grimaced. 'Apparently this Corineus wasn't a giant himself, but he was eighteen feet tall.'

'That doesn't make much sense,' I commented.

'Very little of this does,' Fin agreed. 'There are a whole lot of different versions, and each one of those has variations. Later on, there's the story that these giants were descended from demons and the thirty daughters of some long-ago king of Greece, or possibly Syria, who planned to murder their husbands in some sort of protest against arranged marriages and the patriarchy generally. They were found out because the youngest girl gave the game away, and as punishment, they were set adrift in a ship to starve or drown or suffer whatever fate might befall them. As it turned out, they washed up on the south coast. The eldest was called Albina, so they called this island Albion after her.'

'Giants in these fairy stories have a nasty habit of kidnapping princesses who don't seem to end up being eaten,' I said thoughtfully. 'Presumably that means the giants have something else in mind. You said whatever you saw reminded you of a shuck somehow?'

'It did, though don't ask me why.' Fin was curious to see where I was going with this.

'Well,' I said slowly, 'shucks are creatures of shadow, according to the dryads and naiads anyway. Don't ask me what that means exactly, but I do know shucks can be all sorts of different sizes when they show themselves to humans. I once saw one pretending to be a black Labrador.' Catching a glimpse of that dog's true nature had been a nasty shock.

Fin tapped her pencil on the desktop. 'Any sort of shadow will be different sizes depending on the time of day and the angle of the sun.'

'So if your instincts are right, maybe giants aren't always the same size? Which would make sense if they were kidnapping women and threatening to force them into having sex. We know these monsters that live in the darkness can feed on fear and misery...' I didn't want to continue that thought.

I didn't need to. Fin was looking revolted as she scanned her notes. 'That would explain why no two sources can agree on what height they really are.' She looked up. 'But I don't think we'd better rely on you beating this one in a wrestling match.'

'There really are no clues anywhere about the best ways to defeat them?' At least Eleanor and I had found plenty of stories about how to kill wyrms, even if the answer turned out to be 'hack them to bits'. That might be unsubtle, but we'd found out it was effective. Unfortunately, these days I knew there were a whole lot of other things out there that were a whole lot harder to kill.

'It must be possible,' Fin insisted. 'The Green Man told you to subdue it anew. That means someone's done that before.'

I picked up one of the fairy tale books. 'Cutting off a giant's head seems to be the preferred method, ideally with a magic sword. The one you saw must have been in hiding for a few thousand years, or it's spent the last couple of centuries getting better after the last time.'

I tried to remember where I'd put the reproduction halberd I'd used to kill the wyrmling. That weapon might be a Victorian fake, but it had done the job. Unfortunately, I wasn't at all sure I'd be able to fit it in Fin's Toyota. I considered other options.

There were replica longswords at Blithehurst, but any tool is only useful if you know what you're doing with it. I remembered the Historic European Martial Arts displays Eleanor had arranged for last year's bank holidays. After watching a lithe, curly-haired woman demonstrate how to fight with a sword nearly as tall as she was, I knew that took training and practice. If I was going up against a giant hand to hand, I'd be using an axe, or possibly a chainsaw. I know how to handle both of those.

Fin got up and stretched, looking out of the window. 'We've still got some daylight left. Maybe it's worth trying to talk to Asca or Frai again? They might know something they'd be willing to share.'

I shrugged. 'It can't hurt to try.'

'How's the path?'

I looked at Fin's leather ankle boots. 'A bit muddy, but you'll be okay.'

We got my coat and Fin's jacket and walked up the hill to the temple. Just as we arrived, Asca walked down the steps of the plinth.

'Good afternoon, Daniel.' She looked like a handsome forty-something woman in jeans and a Blithehurst employee's fleece. If any determined walkers out on the public footpaths through the pasture saw us, they wouldn't give her a second glance.

I reminded myself that she might not be as abrasive as her mother, but we should still watch what we said. 'Hello.'

Asca got straight to the point. 'Finele, you have truly seen a giant?' She was astonished.

I decided to be just as direct. 'What can you tell us about them?'

'Very little, but what I know, I will share.' The dryad sat down on the closest stone bench.

Fin and I sat on the next one. Asca laced her hands together in her lap as her gaze grew distant. I saw her eyes shift from a facsimile of human to the deep green of summer leaves.

'There were stories told of the days when the first of us came to these lands. That was after the snows retreated and the trees returned. Before the floods drowned the great valley that lay between the hills that became these islands and the forests far away to the south.'

It took me a moment to work out what, or rather, *when* she meant. Asca was talking about the long-lost days after the last Ice Age, before rising sea levels formed the English Channel. Maybe I owed Frai a bit of an apology. I was pretty sure even the old dryad's memories didn't go back that far.

'There were giants here then. At least, so it was said when my foremothers told tales of the past,' Asca mused. 'Creatures of the dark places under the earth. They were solitary and given to rage and violence if another of their kind strayed into their domain. Those of us born of wood and water shunned the lands they claimed rather than fight them. The humans who followed the herds here and chose to settle soon clashed with the brutes.'

She shrugged. That didn't surprise me. Dryads have little interest in things that don't directly affect them or their trees.

'But those humans stayed,' I prompted. 'The giants didn't drive them back to wherever they had come from.'

'Indeed,' Asca agreed. 'Your father's people must have found a way to overcome such foes. Of course, mortals have always been inventive and resilient. How else would you make the most of such short lives?'

'But do you know how?' Fin persisted. 'How did they defeat the giants?'

That was the million-pound question as far as I was concerned.

Asca looked thoughtful. 'Mortal men's greatest strength has always been in working together, like crows driving off a goshawk that could easily kill any one of them caught alone.'

'Right.' That might be true, but it wasn't much use to me. The days when some woodcutter's son could recruit a mob with flaming torches and pitchforks were long gone – if they had ever existed outside the movies. These days, telling people I needed their help to kill a giant would get me locked up under some mental health legislation.

Asca seemed to know what I was thinking. She looked at me, her eyes narrowing. 'The master of the forests would not send you to do this if there was no way for you to succeed.'

I nodded, but I stopped short of agreeing. Just because I *could* win some fight, that sure as hell didn't guarantee that I *would.* As a dryad's son, I'm tall and strong, I'm almost never ill, and I can expect to live a long and healthy life, but I have no more or less good luck than anyone else.

I'd already come far too close to failing this sort of challenge. Sooner or later, everyone's luck runs out. I needed inside knowledge to tip the scales in my favour. One thing I've learned the hard way – and not just from fighting monsters – is fair fights are for fools.

Fin was remembering our conversation in the library. 'Are giants creatures of shadow, like shucks?'

'Yes.' Asca seemed surprised she needed to ask.

'Do you think Kalei might know something more about them?' I interrupted. 'Have you seen her lately? Could she find out what other naiads might remember?'

I know even less about river spirits than I do about dryads, but I knew Kalei spent time underground where centuries of flowing water had carved caves and channels through the Peak District's limestone crags. She had also helped me out in the past. Of course, that was on the understanding I would repay the favour. Even so, I reckoned owing her would be less risky than going up against a giant without some advantage. Besides, Kalei was the only naiad I knew, and as far as I was aware, the only one who ever visited Blithehurst's river.

'I will see if I can reach her.' Asca rose to her feet. 'I will see what the trees remember. Be careful. Giants are merciless and they are killers. That much I do know. Just as I know we cannot afford to lose you, Daniel.'

That was unexpected. Then I reminded myself she was just as single-minded as her mother when it came to safeguarding Blithehurst. To do that, they needed human help.

'I'll watch out.' But I was speaking to empty air. The dryad had vanished like a leaf blown on the wind.

'That was more than you got from Frai.' Fin tried to sound encouraging.

I nodded, non-committal. 'Let's hope she can find out something useful from Kalei.'

Fin looked around. 'What do we do now?'

'I should ring Eleanor and let her know what's going on.' I sighed. 'She'll need to get someone else to stay in the house if I'm not going to be here for... however long this takes. I can't leave just yet.' I looked at Fin. 'Are you okay to stay overnight? There are plenty of guest rooms...'

She nodded and answered before I could work out what to say next. 'I've got what I need in my backpack. What are we going to do about dinner? I don't suppose any takeaways deliver all the way out here.'

'I've got a stash of ready meals in the freezer. I'm fairly sure there's a fish pie.'

'Sounds good.' Fin stood up.

Since I still couldn't think how to ask whether or not she wanted to share a bed, I did the same. Also, sitting on the cold stone was making my arse ache. We walked back to the house. Fin unzipped her jacket as I locked the side door behind us.

'Why don't you call Eleanor while I put the kettle on?' she suggested. 'Tea or coffee?'

'Tea, please.' I headed for the library and took out my phone.

Thankfully it was late enough in the day that I reached Eleanor herself, not her voicemail telling me she was in a library. I explained how my day had started, as well as what Fin had seen. I told her what we'd learned – and had not learned – from the books here, and from the dryads.

'The thing is, at the very least I need to go and see what's down there. That means being away for a night, maybe longer.' I didn't need to explain to her that if the Green Man was telling me to do this, I wouldn't get any peace till I did.

There was a longer wait than I expected before Eleanor answered.

'Well, that's not what I expected to be talking to you about today,' she said heavily.

That worried me. 'What's the matter?'

There was another long pause before Eleanor replied. 'I was going to give you a ring this evening. I need to call a family meeting. The Blithehurst Trust needs to make some decisions.'

Hard decisions, by the sound of her voice. That worried me even more.

'I'll make a few calls to set things up this evening, and then I'll come down tomorrow,' she went on. 'You can set off any time you like.'

'Thanks. I'll let you know how we get on.'

'Good luck. Be careful.' Eleanor sounded even more grim. That was understandable. She'd lost a brother to what the mundane world thought was an accident. She and I knew his death was no such thing.

'I will be,' I assured her.

'I'll talk to you soon.' She ended the call.

I stood there wondering what I was going to come back to, assuming I found a way to deal with this giant. Assuming I'd still have a job here.

Chapter Four

There was a fish pie in the freezer as well as the chicken casserole I'd planned on eating. That was a relief, since Fin doesn't eat meat and I didn't fancy heading out to the shops. After dinner, I brought my laptop down to the library and we watched a film about two young soldiers in World War One. Things could be worse, I told myself. Presumably giants didn't have heavy artillery. We shared one of the sofas as we finished the bottle of white wine we had opened, though Fin sat at the other end to me, and I didn't try putting my arm around her.

She took one of the other guest rooms when we went upstairs. I expected knowing she was a few doors down the corridor would give me yet another restless night. As it turned out, thinking back to a weekend we'd spent together in the Cotswolds soon put a smile on my face. I dozed off and slept like a log.

When I got up, I dragged my holdall out from under the bed and packed clothes and a wash-kit for a few days away. Thankfully, I was up to date with my laundry. On the other hand, I wondered if I should go down to the cottage and bring back a few more things. I usually travel light on the basis that if I need something I haven't got, there are always shops and I've got a credit card. Now, though, I wondered what I would do if I got stuck somewhere when another lockdown was declared.

I hesitated, then decided, fuck it, I'd just have to cope with what I had with me. I put the charger for my phone into the holdall and zipped it shut. Then I opened it up again and added the box of condoms that had been sitting unopened in my sock drawer. I was never in the Scouts, but I know it's a good idea to be prepared.

I went downstairs and got my laptop out of the library and put that in the holdall as well. Leaving the bag by the side door, I went into the kitchen. I found Fin looking at the washing machine as it filled with water.

She glanced at me with a faint frown. 'I didn't think this through. I've just put the bed linen I've used in to wash, but that means we've either got to wait until the programme finishes or I need to leave Eleanor a message to tell her I've left her a load of laundry to deal with.'

I was simply relieved to see she was irritated with herself and not at something I had done. 'It's not a problem. It's not as if we've got to be anywhere particular at a specific time. We can see if there's anything else in the library while the sheets wash. We might as well walk up to the temple as well, to see if there's anything new the dryads have to share.'

Fin looked a bit less stressed. 'You're right. Yes, let's do that.' She pressed her palms to her face with a wordless growl of frustration, exasperation or both. When she lowered her hands, red marks were slow to fade on her pale skin. 'I don't know why I'm being like this. I can get in a state about the stupidest things at the moment.'

'Same here,' I said with feeling. 'It's all this...' I gestured, failing to find the right words. 'Not knowing when all this utter bollocks will end.'

Fin managed a brief laugh. 'That's a good way to put it. I keep trying to remember that saying about do what you can and accept what you can't change? For the moment, anyway.'

'I know what you mean.' I looked round the kitchen. 'The first thing we should do is have a decent breakfast. I don't know about you, but unless we need a pee or some fuel, I'd rather not stop at a motorway services.'

'Me neither,' Fin agreed. 'Have you got enough bread for us to make some sandwiches? How about something to drink? I'll be okay for petrol, though we will need to fill up once we get down there.'

'Where is "there", exactly?' I realised I hadn't asked the most obvious question. She wasn't the only one being a bit slow at the moment.

Fin leaned against the kitchen cabinet as I filled the kettle and switched it on. 'The village where we're working, where the salad packers are polluting the stream, is Bockbourne Magna, and there's a smaller place, I suppose you'd call it a hamlet, higher up on the downs. That's Bockbourne Parva. The stream itself is called the Bock. That's probably from the Old English word for "beech", since there are a whole lot of beech woods in the area.'

'I wonder if there are any old local legends that might give us some clue what we might be dealing with.' I got a couple of mugs out of the cupboard. 'And how to deal with it, come to that.'

'We should take a look,' Fin agreed. 'I haven't come across anything so far, but I've been reading about the geology of the area, not the folklore.' She moved to let me get to the fridge.

'Are there any local museums? Any other historical sites that might have a bookshop where we could find local legends to follow up on?' I took out the eggs and butter, and realised I was going to have to make a run to the supermarket before we left. If I didn't, Eleanor would get here to find she had enough milk for a cup of coffee and not much else. Sandwiches for Fin would use up the last of the cheese.

Fin passed me the frying pan from the draining board. 'There's more history than you can shake a stick at, though most of it's outdoors and a bit short on book stalls. Bock Down is pretty close to the Ridgeway, and people have been coming and going along that since forever. The stone circle at Avebury's not so very far away, and that goes back to Neolithic times, along with Silbury Hill. There are long barrows all over the place, and a couple of Roman villas. King Alfred beat the Danes at the Battle of Ashdown, which was probably somewhere not too far away, though no one's exactly sure where. What can I do to help?'

'Get some toast on?' I cracked eggs into the pan.

Fin got the loaf out of the bread bin and began cutting slices. 'When the Normans turned up and beat the Saxons, they built castles at places like Marlborough and took over the royal hunting forests that covered the area at the time. The locals mostly just carried on doing their own thing, farming and grazing their animals. Later on, the downs were used for raising sheep, so the villages and towns spun the wool and wove a lot of cloth. Parliament's armies passed that way, when they were heading out of London to fight the Royalists for control of Bath and Bristol during the English Civil War. When the Royalists got the upper hand, they chased the Roundheads right back to Newbury, so there was a fair amount of skirmishing in the area, one way and the other.'

'That's an awful lot of people not to notice a giant if there was one strolling around.' I wondered if this monster really had been sleeping since the last Ice Age. If so, what the hell had woken it up? 'Do you want some baked beans with this?'

'Might as well.'

I didn't have anything else to say, so I concentrated on cooking the eggs. Fin started buttering the toast when that popped up. We ate our breakfast and finished up the last of the loaf as toast and jam since I was going to have to go to the supermarket anyway. I didn't only need to restock the fridge for Eleanor. I'd realised there were no bottles of water or anything else for Fin and me to drink on the journey. I only had cans of sparkling orange, and anything we had to drink all of once it was open would be a pain in the car.

While I did that, Fin walked up to the temple to see if either of the dryads would show themselves. When I got back, she told me they hadn't turned up, so we went to see if Blithehurst's library had anything interesting to tell us about the North Wessex Downs. That really was a long shot, so neither of us were particularly surprised when we only found the sort of general information that crops up in travel guides.

I started putting the books that I'd left on the desk back in their places on the shelves. 'Do you want to start looking online? For legends around the Bockbourne villages specifically, I mean, not just for stuff about giants. Or shall we do that once we're down there?'

'Let's leave it for now.' Fin gathered up more books from the low table between the sofas. 'We could waste half the day finding out nothing much at all.'

'Easily,' I said. 'Let's get on the road.'

I glanced up at the corner of the ceiling to see if there was any sign of the Green Man's presence in the closest carving. There was no hint of an emerald glint, which was probably just as well. If there had been, we'd have had to decide if that meant we should stay or if he wanted us to get a bloody move on.

We brought our bags downstairs. Fin took the bed linen out of the tumble dryer while I went round and checked all the doors and windows were secure. I set the alarm and texted Eleanor to let her know we were leaving. She didn't answer, so I guessed that meant she was already driving, on her way here.

Fin carried her backpack and the bag with our sandwiches. I had my holdall and the bag with the drinks and other things I'd bought for the journey. We walked up to the car park, and there were a few other cars there. I could see some customers wandering around the garden centre. Normally there'd be a whole lot more than a few people here, even this late in the year. I wondered uneasily just how bad things were getting for Blithehurst.

Well, that was one of those things I could do sod all about. I needed to focus on dealing with this giant. That was simple enough. Of course, saying that something is simple sure as hell doesn't mean it's easy. I wondered if I should have packed my chainsaw. Well, if we decided I needed it, I could always come back and pick it up.

We got into the car and Fin set up her phone in a bracket stuck to the windscreen, so she could use it as a satnav. I adjusted the passenger seat as far back and as low as it would go. That was just about comfortable, even if I didn't have as much leg room as I'd like. At least Fin could see past me easily enough when we came to a junction. We made our way cross-country and joined the motorway, heading south.

'See what I mean about the traffic?' Fin remarked after a few miles.

'I do.' I was still getting used to being on a major road again, after so many months barely leaving the Blithehurst estate. That was just one reason why it made sense for Fin to be driving, even if I'd usually prefer to be behind the wheel, given the choice. Besides, this was her car, and she knew where we were going.

She put the radio on, and we listened until the news bulletins got too depressing and infuriating. I found some Frank Turner CDs in the glove box and a Red Hot Chili Peppers, so we listened to those instead.

There might have been hardly any cars compared to normal, even though it was a Friday, but someone still got something badly wrong on the M6 where it passes Walsall. Gantry signs overhead warned us there'd been an accident ahead as traffic slowed to a crawl. I reached round to the back seat for the food and drink. There are some advantages to having long arms when you're travelling in a small car. We ate our sandwiches. Corned beef and pickle for me. Cheese and pickle for Fin.

'Sprite or lemon tea?' I offered Fin her choice of the drinks I'd bought at the supermarket.

'Sprite.' She took it carefully from me, drank about half and handed the bottle back. 'Do you need a stop at a services?'

'I'm okay for now.' I screwed the cap back on the Sprite and drank some lemon tea. 'Unless you'd like a break from driving?' I reckoned my road sense was back up to speed by now.

'I'm fine, but thanks.' Fin pulled out to overtake a haulage firm's lorry.

We were able to make better speed once we joined the M5, but after everything we'd done before setting out, I realised it wouldn't be that much longer before we started to lose the daylight. We were coming up on Cheltenham when Fin spared me a quick glance, before looking back to concentrate on the road.

It turned out she was thinking the same thing. 'It's later than I realised. Do you want to take a look at Bockbourne tonight, or shall we carry on straight to mine and head over there first thing in the morning?'

I looked at her phone in its holder and saw the line on the map display. We'd need to leave the motorway at a junction near Gloucester to cut across to the North Wessex Downs. If we were heading to Bristol, we'd be going straight onwards.

I hadn't realised Fin was working from home. I'd assumed she would be staying somewhere close to the job she was doing. That was stupid of me, especially at the moment. Why would she do that when she could use the M4 to go there and back when she needed to visit the site? I guessed the commute would be about an hour and a half? Quite apart from anything else, the cost of fuel would be cheaper than paying for accommodation.

'Well?' Fin prompted, breaking into my thoughts. 'We need to decide if I'm turning off at the next junction.'

'Let's go to Bockbourne and see what there is to see.' It would be twilight by the time we got there, but I could still get some idea of the place.

'Okay then.' Fin hit the indicator and changed lanes to head for the slip road. We left the motorway, and a decent road took us through the Cotswolds, heading for Cirencester.

I switched off the CD. 'I wonder how Sineya is getting on with reviving the woodlands at Brightwell.'

Fin didn't need me to explain what I was thinking. 'I can't imagine she knows anything about giants that her mum and gran don't know.'

'She might have heard something since she left Blithehurst. I grant you, that's a long shot, but there's a naiad in the lake there as well now. Did you ever speak to her?'

Fin and Blanche had done a lot of work sorting out the blocked and diverted watercourses for Brightwell Hotel's owners. That was after she and some more of her family had helped me kill the monster that had screwed up the drainage as well as spending centuries preying on the locals.

'Tireis?' Fin shook her head. 'I never really got to know her. She kept pretty much to herself.'

'It might be worth seeing what she knows,' I persisted. 'We can ask Sineya to be our go-between.'

Fin shrugged. 'Maybe, but not today.'

'Fair enough.'

The next sizeable place after Cirencester was Swindon. The route we were on skirted the sprawling suburbs. Fin took a turn-off heading south-eastwards, and the narrower road she was following cut under the motorway. The line on the map on her phone took us along the flank of the high ground, through winding lanes. I realised these linked the little valleys that ran down towards the river to the south.

I really hoped we wouldn't meet a tractor coming the other way. There was no way another vehicle would get past us, and even the passing places looked a tight squeeze. I was relieved when Fin flicked on the headlights as the dusk drew on.

'Here we are.'

She turned a corner and I saw a scatter of buildings ahead. We passed a sign asking us to please drive carefully through Bockbourne Parva. I could see why the locals might want people to do that. The single-track road snaked erratically through houses which seemed to have been built without any sort of overall plan. Some roofs were thatched, others were tiled. Some houses were brick, others were painted white, so I couldn't tell what they were made of. None looked particularly recent.

I grabbed the door handle as we reached what I guessed was the village green, and Fin threw the Toyota round a sharp left-hand bend. 'Did they just build a house anywhere the ground was flat enough to take a foundation?'

'It's more likely they were trying to avoid unexpected streams.' She took a right turn to head across the upper side of the roughly rectangular green.

'How do you mean?' I looked to see if there was a pub or anything else here, but Bockbourne Parva didn't even seem to have a church.

'We're on the spring line here.' Fin headed down a lane so tight I honestly expected the hedges on either side to brush against the doors of the car. 'Rain on the top of the Downs soaks into the chalk and filters down through it until the water meets an impermeable layer of rock or clay. Then it goes sideways until it comes out on a hillside somewhere.

Water always goes somewhere. Depending on the geology, as well as the time of year and the amount of rain there's been, a spring can come and go. That's why a winterbourne is a stream that only flows in the winter.'

She broke off as she negotiated a hairpin bend. The lane also went down a slope steep enough to make the Toyota's headlights lurch alarmingly. I stopped asking questions and wondered when another vehicle had last been along here. I could see grass growing in the middle of the crumbling tarmac.

Fin pulled into a field entrance and stopped the engine. She looked at me. 'We can get a decent overview of the valley and both villages from here.'

'Lead on.' I reached for the door release.

Getting out of the car was harder work than I expected. I wasn't stiff exactly, but my back and legs are too long for me to enjoy sitting in the same position for so many hours. I hauled myself to my feet, raising a hand to the roof sill. Once I was sure I was standing on something solid, I did a few knee bends and stretches.

On the other side of the car, Fin was arching her back and rubbing the back of her neck. 'It's nice to stop moving,' she said with feeling.

I was enjoying the soft silence after the non-stop sounds of the engine and the wheels on the road. The clean, cool air was welcome too. The breeze carried the merest hint of rain, and I caught the sleepy scent of woods settling into their seasonal torpor as autumn deepened. It wasn't home, but it was reassuringly familiar.

I looked across the car's roof. 'Where do we go from here?'

Fin got her jacket off the back seat and pointed at the stile beside the farmer's metal gate. 'There's a footpath.'

'Right.' Now we were out of the car, my eyes were adjusting to the fading light. I saw a signpost half hidden in the hedge. Taking my coat out of the car, I waited for Fin to take the lead. We climbed over the wooden stile.

'Watch your step,' she advised.

'Sheep shit?' I could see a flock of them scattered across the field, idly nibbling grass. The ones closest looked at us with mild curiosity and lost interest just as quickly.

'And rabbit shit.' Fin pointed at a long-eared shadow darting away as it caught sight of us.

Seeing the length of its legs, I thought it was a hare, but I could have been wrong. It didn't really matter, so I didn't say anything.

We headed along the faintly darker track across the turf that marked the public footpath. I did my best not to tread in anything unpleasant as we approached the next hedge. There was another stile for walkers. Once we were over that, Fin stopped and turned to look back the way we'd come.

'There's Bockbourne Parva.' She pointed towards the cluster of house-shaped silhouettes against the pale sunset sky to the west. A few lit windows looked like holes cut right through them.

'Right.' I realised we were some way below the smaller village now, on the side of the downland where this steep-sided valley cut a sharp crease in the landscape.

Immediately below us, on the far side of the field where we were standing, the hedge had either been left to its own devices for several years or that was the edge of a small copse. Either way, as we got closer, I realised the land fell away sharply, down a slope that mountain goats wouldn't fancy, never mind these sheep.

'That's Bockbourne Magna.' Fin pointed towards a considerably bigger settlement which lay below us, where the landscape opened up. I could just make out a stretch of substantial woodland beyond the village. Those must be some of those beech trees Fin had mentioned.

Even though the shadows were thickening, I could make out proper streets and a tall, long-roofed building that I guessed was the church. That was on the far side of the valley, and most of the village was on the far side of the stream Fin had been hired to get cleaned up.

That made me think of something else I'd been meaning to ask. 'Who exactly are you working for? Who got in touch to ask you to investigate the salad company?'

'The Parish Council, officially. In practice, there's a pretty small group of people who take the lead in running everything from the residents' association and the neighbourhood watch to quiz nights at the pub. They're putting up the cash to pay us.'

'From families who've lived here since before the Romans rocked up?' I wondered if someone with deep-rooted blood ties had something to do with the giant stirring.

But Fin was shaking her head. 'There's a handful of fairly new arrivals who've moved out of Swindon, and who drive back in every day for work. A couple retired here from somewhere near Leicester. There's a solicitor who works in Marlborough, but he wasn't born in the area. He was at the boarding school when he was a boy, and he came back a few years after university. Then there are some weekenders who work in places like Bristol or Bracknell.'

So much for that theory. 'Where exactly did you see the giant?'

Fin pointed up the hill. 'I started out on the top of the down, above Bockbourne Parva. I wanted to see if I could trace the springs that meet to make the stream, including ones that are dry at the moment. I was flying down the line of the Bock when I saw it walking right over here.'

She swung her hand around to indicate the field we had just gone through as well as the one where we were actually standing. 'It went on down the hillside, past that stand of trees, and then I lost sight of it in the woods.'

'What did the sheep do?' I was curious.

'They ran off as far and as fast as they could, and I don't blame them. They huddled up by that far fence line, as tightly as they could.'

She shivered violently. It certainly wasn't warm out here in the open, but it wasn't cold enough to justify that.

'It was—' She struggled to find the right words. 'Like that "a goose walked over your grave" feeling, only twenty times worse. And I wasn't anywhere close to the thing.'

I looked back at the sheep. They were still eating grass or staring vacantly into space. I hoped that meant the giant wasn't anywhere close.

A pale shimmer caught my eye. For an instant, I thought it must be the moon, rising over the swell of the land. Then I realised the white shape was moving, and it certainly wasn't a sheep.

It was a horse, a white horse, and it wasn't someone's weekend ride out for a stroll. My first thought was it must be some thoroughbred that had got loose from one of the racing stables I'd learned were scattered around here. Then I realised it was roughly twice as tall as the average horse. I could see that from the size of the sheep it was walking past. I saw a few of them get out of its way, but the rest weren't bothered by its arrival. That was a relief, sort of.

I'm not sure if the horse even noticed the sheep. Its ears were pricked forward and its head was raised. Its eyes shone bright as stars, and it seemed to be looking for something. If it was, that something was far ahead of us, away down the hillside.

It reached the hedge that we'd climbed over using the second stile. The horse walked straight through the hawthorns. I don't mean it forced a path through the spiky twigs and leaves. It just carried on at the same steady pace, like a ghost walking through a wall on TV. It wasn't translucent like a ghost though. This beast looked solid enough to do damage.

A wordless squeak told me Fin had seen it too. I reached out towards her, though I didn't take my eyes off the horse. I felt her lace her fingers through mine, and together, we backed slowly away. I'm not sure that was necessary, since the horse's unhurried path wouldn't bring it particularly close to us. Never mind. It felt like the right thing to do.

The horse passed by, with its tail idly swishing, not giving any indication it had seen us. That meant we got a better look at it, and I remembered learning somewhere that white horses with black muzzles are called greys. Technically they're only white if they're pink around the nose and mouth.

Well, this horse was white, even if there were shades of pale grey around its muzzle and in the hollows of its ears. White and gleaming, like a hunter's moon on a clear, cold night. As I thought that, the dapples on its muscular haunch seemed familiar. I realised the pattern looked like the scatter of craters on the surface of the moon. I blinked away sudden dizziness as the horse went on its way.

It shone bright against the dusky outlines of the trees growing untamed at the edge of this field. We stood there until it went far enough down the steep hillside to pass out of sight. Fin was trembling. I could feel the shivers through her fingers. I wasn't about to feel superior. I was shaking as well. I wasn't afraid, not exactly. All the same, I knew I didn't want to get on the wrong side of that horse, and not just because it was so huge.

Fin untangled her hand from mine as the last lingering glow faded away. The evening shadows closed around us. I held my arms out and she walked into my hug. She hugged me back, and I'm honestly not sure who was holding on for most reassurance.

She said something, but she had her head tucked under my chin. Whatever it was got lost in my coat. I relaxed my hold on her now that my legs felt stronger.

'What was that?'

Fin looked up. 'I said, we've been looking up the wrong legends, haven't we?'

Chapter Five

I plucked a small feather out of my chest hair as I walked quietly towards Fin's bedroom door. Before I could decide what to do with the curl of white, it slipped out of my fingers. I turned to see it fly through the air, straight as an arrow. It floated down to rejoin the other feathers clinging to Fin's back as she lay in bed, sound asleep.

Folk stories about swan maidens generally involve shawls or shifts with feathers stitched or woven into them. Fin said those stories were true. In the olden days, owning something like that might seem eccentric, but the reality was far too risky to share, even after fear of witchcraft had faded away. In reality, downy white feathers cling to a swan maiden's skin, appearing around puberty along with their ability to transform into a bird. I still wondered what that must have been like. It had been bad enough learning to shave with my face breaking out in spots.

Thankfully, these days, Fin and her family have a lot more say about who will see them undressed. Sometimes she threads her feathers into a vest's fabric. A lot of the time, she keeps them safely locked away. None of them will risk anyone else getting hold of their feathers, and I knew better than to joke about it. Those other stories are true as well: where men are so determined to keep a swan maiden as an unwilling wife that they steal and hide whatever their feathers are attached to, so they can't shift shape and fly away.

I know a bit about dealing with besotted lovers. Being a bit more than ordinarily human gives you an unexpected allure. Other people respond without even realising. My mother's ancestors – among others – have been seducing mortal men to get their own way for at least a couple of thousand years. Fairy tales make that very clear. So it was hardly a surprise to find out I had no trouble getting any girl I wanted into bed. I didn't use to think it was a problem.

Thankfully I'd grown out of that before I met Fin. From her point of view, being inexplicably attractive led to far too much unwanted attention. She told me in no uncertain terms that men have enough trouble taking no for an answer from a woman, without her swan nature sending the blood from their brain to their cock.

As I got my wash-kit out of my holdall and headed for the bathroom, I wondered about the faint tension that I'd sensed between me and Blanche, the couple of times we'd met. I had a pee and cleaned my teeth, but I still couldn't think of a subtle way to let Fin's sister know I was as immune to Fin's inherited charm as she was to mine. That was one reason why she meant so much to me. Fin knew me for who I was, and nothing but her own desire was influencing her choice to be my lover.

When I walked back into the bedroom, Fin rolled over onto her back. She yawned, stretched and rubbed her eyes. The duvet was pushed down to her waist, and I took a moment to admire the pale curves of her tits as drifting white feathers caressed her nipples. When the two of us were alone, she wore her feathers loose next to her skin. I found that incredibly erotic. Maybe I wasn't as immune to her charms as I thought. Maybe we didn't have to get up just yet.

Fin looked at me and laughed. 'I can see what you're thinking. Put your underpants on. We've got a day's work to do.'

'If you say so.' I grinned. 'If you're sure?'

Fin sat up. 'I'm sure Blanche will be on her way back from Southampton. I don't want the sound of her key in the lock putting you off your stroke.'

'Good point.' I reached for my underwear and combat trousers.

My T-shirt was still in the lounge, where we'd started taking each other's clothes off the night before. After I'd offered to sleep on the sofa, to keep my distance, just in case. Fin had pointed out we'd spent at least half the day in the same small car, breathing the same air. If either of us was going to infect the other, that had already happened. We might as well make the most of having the flat to ourselves, she said as she started kissing me.

I put my shirt on and cleared the dining table, where we'd abandoned the remains of last night's takeaway. Cainescombe is just big enough to have a decent chip shop, and just far enough outside Bristol to avoid being swallowed up by the city. On the other hand, it's close enough to the motorway for builders to make a good few quid developing bits and pieces of land where local businesses, workshops and garages have given up the struggle. Fin and Blanche were sharing a three-bedroom flat on the upper floor, left-hand side, of a low-rise block of four. There were four identical blocks at the end of a cul-de-sac behind farm buildings that had been converted into bigger, pricier houses.

There was a food-waste caddy by the sink, so I dumped the abandoned chips and scraps of batter in that. I bundled everything else into the big paper bag we'd been given our food in. When Fin got out of the shower, I'd ask if she wanted me to take that straight down to the outside bins. If she told me where to find the outside bins.

I carried the plates, cutlery and glasses through to the small kitchen that opened off the good-sized living room. The flat's layout was very straightforward. The front door opened into a hall with the bathroom at the far end. In between, the bedrooms on the left overlooked the parking spaces at the front. Fin's room was the first door, they shared the middle one as an office for their business, and Blanche had the bedroom near the bathroom. On the right, the lounge diner ran almost the full length of the flat, with doors into the hall at each end. The windows were floor to ceiling, with a glass door opening onto a balcony. These upper apartments had a great view over the ground-floor flats' small gardens to the farmland beyond.

As I did the washing-up, I heard Fin showering. I wondered what happened to her feathers under the spray. I wondered when we'd be able to spend some time in a hotel with a shower big enough for me to join her and find out.

She was soon walking back to her room wrapped in a towel. 'There's cereal in the cupboard next to the cooker,' she called out. 'Milk in the fridge.'

I was finishing a bowl of muesli when she joined me, twisting her wet hair into some sort of complicated black plastic clip. 'What's Blanche doing in Southampton?'

'Taking some water samples from Bockbourne to the lab we use for analysis.' Fin grinned as she stirred her own muesli. 'And shagging the lab tech she fancies. I can't think of another reason for her to stay overnight. I don't think he's an infection risk. He spends his working life wearing gloves and a mask.'

I didn't know what to say to that, so I reached for my phone. 'I got a text from Eleanor last night. She says, "Good drive down. Thanks for stocking the fridge. Saw F. She says K is asking around."'

'I wonder if we should see what the naiads and dryads know about white horses.' Fin put down her spoon and fetched a card that was tucked behind a clock on the sideboard. 'Let's see what we can find out for ourselves first.'

The card had the flat's Wi-Fi network details and password. I fetched my laptop and set it up on the dining table while Fin finished eating. She took our cereal bowls out to the kitchen, and I heard her put the kettle on.

I got online and was soon surprised. 'Did you know there are nine white horses carved into the chalk in the area around Bockbourne?'

Fin appeared in the kitchen doorway. 'I knew there were a few, but I wouldn't have said that many. Tea?'

'Please.' I read out the list I had found. 'Alton Barnes. Broad Town. Cherhill. Devizes. Hackpen. Marlborough. Pewsey. Uffington. Westbury. Those are all places with a white horse.'

Fin came out of the kitchen with a tray holding a mug of tea for me and a cafetière with a mug for herself. 'Do you want to start at the beginning of the alphabet or the end? I'll go the other way and meet you in the middle.'

'I'll start at the end.' I wanted to know more about the Uffington Horse. That was the only one I'd heard of, even though I'd never visited the place. I had no idea why, now I came to think about it. It's only at the other end of Oxford-shire from the Warwickshire border where I grew up. But I've always been more interested in visiting old woods than climbing the downlands.

Fin fetched her own laptop and I emailed her the link to the list. We began seeing what else there was to learn. That meant looking beyond the first pages of search results, for tourists looking for a scenic drive and just recommending places to stop and see these dramatic sights. Fortunately, after a bit of lateral thinking about how to phrase my ques-tions, I found local enthusiasts were keen to share what they knew on blogs and other websites.

I was surprised to learn there was a whole lot more to carving a horse than just scraping off the turf to reveal the pale chalk underneath. Doing it properly meant digging out the lines, or the shape, as deep as a metre, and packing that trench with chalk rubble that was quarried elsewhere and brought in. That wasn't the end of the hard work. Traditionally, the horses were scoured every seven years. That meant digging out any weeds, recutting the edges of the turf and adding a fresh top layer of crushed chalk.

That was a hell of a lot of effort for local people, all done with hand tools, on unhelpfully, even dangerously, steep slopes. But it had been done for centuries, maybe as far back as the days when those tools were made of flint and antler, through to the 1800s when at least metal picks and trowels could be used. What no website could tell me, though, was *why* people were prepared to put in so much work. At least until the twentieth century, anyway.

If there were other people working from home in the other flats, they were being very quiet, considering the whole place had wooden floors. Hearing footsteps coming up the stairs in the silence made me look up. Fin did the same, and our eyes met.

'Blanche.' She'd barely spoken when we heard the flat's front door open.

'Hiya!' Fin's sister called out from the hallway.

'In here!' Fin called back.

The far door opened, down at the end where two sofas at right angles faced the TV in the corner.

'Why are you—?' Blanche halted, surprised. 'Oh, hello, Dan.'

'Good to see you.' I hoped I sounded friendly.

Blanche looked at Fin, clearly expecting an explanation. She was simply curious, as far as I could tell. That was good.

Fin rubbed the back of her neck. 'We've had an eventful day and a half.'

'Do tell.' Blanche dumped her hefty messenger bag on the sofa that effectively divided the long room into two halves. She leaned against the back of it, looking at the two of us sat facing each other across the dining table.

Fin started telling Blanche about seeing the giant in the Bockbourne valley. I left the four most informative web pages I'd found open on my laptop and went into the kitchen to put the kettle on. I wondered if there were biscuits anywhere, but I wasn't about to start opening cupboards to find out.

I turned back to the doorway while I waited for the kettle to boil. That meant I could look at Fin and Blanche together. No one would ever doubt they were sisters, though Blanche was a bit taller. She'd also had her hair cut nearly as short as mine, which was a surprise. Even so, an unbiased observer would probably say they were equally attractive. I'm definitely biased, so I wasn't making any comparisons.

Fin finished telling her sister about us seeing the white horse last night. Blanche had no idea what to say to that, so I spoke up.

'Do you want more coffee, Fin? Can I get you anything, Blanche?'

'I'm fine with this.' Fin refilled her mug, though what was left in the cafetière must have been stone cold.

'Ginger and lemon grass tea, please, in the brown tin by the kettle.' Blanche was frowning now. She looked at Fin. 'Okay, that's unexpected, but in what sense is it our problem? I mean, as far as we know, nothing has actually happened. Nothing that's going to get the locals worked up. Shouldn't we leave well alone?'

'There's a bit more to it than that.' Fin explained why I was there, thanks to the Green Man.

I made drinks for me and Blanche and carried them through to the dining table. I saw her expression and could make a fair guess at what she was thinking. The Green Man might have sent me to Bockbourne, but Fin didn't have to get involved.

'So nothing's happened so far, but you're sure it will.' Blanche grimaced as she reached for her mug.

Fin nodded at our laptops. 'We're seeing what we can find out while we wait.'

Blanche shrugged. 'Do you want me to help?'

'Honestly, the most useful thing you can do is write up the Mendips site visit and chase some invoices.' Fin looked apologetically at her sister.

To my relief, Blanche grinned. 'I can do that. I'll be in the office. Give me a shout if you need me.'

She picked her messenger bag up from the sofa and headed for the door to the hall, careful not to spill her tea. We heard doors opening and closing.

Fin looked across the dining table. 'So how have you got on?'

'Here's what we do know. Uffington is the one chalk horse that's definitely been proved to be ancient, and experts reckon it was the first to be cut, around three thousand years ago. There are similar designs in Bronze Age art and on Iron Age coins, apparently. Who cut it, and what's it for? That gets us into guesswork. There's a lot more information available about what it can't be.'

Fin was puzzled. 'How do you mean?'

'The idea that King Alfred had the horse made to celebrate his victory over the Danes was finally binned quite recently, when a way of analysing soils was developed.' I checked the relevant tab on my laptop. 'Optical Stimulated Luminescence Dating, apparently. How much would you like to know about that?'

Fin waved it away. 'What about the other horses?'

I read what I'd found aloud, summarising as I went. 'The one at Westbury is also known as the Bratton Horse, because it's on a slope below an Iron Age hillfort called Bratton Camp. The current horse was cut in 1778, but that was done on the site of a previous horse which seems to have looked like the one at Uffington. That's as much as anyone knows for certain, if you can call that much "certain". Some people are convinced the original was another Bronze Age or Iron Age horse. Other people say it was a fake, the equivalent of the ruined bits of castles that landowners were having built around then.'

'That's a bit of a theme in what I've read.' Fin looked at her own screen. 'There are pretty firm dates for the Alton Barnes, Broad Town, Cherhill and Devizes horses. They were cut from the 1780s through to the 1870s, roughly anyway, though the Devizes Horse was as good as lost until it was recut to celebrate the millennium. What no one can be sure of is if there were horses on those sites before. Some of the arguments are basically, well, there's an Iron Age hillfort there too, and the slope would be such a good place for a horse, there must have been one.'

I swallowed a mouthful of tea. 'The Pewsey Horse was cut on the site of an old one, but details about whatever was there before are pretty vague. The only one that seems to have been cut on a greenfield site is the Marlborough Horse. That was a schoolmaster's idea, and he had his pupils for a workforce. He wasn't anything to do with the boarding school that's there now though. There was an earlier one.'

Fin's mouse hand was busy again, and I could see her eyes searching her laptop's screen. 'It's the same story at Hackpen. "Not much is known, but it's generally believed" and so on. The horse there now was cut in 1838, possibly to commemorate Victoria's coronation.'

'Or just because someone thought it was a good idea.' I shook my head, frustrated.

'There's got to be more to this.' Fin was certain. 'There are local folk tales of different chalk horses coming down from their hills, to drink from the rivers or graze. I'd say we're not the only people who've seen... whatever we saw last night.'

I'd noticed those stories as well as I'd clicked from website to website. 'So there's more to these horses than the locals just copying some other village. But what do they mean? How do we find out?'

Fin sighed. 'I don't suppose any little local museums are open at the moment, or second-hand bookshops. The branch library here closed the year before last.'

We both know there's a vast amount of local history and folklore written down in days gone by that's not on the Net and probably never will be. That makes it easier for people like us to keep our secrets, but it doesn't help when we're trying to unravel a mystery.

'We could look for old books online, I suppose,' Fin said dubiously, 'but there's no way to know if we'd get what we needed, and I don't know about you, but I don't have cash to spare buying some antiquarian's memoirs that turn out to be useless.'

'And there's no saying how long deliveries might take at the moment.' I looked at Fin. 'Here's a different question. How much more do we need to find out about these chalk figures?'

She was surprised. 'Don't you want to, after seeing that horse?'

'Does it have anything to do with the giant?' I countered. 'We both felt its power, but we didn't feel it was any threat, did we? Not like the giant. You knew that was dangerous all the way from the other side of the valley. That's got to be the menace the Green Man wants dealt with, don't you think?'

'You don't think they're connected?' Fin's pale eyebrows arched. 'Seriously? It's pure coincidence we saw that horse the day after I saw the giant?'

'Fair point,' I conceded. 'But there's no mention of a chalk horse anywhere near Bockbourne Magna or Bockbourne Parva.'

'That doesn't mean there wasn't one in the past. These things disappear surprisingly fast if they're not maintained. Traces of lost horses have been found at Tan Hill and Rockley.'

'So how do we find out?' I still couldn't see an answer.

'We go to the pub,' Fin said promptly. 'The White Hart in Bockbourne Magna. There are a load of old posters, newspaper clippings and photos framed and hung on the walls.'

'It can't hurt to take a look,' I allowed.

Fin closed her laptop. 'If we go now, we can get some lunch.'

'That's a good idea.' I shut down my computer as well.

Fin stood up. 'I'll tell Blanche while you wash up the mugs.'

I must have looked surprised. She grinned at me.

'House rules. We clear up after ourselves, because if we don't, the other one has to choose between being a nag or a skivvy, and that's a crap thing to do to your sister.'

'I could have done with that rule in a few house shares.' I collected everything and headed for the kitchen while Fin went to speak to her sister. I could hear their voices, though not what they were saying.

As I dismantled the cafetière, I wondered if Blanche was concerned about losing her flatmate, if Fin and I got serious enough to think about moving in together. Maybe that explained her coolness towards me. I had no idea what sort of mortgage they had on this place, but it was hard to imagine one salary would cover it. How would Fin moving out affect their business? What strains would that sort of fallout cause between me and Fin? I'd never had to think about things like that before. There are some advantages to being a loner – until you want to stop being alone.

'Let's get on the road,' Fin called out from the living room.

'Right.' I rinsed soapy water off my hands and dried them on the towel. Do the job that's in front of you. Worry about what's next when it's done. That's what my dad always says.

Chapter Six

There's a petrol station on the outskirts of Cainescombe. Fin headed there to fill up the car. Once we were on the motorway the trip seemed a lot quicker than it had done last night. The roads down to the bottom of the little valley felt wider and less winding as we passed under the motorway and ignored the sign for Bockbourne Parva. You could hardly call Bockbourne Magna a big place, but I could see it had a primary school as well as a decent-sized village shop that doubled as a Post Office. That must help persuade people with well-paying jobs to trade a longer commute for evenings and weekends outside the towns and cities where they worked.

I was glad to unfold myself from the Toyota's passenger seat when Fin pulled up in the White Hart's car park. The pub was a handsome Georgian building across the road from St Melor's church. That was one of those sizeable Victorian Gothic barns without a tower or steeple. It was impressive enough, but there wasn't a trace of whatever had been there originally. I reckoned there'd always been money for rebuilding here, while the smaller, poorer village higher up on the hillside had been left much as it was. I could see plenty of replacement windows and tasteful extensions, as well as newer builds on what had been paddocks or orchards between the older houses.

The pub's car park was half full, and plenty of customers sat at the socially distanced tables outside in the garden. Each table had an umbrella, though there was no sign of rain at the moment. That was a relief. The grass in the beer garden was getting trampled into bare earth by more shoes than it was used to. If much more than a shower hit, the mud would be slick underfoot.

Fin took the path between the tables, heading for the porch that led into the pub. I followed, aware of mildly curious glances coming my way. I was wondering what that was about when a waitress in her forties came out of the pub door. She was wearing black trousers and a padded waistcoat over her white shirt. I caught the scent of the steak and ale pie on one of the plates on her loaded tray, and my stomach rumbled.

'Table for two, is it? Over there will be fine.' The waitress smiled as she gestured with her tray. 'I'll be with you in a moment.'

'We'd like to sit inside, please, if that's okay.' Fin stepped aside to let the waitress pass.

The woman didn't move. 'Oh, no, sorry, we're only serving outside at lunch times for the moment. We open up the bar and dining room in the evenings.'

She was perfectly polite, but that clearly wasn't up for debate. I guessed she was management, maybe the pub's owner, rather than hired staff. Whatever, she wasn't local. Her accent was pure Essex, no trace of Wessex.

'Oh.' Fin looked blank.

'That's not a problem,' I said quickly. 'Thanks. We'll sit over there.' I led the way to the vacant table.

'I suppose we may as well have something to eat while we're here.' Fin sat down and reached for one of the freshly printed paper menus. 'We can always come back this evening. The food is very good. Decent vegetarian options too.'

'Good to know.' I'd already decided I was having the steak pie, with carrots and broccoli and mash, but I studied the list of local beers. I wasn't driving, after all.

Fin looked up. 'Try the Summer Lightning. That's from a good local brewery.'

I nodded. 'I will.'

An irritated voice rose from a table on the other side of the path. 'Whatever I saw, it wasn't him!'

I looked up. Four middle-aged men in walking gear with binoculars and cameras were looking at me. They looked horribly embarrassed when they realised I'd overheard them. To be fair, so had everyone else in the beer garden, thanks to one of those sudden silences that invariably crop up when someone says something stupid.

'Our friend thinks he saw Bigfoot in the woods last weekend.' One of them laughed like a man well down his third pint. He gestured with his nearly empty glass. 'I was wondering if you were out for a stroll.'

'No offence meant,' the man with the mineral water next to him said hastily.

'None taken,' I said mildly. 'I've been called worse.'

That's true. My nickname's been Lurch on several building sites, and I was called Bigfoot often enough at school. Until everyone saw what one of my big feet could do, booting someone's backside unexpectedly. I may take a size-fourteen shoe, but I can move quickly and quietly when I want to.

The waitress came back and took our order. As she walked away, Fin drummed thoughtful fingers on the table. 'I wonder what we might see, if we go down to the woods today.'

I could see in her eyes what she wasn't saying, in case anyone overheard us. So she wasn't the only one who'd seen the giant. More than that, it looked as if the thing had been wandering about for at least a week. I wondered what it wanted with this place or its people. Nothing good was a safe bet, for middle-aged birdwatchers or whoever else the creature might stumble across.

I wondered exactly what this particular man had seen. If he had an unsuspected ancestor like my mum or someone similar, the giant might still have been in its shadow form, scary enough but with no real weight or substance. Unfortunately, greenwood or river spirit blood unknowingly inherited isn't immediately obvious, not to me anyway,

If the birdwatcher was human through and through? Ordinary people can only see those who normally live unseen when they choose to manifest, like the Blithehurst dryads pretending to be tourists, or that black shuck playing at being a Labrador. If the giant was setting solid foot in these woods, that was very bad news. I hated to think what might happen if half the fairy tales I'd read held anything like the truth.

I did my best to study each of the four men in turn without them noticing. Unfortunately, I couldn't be sure who'd spoken first. So I didn't know who'd seen the giant. The only one I could discount was the one who'd mentioned Bigfoot. Thankfully, none of the birdwatchers noticed me looking at them. Their conversation was becoming more and more intense. Unfortunately, they were keeping their voices down after embarrassing themselves earlier.

Our food and drinks arrived. My pint of beer was very welcome, and Fin was right. The Summer Lightning was very drinkable. We started eating, even though it made listening in to the other table more difficult. A few moments later, I nearly choked on my mouthful. I'd just heard something really bizarre from the other side of the path.

'What do you mean, universal monsters? Like Dracula and the Wolfman? That sort of thing?'

The bearded man opposite the man with the mineral water looked bemused. 'What?'

Mineral water man persisted. 'Universal Studios. The great black-and-white monster movies. The classics.'

The four men stared at each other, sharing a moment of mutual confusion. I looked across the table. Fin's gaze met mine as she ate her red onion and chestnut pie. I could see the word 'monster' had got her attention too.

'No, no, no. It's got nothing to do with the movies.' The bearded man took a long swallow of what looked like cider. 'I'm talking about the universal monster template theory.'

'Never heard of it,' Three-pints-in said emphatically.

The fourth man spoke up quickly before his bearded friend could get annoyed. 'What's that then?'

The bearded man took another drink. I guessed he was weighing up the urge to keep his irritating friend guessing against his desire to share what he knew with the others. Thankfully, he chose to display his superior knowledge.

'There are six sorts of monsters that crop up in folklore all over the world,' he began. 'Big flying things, big snake or lizard things, big dog things, big cat things, big humanoid things, yes, like Bigfoot, and small humanoid things like goblins and pixies and so on. These are the universal monsters, and they crop up time and again in mythology, and in places where there have never been similar creatures that could have got people's imagination making up stories about them. I mean, there have never been giant snakes or crocodiles in England, but we still have legends about dragons. Where do those ideas come from?'

Three-pints-in looked as if he was about to answer. He suddenly jerked and looked indignantly at the fourth man. I guessed he'd got a kick in the shins under the table.

Bearded man went on. 'The universal monster template theory says that these stories stem from deep-seated ancestral memories held in the most primitive parts of our brains. Memories that go all the way back to the days when our ancestors were early hominids roaming the African savannahs. Think about it. Australopithecus-whatevers were what, about four feet tall? There were plenty of lions and wolves and snakes and crocodiles that were easily big enough to eat them. Archaeologists have found hominid fossils to prove it, with animal bite marks on them. There were other hominids around then as well, who didn't make the evolutionary cut. They died out while Homo Sapiens survived. Some of them were bigger than our ancestors, and some of them were smaller. There are fossils of them too.'

Mineral water man snapped his fingers. 'Like those Indonesian hobbits. Homo Flore-something.'

'That sort of thing, yes,' the bearded man agreed. 'Anyway, the monster template theory goes, for all our modern progress, we still share these ancestral fears. So when someone catches a glimpse of a stray cat in Cornwall, especially without anything to give it scale, their subconscious tells them it's the Beast of Bodmin.'

Three-pints-in was determined to have his say now. 'That sounds pretty far-fetched to me.'

The bearded man just shrugged and finished his cider.

He had an ally in the fourth man. 'I can see how that could make sense. It's a bit like that, what do they call it, the way people see faces in light switches, or the arrangement of windows and doors in buildings. There are loads of those photos online.'

The film fan with the mineral water nodded. 'And it might help explain why horror movies are so popular – the creature features at least.'

Three-pints-in still looked sceptical. 'So where did you come across all this?'

The bearded man grinned. 'A cryptozoology website.'

Three-pints-in grimaced. 'Crypto—?'

His bearded friend was already explaining. 'Cryptozoologists. They go looking for animals that are supposed to be extinct, or ones that have escaped from zoos and started living wild, and yes, they hunt for evidence of things like Bigfoot or the Loch Ness Monster. I found an expert's site and put up a post a few days ago, saying I thought I'd seen something strange around here. Some of the replies got quite excited. There were stories of giants roaming around Salisbury Plain in medieval times, and that's not so far away. Some legends say they built Stonehenge.' He looked around the table. 'Are we finished? We should probably be making tracks.'

They stood up and gathered their cameras and other stuff. The fourth man wasn't ready to let things drop quite yet though.

'So did this website explain what you saw in the woods last week?'

The bearded man shrugged again. 'A tree's shadow. Some trick of the light. Ancestral memory does the rest.'

The fourth man nodded, thoughtful. 'I wonder if this might have something to do with the uncanny valley. You know, the way we recognise robot faces as nearly human, but not quite, and that makes us uneasy. Could that be some residual instinct warning us to be wary around other human-oids competing for resources?'

Mineral water man shrugged. 'If it is, I can't see how we can write algorithms to get round it.'

The four of them headed for the car park, so I guessed they had already paid their bill. I ate the last of my lunch. I thought about instincts warning people to be wary of faces that looked human but weren't. I reckoned that unconscious unease came from far more recent encounters that had happened much closer to home.

Fin finished eating and looked at me once the four men were safely out of earshot. 'Let's hope we won't be tripping over monster hunters in the woods.'

'With luck.' I still felt apprehensive. 'Do you know anything about cryptozoologists?'

'Not a thing.' Fin broke off as the waitress approached our table with an empty tray.

'Can I get you anything else?' she asked brightly. 'Can I clear these plates away?'

'Please, go ahead.' I leaned back so I wasn't in her way and looked at Fin. I wouldn't say no to a dessert, but I could wait if we were coming back here this evening. 'Do you want anything else?'

'I'm fine.' She smiled at the waitress. 'That was lovely, thanks. Could we have the bill, please?'

'Of course.' The waitress loaded up her tray and crossed the path to collect the four men's empty glasses.

'So what are we going to do now?' I asked Fin.

She chewed her lip for a moment. 'How about we go and take a look at the Uffington Horse? As far as I can tell, that's the easiest one to actually get close to.'

'Fine with me.' I had no idea what Fin expected us to find there, but it seemed as good a way as any to pass the afternoon, before we could come back and get inside the pub. 'How far away is that?'

'It's on the other side of the downs.' She was already checking the route on her phone. 'About forty minutes from here.'

The waitress came back with our bill and a hand-held credit card machine with the keypad wrapped in clingfilm. I got out my wallet.

'I'll get this,' I said as Fin reached for her backpack. 'You've paid for the petrol so far.'

'Oh, okay.' She grinned at me. 'Thanks.'

I paid up and pointed at the signs showing the way to the loos. 'I'll just use the Gents.'

'Good idea,' Fin agreed.

The toilets were at the back of the pub, off a lobby with glass-paned inner doors that opened into the bar. I could see what Fin meant about old posters that had been framed and hung on the walls. There was a good display of black-and-white photos in the lobby itself, but I couldn't stop and study them when I came out of the Gents. A bloke was waiting outside the door, by the sign that said one at a time. He was holding a small boy's hand, and the kid was shifting from foot to foot with a face that said he really needed a pee.

I went to wait outside. Fin soon appeared from the Ladies, and we headed back to the car park. As we walked towards the Toyota, a muddy white Ford Fiesta pulled up. A woman with short dark hair got out of the driver's seat and opened the rear door to get a coat out of the back.

I wouldn't have given her a second look, except for the way she stiffened when she turned around and saw the two of us. Her eyes widened with what could have been recognition or might have been something else. Either way, I wanted to know.

I halted. 'Can I help you with something?'

'No,' she snapped.

I raised my hands and took a step back. 'No need to bite my head off.'

The woman didn't answer. She hurried past us towards the beer garden, with her face turned away.

'Charming.' Fin was as surprised as I was.

'Maybe she recognised me from all that shit online about me,' I said uneasily. 'You know what they say. The Internet is forever.'

A few years ago, I'd been suspected of a murder. That had been the first time the Green Man expected me to sort out a clash between the ordinary world and the scary things that live in dark woods. When a girl turned up horribly dead a few miles from where I was working, that definitely hadn't been a good time to be a loner who moved from place to place every few months. The police had taken a long hard look at a carpenter with access to a lot of sharp tools, and I could hardly explain I was there to deal with a problem no coppers could tackle. The tabloids and twenty-four-hour news channels had had a field day, not giving a fuck about the actual facts.

I did my best to shrug it off and headed for the Toyota. I remembered to go around to the passenger side at the last minute.

'So what do you make of that universal monster theory?' Fin clipped her phone into the bracket fixed to the windscreen and reached for her seat belt. 'Have you ever heard of it before?'

'Never.' I waited for her to pull safely out of the car park's narrow exit. 'I've no idea if it's plausible, but it could be a useful way to explain away sightings of things like the shuck at Blithehurst.'

Fin still looked troubled as she concentrated on the road. 'I can't say I like the idea of Bigfoot hunters turning up, even if they're just out to disprove any rumours of sightings.'

'At least that gives us an excuse to be out in the woods ourselves.' I looked at the trees on either side of the road. The leaves were somewhere around the halfway point of turning from green to gold. A fair few had already fallen, and bad weather would soon bring down more. Tufts of long grass were still flourishing among the drifts of sodden brown. The duller green of ivy straggled in tangles across the uneven ground.

I could see through the trees for a fair distance. Beech woods are comparatively open and airy, with their lack of undergrowth and the tall, straight trunks of the trees standing well spaced apart. I'm more familiar with the denser, darker security of oak woodland. I felt uncomfortably exposed, even being driven along in the car.

Chapter Seven

Fin followed the online map's route up the valley, and the road got narrower. She didn't take the turn for Bockbourne Parva but drove up the great slope of the downs instead. We left the trees behind and were soon driving past open pasture. I wondered if there was any trace of a chalk horse under all the sheep. If there was, how would anyone find it?

I hadn't come up with any bright ideas by the time Fin turned into the National Trust car park. That was tucked in a tree-ringed hollow where I guessed chalk had once been quarried. There were plenty of empty spaces, as well as more cars than I had expected, even at the weekend. I supposed with so many places closed, people were making the most of days out to go walking and see something interesting. I got out of the Toyota and went to buy a ticket. Then we followed the signposts towards the horse, leaving the scrubby trees around the car park behind.

After we negotiated the gates designed to foil escaping sheep, we walked out onto the top of the downs. The skies above us were vast and empty. Empty, but not cloudless. The day had turned overcast, and a darker line that promised rain was heading towards us from far away in the west.

Far, far away. The view was spectacular, even on this grey autumn day. We were right at the end of the chalk ridge that makes up those downs. Behind me, the high ground carried the Ridgeway through the borderlands of Oxfordshire, Berkshire, Wiltshire and beyond. Ahead of us, the sheep-cropped turf fell away down steep slopes that looked like a rumpled blanket. Far below, miles and miles of flat farmland stretched towards the distant horizon. The squares and rectangles of green and brown were criss-crossed by the lines of hedges.

The landscape looked like a patchwork quilt. Though patchwork quilts don't have the stark white lines and angles of wind turbines to snag the eye here and there.

Setting aside the novelty of being able to see bad weather coming from such a distance, I tried to calculate how soon the rain would reach us. I tried to calculate the wind speed, turning my face into the strong, steady breeze. It was no good. I'd just be guessing. Most of the other people I could see had decided they'd prefer to be safe and dry than sorry and soggy. They were heading back to the car park.

I turned to Fin. I was about to ask if she had any idea how soon we might get soaked, or did she think the wind might sweep the clouds over us too fast for rain to fall. I stood and watched her instead. She'd pulled that clip out of her long blonde hair, and the wind sent it streaming out behind her. She was taking deep breaths as her lips curved in a blissful smile. Her eyes were closed, and I saw her flex her hands, opening and closing her fingers.

She glanced at me, and her blue eyes were bright with delight. I was convinced if there'd been no one around, she would have handed me her backpack with her keys and wallet and turned into a swan there and then. She would have flown away on her wide white wings, for the sheer pleasure of soaring over this landscape.

I grinned at her. 'Take all the time you like. Whenever you're ready.'

She laughed. 'I'm fine, thanks. Let's look at this horse now we're here.'

I started walking towards the vantage point where the signs said we'd get a good view of the horse. When we reached the marked spot, I decided Fin would get the best view of the mysterious design if she did take flight. I could make out the sweep and curve of the wide chalk lines from where we were standing, but I realised why the tourist websites had said it was best seen from a distance, from somewhere in the vale below.

Those websites had said a few other interesting things as well. I pointed down the hillside, into the broad hollow directly beneath the horse.

'That dry valley's called The Manger. It's where the horse is supposed to go and graze. Those ridges over there are called the Giant's Steps, and one website I read says they were caused by the permafrost melting at the end of the last Ice Age.'

Fin pursed her lips. 'The dryads could be on to something then. I don't know about ancestral memories from aeons ago in Africa, but I could be convinced that lost truths linger in ancient names in the landscape.'

I pointed to the other side of the hollow, where a small round hill had a flattened top that couldn't possibly be natural. A bare patch of chalk was stark white against the green turf. 'That's Dragon Hill, where St George supposedly killed his dragon. Grass won't grow where its blood was spilled, apparently.'

'How likely is that?'

Fin wasn't being sarcastic. She knew I'd killed the wyrmling at Blithehurst, and that I'd seen two other, bigger wyrms, though fortunately killing them hadn't been down to me.

I looked around to make sure no one was close enough to hear me. 'Wyrmling blood stinks like hot tar, and it's about as hot and thick. I could believe it would scorch grass so badly that nothing would regrow. I don't know about St George getting involved, but I could be persuaded a wyrm died here. This would be a good place to fight one, if it could be lured up so high. There's no water anywhere close for it to dive into and heal its wounds.'

I nodded towards the chalk figure. 'Horses can kill snakes. Don't they trample them to death? I bet the horse we saw last night could make a hell of a mess of a wyrmling.'

'Maybe.' Fin looked around. 'Can you feel... anything?'

I thought back to the eerie sensation of watching the luminous white horse in the twilight. There was nothing like that here, not at the moment, anyway. 'No,' I admitted.

Fin shivered. 'Me neither, though I have no idea if that means something or nothing. Let's get out of this wind.'

'Fine by me.'

She didn't head back to the car park though. We went up the slope towards what the signs called Uffington Castle. It's a hillfort, and a big one, surrounded by an outer earth bank and a wide ditch about three metres deep. Any attackers crossing that would meet a taller, steeper inner rampart that I guessed had been built from the spoil when the builders dug out the ditch. That was a hell of a lot of man-hours of work by hand. We walked alongside the outer bank and reached a place where a narrow earth bank crossed the ditch to an entrance.

'A fair used to happen here,' I told Fin, 'back in the days when the horse was scoured every seven years. Well, they called it a fair, but it sounds more like a temporary small town was set up.'

I'd found a website that had gone into endless detail about the festivities, but I'd resisted the temptation and just scanned it. 'Stalls were set up so people could spend the day eating and drinking if they wanted to. The competitions ranged from horse races along the Ridgeway to the locals chasing pigs and climbing greasy poles. There were poetry and singing competitions and singlestick fighting.'

Fin was curious. 'What was that?'

'A way of training men to use the sword they'd be handed if they joined the army or the early police.' I'd had to look it up. 'The stick had a basket-work hilt to protect your hand, but it still sounds bloody dangerous. Literally. You won by hitting your opponent's head hard enough to make them bleed.'

'The good old days,' Fin remarked. 'No such thing as risk assessment or health and safety.'

We stood for a moment, looking at the deserted expanse of windswept, tussocky grass. I estimated the inside of the fort was a bit over two hundred metres by one fifty. It was hard to imagine the space crammed with people and uproar, like something out of a Dickens drama on telly. The only sound now was the wind, and snatches of birdsong from the small brown shapes darting along the ditch where they had some shelter. They were moving too fast for me to see what they were, and I didn't blame them. It was too chilly to be hanging about.

'Where to?' I asked Fin.

She turned to look eastwards along the downs. The land-scape didn't fall away on this side, but we could still see for a spectacular distance. She pointed. 'That's the Ridgeway. Wayland's Smithy is about a mile's walk over there.'

I knew what she was thinking. Back at the start of the year, we'd stopped a greedy bastard digging up a whole lot more than he bargained for near her mum's house in the Fens. I'd nearly ended up drowned when my Land Rover had been swamped. I'd survived because I was rescued by a mysterious figure poling a hollow log boat through the floods.

He'd told me his name was Wade, but he'd said nothing else about himself. When I was back on dry land, I'd gone looking through old books and stories. I hadn't found much about him. Oh, once upon a time, the tale of Wade and his boat had been widely told. Geoffrey Chaucer certainly knew all about him, but if anyone ever wrote down the full story, it's been lost in the mists of time. Eleanor had gone looking in the university libraries she could access online, but the references that lingered here and there only offered fragments of his legend. Some of those scraps said that Wade was Wayland's father. I knew Fin knew that, because I'd told her.

'Do you think we'll find some answers there?'

She shrugged. 'It can't hurt to take a look, can it?'

I shoved my hands in my coat pockets. 'Okay.'

We started walking towards the path that would take us there, following the wooden signposts. I wondered if this was the right thing to do.

Wade had given me a message for the Green Man. 'Tell him that more than the waters are rising.' That's what the mysterious ferryman had said before he dissolved into mist and starlight. Could he have meant this giant was going to be on the move? Or was he talking about the white horse that we'd seen? I had no idea, and I didn't like it.

I wasn't even sure the Green Man had got the message. I'd stood in the library at Blithehurst and repeated Wade's warning four times, looking up at each of the carved faces in turn. Had I seen a flicker of emerald light as I finished speaking, or had I imagined that? I still wasn't sure. I'd told my mum and the dryads at Blithehurst, asking them to pass on the message if they saw the Green Man. None of them had told me they'd done so, though to be fair, I hadn't asked.

We walked along the broad groove worn into the chalk by countless generations of human and animal feet, and maybe stranger creatures than that. I wondered if we'd find more ordinary ramblers at Wayland's Smithy? If we didn't, I wondered if I was going to get a bollocking from Wade or Wayland for not doing as I was told. What was I? The Green Man's sodding voicemail?

We reached the Ridgeway and headed east. Now we had thin soil and a bit of grass underfoot, though I could see that it didn't take much to wear through to the chalk beneath.

I noticed ruts from wheels and wondered how long they'd been there. Uncompromising metal notices told anyone who cared that this was a restricted byway, in black and white and red. I wondered how often they were ignored. My dad occasionally has trouble back home with tossers determined to go off-roading in their shiny new four-wheel drives. There are always some arseholes who think that rules only apply to other people.

Fin was looking from side to side as we followed the path. The Ridgeway carved a pale, barely wavering line up the long, shallow slope ahead of us. The hedges that topped the low banks on either side were mostly blackthorn and hawthorn. The low trees were still mainly green, though I could see where the leaves were starting to yellow. Other foliage was spotted and edged with autumnal brown. All the branches were heavy with fruit. It was a good year for deep red hawthorn berries as well as blue-black sloes. The birds and any other animals around here would be glad of that food once winter came.

'What are those? Do you know?' Fin was looking at another hedgerow tree. These twigs were already leafless, which made their bright pink fruits all the more startling.

I knew I'd seen something like that in a book somewhere, but it took me a moment to remember its name. 'I think it's called spindle. The wood was used for, well, spindles for wool, and for knitting needles, things like that.'

Loud, excited barking interrupted me. I turned around to see where the noise was coming from, and so did Fin. A sizeable hare was bolting along the path. I honestly thought it was going to run into my legs. The animal wasn't looking where it was going. It was just desperate to get away from the dog chasing it. I took an incautious step backwards and nearly fell flat on my arse as my foot slipped.

The hare jinked and dodged past me, barely slowing down. As I recovered my balance, I tried to grab the dog when it came within reach, but the bastard thing wasn't wearing a collar. It was some sort of mixed breed, from what I could tell as it raced after the hare. It was greyhound-shaped, but it was smaller and black-coated, with a definite look of Doberman about its head. If either of those breeds were in its ancestry, I guessed there was room in its tiny skull for two instincts and not much else. Those instincts would be 'chase' and 'kill'.

The hare knew that. It was racing away as fast as it could, trying to open up a lead. That meant staying on the path. The fleeing animal looked like some action-movie halfwit running down the middle of the road while the villain chases them in a car. But the hare wasn't stupid. It knew if it slowed to try to hide in the hedge, it would feel that dog's teeth grab its leg.

Someone was hurrying up the track, shouting and waving what I guessed was the dog's lead. I left him to Fin and started running after the dog. I didn't think I could stop the damn thing catching the hare, but I might be able to get it off before the poor thing was too badly injured. There had to be a wildlife rescue place somewhere around here. A vet might be able to give the hare a chance.

I saw a crossroads up ahead, where a strip of tarmac crossed the Ridgeway. The dog's black backside disappeared as it turned right. Its hind feet skidded, nearly losing their grip. When I reached the break in the chalk path, I realised a public road arrived here, dead-ending at the entrance to a farm. There was no sign of the hare. The black dog was standing in the middle of the road, looking in all directions. It was thoroughly confused.

Several cars had parked along the broad verge, in the shelter of the stand of trees. I guessed this was a place where walkers in the know came to park for free instead of paying for the National Trust car park. One of the vehicles was a muddy white Ford Fiesta. A woman with short dark hair was hurrying towards it. A few moments later, as she went around the front to reach the driver's door, I realised who she was. That was the woman we'd seen in the White Hart car park. The woman who'd given me that strange look. What was she doing here?

'Hey!' I took a step, ready to go after her. She ducked down behind the car, as if she was trying to hide from me.

I had second thoughts about going any closer. A man my size confronting a woman on her own never looks good. There might be someone sitting in one of those cars striped with tree shadows. I couldn't see past the shine on their windscreens.

That moment's hesitation cost me any chance I might have had to find out what the hell she was up to. Wrenching her car door open, she scrambled inside and started the engine. She threw the Fiesta into a tight, fast U-turn and accelerated so hard that the tyres spun before getting a grip on the tarmac. The dog had had better traction.

I heard a whine. I looked down and saw the hound looking up at me. It was a young dog, not much more than a puppy. Its ears were pricked and its expression was eager, as if it expected me to tell it where the hare had gone. It didn't know it had done anything wrong.

It wasn't the dog's fault it belonged to a tosser, but someone had to teach it a lesson. I vented my frustration at not being able to talk to that woman.

'Bad dog!' I told it, with plenty of full-throated menace.

The mongrel got the message. It cowered away, pressing its belly low to the ground. I got no pleasure from seeing that, but I hoped it might think twice before chasing after a hare again – or any other wildlife, come to that.

'You – you don't need to scare him.' The dog's owner had arrived. He was about my own age, about a foot shorter than me and pudgy around the middle under layers of outdoor gear. He was out of breath and indignant.

I was about to give him a piece of my mind, but Fin got in first.

'Do you realise you could be fined five thousand pounds if your dog had killed that hare? Wild mammals are protected by law. You have absolutely no control over him, do you? If you're going to own a dog, you should damn well know how to handle it. The first thing you do is train him to obey you. What was he doing off his lead anyway? How could you be so irresponsible? What if he had gone after a sheep?'

The dog owner stood open-mouthed as he tried to decide which question to answer first. I didn't give him the chance.

'Where I grew up, dogs that go after sheep get shot.'

He looked as shocked as if I'd slapped him. I don't know if he would have tried to argue with me, but that's when those clouds I'd forgotten about arrived. The rain didn't fall so much as come lashing at us sideways. The downpour hammered the road and the trees around us. The noise alone made trying to carry on talking completely pointless.

The dog owner got the hound's slipped collar back over his pet's head with shaking hands. He patted the subdued animal and it pressed itself against his leg with what looked like genuine affection. They started walking back towards the White Hart. It's fair to say they both had their tail between their legs. Man and dog both ducked their heads as they headed into the merciless squall.

I was looking down to stop the rain getting into my eyes. Milky streams of chalky rainwater swirled around my boots and ran off the footpath to straggle across the dark grey tarmac. I moved into the shelter of a flourishing hawthorn. We might as well wait for the worst of the weather to pass overhead before we decided what to do next.

'Do you think he'll find a dog-training class?' Fin had to raise her voice, even though she was pressing up against me.

'I hope so,' I shouted back. 'I think the idea that a farmer could shoot his pet gave him a hell of a scare.'

I saw that Fin was shivering. Her shower-proof jacket wasn't doing much to keep her dry in this downpour. Come to that, while my expensive new coat was living up to its advertising, my combat trousers were soaked, cold and clinging to my legs. 'What now?'

She wiped rain and strands of wet hair out of her eyes. 'I'm absolutely drenched, and it'll be ages before the pub's serving dinner. Let's go home.'

Chapter Eight

I'd never realised sheep can look so smug. When we'd left the field by the car park, the flock had been wandering across the hill, idly nibbling grass. When we got back, they were sheltering in the lee of the trees that edged the hollow. The sheep watched me and Fin approaching but didn't move. I couldn't see a drop of rain on their nice, warm woolly backs.

Down in the car park, most of the other vehicles had already left. There was no sign of that bloke and his dog. At least the rain was easing off. There was enough shelter in the hollow for Fin to get some lengths of plastic sheeting out of the Toyota's boot without everything else in there getting soaked.

'Stick this on your seat.' She handed me one of the sheets with a wry smile. 'Getting unexpectedly wet is a regular hazard in my line of work.'

We got into the car and Fin searched in her backpack for her phone. Thankfully, the lining was properly waterproof. I was glad I had my own wallet and phone in the inside pocket of my new coat.

Fin was ringing Blanche. 'We're heading back now... Yes, we did.' She laughed and listened for a moment. 'Okay, if that's all right with you. Do you want me to get anything from the supermarket?... Fine, if you're sure.'

She ended the call, dropped her phone in the backpack and handed the whole lot to me. She turned the key in the ignition but didn't drive away, turning on the car's fan and heater instead. Though she'd only spent a few minutes on the phone, the windows were already steaming up. Fin reached under her seat and pulled out a ragged length of old towelling.

I waited for her to wipe all the glass she could reach and held out my hand. 'I'll do this side.'

The advantages of long arms in a small car came in useful again. When Fin was satisfied she could see clearly, she drove out of the car park. We were soon back on the motorway, heading westwards while the bad weather went on its way to dump the rest of its rain somewhere to the east. Sitting on plastic in wet trousers wasn't particularly comfortable, but the Toyota's upholstery would stay dry.

When we pulled up in Cainescombe, I guessed the dark blue Honda in the flat's other designated space belonged to Blanche. When we got upstairs and Fin opened the front door, her sister was in the hallway, getting a stack of towels out of a cupboard.

Once we'd hung up our coats, she handed a couple of towels to me. 'You two look like drowned rats.'

I wasn't sure how to respond to that, but I didn't have to. Blanche had turned to Fin. 'You're welcome to use the en-suite.'

'Thanks.' Fin took the rest of the towels.

Blanche gave us both a brief smile and went back into their office. I followed Fin into her room and we each found ourselves some dry clothes.

'If you leave your wet stuff here, I can get everything into the wash.' Fin peeled her damp sweatshirt over her head.

'Thanks.' Stripping off, I wrapped one of the good-sized towels securely around my waist. Picking up the other one and my dry clothes, I headed for the bathroom. A hot shower was very welcome, though I didn't linger. Leaving the towels to dry on the heated rail, I got dressed and went in search of a cup of tea.

Out in the hall, I heard running water coming from Blanche's room. So Blanche had got the en-suite when she and Fin had moved into this flat. I wondered whose idea that had been. Had she claimed the better bedroom on the grounds of being the older sister? Well, it wasn't any of my business.

I found Blanche was in the kitchen, standing with her back to the door as she cut up some aubergines on a chopping board next to the cooker.

She paused, half turning, knife in hand. 'We take turns to cook at weekends. I'm doing caponata and a cheese and spinach pie. I'll cook some sort of meat for you if you want it when you're here, but I warn you, whatever it is probably won't be very good. I'm not used to doing things like that.'

That wasn't any sort of apology, but she wasn't picking a fight either. She was simply stating a fact. So I gave her a straightforward answer back.

'Vegetarian's fine with me, thanks. Okay if I put the kettle on? Can I make a cup of anything for you while I'm at it?'

'Sure.' Blanche moved what she was doing to the other side of the cooker, so I could get to the sink under the window more easily. Once I'd filled the kettle, she started chopping again. 'Lemon grass and ginger tea, please. Brown tin.'

I made the two drinks and took my actual tea out to the dining table. That small kitchen felt uncomfortably crowded with the two of us in there.

My laptop was still set up, so I sat down and switched it on. The first thing I looked up was the spindle tree. I was pleased to see that I had been right when I identified those bare twigs with the bright pink fruits. I also learned that anywhere spindle grew in the wild was likely to be an ancient woodland. I told myself I needed to remember that. Finding old trees didn't necessarily mean looking through remnants of oak forests.

I looked up Wayland's Smithy next. One legend in particular caught my eye. The Smithy is where the Uffington Horse goes to get a set of new shoes. It gallops through the sky to get there, once every hundred years. Apparently, the last time that happened had been around a century ago, though the web page I was reading scrupulously noted that no eyewitness accounts could be found. I'll bet. I couldn't imagine anyone who could see something like the horse we had seen would be fool enough to draw attention to themselves in the 1920s.

A hundred years ago, as good as, anyway. And now things were stirring again. This timing didn't feel like a coincidence to me. Come to that, I was wondering how come Fin and I had just happened to end up having our lunch a table away from those four blokes who had been talking about seeing the giant, even if the bearded man hadn't believed his own eyes. Yes, I know timing in real life can be so remarkable that you'd never believe it in a book or a film, but I wasn't convinced that had just been luck. I wondered if the Green Man had been lending us a hand, or maybe Wayland's influence reached right across the downlands, as far as the Bockbourne valley?

If either of those mysterious figures was getting involved, I needed to find a way to let them know I could do with a lot more help. I'd been sent here to subdue the giant. I'd accepted that challenge. I'd do my absolute best. I still had no sodding clue where to even start.

Fin came in from the hall, carrying a laundry basket full of wet clothes. She went into the kitchen and I heard her telling Blanche about our day as she loaded the washing machine. When Fin started explaining the monster template theory to her sister, that gave me an idea. I tuned out their conversation and went looking for cryptozoology websites. Maybe one of them would have ideas on how to kill a Bigfoot. That might give me some sort of lead to follow.

The first thing I found was the answer to a different question. Something had occurred to me in the beer garden. I knew there really were monsters, but as far as I was concerned, there was one on that universal list that still needed a lot more explaining. I could tick off three of the others, because I'd seen them for myself. I'd encountered more than one black shuck, as well as several wyrms. I'd met the hobs who live near Fin's mum in the Fens, and Fin had seen this giant, so that made four that I could believe in. I was prepared to accept there was some cat equivalent of the shuck, given the regular sightings of Beasts of Bodmin and wherever else. The fact that no one had ever caught one just confirmed they were supernatural, as far as I was concerned.

But what about flying monsters? I hadn't ever seen or heard anything about things like that being real, at least as far as people like me and Fin are concerned. How did cryptozoologists explain them?

After a bit of looking, I found an explanation. It had to do with lemurs in Madagascar, and I had to read it twice. Apparently, if any sort of shadow sweeps across a lemur, it freezes like a prey animal that's afraid that some passing raptor is about to have it for lunch. Only there are no hunting birds anywhere around there that are big enough to do that, certainly not as far as the biggest lemurs are concerned. That doesn't matter. Even those biggest lemurs act as if they're afraid of being eaten. And excavations have discovered fossils that prove there had been massive eagles on Madagascar aeons ago.

If I understood what I was reading, this was where the whole idea of inherited memory in primates got started. Cryptozoologists reckoned modern lemurs were still afraid of the flying predators that were eating their remote ancestors countless ages ago. Lemurs pre-date australopithecines. Truly gigantic birds of prey have been found in other parts of the world as well, or at least their fossils have been unearthed. As far as I could work out, cryptozoologists drew a few dotted lines to join all these things together, and flying monsters joined the universal monster template theory.

It would be good if that was true, I decided. I'd much prefer to think that dragons with wings were the remnants of some scared monkey's nightmare, instead of something I might actually come across. The thought of trying to fight a giant was bad enough.

Which reminded me of what I was actually supposed to be looking for. I tried a few different ways of asking Google to show me what cryptozoologists might be saying about giants. I must have got something right. I found myself looking at a website where a lively discussion was going on. There were a whole load of comments below an account of someone seeing a gigantic shadowy humanoid walking through a beech wood. I realised this had to be the post that the bearded man had mentioned. Every detail of the date and place fitted. Coincidence? Lucky break? I really didn't think so.

I was about to call out to Fin and tell her when I realised there was also a lively discussion going on in the kitchen.

'If there's any chance there's anyone out in those woods looking for something supernatural, then we don't want to go within a mile of there.' Blanche was adamant. 'The Bockbourne job's nearly done, and we can do most of the rest remotely. You need to stay well away from this.'

'That's not an option for Dan,' Fin protested. 'The Green Man sent him here to tackle the giant.'

'No, he was sent to Bockbourne, not to anywhere around here. Lend him your car keys and he can go looking for trouble on his own.' Blanche broke off as she realised I was looking at the two of them though the half-open kitchen door.

'I'm sorry, Dan, but we stay safe by not taking risks.' She didn't sound remotely apologetic. 'It's different for you. No one can ever prove you're a dryad's son. All you have to do is deny it, even if someone was prepared to believe such a thing is possible. What happens to our family if someone sees one of us shifting?'

'None of us have ever been caught out,' Fin objected. She was seriously annoyed. 'We're always careful. I'm always careful. It's the first thing Mum taught—'

'How do you know you haven't been seen? I bet people used to sneaking around after animals are bloody good at not being noticed.'

Since Fin had no answer for that, Blanche pressed harder. 'You can't be certain. None of us can. Yes, we're always careful, but this is different. We can't take any risks at all, not around Bockbourne, not now everyone and their dog has a camera on their phone. As for these cryptozoologists, if one of them gets suspicious, I hate to think where we could end up. What might DNA analysis show if someone gets hold of a feather from one of us? I have no idea, and nor do you. '

I tried to reassure her. 'I don't want Fin taking any risks. Not tripping over some monster hunter. Not getting too close to this giant.'

'Excuse me.' Fin was really cross now. 'I'll do whatever I damn well like, thank you both very much.'

'I never said I don't want your help,' I said hurriedly. 'I'm talking about not taking risks that can be avoided, for both of us.'

'Like what?'

As she challenged me with an unblinking look, I realised I had no actual idea, any more than I knew how to subdue the giant. I changed the subject, gesturing at my laptop screen.

'I don't think we need to worry too much about monster hunters. The cryptozoologist who runs this website seems a lot more interested in debunking any stories of a Bigfoot sighting. There's a thread here about something in the woods at Bockbourne that goes into all sorts of details about depth perception and colour vision during twilight. It ends up with pretty much everyone convinced this supposed monster was just a trick of the shadows.'

'Let me see.' Blanche came out of the kitchen, wiping her hands on a tea towel.

'Scroll for yourself.' I let go of the mouse and tilted the screen a little bit further back, so Blanche could read at her own pace. I can't stand it when I'm trying to look at something and someone else keeps shifting it up or down.

Blanche leaned on one hand, taking the mouse in the other. She read the original post, then clicked to expand the various comment threads beneath it. Finally, she made a non-committal noise.

'So who is this person, anyway?' She clicked on the tab labelled 'About' in the row at the top of the screen.

'Shit!' The word was out before I could stop it.

'What?' Fin had been standing in the kitchen doorway. She came to stand beside me, looking at the web page and the photo.

'Bloody hell. That's her, isn't it?' Her voice went from surprised to certain. 'She's the woman from the White Hart car park.'

'What are you talking about?' Blanche demanded.

Fin explained. Then she looked at me, biting her lower lip. 'She gave us a really strange look, didn't she, Dan?'

There was no point denying it, even if neither of these swan maidens had a dryad's talent for hearing lies. 'Yes.'

Fin heard something in my tone, even in that single word. 'What? What is it?'

'I saw her again.' I shrugged. 'You know where we caught up with that dog? Where there were some cars parked up? One of them belonged to her. I saw her driving away.'

'You're only just mentioning this now?' Blanche demanded.

'If I hadn't seen her photo, I wouldn't have thought seeing her again was important,' I protested, waving a hand at the laptop.

Though as I said that, I wondered if it was entirely true. Something about the woman's odd behaviour had made me uneasy. Had I put us all at risk by ignoring that? I hoped Fin wouldn't ask if I'd been going to tell her about seeing the woman later. I honestly wasn't sure.

Blanche had already made up her mind. 'It's obvious what she's up to. She's using her website to trawl for potential supernatural sightings. Then she persuades these people that they must be mistaken to stop them from carrying on looking. Meanwhile, she's busy investigating for herself. If she does ever discover—' she gestured, exasperated '—*something*, she stands to make a fortune from selling the story and the pictures to the papers or the telly, or even just putting it up on bloody YouTube.'

'Why was she near the Smithy?' Fin objected. 'That's miles from Bockbourne. No one's seen a giant around there.'

'As far as you know,' Blanche shot back. 'Maybe she was following up on some white horse sighting in that area. Maybe she was following you two. If this—' she glanced at the screen '—this Hazel Spinner heard about the giant a week ago, who's to say she wasn't skulking about the other morning when you were out there flying over the valley. She might not have seen you shift, but she could still be wondering what you were up to, out and about so early. She could be stalking you, trying to find out.'

Fin laid a hand on my shoulder and looked at the laptop instead of her sister. 'Are there any posts on that site about any sort of sighting close to the Uffington Horse?'

'It doesn't matter if there are.' Blanche spoke before I could even move the mouse. 'Look there, at her bio. That says she's based near Exeter. If she's here, she's come all the way from Devon to hunt for whatever she's after. That makes her dangerous, any way you look at it. You need to steer clear of her, for all our sakes.'

Fin's hand tightened on my shoulder. I looked up to see she would really like to argue, but Blanche was right – about one thing at least. This wasn't just about Fin. If her secret was uncovered, her whole family would be under the spotlight. When I ran risks, I was the only one who could get hurt.

And Blanche had made another good point. We didn't know why this cryptozoologist woman was here. But I couldn't work out how to say any of that without Fin thinking I was taking her sister's side. I wasn't, and I wasn't going to stop trying to tackle the giant. That's why the Green Man had sent me to Bockbourne. I couldn't work out how to say that either, without making this unexpected argument worse.

I thought of something else. 'Can anyone smell burning?'

'Shit.' Blanche hurried back into the kitchen.

Chapter Nine

All I could actually smell was the promise of a good meal. At least that interruption stopped Fin and Blanche getting into a blazing row. Though I saw Blanche glance over her shoulder as she stirred a pot of something on the stove. Her expression told me she knew exactly what I'd done. What I couldn't tell was how she felt about that.

I concentrated on my laptop screen. I wanted Fin's help, but that had to be her choice. I wasn't going to be responsible for her putting herself and her family at risk. Equally, I wasn't going to tell her to stay safely out of the way. I knew she could handle herself when she was facing some danger.

Fin walked around the table, sat down and switched on her own computer. 'So what do we do now?' She sounded exasperated but determined.

'See if we can find any mention of a lost chalk horse near Bockbourne?' I suggested. 'Failing that, see if we can find out how archaeologists or whoever go looking for something like that, once the exact location's been forgotten.'

'Why?' There was a faint edge to Fin's voice.

'Because that will give us a great excuse if this Hazel Spinner woman or anyone else wants to know why we're out and about in the woods. Add to that, we'll be telling the truth. There has to be some connection between you seeing the giant and us seeing that horse. I can't believe it's just a coincidence. I think it could be important. Neither of us felt that horse was a threat. I'd like to know if we can get it on our side before we go looking for a giant.'

I lowered my voice. 'And if you want to make quite certain that crypto woman can't get any proof of who you really are, you just need to leave your feathers here, don't you?'

I didn't particularly want her to do that. If we did find ourselves neck-deep in the shit, I'd like her to have the option of flying away – to get herself out of trouble and to get some help for me, if that was possible. But if she needed to leave her feathers behind to keep the peace with her sister, we could work around that.

'I'll think about it.' Fin glanced at the kitchen, where Blanche was making enough noise to drown out anything we might say. 'Okay, let's see if there's ever been a Bockbourne Chalk Horse.'

As she began typing, I decided to see what I could learn about rediscovering lost chalk horses in general. I soon found I was reading about something completely unexpected.

The lost Red Horse of Tysoe had been a figure carved into the Edgehill escarpment, where the red clay of the area gave the horse its colour. Or rather, there had been a whole series of horses. Cutting into clay didn't give an outline that was nearly as clear or long-lasting as a trench cut deep into the chalk of the downs. Undergrowth and scrub could reclaim the land in as little as a couple of years if the horse wasn't scoured every year. The whole thing got completely lost several times, so an entirely new horse had to be cut.

Once, the horse at the time had been deliberately destroyed. A local pub landlord who didn't give a toss about feudal obligations ploughed it up in 1800 when he bought the land from the Marquess of Northampton. He soon found that was a mistake. His pub, the Rising Sun, had made a lot of money from the Palm Sunday fair that went with the annual scouring. Without everyone turning up to tend to the horse and have some fun, his takings went way down. He soon had another horse cut. That was probably the fourth and last one, and it had vanished by 1910. There might have been some attempt to cut another one after that, but any trace of it was lost during World War One.

If that's when the horse had been lost, I wanted to know when it had first appeared. There was solid evidence for the figure being there in 1607. An antiquarian called William Campden was surveying the British Isles and noted it down as a point of interest. In 1612, a Warwickshire poet I'd never heard of called Michael Drayton complained that Uffington's white horse got all the attention while his local red horse didn't get anywhere near the recognition it deserved. He felt his own work was undervalued as well.

There were plenty of other mentions, according to the webpage I found, until the final horse disappeared. The last people to take any real interest were a bunch of archaeologists in the late 1960s who were keen to try out new technology like resistivity surveys, as well as soil and plant analysis. One way and another, they'd found enough traces of the various horses to show just how much the site had moved around. That was all very interesting, but not really what I was looking for.

I backtracked and followed a different set of links, looking for any earlier history. I found several theories. One explanation was that Richard, Earl of Warwick, had the first horse cut during the War of the Roses, to commemorate his victory at the Battle of Towton, way up in Yorkshire. Apparently, things weren't going his way, so he jumped off his horse, killed the poor beast with his own sword and told his men he'd fight on foot or die beside them. If that was true, it would certainly have been bloody memorable.

Other, less dramatic proposals linked the horse with local place names that linguists reckoned were tied to ancient gods. Archaeologists and anthropologists reckoned Roman and earlier rituals celebrating the links between gods, goddesses and horses had been part of spring festivities. A few suggested these celebrations were forerunners of the Palm Sunday scourings. Draw some of those dotted lines I'd come across earlier between these ideas, and the Red Horse could be attributed to the Angles. They had settled the fertile land below the scarp sometime around 600 AD. Join the dots in a different pattern, and the Saxon leader Hengist was responsible. I could take my pick of these theories, because when it came down to it, no one really knew.

Maybe not, but Edgehill wasn't too far from where I had grown up. That had to mean I had a good chance of a better source than pages on the Internet which might be genuinely well-researched information or might be complete bollocks. I looked across the table. Fin was intent on whatever she was reading on her screen. Out in the kitchen, Blanche was listening to the radio as she did something or other.

I got up and went through to Fin's bedroom. Finding my phone, I was relieved to see it still had a decent charge. I closed the door and called my dad.

He answered after a few rings. 'Dan? How are things?'

'Fine. How about you?' I didn't really need to ask. I could hear from his voice that he was fit and cheerful. A wave of relief hit me. I hadn't realised how much I'd been worrying that something might be wrong. Not for any particular reason. Just because everything was so uncertain and confused.

'Oh, we're just carrying on carrying on.' Dad didn't sound particularly concerned. 'Dave Fulbrook brings over the groceries and my library books. We have a chat across the gate, not that there's much local news for him to share. Even the usual troublemakers are staying at home. Your mum and I walk around the reserve most days if the weather's okay. We usually see a few dog walkers, but everyone keeps their distance. Other than that, it's a bit like that film, *Groundhog Day*.' He laughed. 'I said that to your mum, and of course, I had to explain what I meant. That went as well as you can expect.'

'I can imagine.' Dryads have their own relationship with time. It's linear, but that's about all they have in common with humans. Dryads live in the moment, and if they want to, they can stay in that moment while years go past around them. On the other hand, a century passing by can mean no more to them than a couple of months might signify for you or me.

'So is anything new with you?' Dad asked. 'Or did you just ring to check in?'

'A bit of both. Is Mum around?'

'I'm here.'

I'd half expected her to be listening in to the call. She'd learned to pick music out of the air years ago, when my dad had been listening to a transistor radio while he was hedging and ditching around the nature reserve. When mobile phones came along, she soon worked out how to join in our conversations. Don't ask me how she does it. I've asked her and she says it's so obvious she doesn't understand why I can't do it too. Then she starts talking about even pigeons being able to sense which way's north and south, and they're the stupidest birds she knows.

'Mum, do you recall when there was a red horse carved into the hillside over Edgehill way?' I mentally crossed my fingers. She might not have seen it. If she had, but she hadn't been curious, she probably wouldn't have bothered remembering.

'Oh, yes,' she said readily. 'It was a lovely sight, especially when the dawn light spilled over the hill behind it. Well, the first horse was beautiful,' she corrected herself. 'The last one looked like a cat trying to wear someone's lost gloves.'

I wondered what the archaeologists had made of any traces they had found of that. 'What else can you tell me about those horses? Anything you might have heard.'

There was a long silence. Fin opened the bedroom door, curious to see what I was doing. Seeing I was on the phone, she kept her interruption short and quiet. 'Dinner's ready.'

As I gave her a thumbs up, Mum finally answered. 'I was told such things were cut into the land to signify a guardian was asleep close by, to be called on in time of need.'

'A guardian? A horse guardian?'

Me saying that got Fin's attention. She paused in the doorway. Mum was still talking. I didn't want to interrupt her to put the phone on speaker.

'Such guardians are great spirits linked to the land and the light, or so I have been told. A horse is the form they take.' She sounded as if this wasn't anything particularly remarkable.

'Who cut the figures?' I asked. 'Who called on the horses when they were needed, and how?'

'Mortals would mark the lands where they lived, and tend the sites. When the guardian's image was renewed, there would be feasts and music to draw the people from far and wide, so that the horse would know its own. My sisters and I would join in from time to time.'

That made sense. Dryads always like a party.

'The wise women held the lore,' Mum went on. 'They knew how to raise the guardians of the land when hearth and home were threatened.'

'Wise women?' I grimaced. 'I don't suppose you have any idea where we might find one of those these days?'

'I'm sorry, I don't.' Mum regretted a whole lot more than just disappointing me. 'They were hunted or they went into hiding a long, long time ago, as humans reckon these things anyway.'

Hunted down as witches, I guessed. Wise women was a name I'd come across before, for local midwives and healers in days gone by, as well as some who might have insights into something more thanks to greenwood blood or some other inheritance.

So much for the olden days. There had to be someone in one of the Bockbournes who knew some ancient lore. Some-one who had roused the horse that we'd seen, presumably because they'd seen the giant first and felt the same threat as Fin. Whoever they were, they wouldn't be easy to find. They'd be as keen to keep their secrets as Fin and me.

'What's this all about?'

Dad spoke at the exact same time as Mum did, so I nearly didn't hear what she said.

'You could always ask the hares.'

'The hares?'

Fin's eyes widened as she heard me say that. She opened her mouth, about to speak. I held up a hand, making what I hoped was an apologetic face. My dad was talking now, and he sounded wary.

'What's going on, Dan? Is there more trouble at Blithe-hurst?'

Okay, I'd expected this. I couldn't talk to Mum without calling Dad, and he's no fool.

'I'm staying with Fin for a few days. We saw a great white horse on the downs. I don't mean a chalk carving. It looked as if it was made of moonlight.'

'Where did you see that? Fin lives near Bristol, doesn't she?'

Like I say, my dad's no fool, and he's pretty good on geog-raphy too.

'You know the Uffington Horse? Fin's been doing a job on the other side of the downs. That's where we saw it.'

Dad grunted. He might not have a dryad's unerring ability to know a lie when he heard it, but he could definitely tell when I wasn't giving him the full story.

'So what's going on around there that's got a guardian spirit up and walking around?'

I had no option but honesty. 'Fin saw a giant.'

'A giant?' Dad was as stunned as I had been. Just like me, he didn't doubt Fin. He'd met her and he'd liked her, and not only because she was a girlfriend I could trust to keep our family secrets.

'At the moment it's no more than some sort of shadow,' I told him quickly. 'As far as we know, anyway. The Green Man wants me to deal with it, but I promise you, I'm not going near it until I know exactly how to put it back in its cave or wherever. Mum?' I spoke fast before Dad had a chance to reply. 'Do you know anything about giants? Anything at all?'

'Such monstrous beings were legends even when my grandmother and her sisters were young.' She was as startled as the rest of us. 'From time to time, the wind has carried rumours that the last of their kind stir in their sleep, especially when there's been bloodshed in the land, but I have never seen one. I know nothing more about them.'

'That's okay.' It had been a very long shot. 'But what did you mean when you told me to ask the hares? When you were talking about who knows the lore to rouse these horse guardians.'

'The wise women.' Yet again, Mum seemed surprised that I needed to ask. 'The ones who can become hares, just as Fin can become a swan.'

I didn't know what to say to that. On the other hand, I could see that Fin was desperate to start asking questions. Then, before either of us could say anything, Blanche shouted from the living room.

'It's on the table!'

'Sorry, Dad, Mum, I've got to go. Take care of yourselves. I'll talk to you soon.' I ended the call.

Fin looked at me with her eyebrows arched. 'As soon as we've eaten, you can tell me what on earth that was all about.'

Chapter Ten

Caponata turned out to be chopped-up aubergines cooked with tomatoes, olives, capers and I don't know what else. I do know that I liked it, as well as the cheese and spinach pie.

'Thanks. That was really great.' I offered Blanche a friendly smile.

She sipped her wine. 'You're welcome.' Her voice was as hard to read as her face.

Fin topped up her own glass and mine. 'Right, let's hear it. What did your mum have to say?'

'Your mum?' Blanche looked at me and then at Fin. 'I thought the dryads didn't know anything useful.'

'The Blithehurst dryads didn't,' I explained, 'but I found something worth following up that was close to home, so I made a phone call.'

I told them both about the Red Horse of Tysoe, and what I'd learned from my mother.

'So, that got me thinking. We might be completely wrong about this Hazel Spinner. She could actually be one of these wise women who can turn into a hare.'

At least none of us doubted that was possible. On the other hand, I could see Fin would take some convincing, never mind Blanche.

'We saw what could have been a rabbit or a hare when we were out on the downs last night,' I went on, 'just before we saw that white horse. I didn't think anything of it at the time. Now, though, what if she was the hare that dog was chasing? That would explain where she came from all of a sudden, when I saw her getting into her car. Because she didn't pass us as we walked along the path, and we didn't see her coming towards us from the Wayland's Smithy direction. You can see a good long way ahead on the Ridgeway. We couldn't have missed her.'

No wonder that young dog had looked so surprised. If I was right, I owed him a biscuit, not a telling-off. He'd done us a real favour.

'As soon as she was out of sight,' I concluded, 'she shifted back to human to get away from the dog. Then she ran for her car.'

Where she'd ducked down to grab the keys she'd left tucked out of sight behind a tyre, or in a magnetic holder inside the wheel arch. I guessed a hare had the same trouble changing shape when she was carrying metal as Fin and her relatives did.

'So she was following us,' Fin said uneasily. 'After she saw us at the pub. Why?'

'Just because she's got her own secrets – even if you're right about that – there's still no guarantee she's not a threat,' Blanche said firmly.

'I wonder if the Green Man was lending us a hand. Maybe the Horned Hunter put the dog on her scent.' I wondered how many mysterious ancient powers might be taking an interest in what was going on out on the downs.

'You still haven't answered the question,' Blanche pointed out. 'Why was she following you? How could she know you were anything more than weekend walkers?'

'If she was the hare Dan saw last night, before we saw the horse,' Fin said thoughtfully, 'she probably realised we could see it, from the way we reacted. That would tell her there was something unusual about us.'

'That's a hell of a lot of "if".' Blanche shook her head.

I looked at her. 'If Fin's right, there's no reason to think she knows your secret. There's no reason to ever tell her. We can let her think your family's like Eleanor's. Then she'll assume Fin saw the horse thanks to some ancestor with greenwood blood.'

Fin drank some wine. 'If we are right, that would explain why her website seems more interested in convincing people there are rational explanations for whatever they think they saw. What better way to keep her own secret safe?'

Blanche acknowledged that possibility with a reluctant nod. 'I suppose so. But we still don't know why she was following you today.'

'We're not going to know that until we ask her,' I said.

Both sisters stared at me.

'What else are we going to do?' I asked them. 'We can do that online and we can all stay safe. There's an email address on her website, so we use that to make contact. We set up a throwaway account that doesn't link back to any of us, so there's no way she can track us down.'

'She must know Fin's number plate,' Blanche objected, 'if she was following you today.'

'What's she going to do with that?' Fin countered. 'Go online to check when my MOT and car tax is due? She'd have to be in the police to find out any more than that about me.'

'How do you know she isn't a copper?' Blanche shot back. 'Cryptozoology might just be a hobby.'

I didn't want them to start arguing again, so I raised my voice just a bit. 'We'll send her a message that will only make sense if she is what we think she is. If we're wrong, she'll just think some random nutter has found her website. I bet she gets more messages than she can count from weirdos telling her they've seen the Loch Ness monster.'

'What are we going to say,' Fin wondered aloud, 'that'll convince her it really is us?'

'What are you going to do if she answers?' Blanche challenged us both. 'What's the point of doing this, other than satisfying your curiosity? It's still taking a risk, and that's simply not a good enough reason to put us all in danger of being found out.'

I drank the last of my wine. I was suddenly tired of this. 'Because if she was the one who summoned that horse, then maybe she knows something about the giant. Because we still have absolutely no clue how I'm supposed to subdue it or do anything else. I can't leave it wandering around until it fee fi fo fums into some poor bastard birdwatcher and eats him raw.'

I stood up and began collecting plates and cutlery. 'You cooked. I'll wash up.'

'I'll help,' Fin said hurriedly. 'You won't know where to put anything away.'

Blanche poured herself the last half-glassful of wine and went to sit on the sofa at the far end of the room. She picked the remote up from the coffee table and turned on the TV.

I carried the stack of plates into the kitchen. Putting the plug in the sink, I started the hot water running. Fin came through the door carrying the pie dish and the bowl that had held the caponata.

'I'm sorry if I've pissed her off.' I knew the door was open, and I didn't mind if Blanche heard me. 'We need to do something, not just discuss endless reasons why we shouldn't. That'll get us nowhere.' I squirted more washing-up liquid than I intended into the sink. 'I get why Blanche is concerned, I really do, but we're not idiots. We know when to keep our mouths shut.'

'I agree.' Fin put the remains of the pie into the fridge. 'So what do we put in this email we're sending? "Have you recovered from your hare-raising encounter with that dog yet?"'

I looked around to make sure I had heard that right. Fin grinned at me.

'Or we could go for something like, "Let's meet for a drink, somewhere you can let your hare down?" How about that?' she suggested.

'I'm going to have real trouble not saying something like that when we meet her now, so thanks for that.' I turned back to the sink to start washing the cutlery. 'If we meet her,' I added. 'She may just ignore whatever message we send.'

'Nothing ventured, nothing gained.' Fin grabbed a tea towel and started drying up the knives and forks. 'Though it's probably best if we don't make any hare jokes until we know she's got a sense of humour.'

'Right. She could have a hare-trigger temper.' I put a clean plate in the rack on the draining board.

'She's going to ask how we know what she is, you realise.' Fin turned serious. 'How are we going to explain that?'

'We stick as close as we can to the truth.' I knew Fin's family didn't have any particular talent for hearing lies, but there was no saying the same was true for a wise woman who could turn into a hare. It's not as if there's any sort of book of rules for all this stuff. My life would be a hell of a lot easier if there was.

I carried on doing the washing-up. 'I can tell her I saw a hare when we saw the horse, and then my mother told me about their ties to the ancient lore about the chalk horses being guardians. I don't have a problem letting her know I'm a dryad's son, and we can only let her know our first names, to make ourselves harder to find. And I can let her think I caught a glimpse of her when she turned human to get away from that dog.'

'What then?' Fin picked up a plate and started wiping it.

'Honestly? I think we're going to have to play it by ear. Shit.' I shook my head as I put the caponata bowl into the sink. 'It really is going to be far too easy to sound like I'm taking the piss.'

'Do we tell her we – you – I saw the giant?'

'I don't know.' I gave that some more thought. 'That's got to be what's brought her to Bockbourne. How about we say we overheard those blokes at the pub talking about seeing what one of them joked was a Bigfoot, and that's how we found her website. We don't necessarily have to say we know anything about the giant until we know a bit more about who we're dealing with.'

The less we gave away, the happier Blanche would be, I thought, but I didn't say that out loud.

'Right.' Fin didn't say anything else until we'd finished washing up and she'd put everything away.

She took another bottle of red wine out of the rack under the work surface and unscrewed the cap. I followed her into the living room, where she topped up our glasses. Blanche was watching something Scandinavian-sounding on the telly.

'I've opened some more red. I'll leave it here.' Fin screwed the cap back on and put the bottle on the dining table.

'Thanks.' Blanche didn't look away from the screen. Maybe she was concentrating on reading the subtitles. Maybe she wasn't.

'Here.' Fin handed me both glasses of wine.

I wondered why until she picked up her laptop from the sideboard, where everything had been put out of the way so we could use the table for dinner.

'We'll use the office, so she can watch her Danish murderers in peace.'

'Icelandic, this time.' Blanche still didn't look away from the telly, but she raised her wine glass in what could be a thank you for being left in peace. I hoped it was.

Fin led the way to the central bedroom. It was smaller than either of the others, but there was still plenty of room for two desks, facing the walls on either side. Each desk had a couple of decent-sized monitors ready to connect to a laptop. There was a pinboard on the wall above each set-up, covered in notes and diagrams. A table underneath the window had a map spread out on it, and two filing cabinets stood on either side of the door we'd just come through. It all looked very efficient.

Fin put her laptop on the desk that faced her bedroom. She opened it and sat down, though she didn't hook up the monitors. 'Okay, what name are we using for this email address?'

I'd been thinking about that. 'BockbourneMan should get her attention.'

I put the wine glasses carefully down on the desk and fetched the spare chair from over by the map table. Once I was settled, I picked up the wine again. Any sort of spill in here wouldn't help smooth things over with Blanche.

Fin set up a free email address pretty quickly. 'Right. What are we going to say?'

She took her glass from me and looked thoughtful as she sipped. I took a drink myself, and wished I knew the best way to do this.

'It's got to be more than just "hello",' I said slowly. 'She has to want to meet us.'

'She'll want to find out what we know.' Fin handed me her glass and started typing. 'How about this? "We saw you the other night, and again today, but we didn't get a chance to talk. Any chance we could swap notes about local horses and maybe other things?" If you don't know what we're talking about, that looks perfectly innocent.'

'That's good,' I agreed. 'If you change the start to "I". We want her talking to me.'

Fin gave me a sideways look. 'I'm just the dumb blonde you've got in tow, am I?'

'Would it be so bad if she thought that?' I was serious. 'If she does, that means she's not as bright as she thinks she is. That would be useful to know. Besides, if I'm doing the talking, you can be watching her, and listening. That way, we won't miss anything important. Then we can decide if we trust her. Until we're sure of that, we don't want to give up any more of our own secrets than we have to.'

Fin pursed her lips, looking at the screen. 'That makes sense, I suppose.' She moved the cursor and hit the keys to change the email. 'Am I putting your name at the end? Best wishes? Regards? Yours sincerely?'

'Good question.' I gave it some thought. 'It needs my name. If it's anonymous, there's a bit of a "we know who you are and where you live" vibe. Let's just go with "Dan" for a sign-off.' That's how I end most of my emails anyway.

Fin typed. 'Anything else?'

I shook my head. 'Hit send.'

She did that, and took her wine glass back. 'I wonder how soon she'll reply. If she'll reply. How long do we wait before we give up on this idea?'

I grimaced. 'Hard to say. We don't know how often she checks for email to that website address. Then she's got to decide what to do. We've got to give it a couple of days at the very least.'

'What are we going to do in the meantime?' Fin glanced at the pinboard on the wall above her desk. 'I can't leave Blanche to do all the work here. We have clients we need to keep happy.'

'Right.' I took a swallow of wine. 'If you're okay with me borrowing your car, I can go and take a walk through the Bockbourne Woods while you're busy. The Green Man might give me a hint about what to do next.'

'What if you see the giant?' Fin asked, apprehensive.

'Then I'll leg it,' I assured her. 'Seriously, I'm not going up against something like that until I know how to take it down.'

The more folklore I've read, the less I agree with the theories that say fairy tales were only supposed to scare the shit out of children to stop them wandering off. The older versions are as bloody and violent as any horror film. Now I wondered how many of those stories started out being told by people like me. A dryad's son who'd had a narrow escape could warn anyone else who could see the unseen what they might find themselves going up against.

Fin still looked concerned. 'You should head over there in the middle of the day. If this giant's still only a shadow, maybe it's only around at dawn and dusk.'

'Good idea. I should ring Eleanor as well, and let her know what's going on. Who knows, the dryads might have something to say about hares and carvings of guardians in the landscape.' I wondered what was going on at Blithehurst that had nothing to do with giants or chalk horses. How much might Eleanor be willing to tell me about whatever trouble the business was in? Was there anything I could do about it if she did?

I checked the time in the corner of Fin's laptop screen. 'Not tonight. I'll ring her in the morning.'

'We could both go over for a walk in the woods tomorrow. Blanche and I always take the day off on Sundays.' Fin shrugged. 'House rules. It's too easy to end up working all day, everyday, when you're self-employed.'

'Right.' I was used to working weekends. I'd got into the habit when I'd spent Monday to Friday on building sites and Saturdays and Sundays at craft shows. It had never bothered me. Then again, I hadn't had anything better to do.

'So what do you want to do now? Have an early night?' I said hopefully.

'That sounds like a good idea.' Fin hid her grin with her wine glass as she took a drink. 'Though we should probably wait until Blanche has finished with her Scandi noir murders.'

That made me think of something completely different. 'There are giants in Norse folklore. Do you suppose we might find something useful if we read up on those?'

'I have no idea.' Fin looked dubious. 'Do you suppose that means other things in those stories are real, like trolls for instance?'

Before I could answer, the laptop chimed.

'We've got a reply.' Fin sounded as if she couldn't quite believe it.

Neither could I. 'What does it say?'

She opened the email and read the single line aloud. 'Who are you?'

We looked at each other.

'Say we – that I'm a friend?' I shook my head. 'No, that sounds like a stalker.'

'Not necessarily.' Fin bit her lip, thinking. 'We can say you share her interests in lost lore?'

That sounded a bit vague to me, but I couldn't think of anything better. 'Okay. Try that.'

Fin typed and hit send. We sat there waiting, staring at the laptop screen. I resisted the temptation to time how long it took to get a response. When it came, I wondered what had taken so long. All we got back was one word.

'Why?'

We looked at each other again.

'Shall we try something about old stories being handed down through your family?' Fin didn't sound convinced.

I certainly wasn't. 'Tell her the Green Man sent me to Bockbourne to see what's woken up in the woods.'

Fin blinked, startled. 'Seriously?'

'Why not? Let's get things moving. Otherwise we'll be here until midnight swapping one word every five minutes, then spending ten minutes trying to work out what each answer might mean.'

Fin couldn't argue with that, or at least she decided not to try. She sent the message. We stared at the screen again. We waited, and waited some more.

'Maybe she's decided I'm just a nutter.' I finished my wine.

A few minutes later, the laptop told us we had an answer.

'Why you?'

Fin looked at me and raised her eyebrows.

'Tell her my mother's a dryad.' I shrugged. 'She'll believe me or she won't.'

'Fair enough.' Fin typed and hit send.

This time we got an answer almost at once.

'Where can we meet and when?'

Seeing my direct approach get results was very satisfying.

'Let's say noon tomorrow.' Fin was already busy at the keyboard. 'There's a place where the trees come down to the river. There's a ruined eel house there, so she'll know exactly where to go.'

I wanted to ask why eels needed houses. I asked something a lot more relevant. 'What makes this such a good spot?'

'It's off the beaten track for one thing.' Fin hit send. 'For another, if you're on your own, she might be more willing to talk. If I'm there, well, two against one is a whole different dynamic.'

'Except you will be there, won't you?' I realised what she was planning. 'You'll be paddling along by the bank.'

She smiled with satisfaction. 'We won't tell her I can change into a swan if we don't have to. That doesn't mean I can't be a swan around her.'

I wondered what Blanche was going to say to that. I wondered if Fin was going to tell her. Well, that was between the two of them, and no business of mine.

The laptop chimed one last time. We were back to one-word answers.

'Okay.'

'Good.' Fin shut down the computer and turned to me on her swivel desk chair. 'How about that early night?'

She leaned forward and kissed me. I had my hands full of wine glasses, so all I could do was kiss her back. She ran her hands up my thighs. Feeling her touch, I wanted to do a whole lot more than kiss her.

Fin took the glasses out of my hands. 'I'll just take—'

Now that my hands were empty, I could cup her breasts. I stroked her nipples with my thumbs through her sweatshirt. She pressed against me with a murmur of pleasure. Then she kissed me briskly and stood up.

'As I was about to say, I'll go and wash these up while you get clear of the bathroom.'

'Okay.' I went to have a pee and clean my teeth.

As soon as I was back in Fin's bedroom, I made sure I had that box of condoms close at hand as I got into bed. Then I waited for longer than I expected. How long did it take to wash up a couple of wine glasses?

Listening hard, I could hear voices. I didn't think that was some Icelandic detective. I wondered if Fin was telling Blanche we had a plan to meet the wise woman tomorrow. I wondered if Blanche would try to forbid it.

I heard the door to the hall open and close. Fin went into the bathroom. A few moments later, she came into the bedroom and closed the door. There was a slight blush of colour on her cheek bones, but she looked satisfied with herself.

I thought about asking if everything was okay with Blanche, but changed my mind. If things were fine, I didn't need to ask. If they weren't, I couldn't see what I could do about it.

Fin stripped off her clothes, efficient rather than seductive. 'So, where were we?'

I smiled at her and threw back the duvet. She joined me on the bed, straddling my thighs. I reached for her tits, brushing white feathers aside. This time, they flowed up my arms as far as my elbows. The swirling sensation made the hair on my forearms stand on end.

Fin looked down, surprised to see what was happening. I was as startled as she was. Before I could say a word, she shrugged and bent down to kiss me. I lost all interest in anything else.

We may have gone to bed early. We didn't get to sleep till gone midnight.

Chapter Eleven

I found out what an eel house is the following day. It's a small brick-and-timber structure with a tiled roof built across a river. There are brick-lined channels underneath, where the water flows through for most of the year. In days gone by, there were also grilles and sluices that could be used to set traps on moonless nights from August to November. That's when adult eels would be heading downstream, intent on swimming back to the Sargasso Sea to spawn the next generation. Instead, they'd end up in tanks of fresh water, carted off to Billingsgate Fish Market.

At least, that's what the information board on this grassy stretch of riverbank said. It stood beside an ivy-covered heap of rubble reaching halfway across the stream and forcing the water to scour out a hollow in the opposite bank. The Bockbourne Magna Town Trust were intent on restoring this bit of local heritage to its former glory, and unsurprisingly they were appealing for funds. There were photos of another eel house that had been restored over in Hampshire, to show people what they would be getting. Another board had pictures of little school kids holding jars of elvers for release. Fin had explained there were projects along the River Kennett aiming to reintroduce eels. This was one reason why the locals were so concerned about pollution from the salad-bagging operation.

I finished reading the history of the eel house for a second time, and wondered how much longer I should hang around here. How long before some coppers turned up to investigate reports of a suspicious individual loitering in the woods? Though Fin had been right when she said no one really came out this way. We hadn't seen anyone else so far. Maybe the birdwatchers and dog walkers were all eating their Sunday lunch at the White Hart.

I took another look at the ruined eel house and wondered where they would start rebuilding it. To be fair, the job would be a whole lot clearer once that ivy was stripped away. Though it was anyone's guess how stable the tumbledown walls would be without that support. Whatever. It wasn't my problem.

Unless I found myself looking for work again. At least Fin could give me an introduction to the Parish Council if I did end up needing a job. I looked at the swan poking its beak into nooks and crannies where the creeper-covered bricks met the swirling water. I was pretty sure that was Fin. I hoped it was her. We'd split up once we'd parked the car in a secluded spot and she'd shown me which footpath to follow. That way, if Hazel Spinner was on the lookout for anyone approaching, she'd see I was on my own.

We hadn't thought everything through, I realised. We needed some signal so Fin could let me know which swan was her. That, or I needed to get a whole lot better at telling one swan from another. Weren't their beaks and faces supposed to be unique?

Checking my phone, I saw that it was twenty past twelve. Fuck this. Either Hazel Spinner wasn't coming or something had come up to stop her. Fin had her laptop in the boot of the car. We needed to find somewhere with Wi-Fi and check the throwaway email address. I put my phone back in my pocket and started walking back along the path. Fin would realise what was happening soon enough. We'd agreed to meet back at the Toyota.

I had just about reached the beech trees when the woman I'd been waiting for stepped out onto the path. Now I got a proper look at Hazel Spinner, I realised that photo on her website was an old one. There was grey in her shoulder-length dark hair now. She was in her mid-forties, with fine lines around her chestnut-brown eyes. She was middling height and solidly built in jeans, walking boots and an all-weather coat.

'You're satisfied I'm on my own? Do you want to check me for a wire?' I can get sarcastic when I'm annoyed.

She didn't seem to notice. 'I was waiting to see if a hamadryad would want to talk to you.'

That wasn't what I expected. 'Really?'

'If you really are a dryad's son.' She looked at me, challenging. 'Can you prove that?'

'How?' I challenged her back. 'If you're expecting a secret greenwood handshake, no one's taught it to me.'

Her lips twitched in what might have been a smile. It was gone before I could be sure. 'So what can you tell me?'

'About what?' I was in no mood for this. 'Let's not piss about. You know I saw that horse the other night, and I know you were the hare that dog was chasing yesterday. I'm guessing you're the one who roused the horse. My mother told me that wise women who turn into hares know how to summon such guardians of the land. How would I know any of that if I wasn't what I say I am?'

She looked at me for a long moment. 'Where's your friend? How could she see the horse as well?'

'You can ask her when you meet her.' I forced myself not to look at the river. How good is a swan's hearing anyway? That's not something I'd ever needed to find out.

Hazel Spinner pursed her lips. 'You say the Green Man sent you here. How does that work?'

'He comes into my dreams.' Saying that out loud sounded completely nuts. 'He said there was an evil rising here. When I overheard some men talking about seeing some sort of giant in the woods, I reckoned that must be a clue. They were in the White Hart's beer garden yesterday lunchtime, when you saw me in the car park. They were talking about some sort of universal monster theory. I went online to learn more about that and found your website. I found the post that one of them had written. Then I recognised your photo.'

If this wise woman could hear when someone was telling lies, she'd know all that was true. Hopefully, she wouldn't realise it wasn't anywhere near the whole story.

'That monster theory of yours is a good way of putting people off the scent of things they shouldn't tangle with,' I added. Maybe a compliment would get this conversation moving in a useful direction.

'Oh, it's a perfectly respectable cryptozoological theory. I don't claim any credit.' She smiled briefly. 'Though yes, it does come in handy when I need to convince someone not to believe their own eyes. When the website flags up something that could be a threat. They're mostly false alarms, thankfully.'

She looked serious again. 'Not this time. So, you know there's a giant. Do you have any idea how to—' she waved a frustrated hand '—shut it down, lock it up, do whatever it takes to get rid of it?'

'Not yet.' This didn't sound good. 'I was hoping you could tell me.'

She shook her head. 'I can only rouse the horse.'

I couldn't help myself. 'How—?'

She shook her head, more curtly. 'That's between me and mine, and the moon and the land. Even if I could tell you, you couldn't understand.'

'Right. Sorry.'

She wasn't interested in my apology. 'The guardian should keep the giant lurking in the shadows for the moment, but folk stories say they're hungry beasts. It won't stay wary for long.'

'Right. What were you saying about hamadryads?' If this not-so-wise woman couldn't help, I needed to look elsewhere. 'You've seen one around here? More than one?'

'Yes.' She was surprised. 'Haven't you?'

'I haven't been looking. Where should I start?'

'Do you know where Feden Hanger is?'

'I can find it.' As soon as Fin had fingers, not wings, to hold a map and show me.

'I've seen them over there, but they won't talk to me.' She scowled.

'I'll see what I can do. How do I get hold of you, to let you know what I find out? There has to be a better way than going through email.'

She looked at me for another long moment. Then she held out her hand. 'Phone?'

I took it out of my pocket and swiped to unlock the screen. I passed the handset over.

Her fingers worked busily for a few moments. She handed the phone back. 'I sent myself a text, so I've got your number as well.'

I nodded. 'Can I ask what you'll be doing while I'm wandering round the woods looking for help?'

'Keeping watch for our friend,' she said grimly. 'Though there's not a lot I can do if he does start grinding some rambler's bones for a bit of baking.'

Like I say, old folk tales can be real horror stories.

'Let's hope these hamadryads have some answers.' I offered her my hand. 'Call me Dan. Do I call you Doctor Spinner or what?'

She looked a bit surprised but shook my hand briefly. 'Hazel will do.'

'Right.' I realised she wasn't about to leave. That meant I was going to have to be the one to walk away. Fin would just have to work out what was going on. 'I'll be in touch.'

I headed down the path that ran along the bank between the beech woods and the river. The back of my neck prickled with an unpleasant sensation. I was convinced Hazel was watching me walk away. I resisted the temptation to look back and see. I wanted her to trust me. We couldn't afford to lose any allies at the moment.

The path veered away from the river, cutting back towards the road through a stand of trees. I hadn't paid much attention to these beeches going down to the water. I'd been more alert for hares and swans. Now I looked more closely, hoping for some hint of an unexpected presence.

I wondered if a hamadryad would recognise me as my mother's son. The dryads at Blithehurst had done that easily enough, just as they'd known Fin for what she was. I wondered if they could see it just as easily when she was a swan. That was something I should get Eleanor to ask them.

Something caught my eye. My subconscious told me it was a face. I looked, hoping to see the Green Man. I could do with some confirmation that I was on the right track here.

It wasn't him. I saw a twisted and swollen burr on the side of a tree. Sometime, a good while ago, something had hurt this beech. Maybe a storm had snapped off a branch, or perhaps a rope tied around it had cut a deep wound through the bark. The tree had tried to heal itself. Somehow, it had tried too hard, and a bulbous growth had formed on the trunk.

It was head height and head sized, with deep creases where eyes would be shadowed by a scowling brow, and mimicking a grimacing mouth. My subconscious had turned these into a face. It was that pattern-recognition thing those men in the pub had mentioned. Pareidolia. I'd looked it up.

When this tree was felled – if it was ever felled – a wood-worker would pay a top price for the burr. The cluster of dormant buds under the bark would give the wood a wild grain. It would be dappled and dotted with dark spots and swirls, to make a striking and unique pattern on a bowl or a platter or whatever. A furniture maker would slice the burr into fine sheets for veneer, matching the pieces to reflect each other in highly polished designs on expensive items.

They would need to be an expert. Burr wood is unusually hard and dense, and the wild grain makes it prone to splitting unpredictably. One slip of a chisel, or an incautious move in just the wrong place, and all you would be left with was very expensive firewood.

That feeling I had, of being watched, grew much stronger. This burr really looked like a face, and it didn't have a friendly expression. It looked like it knew what I'd been thinking, and it didn't like the idea of being carved up. I remembered a theory I'd read somewhere once, about beech trees communicating though underground networks of rootlets and hair-fine strands of fungus.

'Sorry,' I said to the tree, and walked out of that wood as fast as I could.

Back on the road, I headed for the Toyota. It was parked a short distance away, where a lane turned from tarmac into a track that headed up to the downs. Fin was already standing by the driver's side door.

I dug her keys out of my pocket and tossed them over. 'How much of that did you hear?'

'Enough.' Fin pressed the remote to unlock the car. 'Feden Hanger isn't far away.'

So swans do have sharp ears, even if no one can see them on those sleek white heads.

We got into the car and Fin drove off. After she'd negotiated a blind bend, she spoke to me. 'I should probably have looked this up sometime before now, but it's never occurred to me. What exactly is the difference between a dryad and a hamadryad?'

I told her what little I knew. 'Dryads look after their oak trees, and any other trees and animals in the area, but they're not bound to any one tree. They'll have favourites, like someone will have a cow or a sheep they're fond of in a herd or a flock, but if that tree dies, the dryad won't be physically harmed. Hamadryads are different. They live and die with a particular tree. They're bonded at birth, but don't ask me how that happens, because I don't know. I asked my mum once, but she couldn't explain it.'

I'd never had any reason to ask the Blithehurst dryads what they knew about hamadryads. That was something else I needed to ask Eleanor to do. If I could get hold of her. I'd tried to ring her this morning before we'd left Cainescombe, but the call had gone straight to voicemail. I'd left a message asking her to call me, but she hadn't done that so far.

I got out my phone and tried again. Still no answer. I didn't leave another message. I hoped nothing was wrong, or not too badly wrong.

Fin took a turn signposted to Bockbourne Parva. 'Have you ever met one?'

'No. As far as I know, they're rarer than dryads. I've met a grand total of five of those, and that's after years of looking.'

'Do they live in beech woods, in the same way that dryads favour oaks?'

'Not necessarily. They're associated with quite a few different trees in the stories. Oak as well as beech, walnut, elm, mulberry, poplar and dogwood.'

Fin was surprised. 'That's a real variety.'

'And vines and figs, according to the books, but I don't think we'll find those growing wild around here.'

'Give climate change another couple of decades and you never know.'

She ignored another sign to Bockbourne Parva. We went straight ahead down one of those lanes with hedges that brushed both sides of the car. This took us over a grassy shoulder of the downs and on into a hollow. A beech wood rose up the steeper slope ahead and stretched out along the ridge. In summer, the trees' leafy canopy would overshadow the pasture below. Now the wind was stripping away the autumn foliage to leave bare branches clawing the sky.

'Where can I drop you off without blocking the road?' Fin muttered.

'Aren't you coming with me?' I realised we should have discussed that.

'I wasn't planning to.' Fin seemed surprised I asked. 'If these hamadryads weren't willing to talk to Hazel Spinner, I don't suppose they'll talk to me. There's nowhere up here where anyone would expect to find a swan either. You're on your own with this one.'

I can't say I was thrilled, but I couldn't see we had any other option. 'Okay, then you drop me off and find somewhere safe to park. I'll ring you when I want picking up.'

Fin pulled into a gateway. I got out of the car and she drove off. I lost sight of the Toyota as the lane snaked away. As the sound of the engine faded, I was left alone with the birdsong and the wind rustling through the trees.

Thankfully the field gate wasn't locked. I went through it, closed it behind me and walked across the turf. The ground sloped steeply up to the trees. By the time I reached the beech wood, I was really feeling the climb in my calf muscles and hamstrings. I hoped this was going to be worth it.

As I walked into the shadows of the wood, I couldn't see a sign of anyone else. Not a hiker. Not a hamadryad. I paused to ease the strain in the backs of my legs and looked around. Nothing was stirring. That was odd. The twigs overhead should be shifting in this breeze. There should be birds flitting about. At this time of year, I'd expect some chance of a squirrel searching for beech nuts in the fallen leaves. Instead, everything around me was as still as someone holding their breath. I got that feeling of being watched again.

Since there was no one to see me make a fool of myself, I spoke out loud. 'We need to talk. The wise woman who roused the white horse said I would find you here.'

Somehow, the silence grew more intense. Maybe that was my reply.

'I know you're watching, and you know who I am.' I walked further into the trees. 'You know who my mother must be.'

Still nothing happened. I shrugged.

'The Green Man sent me here to subdue the giant. I hoped we could help each other. You can explain yourselves to him.'

I turned to leave, careful not to slip on the uneven ground. The fallen leaves were slick underfoot after yesterday's rain. I wondered if the hamadryads were still here. Just because Hazel had seen them in these trees, that didn't mean – what did it mean?

One stepped out of a beech tree to block my path. I stopped and folded my arms. Nice try, but if this hamadryad expected to startle me, she would have to do a lot more than that. I've seen my mum stepping in and out of oak trees for as long as I can remember.

She reminded me a bit of my mum, and a lot more of Sineya, the youngest of the Blithehurst dryads. There were differences. All the dryads I've ever met have green eyes apart from Frai. This hamadryad's eyes were steely grey, a few shades darker than the bark of the tree beside her. In my experience, a dryad's hair is some shade of brown, from the light colour of spring oak buds to the richer darkness of autumn leaves. The hamadryad's hair was the rich gold of the inside of a fallen beech nut. Loose curls brushed her shoulders, and the faint golden sheen to her skin wasn't remotely human. Dryads who aren't masquerading as human tend to favour flowing dresses and wraps. She was wearing what looked like a pale grey sleeveless tunic and leggings. If she'd been human, she'd have been shivering at this time of year.

'Good day to you, dryad's son.'

That voice was behind me. The hamadryad blocking my path was simply smiling, and not in a particularly nice way.

I turned slowly around, and I saw a third hamadryad standing some distance away to my left. If I was going to face the one who'd just spoken, I'd have at least two I couldn't see behind me. I wished Fin had come along to back me up, even though we'd still be outnumbered.

'Hello.' I focused on the one who had just spoken.

I guessed she must be their leader, though she didn't look much older. The three of them could easily be sisters, around the same age as me.

'Why do you expect us to help you?' She didn't sneer exactly, but she looked as if it wouldn't take much for her to tell me to sod off.

'I expect nothing,' I said carefully. 'I hoped we might help each other.'

'Why should we help mortal men?'

Oh, great. The hamadryad would be asking questions and not giving straight answers until she thought she'd won some advantage that meant I had to do what she said.

138

'Isn't the giant a threat to you too?' I may find this bollocks tedious, but that doesn't mean I haven't learned how to play the game.

'Not as dangerous as mortal men.' There was an edge to her voice. 'Men who bring axes and worse to our woods, who kill my sisters without knowing or caring what harm they do.'

I supposed she had a point. Giants hadn't turned up here for hundreds of years, but these beech trees would have been felled for building materials and umpteen other things for as long as anyone could remember, human or not. I wondered why the hamadryads hadn't allied themselves with the foresters, to make sure their special trees were left alone. That's what dryads had done for millennia.

'We have not been as fortunate as your mother and her sisters,' the hamadryad said acidly.

For a horrible moment, I wondered if she was reading my mind. Were hamadryads telepathic? I really needed to find out what Frai and Asca knew. But the hamadryad was still talking.

'One of my grandmother's sisters took a human lover. The last of our kin to be so foolish. She learned he could never be trusted. He threw the baby she bore him into a fire. The child had barely drawn breath.'

'Fucking hell.' I knew she wasn't lying. Then I saw the hint of satisfaction in her face as she waited for me to say something. Something she could use to her advantage.

I reminded myself to think before opening my mouth. That horrible story was true, but telling me had still been a tactic. She wanted to make me ashamed of my human blood. Not a chance. That child's murder wasn't my fault, and that wasn't my debt. But if she wanted me to think that I owed her people, that meant she wanted something from me.

'Men can be vicious,' I agreed. 'Regardless, this giant's a danger to you too. It's a creature of the shadows. I know something not so very different that killed a dryad once.'

That wasn't a lie either. Once upon a time, there had been four dryads at Blithehurst, until Tila had gone off on her own because of some row that none of them would explain.

'The Green Man sent me to avenge her,' I added.

I thought I saw a flicker in the hamadryad's eyes. It could just have been a glimmer of light as the leaves shifted overhead. She wasn't about to yield. I could see that.

She folded her arms, lifting her chin. 'Why should we care when the giant catches some human unaware in the darkness?'

'Because you'll see hundreds of humans in these woods searching for a killer they'll never find.'

I wondered how long it had been since these hamadryads had had any close dealings with local people. Did they really have no idea what would happen if some unfortunate dog walker stumbled into a bloody, violent death? 'They might not chop down your trees, but there's no telling what other damage they might do.'

The hamadryad smiled with sour satisfaction. 'Such an invasion would not be pleasant, but it should rid us of parasites which harm us in ways the giant never will.'

I had an uneasy feeling that I had somehow stepped into a mantrap. Oh well. Sometimes the only way onwards is through.

'What parasites?'

'They are filth!'

One of the hamadryads behind me hissed with such venom that my shoulders tensed. All three of them noticed. They laughed, mocking me.

'What parasites?' I stayed focused on the one who had been doing the talking.

'Some men have taken over a woodland that we value.' Now she'd got me where she wanted me, the head hamadryad was far more willing to talk. 'They live in squalor, indulging in strong drink and violence. They cut down trees and burn them. They dig pits and fill them with vileness. We want rid of them, whatever it takes. If we can do that without innocent blood being shed, so much the better. One way or another though, we will see them gone.'

So that was the deal to be done. If I did the hamadryads this favour, they would do... what exactly? I reminded myself of those folk tales where some human comes badly unstuck because they didn't check the small print.

'If someone were to get rid of these parasites,' I said carefully, 'would you be willing to share what you know about giants?'

The head hamadryad smiled with sudden charm. 'We would. Shall we make such a bargain?'

I raised my hand. 'Not so fast. Does what you know about giants include knowing how to subdue them?'

There's always a time for asking someone who can't lie direct questions. The trick in these conversations is seeing it.

Now the hamadryad's smile looked forced. 'If I tell you now, what guarantee do I have—?'

'I'm not asking you to tell me what I need to do here and now. I'm asking if you know. Can you tell me how to send this giant back to wherever it came from? Maybe get rid of it for good? Yes or no?'

She glared at me, but didn't answer. Bollocks. This whole day had been a waste of sodding time. We were no nearer finding out what we so desperately needed to know.

I turned back around. The hamadryad who'd called the men in the woods filth was still standing on the path, and she wasn't moving.

'Get out of my way,' I advised her calmly.

She glanced past me, apprehensive. She was right to be nervous. I was willing to walk straight through her, and she could see it.'

'Wait,' the head hamadryad called out. 'We can ask the trees what they recall from the days of the giants. If you rid us of these parasites.'

I made her wait for a moment. 'I'll think about it.'

'Don't think for too long.' The hamadryad who hadn't said anything so far spoke up. She stared at me. 'Or the giant's path may cross that of some innocent sooner rather than later.'

She glanced at the hamadryad standing in my way, who stepped aside to let me pass. I realised I'd been wrong about who was in charge here.

I left the wood and went back down the hill as fast as I could without falling arse over tit. I really needed to talk to Fin.

Chapter Twelve

Wherever Fin had found to pull in out of the way of local tractors couldn't have been far off. I heard the Toyota approaching soon after I'd called her. I looked around as she arrived. I couldn't see any hamadryads, but that didn't mean they weren't still watching.

'Well?' she asked as I got in and fastened my seat belt.

'Head for the White Hart.'

As she drove, I told her everything that had happened. 'Have you got any idea who these mysterious men might be? Or where they might be, come to that?'

'Not a clue. Could they be some Travellers, maybe, or some idiots thinking they're entitled to go wild camping wherever they like?'

'Could be. Either way, I want to know what we're going up against before I agree to anything.'

There was a world of difference between those possibilities. Scaring off townies who'd decided to try getting back to nature should be easy enough. The weather had probably already half convinced them to pack up and go home. Travellers would be a whole different story.

A few years ago, I'd worked on a brownfield site that had been some sort of old council depot. The foreman had done a deal with some blokes parked up not far away with their families, battered lorries, caravans and dogs. Those blokes had cleared away the old fridges and other scrap metal that had been fly-tipped there, no questions asked. They had been friendly enough, but I wouldn't have wanted to get on the wrong side of any of them. Though I couldn't blame them for being defensive if they spent their lives being treated like shit.

'Gyppos', 'pikeys', 'tinkers'. I'd heard all those insults and worse when I was working on different building projects. I was usually warned that they all carried knives. My dad said that was ignorance and prejudice. I was willing to take his word for it until I had good reason to think different. So far I hadn't found that, but I was still wary.

'So, what now?' Fin asked as we headed for Bockbourne Magna.

'I need to talk to Hazel Spinner.' I glanced at her. 'If we do that together, she'll want to know who you are and what you can do.'

'I'll show her mine if she shows me hers.' Fin didn't seem particularly bothered. 'Give her a call.'

I did that, and by the time I'd finished explaining, we were approaching the village.

'We'll see you at the pub as soon as you can get there then.' I ended the call and glanced at Fin.

Keeping her eyes on the road, she nodded. We reached the White Hart car park a few minutes later.

'Are we going to get something to eat while we're here?' I unfolded myself from the passenger seat. I was really missing my Land Rover.

Fin shut her door and clicked the remote to lock the car. 'Sandwiches, not a Sunday roast.'

'Fair enough.'

As it turned out, roast beef and all the trimmings wasn't an option anyway. Every table was taken, in the beer garden and inside. That could only be good for the owners in such a horrible year for their business, but I was still hungry. We'd also missed another chance to see if any useful information was framed and hung on the dining room walls.

'I'll use the Ladies while we're here,' Fin said. 'You'll wait for Hazel?'

'Sure.' I leaned against the beer garden wall.

Hazel arrived almost at once. She wasn't driving, and I wondered where her car was. Maybe she was staying somewhere within walking distance. I was pretty sure she wasn't driving up here from Exeter every day. If I asked, I wondered if she'd tell me.

She saw me waiting and raised a hand. 'Where's your—? Oh, there she is.'

I turned and saw Fin coming out of the pub. She was holding a paper menu. She handed it to me as she reached us. 'They'll do us coffee and sandwiches to take away.'

'Sounds good.' I scanned the page of options. 'Roast beef and onions in a panini for me.'

I offered the menu to Hazel. She waved it away.

'I'll have a latte, no sugar.' She looked at Fin, not bothering to hide her curiosity. 'Hi, I'm Hazel. I think you've already seen me in my fur coat.'

'I'm Fin. I'm a swan when I want to be.' She took the menu and walked off before I could ask her what sandwich she wanted and offer to get the food.

Hazel was clearly intrigued to meet a swan maiden, but she didn't waste time asking me questions. That was a relief. I wasn't going to give her any answers. That was for Fin to say.

'So what are we going to do now?' Hazel focused on the problem in hand. 'Help the hamadryads, so they help us?'

The trees that ringed the car park were all mature beeches. I wondered if there was a hamadryad hiding in one to listen to whatever we said. I decided it didn't matter if they knew what I thought about the deal they were offering.

I repeated what I'd said to Fin. 'I want to know what we're going up against before I agree to anything.'

Hazel nodded. 'I've been asking around. I may have some idea where to look.'

'That was quick work,' I observed. 'You must have some useful local contacts?'

'I do.' Her tone told me that was all I was going to get.

I could hardly complain about her keeping secrets when we were doing the same. We'd read her website, but she didn't even know our surnames. We waited for Fin. She soon came back with a cardboard tray holding three coffees and two brown paper bags.

'Let's go and sit in the car,' she said briskly. 'Then we know we won't be overheard.'

Not by anyone in the beer garden, at least. I followed her across the car park and took the food and drink off her hands so she could find her keys. We ended up with both passenger-side doors open and Fin sitting sideways on the front seat while Hazel took the back. I stood facing them both.

'That story about a baby?' Hazel sipped her coffee as we ate our sandwiches. 'I think you may have found the answer to a puzzle that's been a local legend for a few centuries. There's a tale about a village midwife who was woken up in the middle of the night. She was told that a woman in labour needed her, but she must agree to be blindfolded. Anyway, she was taken to a big, fancy house, where a masked woman gave birth to a baby. Then the bastard who was presumably the father killed the child by throwing it into the fireplace, just like the hamadryad said. Only the midwife managed to take a piece of the bed hangings away with her. The fabric was traced back to a place called Littlecote House.

'That's not so very far away from here, and in the 1570s, the heir, Will Darrell, had been disinherited. That didn't stop him seizing the place once his father died, and generally being a complete swine. Anyway, even though there was no trace of the woman or the baby, Wild Will was put on trial for the murder. He was acquitted, possibly because the judge was his cousin and Will Darrell had promised to make him his heir. He came to a bad end eventually though, Will. He had a fall when he was out riding and broke his neck. Some said a flash of lightning startled his horse. Other versions say it was hell hounds, and that they can still be seen chasing his ghost.'

Fin and I exchanged a glance. We could both guess what had really happened. I hoped a whole pack of black shucks had scared the prick witless before he died. I hoped that had been a really painful death.

Fin caught a prawn that was falling out of her panini. 'You can see how the hamadryads wouldn't trust humans after something like that.'

Hazel nodded. 'And Will Darrell could kill the mother without leaving a trace by simply cutting down her tree. If he knew what she was, of course, and where to find her particular beech. Or she just fled. Either way, that explains how she disappeared so completely.'

I swallowed my mouthful. 'The hamadryad said this mystery woman was one of her grandmother's sisters. So that gives us, what, around two hundred and fifty years per generation, however little hamadryads are made. That fits with the average lifespan of a beech tree, roughly anyway. That could mean we have a problem. I'm not convinced these hamadryads' memories go back far enough to tell us anything useful about giants. Even if there have been stories passed down. Not if the dryads can't help us, and what they know goes a whole lot further back, as far as the Romans.'

'So what are you saying?' Hazel asked warily.

'I've been thinking about something Asca said. She's one of the dryads I know,' I explained hastily. I needed to remember that Hazel knew nothing about me, or where I worked.

'Asca said she would see what the trees remembered. Maybe she or one of the others could tell us how to find out what the oldest trees in this neck of the woods might know. Then we wouldn't have to make a deal with these hamadryads at all. We might be able to find out how to deal with the giant without having to tangle with mysterious men messing up some part of their forest.'

Though I didn't fancy explaining to my mum that I'd refused to help solve a problem like that.

'Do you think the hamadryads will take kindly to being let down?' Fin clearly had her doubts.

'I haven't agreed to anything yet,' I reminded her. 'And I'm not going to be much use doing whatever we need to do to deal with this bloody giant if I'm in hospital because I got beaten to a pulp by some thugs, or if I'm on remand for ABH.'

Fin and I exchanged another look. She knew I had a criminal record for breaking a man's arm with a spade. He'd been part of a gang out badger baiting in the nature reserve, and the bastard had gone for my dad, but mitigation only goes so far when you put someone in hospital. At least it had gone far enough to get me a suspended sentence and probation instead of jail time. Even so, that was the first thing any copper would see if he had some reason to look me up on his police computer.

Hazel was looking from me to Fin and back again. I saw her realise she wasn't going to get any explanation.

'So what are we going to do?' she asked again.

'You said you had some idea where these mysterious men might be?' I asked that for Fin's benefit. 'We can take a look at least.'

We might as well do something while I was waiting to hear back from Eleanor. As soon as she called me, I'd ask her to ask for Frai's or Asca's help with talking to old trees. Then we'd know what our options were. Then we could make some decisions.

'I agree.' Fin looked a lot happier. 'Who knows, it may only take a phone call to the cops to get rid of them, if they're trespassing or doing criminal damage.'

'It can take a fair while to get people moved on,' Hazel observed. 'Still, if they're really up to no good, a visit from the boys in blue might be enough to scare them off.'

Fin nodded. 'Then there's a good chance the hamadryads will help us, if we've done that for them.'

'They'll owe us for doing that much,' I agreed. Of course, that still didn't mean they would be able to tell us what we needed to know.

Hazel stood up. 'Do you have a map? A decent one, on paper? We don't want to risk relying on a phone signal.'

'Ordnance Survey Explorer?' Fin got up and handed me her empty cup and sandwich bag.

As she went to the back of the car, I held out my hand for Hazel's coffee cup. 'Shall I bin that for you?'

'Oh, yes, thanks.' She wasn't doing a very good job of hiding her interest in what Fin might have in the boot.

I was sure if Fin didn't want Hazel to see what she had in the car, she wouldn't have got out the map. In any case, if Hazel's local contacts were any good, it wouldn't be long before she identified her as the blonde who was in the village to test for pollution in the river. Of course, as soon as Hazel knew that, I realised uneasily, she would know about Blanche as well. I hoped that wasn't going to be a problem when Fin's sister found out what we were doing.

When I got back from throwing the rubbish into the bin, the two of them had the map spread out on the Toyota's bonnet. As they both bent over it, Hazel traced a line with her forefinger. She tapped a spot in what looked like the middle of nowhere.

'Sere Stock House used to be here. It was a hunting lodge built by the Victorians, but it was left to go to rack and ruin between the wars. There's still access, even though these are all private roads. There are notices and barriers, but those wouldn't stop anyone determined to ignore them.'

She looked up before I could ask what made her think this was the place we were looking for.

'There has definitely been more traffic on this road than there should be in the past few months. It's not somewhere you'd go without a good reason. If you wanted to set up some sort of illegal camp, it would be a good spot.'

I reckoned she knew a lot more that she wasn't sharing. I guessed someone she knew had gone to see why there had been more cars than usual around there.

Fin nodded, still looking at the map. 'You could go out this way and get onto the motorway easily enough.'

I was more interested in getting there than potential ways out. 'How do we get close enough to see what's going on without anyone seeing us? We still don't know what we might be walking into.'

Hazel's finger followed another line on the map. 'We can park here, then walk through this way.'

Her confidence convinced me someone had already taken a look. I wanted to know what Fin thought, but there was no way to ask her with Hazel standing there. We couldn't risk pissing off our only ally.

Fin was folding up the map. 'Are we going in one car?'

'If we'll all fit.' Hazel sized me up, as if she'd only just noticed my height. 'I'd be better in the front to give directions, if you can sit in the back.'

'I can try, if you pull the seat right forward.'

We managed – just. I was uncomfortably cramped, even with Hazel's shins right up against the dashboard. I hoped to hell Fin wouldn't need to make an emergency stop. If she did, Hazel would lose both her kneecaps.

I hadn't got a very good look at the map, and I wasn't happy about that. Wherever we were going was a lot further than I expected as well. Maybe it just felt like that to me. It wasn't as if I could see the roads and signs at all clearly, squashed into the Toyota's back seat. I was soon thinking we'd need the world's biggest shoe horn to get me out of the little car when we got there.

We were certainly heading away from the chalk hills of the downs, into the broad vale that had been slowly carved out by the river. This fertile land had been claimed by the beech trees, at least until the forests were cleared. Now only isolated pockets of ancient woodland remained between the villages and farms.

Finally, thankfully, Fin pulled up by an indistinct turning. Hazel got out to raise the pole barrier that barred access to the single-lane road heading into the woods. A red-and-white sign nailed to the pole said 'KEEP OUT', and at first glance it looked as if the whole thing was solidly chained up, complete with a padlock. Hazel didn't hesitate as she pulled the tangle of chain aside. She pushed down on the weight on the end of the pole.

Fin drove through and pulled up to wait for Hazel to reset the barrier.

'If she hasn't been here, she knows someone who has,' I said before she got back to join us.

'Oh yes.' Fin had no doubts about that.

She didn't get a chance to say anything else. Hazel opened the car door and got in.

'Go down here until you reach a fork in the road. Then bear left.'

Fin drove on. I looked out of the windows on each side. At least I could see a fair distance, thanks to the well-spaced beech trees. There was no sign of anyone out in the wood, human or otherwise. That didn't mean no one would hear the Toyota's engine. That sound would definitely carry. The sooner we were parked and away from the car, the happier I would be.

Hazel pointed. 'There's a place to pull in just past that big oak.'

That made me feel a whole lot better, as Fin stopped the car and we got out. This oak was a magnificent, ancient specimen, and its presence in this beech wood was no accident. It had been planted here to signify some long-lost boundary or perhaps to mark a gathering place. It might even have been intended as a gallows tree.

Centuries ago, it had been pollarded. The branches of the crown had been cut back, so that regrowth would produce a regular harvest of wooden poles for countless uses. The trunk had continued to swell, and I estimated it was eight or more metres around by now. Without regular cropping in recent decades, the branches that ringed the top had grown outwards like stag horns. Thrusting spikes warned off foes from any direction, and the summer's leaves were still defiantly green. This tree wouldn't surrender to the arrival of winter without a fight.

'Is there any way we can hide the car a bit better?' Fin was looking around, apprehensive. 'If these squatters or whoever they are find it and trash it, we're buggered.'

Not to mention the cost to her of losing all the stuff in the boot, starting with her laptop.

'Let's see what the Green Man can do.' I looked straight at the oak, resolutely expectant. I told myself it couldn't hurt to ask. He'd sent me here, after all. Add to that, he'd made me as good as invisible at least once before now. Fin deserved his help today.

A shiver ran through the twisted branches. For an instant, a cluster of leaves formed themselves into a foliate face. I took the glint of green light beneath those bushy brows for a yes. The face was definitely smiling.

'Did you see—?'

I turned to see Hazel staring at the tree, open-mouthed. I grinned, and tried to look as if this was no big deal. As a matter of fact, I hardly ever asked the Green Man for anything. Just thinking about doing it was unnerving.

Hazel looked back at me as if we'd never met before. As if she wasn't entirely certain she liked what she saw.

'How are we going to do this?' Fin was focused on the task in hand. She put her keys in the outer pocket of her backpack and went to sling the straps over her shoulder.

I held out my hand. 'How about I take that? In case you need to make a quick getaway?'

'This is hardly flying country.' She looked around at the beech trees and up at the lattice of branches between us and the sky. 'Besides, what good will that do, if I leave you out here on your own with my car keys?'

'I'll find some way to hold them off until the cops turn up. You get away and ring 999.' I'll admit the police do have their uses.

Fin shook her head. 'I'll need a phone to do that.'

Hazel was getting impatient. 'How about we just see what there is to see?' She started walking away along a narrow track without waiting for an answer.

Chapter Thirteen

As we followed Hazel along the path, Fin got out her phone. 'How much battery have you got?' she asked quietly. 'We should be ready to take pictures. We'll want evidence for the police if we turn whatever this is over to them.'

I wasn't sure I liked that idea. Don't get me wrong. I was all in favour of the police handling whatever this was, but Fin supplying photos would mean her giving a statement, maybe even evidence in court. That was a lot more involved than I wanted her to be.

'Hush.' Ten paces ahead, Hazel rounded on us with a scowl.

We kept quiet after that. I let Fin go ahead of me. She started following Hazel's lead in moving from the shelter of one tree to the next, to make it harder for anyone up ahead to see that we were coming.

I did my best to do the same, though there's a hell of a lot more of me to hide. Still, growing up with a nature reserve warden for a dad, I'd learned a fair bit about moving quietly and unnoticed through woodland. I glanced over my shoulder from time to time, but there was no sign of anyone following me, or of any movement by the car. That was good to know.

I had lost sight of the ancient oak by the time a muffled cough echoed through the wood. It was definitely a human cough. Sometimes deer can make a similar sound, but they don't carry on spluttering like someone in serious danger of bringing up a lung.

Hazel was a fair bit further ahead of us now. She stopped and beckoned. Fin and I joined her. We moved together, cautious. Hazel was waiting where a great grey beech had

fallen in some past winter storm. It had grown too tall to re-
sist the brutal winds, unlike the squat, defiant old oak where
we'd parked. The beech's loss had opened up the canopy of
branches overhead. Dozens of its fallen nuts had seized their
chance to sprout, racing upwards to claim the daylight.

The saplings were as thick as my wrist, and about as tall
as Fin. Clustered so closely together, the young trees made
a very effective screen, as long as I crouched down a bit. We
could see through the spindly trunks, but a casual glance
from the other side would hopefully slide right over us. Even
if we were spotted, anyone wanting to lay hands on us would
have to skirt around that barrier. There was no way they
could force a way through those tightly packed saplings.

'Wait here.'

Hazel had barely spoken when she vanished in a flash of
amber light. As I blinked away the lingering smudge across
my vision, I saw a sizeable hare bounding away. I soon lost
sight of her. A beech wood might not be their natural habitat,
but that brindled fur was still extremely effective camouflage.

'What can you see?' Fin spoke so quietly that I barely
heard her.

I risked standing a bit taller and assessed the view ahead
of us. My eyes picked out the details that didn't belong, and I
started to make sense of what I was seeing through the trees.
Those ruddy straight lines that had no place in nature must
be remnants of the ruined house's brick walls. Larger, darker
shapes were harder to understand.

Whatever they were, they weren't vehicles. I reckoned that
meant we weren't dealing with Travellers. The clue is in the
name, after all. For another thing, I'd expect there to be dogs
and maybe horses, as well as caravans with people around
them, whatever the time of day. There was no sign or sound
of anyone here, apart from whoever had that awful cough. It
sounded really painful.

We waited and watched and didn't see a thing, until Hazel came back down the path. I turned away just in time to avoid being dazzled as she changed back to her human form.

'What's the matter with you?' she asked, puzzled.

Fin explained. 'He sees a flash of light when one of us shifts. We think it must be something to do with his dryad blood.'

Whatever it was, I could do without it, and we could discuss that some other time.

'So what's over there?' I asked.

'Huts,' Hazel said simply. 'They're not locked, and there's no one around, apart from that poor bastard with the cough. Shall we have a look for some clues that might tell us what on earth's going on here?'

I looked at Fin.

She shrugged. 'We came all this way to see.'

We followed Hazel down the path. I realised we were approaching the old hunting lodge from the side. If there had ever been lawns around it, those were long gone. At the sides and the back, birch and beech saplings now thrived. The house had been ringed by a hard-packed gravel path, which the woods were doing their best to reclaim next. Thorn bushes and bramble thickets had almost reached the walls. The building itself was a roofless, windowless shell. Ivy had laid claim to the brickwork, with questing tendrils spreading out from dense swathes of glossy dark green.

The gravelled expanse at the front of the ruin was pretty sizeable. I guessed that's where carriages and, later, cars had arrived and turned around to go back the way they had come. I could make out the curving line of a tree-lined drive stretching away to our right.

Any plants that might have seeded themselves in that open space must have been ripped out or crushed. Twelve wooden huts had been set up in two rows of six, facing each other across three or four metres of gravel churned into mud by vehicle tyres. If we wanted to see anything else, that's where we would have to go. There was barely enough space left between the sides of the sheds for someone my size to walk without turning sideways.

As far as garden buildings went, they would be towards the top of any range for size, but they weren't nearly fancy enough to be called a garden office or chalet or anything like that. I reckoned they'd been put up in a hurry. The corners weren't what I would consider square, and nothing had been properly levelled. The roofing felt wasn't straight and the ends had been left hanging ragged. Each one had a central door with what should have been glazed windows on either side. Instead, sheets of thick black plastic had been nailed over the openings.

The doors were secured with a flat black metal hasp that slotted over a staple solidly fixed to the frame. At least, they would be secured when the padlocks that hung open on the black steel hoops were snapped shut. There was nothing to stop us going inside and taking a look to see what was going on. Hazel was right about that.

Well, we could go inside all but one of the huts, that is. The far end one with its back to the driveway was padlocked shut. That was where the coughing was coming from. Locking someone in like that was definitely illegal, whatever else was going on. It was also fucking inhumane. Whoever was in there, they needed to see a doctor.

On the other hand, though... if whoever was in there couldn't get out, they couldn't see us. They couldn't raise the alarm, assuming they were in any fit state to do that. More importantly, as far as I was concerned, they couldn't infect us with whatever was making them so obviously ill.

The three of us exchanged glances.

'I say we take a look at the huts last,' I said quietly, 'once we've assessed the rest of the site.'

Fin nodded. 'As soon as we leave, we call the police and tell them to come and rescue whoever's locked in there.'

'We tell them to bring an ambulance,' Hazel added.

Now we were here, I took the lead. That way anything unexpectedly hostile would have to go through me to get to Fin. The first room we approached on this side of the house had once been a kitchen, or something like that anyway. I could see the floor had once been scrubbed flagstones, and bits of broken green tiles clung to crumbling plaster. There wasn't much of the walls left standing. The tallest remnants barely reached my shoulder.

What must have once been a fireplace was being used as a crude hearth. If there'd ever been an iron range, or some more modern cooker in there, that was long gone. Two-metre lengths of rusted iron bars that looked like reinforcing rods for concrete had been set up in there, raised to about knee height on stacks of salvaged bricks. Metre lengths had been laid across those and secured with twists of wire. That made a grid that would support cooking pots over a fire. There was a sodden drift of wood ash underneath which made that obvious.

Roughly chopped logs were stacked under a tarpaulin, trying to stay dry in the corner. I went to take a closer look. That was green beechwood, hacked down by someone with no real idea how to use an axe. That explained the lingering smell of petrol I had noticed. Fresh-cut wood is hellishly hard to get burning, and when it does catch, the smoke will be choking. Maybe the poor bastard we could still hear coughing had got a lungful, and regretted it.

Fin looked warily towards the noise. Then she gestured towards three modern metal lockers stood against the opposite wall. They were the sort of thing DIY centres sell to store tools in, or maybe bikes, in gardens with no space for a shed. They're solidly designed to foil burglars, and each of these was secured with a heavy-duty chain and a laminated steel padlock. No one was getting in there without the keys.

'What do you suppose they're for?' Fin's voice was lower than a whisper as she got out her phone and started taking photos.

I answered her just as quietly. 'Pots, pans, food.'

I wondered whether those metal doors and locks were to keep out foraging animals or desperate humans. I was getting a very bad feeling about this place.

Hazel looked at the rest of the house. 'I can't see them using any of the other rooms. Can you?'

I studied the interior, where a whole section of the wall above us had collapsed in on itself. I could make out the splintered ends of blackened joists and floorboards. Even with the fading petrol fumes in the back of my throat, there was a powerful smell of rot. 'I reckon a blackbird making a heavy landing could bring down those beams.'

'Let's see what's out the back.' Fin stepped through a gap in the wall where there'd once been a window. Broken edges of bricks were still raw where the last of the masonry had been kicked out to clear the way.

'Mind the thorns.' Though as I followed her, I found the scrubby trees weren't as dense as I had first thought. Either that, or they were letting us pass.

In the corner between the kitchen wing and the rest of the house, we reached what had once been some sort of yard. Brick paviors sloped towards a central drain, but that had been blocked for a long time. The ground was thick with moss. Someone had scraped chunks of it away with a shovel, to make a path to an old-fashioned pump. From the stack of black plastic buckets beside it, that's what these people were using for water, so the house must have its own well. I hoped there were plenty of water purification tablets in those lockers.

Hazel was following Fin, both of them careful on the treacherous footing. 'What is that revolting smell?'

'Fluid for chemical toilets, and everything that goes into them.' I recognised that aroma from portaloos on building sites.

We found a long, single-storey room stretching out from the back of the house. Once, whoever lived here could enjoy views of the forest through tall windows and wide double doors. Maybe it had been a ballroom, or a billiard room or something else. Now it was home to a row of camping toilets under a tarpaulin rigged over what was left of the roof. These weren't the big cubicles that some genius on a building site inevitably calls 'The Turdis', or even the compact cubes that camping shops sell. We were looking at the bargain basement versions that are basically a big, sturdy bucket with a seat and a lid. We didn't go any closer.

As far as I was concerned, we weren't going any further at all. Anyone coming around here for a crap would have a seat overlooking a scene of devastation in the woods. Holes had been dug apparently at random so those stinking buckets could be emptied. Whoever had filled them in had done a half-arsed job. There were heaps of soil beside sunken hollows where clumps of bog roll showed white against the earth and whatever else was down there.

Beyond the shit pits, the smaller trees had been cut down. There was a chainsaw in one of those metal lockers then. Less expert hands had cut up the wood for burning with hand tools, judging by the piles of splinters and rags of bark beside the ragged stumps. Meantime, whoever was in charge of the chainsaw had started cutting the lower branches off the bigger beeches. Whoever had done that was no tree surgeon. These trees had been brutally mutilated.

'No wonder the hamadryads are pissed off.' Fin's voice was muffled.

I saw she was holding the end of her sweatshirt sleeve over her mouth and nose with one hand, taking photos with her phone with the other.

'I'm not sure what they expect me to do though.'

Whatever the hell was going on here, it clearly wasn't a one-man operation. That meant I wasn't going to put an end to it single-handed. This really was a job for the cops.

'Let's take a closer look at these huts.' Hazel turned to retrace our steps.

Fin and I followed. Back at the front of the house, whoever had that awful cough had finally fallen silent. Hazel pulled open the unlocked door of the closest shed. There was barely enough clear floor for any one of us to go in and turn around. None of us went inside regardless. For a start, that would block the others' view, as well as the only light coming through the door.

For a second thing, the place absolutely stank. The reek was a foul mix of unwashed bodies, unwashed clothes and cigarette smoke. Dirty sleeping bags had been bundled up and shoved into each corner along with rolled-up mats, held in place by battered holdalls or rucksacks. It looked like this hovel was home to four men.

Besides a stack of folded-up camping chairs, the floor was covered with plastic crates. Several held clothes, mostly jeans and sweatshirts. One was full of plastic cups and paper plates. The one closest to the door held a four-pack of bog roll, ripped open and half used, as well as a battery-powered camping lantern and a couple of creased and grimy paperback books.

Fin took a couple of photos and put her phone away in her backpack. Then she bent down to pick up one of the books, wrinkling her nose as she flipped through it.

'Anything exciting?' I asked.

'No idea.' She held it out with two pages open so I could see the print.

I realised that wasn't just in a foreign language, but the letters were unrecognisable as well. Russian, maybe, or something close? I seemed to recall quite a few Eastern European languages used the same alphabet.

Wherever the people living in these hovels had come from, I was willing to bet this wasn't the accommodation they'd been promised. I guessed whatever work they were being bullied into wasn't what they expected either, even if it was farm work or something else that wasn't downright illegal. The idea that I could deal with this on my own was laughable – or it would be if this wasn't so serious, and not just for the hamadryads.

Fin dropped the book back in the crate. She stood there with her hands held wide. 'There's some hand sanitizer in the pocket with my keys.'

I went behind her and found the small bottle in her backpack. I squirted clear gel into her upturned palm, put the bottle back and did up the zip. 'I don't think there's anything else we need to see.'

Fin rubbed her hands around each other. 'What are we going to do now?'

Hazel had moved on to peer into the next shed. She looked around at the sound of our voices. 'This is much the same.'

Whoever had been coughing must have heard us speaking. He called out in a language I didn't understand, though his desperation didn't need translating. I looked at Fin, and at Hazel. They didn't know what he was saying either.

The poor bastard started coughing again. Then another, weaker voice spoke up inside the locked shed. Fuck. There were two of them in there. At least two of them.

One or other of them begged for help again. I still couldn't make out if that plea was in some foreign language or English. Hazel stared at the two of us. She was as shocked as we were.

Fin reached for her phone. 'The police can sort this out.'

I nodded. 'No argument from me.'

'No signal.' Fin scowled. 'Bugger.'

'Wouldn't want any of these poor sods getting hold of a phone and calling someone.' I looked around. 'Though I don't suppose they have any idea where the hell they are.'

Hazel came back to join us. 'Let's get out of here. We'll alert the authorities as soon as—'

A hamadryad appeared beside me. 'You should leave. All of you. At once.'

I was pretty sure she was the one who'd blocked my way out of the wood until the one in charge told her to step aside. 'What's going on?'

She shrugged. 'The giant comes.'

What the fuck?

Before I could say that out loud, I heard something crashing through the woods at the front of the house. Something big. Clouds of panicked birds came bursting out of the trees. They barely bothered to squawk an alarm before getting away, wings flapping as fast as they could. Before I could ask the hamadryad what was happening, she vanished.

I moved to get a better look through one of the narrow gaps between the sheds. Some way beyond the edge of the gravel, where the mature beeches loomed over the thickets of thorns and brambles, I glimpsed a dark shape. A very big dark shape, and it sure as hell wasn't Bigfoot.

'Back up.' I began retreating towards the path we'd used to get here from the road where we'd parked the car. 'Get behind me.'

Hazel and Fin didn't hesitate. We reached the path and I thought very hard about keeping on going. Except we couldn't, could we? I couldn't, at least. The Green Man had sent me here to deal with this giant. I still didn't have a sodding clue how to do that, but this was the first chance I'd had to see exactly what I was up against. It might be the only chance I'd get.

'Wait a moment.' Hazel had already turned around to look, crouching behind a hawthorn.

Fin and I hid ourselves among the beech and birch saplings as the giant reached the sheds. I took a moment to silently ask the Green Man to make certain this monster couldn't see us. He owed me that much. I didn't risk looking around for some sign that he'd heard me this time. I've never done any martial arts, but I've watched enough Bruce Lee movies. Never take your eyes off your opponent.

We could see the giant approaching the back of that far row of sheds, the ones with their doors facing the ruined house. Measured against the height of the felted roofs, I reckoned it must have been at least four metres tall. My dad would call that about thirteen feet in old money. It didn't look as tall as it really was, if that makes any sense. The creature was barrel-bodied, broad-shouldered and bandy-legged, walking with a stoop. If the thing stood upright, it would be anything up to a metre taller.

It wasn't interested in standing upright. Now it had reached the sheds, it was running its long-nailed hands over the closest roof. It bent down as if it was sniffing the roofing felt. It really was an ugly fucker. Its features were roughly human, but weirdly coarse and exaggerated, like a particularly vicious caricature. More than that, its face fitted together wrong somehow. Wrong in a way that raised the hairs on the back of my neck. Forget the uncanny valley. Looking at this thing was staring into the uncanny abyss.

What I couldn't see clearly were its eyes. Its face was screwed up in a scowl, and its chin was pressed to its chest.

'I don't think it likes the daylight,' breathed Fin.

'It belongs in the shadows,' murmured Hazel.

It might be as good as blind, but that didn't mean it was deaf. I waved a hand to shut them both up before the sodding thing heard us. At least what little breeze there was at the moment was coming towards us. With luck, the only thing the giant was smelling was the stink of sweat and misery inside those sheds.

A shaft of sunlight shone through the clouds scurrying overhead. I saw what Hazel meant about the giant being a creature of the shadows. For a moment, I could see right through it, all the way to the sunlit trees far behind. As the sunlight swept across the front of the house and the sheds, the monster seemed to shiver and go blurry.

The moment passed and the giant looked as menacing as ever. Menacing, and really strange. For a start, it was just one colour, like a picture someone had only just started painting. Its hair, skin and clothes were all dark grey, like the surface of freshly broken flint. For another thing, its clothes couldn't seem to make up their mind about what they were supposed to be. What looked like a padded tunic shifted into a high-collared coat with broad sleeves. In the next moment, the giant was wearing something as shapeless as a sack.

None of this meant the monster was some insubstantial shade. As it thumped the shed roof with a clenched fist, I heard the wood beneath the felt crack. It wasn't completely stupid either. Since it was too big to get between the sheds, it was working its way along the row. Every long stride brought it closer to us, which I wasn't happy about. I wondered if we'd made a bad mistake stopping to watch it. If we ran now, movement might catch its eye, however limited its sight was.

Even if it couldn't see what we were, that might be enough for it to chase us.

Which was to say, it could chase me. I reached for the strap of Fin's backpack and slipped it off her shoulder. She looked at me, confused. I pulled harder and pointed up at the sky with my other hand. She narrowed her eyes at me and shook her head. I didn't back down, trying to get the other strap free as well. I risked looking away from the giant long enough to whisper into her ear, as quietly as I could.

'Not now. In case you need to leave in a hurry.'

Fin gave in. She didn't look happy about it, but just at the moment, I didn't care. I wound the backpack straps around my hand and clenched my fist. It felt good to have hold of something, even if rip-stop fabric weighted with a wallet, a phone and some car keys wouldn't make much of a weapon.

I spared a second to glance at Hazel. She was still half crouched behind that hawthorn, motionless and unblinking as she watched the monster. I could see she was ready to run, and I had no doubt she'd be haring out of here, to be faster and harder to spot. I could hardly blame her for that.

For now, the giant was only interested in the shed at the end of the row. The shed we had opened up to look into. That didn't seem like a coincidence, I thought with a sinking feeling.

It struck the roof hard and the whole shed shifted on its wooden base. Now the walls were sloping sideways. I knew it. Those flimsy buildings had been thrown up too fast and too carelessly to be properly stable.

The giant roared with triumph, loud enough to make me wince. Fin and Hazel clapped their hands over their ears. The giant roared again, with savage glee. I wasn't just hearing the awful noise. I felt sickening vibration deep in my chest. It was coming up through the soles of my boots. It seemed to freeze me to the spot. I couldn't have run if I'd wanted to.

Thankfully, the sound of ripping roof felt and splintering wood broke through that paralysis. I saw the giant had found some split between the shed's side wall and the roof where it could wedge in a claw-like nail. I watched as it forced its finger in deeper and widened that gap. It brought its hands together and managed to get some purchase with both sets of talons. I saw it hunch those massive shoulders. With a roar like a power lifter, it flung its enormous hands out wide. That wrenched the roof right off the shed. The panels crashed into the hut next door, trailing lengths of roofing felt.

The giant didn't care. Now it was smashing down the walls of the shed. Its clenched fists shattered the panels of over-lapped planks and its great big feet stamped down the re-mains. Its shape was still shifting as it did that. Now we could see its legs were bare one minute. In the next it was wearing what looked like baggy leggings. The giant stamped again, and now it wore heavy boots that went right up over its knees with the tops folded back down.

It crouched down and began ripping through the stuff that had been inside the shed. Literally. It tore the sleeping bags in half, tossing the pieces away. I watched as it stabbed those talons right through the canvas or whatever one of those holdalls was made of. As the bag was pulled apart, clothes, a couple of aerosol cans and a few packs of cigarettes went flying. The giant roared. Now it sounded frustrated. It started kicking and flinging the plastic crates, not caring what was in them or where anything went.

As it turned its back on us in its tantrum, something clutched my elbow. I nearly jumped out of my skin before I realised Hazel had silently crept up beside me. As I looked at her and she met my gaze, she didn't speak. She just tapped her left wrist with her right forefinger and pointed up at the sky.

I realised what she meant. Time was getting on. The sun was low in the sky and the daylight was fading. This giant was a creature of the shadows. I wasn't sure if twilight would make it stronger or more solid or something else that would make it even more dangerous, but whatever happened, it couldn't be good.

I saw Fin watching the two of us. She understood what Hazel was saying. What I couldn't tell was what either of them thought we should do next. Before any of us could do anything about that, one of the sick men in the locked shed started coughing.

Chapter Fourteen

The giant froze in mid-fury. Its great brutish head swung around. Now it lifted its chin, sniffing the air so hard we could hear it snorting.

Fee fi fo fum... Somehow, I didn't think this monster was going to be picky about where the blood of anyone it was eating had come from. That wasn't the worst of it either, if I was right about something else.

The giant took two long strides and started trashing the next shed in the row. Under the cover of the noise, I told Fin and Hazel what I suspected.

'If that thing kills and eats whoever's locked in that shed, I think that'll give it a much stronger tie to this time and place. It hasn't got a foothold here yet. That's why what we're seeing keeps changing.'

Hazel looked at me, horrified. She didn't ask me how I knew, which was a relief because honestly, I was guessing. It was an educated guess all the same, based on what I definitely knew about wyrms.

'What do we do?' Fin was watching the giant.

I saw it had abandoned that second shed as soon as it realised there were no warm bodies inside – or even cold ones. Be he alive, or be he dead... The giant moved on to rip the next hut apart.

'Can you distract it without getting too close? Seriously, I mean it. Don't get within ten metres. I just need a few minutes.'

Fin nodded, confident. Hazel did the same. I still felt sick with apprehension as I left them to it and ran for the wrecked kitchen. I didn't waste time trying to break into the metal lockers, even though I'd bet they held useful things.

I headed for the hearth, though I wasn't there for the iron bars, not yet anyway. I ripped the tarpaulin off the stack of logs. I'd seen a glimpse of red there earlier. Now I saw I was right. A plastic fuel can was tucked against the wall. Whatever was in those lockers, whoever had the keys didn't want their stuff smelling of petrol fumes.

I shoved Fin's backpack through my belt and knotted the ends of the adjustable straps to secure it. Now I had my hands free, I grabbed the fuel can and unscrewed the cap. Picking up the longest length of wood that I could see, I held it over the stack. I poured petrol over the end of the stick as carefully as I could. I wouldn't be any help to anyone if I splashed my clothes and set myself alight.

I laid the stick on the wood and screwed the cap back on the fuel. Safety first. That and I didn't want to waste any petrol that I might need later. There are a few things I know for sure about monsters that live in the shadows. One of the most important is they really don't like fire.

Now I needed something to set the stick alight. Since I don't smoke, and I don't make a habit of casual arson, I don't carry matches or a lighter. But I'd seen proof the blokes who spent their nights huddled in those sheds smoked. Every smoker I've ever known has always had spare lighters, buying a new throwaway one when they realise they've left the last one somewhere.

I ran back out onto the gravel. The giant was standing in the wreckage of the third shed, roaring with outrage. I saw Hazel throw something small that caught the light with a glint of silver just before it hit the monster. Big as the giant was, it flinched and bellowed with pain. It took a wrathful step towards her.

Something hit it on the back of the head and bounced away. That was an aerosol. Looking across the ruins of the sheds, I saw Fin had an armful of spray cans. She must have scavenged those from the wrecked sheds while the giant was looking the other way. That was a risk I wished she hadn't taken.

The giant spun around and took a stride towards her. As soon as its back was turned, Hazel hit it between the shoulder blades again with whatever she was throwing so hard and accurately. I realised she was pelting it with the steel padlocks unhooked from the open shed doors. The giant turned on her again, only to get another aerosol in the back of its neck from Fin.

The monster couldn't decide which tormentor to pursue. It roared with frustration, so loud my ears hurt. Not so loud that I couldn't hear whoever was trapped in that locked shed hammering on the walls and door. However sick they might be, they were desperately trying to break out.

I didn't waste time wondering what the hell they thought was going on. I was searching through scattered clothes in the remains of the first shed. As I kicked things aside, looking for what I needed, I snatched wary glances at the giant. Since I wasn't chucking things at it, the monster seemed to be ignoring me for the moment.

Then Hazel ran out of padlocks. The giant realised that at the same time I did. It roared with triumph as it stomped towards her. She backed away, down the narrow gap between two of the sheds in the untouched row. The giant didn't bother going around to the other side to try to get to her. It forced the sheds with its massive hands. There was a sharp crack of splintering wood. Hazel waited until the very last moment. Then a hare darted right between the giant's feet and bounded away.

The monster spun around so fast it nearly tripped over its own feet. As it staggered, looking this way and that, I thought it was going to chase the hare. Then I thought it was going to come for me. Then I saw its squinting eyes fasten on Fin as she stood waiting to see what happened. A last gleam of sunshine lit up her white-blonde hair. The giant charged towards her.

'Hey!' I yelled, as loud as I could. I was ready to run for the kitchen and grab an iron bar. Let's see how it liked one of those across the kneecaps.

The giant didn't hear me, or it didn't care. It was chasing Fin. She was already racing for the shelter of the beech trees beyond the scrubby thorns and undergrowth.

I took a step, and nearly lost my balance when I stood on something small and hard. As my boot skidded across the plank floor, I looked down. It was a blue plastic disposable lighter. Better late than never. As long as I wasn't too fucking late. As I stooped down to snatch it up, I looked for Fin. My mouth was dry and my pulse was racing.

The giant was gaining on her. Bandy-legged or not, it had a horribly long stride. Why the hell didn't she change into a swan and fly off? I guessed she'd have to stop running to do that. If she did, she risked the giant reaching her before she could get away. As it was, the bastard thing was almost on her, even though she had nearly reached the mature trees.

If she got to that refuge, she should be able to get away. She should be able to run between those big beeches far faster than the giant could force its way through. I stopped breathing as I watched. There was nothing else I could do.

Something made the giant stagger to a halt. It looked down at its feet with a bellow of fury. That gave Fin the time she needed to reach the first of the beech trees. One was standing a little way forward of the rest. She didn't go past it and on into the woods though. I saw a figure crouching on the grey trunk with one hand on a low branch and the other reaching down. No human acrobat could possibly do that, but this was a hamadryad.

Fin leaped. The hamadryad grabbed her wrist. The two of them disappeared up the tree so fast I lost sight of them. Too fast for the giant to grab Fin's feet, though it came far too close for fucking comfort. An instant later, I saw two figures at the top of the tree. My heart was in my mouth. Dryads can skip across twigs that a squirrel would think twice about trusting. I guessed hamadryads were the same, but Fin wasn't either of those.

I saw her fall out of the tree. No, she wasn't falling. She'd jumped or been pushed or both. Gravity didn't care. She was definitely heading for the ground. Only for a few seconds. I saw a flash of white light and a swan flew through the air on wide wings. She swooped low enough that the giant jumped up to try and catch her. Close, but not close enough. Fin soared away as the giant stood watching, screeching with frustration. She didn't come back towards me, but headed past the other side of the ruined house.

I felt something on my leg. I looked down and saw a hare that could only be Hazel standing up on her hind legs. Her long-eared head butted Fin's backpack impatiently, where I had it knotted on my belt. I dropped everything I was holding and got the bag free. Hazel grabbed the straps in her mouth and bolted for the path back to the car.

Now I was on my own. The giant came stomping towards me and its expression was easy to read. It was pissed off and hungry, and I was first on its list to be eaten. Ripping me apart to work off its anger would be a bonus.

I picked up the petrol-soaked stick and the lighter. I checked to see there was some fluid in it and that it hadn't cracked under my boot. All fine. Thank fuck for that. I stood there and waited. As the giant came closer, it slowed. It wasn't that stupid. If I wasn't running, I must be up to something. It had the wits to work that out.

At least I had a good idea of how fast it could move now. I waited for as long as I dared. Then I flicked the lighter. Nothing. I flicked it again. Nothing. Shit. Third time lucky? The giant was getting closer.

I got a pissy little flame. Hoping that would be enough, I held the lighter under the end of the stick, out at arm's length. The petrol-soaked wood caught alight. The giant shied away and raised one hand to shield its face. I caught a first glimpse of its eyes. The monster's gaze was as shiny, cold and black as an ice-covered road, and equally treacherous.

It was absolutely determined to eat me. It circled the wooden floor of the wrecked shed where I was standing, looking for a way to get past the flame. I kept thrusting the burning stick at it. I shoved the lighter into my pocket, thinking a pitchfork for my free hand would be welcome about now. Failing that, a length of iron rebar would do.

We went in a few more circles. As far as flaming torches go, a petrol-soaked lump of wood isn't ideal. The smoke was stinging my eyes and the stick was burning fast. If I wasn't careful, I'd be the one burned, not the giant.

I held out as long as I could. Then I dropped the burning stick into the biggest heap of clothes and splintered wood at my feet. The freshly broken planks caught quickly and the flames spread fast. I retreated onto the gravel as fast as I could without tripping over something. I felt sorry for whoever's stuff was going to get burned, but it was their belongings or me. Besides, I hadn't seen a trace of passports or cash or anything else of value.

The giant was circling slowly, trying to get around the bigger fire. I was circling in the other direction, to keep as much distance as I could between the monster and me. I wondered how long we were going to do this. The daylight was fading faster. With the glare of the fire right in front of me, it was getting harder to see the dark outline of the giant against the gathering shadows behind it. That wasn't good.

The giant made a move first. Not towards me, but in search of an easier meal. It spun around and headed for the next undamaged shed in the row. That meant it had two huts left to trash before it reached the one where those poor bastards were still trying to break out.

I had better hurry. I ran for the ruined kitchen. The first thing I did was pour the rest of the petrol over the stack of wood. Then I ripped that grid of iron bars off the loose bricks supporting it. Thankfully the twists of wire were only there to stop the cross bars shifting. It was easy enough to pull them apart. Now I had a bundle of lengths of rusty iron. I wished I was wearing gloves as the rough metal bit into my hands, but you can't have everything.

I ran back out to see where the giant was now. It had just about finished trashing the shed next to the one with the locked door. I shifted the bundle of rebar to my left hand and weighed a single length in my right palm.

When it came to sport at school, I wasn't built for running. I could manage short, explosive bursts of speed on the rugger pitch or to get a decent time in a hundred-metre sprint. Any distance longer than that was a walk as far as I was concerned. My strengths in track and field events were throwing the shot, discus and javelin.

I stretched my right arm out behind me and leaned back, using the weight in my left hand as a counterbalance. I hurled the rebar as hard as I could, doing my best to recall the technique I'd been taught at school. Thank fuck a giant is a big target, because what I was throwing wasn't exactly aerodynamic.

The iron rod gouged a deep grey-white groove across the darkness of the monster's shoulder before it clattered to the ground. The giant bellowed with pain and fury. It started to run towards me. I launched another length of rebar, and another one after that. Forget technique, I wasn't after athletics medals here.

The first rod bounced off its thigh but left another pale mark. Now the giant was limping. The second rod hit it right in the gut. The metal sank deep into the monster's belly. The giant collapsed to its knees and roared. A moment later it gripped the iron rod and ripped it out. That cost the monster though. I could see glistening grey oozing from the wound as well as dripping from the palm of its hand. Then it staggered to its feet and kept coming.

I chucked two more lengths of iron. One missed completely. The other stuck into its chest, high up and to the right. The monster reached up to grab it, but this time it changed its mind. It stumbled towards me instead. Hatred lit those glistening black eyes. As it snarled, I saw it had fangs like a shark's.

I could see that because grey drool coated its lips and tongue, shining in the light from the burning shed. I'd hurt it badly, no doubt about that. I backed away carefully and snatched up a length of burning plank from the ruins of the hut. I say burning, but the wood was barely smouldering. The giant's mouth curved in an ugly, mocking smile. It still intended to kill me, and a few embers weren't going to stop it.

I moved fast enough to stay out of its reach, and slow enough to lure it towards the kitchen. Once I was by the hearth, I waited and tried to look panicked, as if I didn't know where to go. The giant actually laughed as it staggered through the biggest gap in the broken front wall. The sound made my blood run cold. Now it had me cornered, it was going to take its time.

Fee fi fo fum... This giant might be able to smell the blood of an Englishman, but petrol fumes meant nothing to it. I threw the smouldering plank onto the fuel-soaked wood by the hearth. I hurled myself through the gap in the back wall as the petrol vapour exploded. I felt flash burns on my hands and face. Forget that. I scrambled to my feet to see what was going on.

The giant had recoiled from the burst of flames. It was shielding its eyes with its forearms, out of pure instinct. I saw its wrist knock the iron bar that was still sticking out of its chest. The monster roared with agony. It stumbled backwards, unable to see where it was going. It crashed against the metal lockers and shrieked, staggering forwards again.

Now it started lashing out wildly. Its face was screwed up and its eyes were tight closed. One massive hand brushed against the wall. I have no idea what the giant thought it was attacking. It didn't seem to care as it hammered at the brickwork with brutal fists.

I retreated fast, and just in time. The giant brought down an avalanche of crumbling bricks and rotting wood. I backed off from the cloud of mouldy-smelling dust, not wanting to breathe that shit. A breeze swept the worst away. I saw the heap of rubble that had buried the giant heave – once – twice. Then everything lay still.

Okay, so that was that, for the moment at least. I wasn't so stupid that I thought this was over, not as far as the giant was concerned. What was I supposed to do while it was licking its wounds or whatever it was doing? Open up that locked shed and see who was inside? What good would that do anyone? I couldn't possibly tell those men what was going on, even if one of them spoke some English. I'd only be someone they could describe to the police – or whoever would be looking for payback when they found their camp had been wrecked. Add to that, I sure as hell didn't want to catch whatever was making those prisoners so ill.

What if they ran off into the woods? I had no idea where we were, and I'd bet those men didn't know either. One night out in the cold and the rain and they could be dead by morning, long before the emergency services found them. The thought of leaving anyone locked up made me feel sick, but honestly, they were better off where they were until the police could get here.

Would the police get here first? I really hoped Fin and Hazel had already made that call. There was no guarantee that the pricks who'd set up this camp weren't already on their way back for the night with the other poor bastards they kept here. I really didn't want to meet them.

The pile of bricks shifted with a harsh, grating sound. The rubble collapsed in on itself, leaving that iron bar sticking out of the top. Something as black and viscous as oil oozed out from the bottom of the heap. It slid across the flagstones and disappeared, sinking down into the cracks in the floor.

That made up my mind. Wherever the giant had gone, the monster would be back. It would definitely be coming after me now. I didn't doubt that for a second, even if I had no idea what I was going to do when it did.

For the moment, I wanted the security of a car's metal bodyshell around me as soon as possible. I followed the path to the road and ran back to the oak tree as fast as I could. Fin and Hazel were standing by the Toyota. Relief made my legs so weak I nearly stumbled.

Fin wrapped her arms around me when I reached them. She hugged me fiercely tight, and just as quickly let me go. She had the car keys in hand.

'You stink of—' She shook her head. 'I hate to think what.'

'Let's get out of here.' I looked at Hazel. 'I drove the giant off, but fuck knows where it's gone. This isn't over by a long chalk.'

She nodded. 'We've rung the police and told them they need to get out here.'

'Did you give your real name?' That idea made me uneasy.

Hazel nodded, unconcerned. 'I'm willing to make a statement saying I was out here walking and saw those huts. I took a look and found it all very suspicious, so I thought I'd better report it.'

So these wise women had no problem telling lies, or at least, bending the truth to suit their purposes. I'd better remember that. 'The police will probably tell you there's been a fire. You had better not know anything about that.'

Hazel nodded, still not fussed. Either that, or she was a very good actress.

Fin opened the driver's door. 'Let's get out of here before the cops or anyone else turns up.'

'Hell, yes.' I crammed myself into the back seat.

I'd barely got the door closed before Fin pulled away like a rally driver. Hazel was in and out of the car like lightning to open and lower the barrier. Once the Toyota reached the main roads, we all breathed a lot easier. Fin stuck scrupulously to the speed limit, though we didn't see any police.

I remembered I'd been thinking how inconvenient it was that Fin lived more than an hour's drive away from everything we had to deal with. Now I was massively relieved. Heading away in a car and then travelling down the motorway should mean the giant lost my scent. At least, it should until I had to come back to Bockbourne. Then I would have to watch my back, and double-check every shadow, even at midday.

Chapter Fifteen

The sound of Fin's phone woke me up. As she answered it, I sat up in bed and watched her. I had a nasty hollow feeling in my stomach that had nothing to do with wanting breakfast. I'd only realised when we'd got back last night that Hazel must have used Fin's phone to call the coppers. The wise woman couldn't have had her own in a pocket if she had been able to shift from human to hare so easily. That meant the police had Fin's number now. I guessed that would give them everything else they wanted to know about her.

Were the cops calling her now? We hadn't agreed on a story to tell them if we needed one. We hadn't even told Blanche what had happened yesterday. When we'd got back, it was time for Fin to start mixing a Thai marinade for the salmon fillets waiting in the fridge, and I needed a shower and to do a load of laundry for the second day in a row. As soon as I was clean and dressed, I went to help Fin do the vegetables for a stir fry.

I'd expected Blanche would start asking questions about what we'd been up to when we sat down to eat. She didn't, and Fin didn't raise the subject. Well, if she wasn't going to do that, nor would I. Maybe she'd told her sister as much as she needed to know while I'd been in the shower and raiding their medicine cabinet. I'd found some antiseptic for the grazes on my palms and cream for my flash burns. Thankfully, this morning my face only felt like I'd spent a scorching day outside without sunscreen. I looked down at my hands and saw those were healing as fast as always, thanks to my mother's blood.

So who was Fin talking to? It didn't sound like the cops were asking awkward questions. I studied her face. Fin didn't look particularly bothered as she listened and said yes and no every so often.

She ended the call and looked at me. 'That was Hazel.'

'And?'

'And the hamadryads want to talk to us. Tonight, at Wayland's Smithy.'

'Us, all three of us, or us, you and me? And hamadryads plural?'

'Plural, and all three of us, she said.'

'When tonight?'

'Moonrise. That's, what, about eight o'clock?'

'Something like that. How did she get this message?'

Fin grinned. 'Apparently there was a hamadryad waiting in the garden when Hazel went out at first light. She wanted to make sure the white horse is still roaming the hills, and to see if there was any sign of the giant in the woods.'

'Did she see anything? Did the horse have anything to tell her?'

How did magical guardian spirits tied to the moon communicate with the wise women who raised them anyway?

'She said the horse didn't seem uneasy, so that's good. There wasn't any trace of the giant. I guess she knows what she's looking for.' Fin started doing something with her phone. 'Hang on. She asked me to send her yesterday's photos.'

That brought back my earlier worries. 'Have the police been in touch with her? Do they want to talk to you?'

'She didn't say.' Fin finished forwarding the pictures and looked at me. 'Are we getting up?'

'What time is it?' I realised I had no idea.

'Not quite half seven.'

I still had questions about that phone call. 'Are we going to meet Hazel at the Smithy, or does she want a lift? Is she staying somewhere in Bockbourne Magna?'

That's where she'd asked us to drop her off last night. Only she'd said she'd get out at the pub and have something to eat there, so that didn't tell us anything useful.

'She asked if we could pick her up from the White Hart car park.' Fin shrugged. 'If she wants us to know where she's staying, she'll tell us. We can always reach her by phone. The important thing is this hamadryad turning up. We need to find out what the hell happened yesterday. Why was the giant in those woods? What were they doing there?'

As she spoke, we both heard a door open and close out in the hall.

'Blanche is up.' Fin got out of bed and pulled on a dressing gown. Her feathers slid out of sight at the neck as she knotted the belt.

'What are we going to tell her about yesterday?'

Fin wrinkled her nose. 'I'm still thinking about that. We need to agree what we're going to tell Mum about all this for a start.'

I got out of bed and found my underpants. 'I need to talk to my dad. He'll want to know what's going on here.'

'Are you going to do that this morning?'

'That depends. How badly do we want to know whatever my mum can tell us about hamadryads?'

I saw Fin was as undecided as I was. Neither of us wanted to worry our parents. It wasn't as if there was anything much they could do.

'You could ring Eleanor,' she suggested. 'See if she's learned anything useful from the Blithehurst dryads. See if anyone's been able to contact Kalei or some other naiad.'

'Maybe.' I changed the subject. 'What are you going to do today, if this meeting isn't until this evening?'

'I'd better spend a few hours in the office with Blanche. We can't afford to lose any clients just at the moment.' Fin headed for the door. 'Tea? Toast?'

'Please.' I finished getting dressed and followed her.

Blanche was in the kitchen, making her own breakfast. She didn't look at us as she carefully tipped measured spoonfuls of coffee into a cafetière. 'So is one of you going to tell me what you got up to yesterday?'

I couldn't decide if that was a loaded question or not. I looked at Fin. I thought she had better be the one to answer. She looked a bit irritated, but she began with us meeting Hazel at the pub.

She told Blanche pretty much everything up to the point she'd turned into a swan to escape the giant. Fin made that sound a whole lot more straightforward than it had looked to me. 'When we got back to the car, Hazel rang the police. Then we waited for Dan.'

I picked up the story and did my best to keep things low-key. I didn't hide how bad I had felt about leaving those sick men locked in that shed, and I explained exactly why I had done that. To my relief, both Fin and Blanche nodded.

'I can't see that you had any other choice,' Blanche remarked. 'But this giant's still out there somewhere. Have you any idea where it's gone? How long before it gets over whatever damage you did to it?'

'I have no idea,' I admitted.

'Me neither, but hopefully the hamadryads can tell us.' Fin explained about tonight's meeting. 'So that means I can spend today in the office.'

Blanche looked at me. 'What are your plans?'

I couldn't read her expression at all. 'What do you need me to do?'

'Do the hoovering? Wash the cars? Make a supermarket run?' There was the faintest hint of a challenge in her voice as she poured hot water into the cafetière.

She'd have to work harder than that to get under my skin. My mum had masqueraded as a human woman to satisfy school teachers and other official people when I was a kid, but that pretence never extended to housework. My dad wasn't bothered. He'd lived on his own for decades and kept everything clean and tidy. As I grew up, he taught me to lend a hand. I'm well used to boring household jobs.

'Fine. I'll hoover when we've had breakfast, and then I'll do the cars. Have you got a list for the shops, or do you need to write one? Would you like me to cook tonight? Or I can treat us to a takeaway if there's one you'd recommend around here?'

I smiled at her. After a moment Blanche smiled back. 'There's a decent curry house that delivers.' She sounded a whole lot friendlier.

'We'd better eat early,' Fin pointed out, 'if we've got to be at Wayland's Smithy for eight tonight.'

'That suits me.' Particularly as I know sod all about vegetarian or fish-only cooking. If I was going to take a turn in Fin and Blanche's kitchen, I'd need to go online to find something tasty and foolproof.

The toaster pinged and some crumpets popped up. Blanche spread butter on them and nodded at the bread bin. 'There are more in there. Help yourself.'

We waited while she poured herself some black coffee and went out of the kitchen with her plate and mug. I expected her to sit down at the dining table, but she headed for her bedroom instead.

184

Fin watched her go, exasperated. 'If she puts tampons on that shopping list, buy regular Lil-Lets.' She shook her head and looked at me. 'So, toast or crumpets?'

'Toast, thanks.' I refilled the kettle and switched it on.

After breakfast, I hoovered the flat's living room, kitchen and hallway, as well as Fin's bedroom floor. I wasn't going into Blanche's room without a clear invitation. I found a dustpan and brush in the hall cupboard, so I did the bathroom floor as well, and cleaned the shower, the sink and the loo. I made sure to do a good job. Then I knocked on the office door and asked Fin where I'd find their car-washing stuff. She went to the window and pointed out their garage in the block on the far side of the parking spaces.

'It's this key.' She handed me the bunch dangling from the one she had selected.

I found the outside tap at the end of the garages and made a thorough job of washing the Toyota and Blanche's Honda. Both were carrying a fair bit of mud. I decided one undeniable advantage of small cars is they're quicker to clean than a Land Rover. On the other hand, no one with half a brain ever expects a Landy to look like it's just driven off a garage forecourt.

Since I had Fin's keys, I brought the hoover down the stairs and vacuumed the Toyota's interior. To my relief, there were only a couple of dirty smears on the back seat. A bit of elbow grease and some upholstery cleaner shifted those. I looked at the Honda and decided Blanche could ask me if she wanted her car cleaned inside. It wasn't as if she'd given me her keys.

Since the weather was fine, I stayed outside after I'd put everything away, and called my dad. That way I wouldn't disturb Fin or Blanche when they were working. He listened as I told him about driving off the giant. I made a point of explaining the monster wouldn't be able to find me, not after we'd driven away in a car. I really hoped I was right about that.

'But you're going back there, I take it?' He didn't sound happy about that.

'Not to that camp in those woods.' I explained where we would be meeting the hamadryads. I didn't say anything about the myths that said Wayland was Wade's son.

'I wonder what they'll want you to do for them next.' He sounded very dubious. 'Shall I see if your mum has any advice?'

'Please.' I guessed she was out in the nature reserve some-where, since she hadn't joined in this call.

'Okay, I'll ring you if she knows anything that might help. Be careful, Dan. Let me know how you get on.'

I could hear the concern in his voice, and I hated to think of him sitting there worrying. 'I will,' I promised.

When we'd said goodbye, I went to search the garage for anything that Fin and Blanche might own to help me keep my word to him. Unfortunately, since they didn't have a garden, there wasn't anything by way of long-handled and sharp-edged tools that could be used as weapons. On the other hand, there was a roll of the orange plastic netting that's a familiar sight on building sites. I moved it and found a stack of those metre-long iron posts with hooked ends that can be driven into the ground, so the netting can be hung on them to make a temporary barrier. Presumably there were times when Fin and Blanche needed to fence something off where they were working.

The netting could stay here, but I picked up three stakes. I would definitely ask Fin if we could put these in the back of the car.

My phone rang. I put the stakes down when I saw the call was from Eleanor. 'Hi, it's good to hear from you.'

She didn't waste any time. 'What's going on down there?'

She sounded really tired. My relief at her getting in touch with me evaporated as I told our story for the third time that day. Eleanor didn't ask any questions. She just listened.

'So we'll see what the hamadryads have to say tonight,' I concluded. 'If Asca or Frai has any suggestions on how to handle them, that would be really useful. How are things going there, anyway?'

'Fine, in the sense that we're not fighting off monsters. As far as the business goes?' She startled me with a laugh. 'We may have found a way to fight off the accountants. I'm still not certain, but something interesting has come up.'

'Okay.' I waited for her to tell me more.

She yawned instead. 'Sorry, I was up half the night. Right, I'll see if I can get any sense out of the dryads, and if they've spoken to any naiads yet. If they have anything remotely useful to tell you, I'll call or text.'

I heard the sound of the Blithehurst landline ringing. She must be in the manor house's office.

'Blast. Sorry, Dan, I've got to take that. Listen, good luck, and for heaven's sake, watch yourself. We need you back here in one piece.'

'Right.' I didn't know what else to say. That didn't matter. Eleanor had ended the call.

By now it was lunchtime. Fin and Blanche took a break and we had soup and sandwiches. Then they went back to work. I wondered how easy Fin was finding it to switch from yesterday's dramas to tackling whatever emails and reports she had to write to keep their business afloat.

Over lunch, Fin had given me their shopping list. That gave me something else to do as the day dragged on. The list didn't have anything intended to embarrass me. It did include bacon and beer, as well as a couple of specified bottles of wine.

I headed for the big supermarket that Fin said they used. It was as good as on the outskirts of Bristol. I did the shopping and realised I should have emptied everything out of the Toyota's boot before I set out. I had to stack the shopping bags on the back seat and in the footwell. My Land Rover would have been a lot more practical.

Before I headed back, I sat in the car park and ate a steak and onion pasty that I'd bought for myself. While I was doing that, I used the store Wi-Fi to go online and see if there were any local news stories about an illegal camp going up in flames beside the ruins of Sere Stock House.

I couldn't find anything about it at all. I wondered if that meant the police hadn't turned up, dismissing Hazel's call as a prank. Maybe they had arrived, but everyone had been gone, so there was nothing to tell the press. Or perhaps they'd made a whole load of arrests and that was just the beginning. The authorities could be keeping everything under wraps as part of some ongoing operation. They could be doing a whole load of things and I had no way of finding out.

I told myself it didn't matter. Nothing the cops might be doing would help me fight a giant. I needed to focus on that. Though as I finished my pasty, I wondered idly what some riot cop's gear might do against a monster like a giant or a wyrm. I knew rubber bullets were nowhere near as innocuous as they sounded, but I guessed they were still made of rubber or something like it. But weren't there batteries that were the same size as baton rounds? Those were metal and would pack a punch. Unless that was just an urban myth I'd heard from some bullshitting builder sometime? I couldn't be sure.

It didn't matter either way. I had as much chance of getting my hands on police tactical weaponry as I did of finding a magic, giant-killing sword in Fin and Blanche's garage.

Since the supermarket had a petrol station, I topped up the Toyota's fuel tank. I headed back to Cainescombe, parked the car and carried the shopping upstairs. Fin took a break from whatever she was doing to help me put everything away. She told me she still hadn't had any calls from the cops. I hoped that was good news. She showed me the curry house's website on my laptop and told me what to order for her and Blanche. I did that and added what I wanted, and noticed how much pricier things were in this part of the country for the second time that day.

I spent the rest of the afternoon at the dining table, looking online for something, anything that might give us some clue about fighting a giant. I'd found absolutely sod all by the time our food arrived. I closed down my laptop and put it on the sideboard while Fin laid the table and Blanche got cutlery, plates and glasses.

She hesitated in the kitchen doorway. 'Dan, would you like a beer, or...'

I realised she was on edge. She was worried about what might happen to Fin and me when we went out that evening. I could hardly blame her. I was apprehensive myself.

'Water's fine, thanks.' I had no more idea than Blanche about what we might be heading into, but I knew a clear head would be best.

Before I could decide whether or not saying that would make her feel better, my phone chimed in my pocket to tell me I had a text.

Fin looked up from opening takeaway containers. 'Who's that from?'

I could see she was tense as well. I checked my phone. 'My dad. My mum says we need to ask the yews what they know about giants.'

Fin looked blankly at me. 'How are we supposed to do that?'

'We'll need the hamadryads' help.' I hoped they would cooperate. I wondered what they'd want in return.

'They can do that?' Fin was surprised. 'That wouldn't have been my first thought, I must say. I wonder what they can tell us. I suppose they get moved from field to field, so they might notice things.' She still sounded dubious.

Now I was the one who was confused. Then I suddenly realised Fin had thought I'd said 'ewes'.

'I'm talking about yew trees, not sheep. Sorry.'

Fin went a bit red, then she laughed. 'Yes, that does make a lot more sense.'

Blanche put a jug of water on the table and sat down. She helped herself to some rice. 'What do you think they can tell you?'

'I have no idea, but with luck we'll find out. It's the best lead we've got so far.' I reached for my lamb rogan josh.

The food was as good as Blanche had promised. I was trying to decide if I should finish the Bombay potato or make sure I wasn't too full to run later on, in case I needed to, when my phone's text alert chimed again.

'It's from Eleanor.' I read the message out loud. 'No one's seen a naiad yet. Asca says ask the trees for help. Frai says start with the local yews.'

'That can't be a coincidence.' Fin started putting lids back on the leftovers.

'No.' I wished these texts had come earlier. I could have gone online to see what I could learn about yew trees in folklore.

As far as woodwork goes, I know the timber is heavy, hard and very tough. If you didn't know, you'd never guess it was from a conifer. That said, it's rewarding to work, as long as you've got the right tools and take a great deal of care. I'd got my hands on some offcuts from a furniture maker once. It had a nice straight grain and an unusual, natural lustre. None of which was any use to us here and now.

'You two had better make a move on. I'll do the washing-up.' Blanche gathered up our plates. She glanced from Fin to me and back again. 'If I have to ring Mum and tell her you two have got yourselves hurt, I'll bloody kill you. Just so we're clear.'

'As crystal.' I held Blanche's gaze for a moment. I hoped she could see that anything trying to get to Fin would have to go through me. 'Can I take a couple of those iron stakes you've got for holding up a netting fence out of the garage, just in case?'

'That's a good idea.' Blanche looked a little bit happier.

'We will be careful,' Fin assured her sister.

Since Blanche was busy in the kitchen, Fin and I went to get dressed for a night hike. We went down to the Toyota. Fin opened up the garage and I fetched the three netting stakes I'd picked out earlier.

'It won't exactly look friendly, turning up at a meeting with those,' she observed.

'I'm not suggesting we do that. But I'd rather have them in the car if we need them than all the way back here.'

'Fair enough.' Fin put the stakes behind the front seats and we headed off.

Driving eastwards along the motorway, we were heading away from the sunset. By the time we reached the White Hart car park and Hazel got into the car, we were losing the last of the twilight. As we parked on that dead end road running up to the Ridgeway, where Hazel had so nearly been caught by that dog, I could see the stars were coming out overhead, and the moon was rising.

Chapter Sixteen

'Did this hamadryad say why they wanted to meet here?' I asked Hazel as we began walking along the track. This high up and out in the moonlight, none of us needed a torch. Being a bit more than ordinarily human in our different ways meant we all had excellent night sight.

I looked around, wondering if I would catch a glimpse of one of the tree spirits, or maybe some other mysterious, shadowy figure. Who was Wayland? Did he really have some connection with Wade?

All I could see at the moment were massive concrete blocks lined up to stop arseholes in four-by-fours driving down the Ridgeway and ripping up the ancient route. The lumps looked horribly out of place, but I guessed they must be necessary. I was simply relieved to see there were no other vehicles around. The last thing we needed was finding we'd parked in a popular dogging spot.

When Hazel was satisfied we weren't being followed, she answered me. 'She said it's neutral ground. She said it would be safe ground as well. The giant can't possibly come here, though she didn't say why that might be.'

'Did she tell you that of her own accord, or did you have to ask?'

'She was the one doing all the talking.' Hazel glanced at me, curious. 'Why do you want to know?'

'I'm trying to get some idea of what we might be walking into. Was she friendly? Apologetic? Aggressive?'

Hazel shrugged. 'I only know she really wanted to get us here.'

I wondered what sort of bollocking the messenger would have got from the head hamadryad if we hadn't agreed to come. 'Was she the one we saw at Sere Stock? The one who told us the giant was coming?'

Hazel shook her head. 'I have no idea. I didn't get a good look at the one who warned us yesterday, not enough to know her again.'

'I'm not even sure if the one who warned us was the same one who helped me up that tree.' Fin was walking along between us with her hands in her pockets. She looked at Hazel. 'The horse that's guarding the Bockbournes, does it have anything to do with the one back there?' She jerked her hooded head back towards Uffington.

'What? Oh, no. The Bockbourne valley has its own horse, though no one has any idea where the chalk figure was cut. Fortunately, we don't need to know.' Hazel said that in a way that made it clear she wouldn't answer any questions about who or what was involved in however the guardians were raised.

We walked on in silence, passing a wide, open field that stretched away to our right. A long line of beech trees marked the boundary on the far side. They were cloaked in shadows, making a dark barrier against the moonlit sky.

It's not a long walk to reach the short path off the Ridgeway that leads to the Smithy itself. Of course, it had never been a forge or anything like that. There was an English Heritage information plaque to explain all about it. I'd already looked up the details online, so it didn't matter that there wasn't enough light to read it beneath the shadows cast by the trees.

Two Neolithic long barrows had been built here thousands of years ago, one after another. Nowadays, mature beeches surrounded a long, low ridge of leaf-covered turf that was marked out by what I supposed had to be called standing stones. Personally, I reckon standing stones should be a bit bigger than something I'd consider an irritating trip hazard anywhere else.

The megaliths that flanked the entrance to the later barrow were far more impressive. Four massive, irregular sarsen stones were embedded in a bank of earth that was kept in place by a drystone retaining wall. There was a gap in the centre with slabs of stone holding back the earth on either side. Another, smaller slab obstructed the entrance. Anyone wanting to go down the roofless passage would have to step over that. There wasn't far for them to go. Two stone pillars stood like door jambs with another slab laid across them like a lintel. There was only blackness beyond.

I knew from what I'd read online that there was a burial chamber ahead. It was flanked by two more, one on either side. I knew there was nowhere to go beyond those cramped spaces. Their walls were solidly built of stacked stones backed by the mound of earth. I knew that archaeologists had surveyed and explored every inch of this site.

Standing beneath the moon and the starlit night sky, I didn't believe that was all there was for a second. Not now the sun had set. That dark emptiness between those pale grey pillars looked like an entrance that could lead anywhere. Only an utter fool would step over that stone sill before the sun rose again.

The hamadryads would probably have something to say if any of us tried to do that. Four of them were standing up above us on the earth bank, to the left of the barrow entrance and a few paces behind the sarsen stones. There were more of them among the trees that surrounded the site. Maybe a dozen, in groups of three or four? I was just guessing. There could be twice that many hidden in the darkness. I wasn't going to try counting heads with the one in charge glaring down at me. I recognised her and two of the others on the barrow from our first encounter on the top of the hill in the beech hanger. That was something, at least.

However many there were here, seeing such a gathering of hamadryads was a real surprise. The most dryads I've ever seen in one place were the three at Blithehurst when I'd first arrived. I wasn't used to being outnumbered like this. I wasn't at all sure I liked it. I didn't know anywhere near enough about hamadryads. The ones I could see weren't holding anything that looked like weapons, but that didn't mean a lot. I knew what my mum could do when she was angry. I did know I was glad I hadn't told them my name. I had no idea how they might use that against me.

The one who'd told the others to let me pass in the woods took a pace forward. Her face was hard as she looked down at me. 'What have you got to say for yourself?'

So we were playing this game again. Trick the stupid human into making a mistake. 'About what?'

'You have not kept to your end of our bargain. You owe—'

'What bargain?'

That silenced her for a moment. I went on quickly before she could speak.

'I made no promises. I've made no decision. I said I would think about helping you, in return for—'

'You said you were going to ask the trees yourself.' The fourth hamadryad stepped forward. The one I hadn't met before now. She glared at me, accusing. 'You aren't going to help us at all!'

'So you were listening to us when we discussed what we might do?' I glanced at Fin and Hazel to make sure they realised I was talking about our conversation in the pub car park.

Satisfied we were all on the same page, I looked up at the angry hamadryad. 'You must have left too soon to hear everything we said. Yes, we wondered if my mother's kind might know how we could ask the trees what we need to do to subdue the giant. We weren't sure we were going to be able to help you with your problems, if that was your price for telling us. We decided we needed to know a whole lot more about these men making such a mess of your woods. We were wondering what might be the quickest and easiest way to get rid of them. We went to see if we should call the police and have them arrested. Why else do you think we were there when the giant arrived?'

None of the hamadryads on top of the mound answered me. The one who'd been in charge in the beech hanger shot the angry one a scorching glare. They both knew I was telling the truth, and so did every other hamadryad who'd just heard me. I wondered if the angry one had really left the pub car park early, or if she'd only told the others half the story. She was definitely looking defensive.

Let's see if another question would keep her off balance. 'What was the giant doing there anyway?'

'That's a long way for it to roam without a very good reason.' Hazel looked at both hamadryads. Her face was as hard and uncompromising as her voice.

The angry one tried to hit back. 'We knew we couldn't rely on you. We knew we must deal with this threat for ourselves.'

I shook my head. 'You knew no such thing. You would have known that we needed to know more to be able to help you if you had talked to us.'

I heard a sound like the rustling of wind in the leaves of the beech trees all around us. Except I knew that wasn't the breeze. Our audience in the shadows was stirring. I could tell some of them weren't happy. The question was, were they unhappy with me or cross with the angry hamadryad? The next question was, how were we going to move this conversation on from a repetitive and ultimately pointless blame game? To my relief, Hazel had that covered.

'Do you understand what we mean,' she said sternly, 'when we talk about calling the police to arrest trespassers?'

Up on top of the mound, the two hamadryads I recognised looked at their leader, uncertain. She stared down at Hazel, wooden-faced. Seriously. That's the only way to describe her expression. The angry hamadryad looked furious. But everyone, mortal and human, could see that neither of them was willing to answer the wise woman.

I followed up with another question. 'Do you understand what could have happened if the giant had killed and eaten one of those men who were trapped there, in the woods by that ruin?'

The angry hamadryad wasn't expecting that. She frowned, puzzled.

The one who'd been in charge in the beech hanger looked wary. 'What do you believe the consequences might have been?'

I had to admire the way she sounded as if she wanted me to confirm something she already knew. I chose my next words carefully.

'I know that a wyrm must have meat to bind it to the earth when it hatches. Then it can draw power from the soil and the rocks below as well as from the shadows. I believe the same may well be true for the giant, now it has stirred for whatever reason. I'm afraid it will become far stronger and more dangerous if it kills and eats a mortal.'

Every hamadryad could tell I was being honest about that. The hiss and whisper of arguing voices rushed around the shadows below the trees. There didn't seem to be much agreement. That couldn't be good.

Hazel spoke loudly, to make herself heard. 'Who here has ever faced a wyrm? Who has had to fight a wood wose? Who among you has ever had dealings with anything more dangerous than a boggart?' she demanded, scornful.

I could see the hamadryads up on the mound didn't like her tone at all. It was equally obvious that none of them could answer her without choking on an attempt to lie.

I concentrated on keeping my own face expressionless. Did Hazel know I'd fought a wood wose up in Derbyshire, or was that just the next scary monster she could think of after I'd mentioned wyrms? Had she ever encountered a wose herself, following up some report of wild men roaming some remote part of the country? There was still far too much that Fin and I didn't know about this wise woman.

She was right, though, I realised. These hamadryads had absolutely no clue what they were up against. I realised something else. I'm too used to dealing with dryads who think of centuries like humans think of decades. Who are as hard to kill as the oaks they love. Who have been dealing with mortals for so long that they're experts at walking among us unnoticed.

I wasn't the only one who'd got this wrong. Fin was used to dealing with hobs and sylphs. She'd known some of them since she was a kid. It's anyone's guess how long-lived they might be, but they like to live unseen in and around people's houses, entertained by their comings and goings. They understand mortals just fine.

Hamadryads, though – especially these hamadryads – they were different. Their lifespans were far closer to humans'. If wyrms and giants only stirred once in a millennium, it was hardly surprising they'd never encountered such dangers. Helpful advice handed down from previous generations would only go so far, and that clearly wasn't far enough. I remembered reading somewhere that oral history only goes back reliably as far as a grandparent's stories. Any tale that starts 'in my great-grandfather's day' is already moving into myth.

Add to that, inherited advice must be pretty scarce. These hamadryads were far more vulnerable than the dryads, naiads, hobs and sylphs Fin and I had dealt with. When their beech trees were cut down, they died. That must have happened a lot in the centuries when weaving wool and making furniture and countless other crafts had spread along these rivers and through the valleys overlooked by the downs. Before the industrial revolution brought iron and steel into widespread use, all engineering was done with wood. The hamadryads must have constantly faced the threat of men with axes.

I was starting to understand why they'd wanted this meeting on neutral ground, perhaps under the eye of some unseen power. They needed to protect themselves, not to reassure us. They hadn't asked for our names because they were afraid to surrender their own.

Now I reckoned I'd been wrong about why the Green Man had sent me to the Bockbournes. There was a good chance I wasn't here to protect the local humans from the giant, not directly at least. I had to save us all from some massive hamadryad fuck-up, because they didn't know what the hell they were doing.

'Well? Why was the giant in those woods anyway?' Hazel was still focused on what had happened yesterday. She looked around at the figures in the shadows as well as up at the four on the mound. 'You have no idea what you're dealing with, but you still thought it was a good idea to lure the giant into attacking those men. You didn't give us any time to resolve a problem that those mortals were causing you using the mortal means that we understand.'

No hamadryad was interested in answering her. Rising disagreement under the beech trees sounded like a storm thrashing through the leafy branches. The three allies on the mound were looking accusingly at the angry one. I guessed that sending the giant to smash the encampment had been her bright idea.

I'd been aware of Fin beside me watching and waiting since the start of this conversation. Now she saw the right moment to offer an olive branch, so to speak.

'What's done is done. We have to decide what to do now. We have to work together, to keep us all safe from this monster. There are debts on both sides here. Your sister helped me escape from the giant.' She looked at the spokeswoman, then gestured towards me. 'He risked his own life to drive off the giant, for the moment at least.'

Hazel wasn't ready for anyone to play peacemaker. 'Saving us all from the consequences of your folly.'

That wasn't helping. The angry hamadryad vanished. From the sudden rush of sound all around, so did a good few others who'd been under the trees. A still, tense silence fell. The three left facing us glanced at each other. Even the spokeswoman looked uncertain.

I spoke fast before she decided to disappear too. We still needed hamadryad help. 'The giant is injured, but I have no idea how fast it will recover. Let's not waste any more time. We have to find out how to get rid of it, not just hurt it. My mother says we should ask the yew trees.'

It might help to remind them I was some sort of distant relation. Out of the corner of my eye, I saw Hazel look at me in sudden surprise. Of course. We hadn't told her about those texts. Oh, well, I'd apologise later.

I kept my gaze fixed on the hamadryad. Now it was time for some honest truth. 'I have no idea how to do that, or where we might find any ancient trees around here.'

'Nor me,' Fin said.

'Nor do I,' Hazel admitted, grudging.

'Will you help us?' I asked. 'Please?'

We stood there for a long moment. Somewhere, far away, I heard the distant call of a hunting owl.

The spokeswoman smiled, mocking me. 'We will think about it.'

The hamadryads vanished, every last one of them. We stood alone in the moonlight.

'Bugger,' Hazel said with feeling.

Fin looked around. 'So what do we do now?'

'Wait for them to come to their senses.' Hazel seemed confident that would happen.

'I'm not so sure about that.' I wondered who might still be out there in the shadows under the trees, listening unseen. 'We need them more than they need us at the moment.'

Fin agreed with me. 'How much damage can the giant do to them?'

'We need to remember they're not used to dealing with people, even people like us.' I tried not to sound as if I was accusing Hazel of screwing up. That wasn't easy, because as far as I was concerned, she had done. From the sharp look she gave me, I think she realised that.

To my relief, Fin spoke up. 'Remember what you told us about the legend of Will Darrell? If you're right, the last time one of them had a human lover, that ended in at least one horrible murder. We don't even know if she went to his bed willingly, or if that was some bargain to try to keep her sisters safe. He was an utter bastard, after all. Maybe there were more deaths than just the baby. No wonder they kept their distance from ordinary people after that. We can hardly blame them for not understanding how things work in our world these days.'

Hazel looked as if she would like to argue about that, so I changed the subject. 'I wish I knew if the cops turned up to deal with that camp in the woods. I haven't found any news online.'

'Me neither.' Fin shook her head.

'If the cops have cleared everyone out of there, then at least the hamadryads would owe us for that much. They can settle that debt by helping us talk to the yew trees.' I really hoped there was one of them lurking close enough to hear me say that.

'I'll see what I can find out.' Hazel's expression told me that was as much of an apology as I was going to get.

'Thanks. Well, I don't see any reason to hang around here any longer tonight.' Fin looked from me to Hazel. 'Shall we drop you at the White Hart?'

Hazel didn't answer immediately. 'I'm actually staying in Bockbourne Parva,' she said eventually. 'Anywhere on the green will be fine.'

'Okay.' Fin was already walking back up the path to the Ridgeway.

None of us spoke as we walked along the track to the car. There wasn't really anything to say. Fin put the netting stakes in the boot so Hazel could sit in the back without them in her way. We got into the Toyota and headed off, still in silence. Fin found her way through the dark, twisty lanes to Bockbourne Parva and pulled up at the lower end of the village green.

'Thanks.' Hazel got out, but she didn't immediately close the car door. 'I'll let you know as soon as I find out what's happened at Sere Stock House.'

'Thanks.' Fin waited for a moment and then drove away.

I watched Hazel in the wing mirror. I saw she wasn't going to walk away until we were out of sight. 'She still doesn't want us to know where she's staying,' I observed.

'I don't particularly want her knowing where I live,' Fin retorted. 'These things cut both ways.'

'You don't trust her?' I might not agree with Hazel's methods, but I was pretty sure we were on the same side.

'I don't know her,' Fin said without heat. 'What she doesn't know, she can't let slip by accident.'

'Fair enough.' I waited for Fin to get across a nasty little junction. 'Where do you suppose she gets her information?'

'She seems pretty active online. That's how we found her, after all.'

'I wonder how the hamadryads know how to find her.'

Fin didn't think that was any surprise. 'Have you seen how many beech trees there are around the Bockbournes? They must know every inch of that valley.'

'I wonder if they know where the lost horse is.' I decided that wasn't relevant. 'So what are we going to do if the hamadryads won't help us?'

Fin sighed. 'Start by finding out whatever we can about yew trees. See if your mum has any suggestions?'

I had another idea. 'I wonder if Sineya would be willing to come here to help out. Brightwell's a lot closer. She might know how the hamadryads lured the giant to those woods for a start.'

'It can't hurt to ask.' Though Fin didn't sound too hopeful.

We soon reached the motorway and had a straight run back to Cainescombe.

Blanche was watching something on the telly. Whatever it was, she switched it off as soon as we opened the living room door. 'How did it go?'

I let Fin tell her sister what had happened. When she finished, Blanche looked at me.

'So there are two factions of hamadryads?'

I nodded. 'Good copse, bad copse.'

They both looked blankly at me.

'Copse? Trees, thicket, spinney?' I wished I'd kept my mouth shut. A joke's never as funny when you have to explain it.

Fin headed for the kitchen. 'I'm going to put the kettle on.'

Blanche looked at me. 'So what happens now?'

I managed not to swear despite my frustration. 'We wait for the hamadryads to decide if they're going to help us or not.'

Chapter Seventeen

We didn't get an early-morning call from Hazel. After Fin's alarm went off, we got up and had breakfast. Then we all started work. Fin and Blanche went into their office. I could hear them talking quietly as I sat at the dining table with my laptop. I closed the living room door and went online to learn whatever I could about yews.

I soon realised why the dryads were telling us to ask these particular trees. They might well know something that could help us. A single yew tree can thrive for a thousand years, but that might only be the start of its lifespan. Where an ancient tree's branches droop and touch the ground, they can take root. Those branches become trees in their own right and take on a whole new life. As they grow old and their branches sag, the cycle can repeat itself. There are places where a circle of yews are reckoned to go back to an original tree that flourished as long as nine thousand years ago. No wonder they've been associated with resurrection from the days of the druids onwards.

Associated with resurrection and death, and not just because yew was the wood of choice for the medieval longbows that were so good at slaughtering enemies in battle. I already knew that yews are often found in churchyards, and following different links, I discovered different theories about that. I also found there's a whole lot of arguments.

Some websites stated the trees were grown there to make sure of a good supply of bow staves for those medieval armies. Other people insisted the trees were simply inside churchyard walls in an era without fencing or hedges to stop grazing animals killing themselves by eating the foliage. A third group reckoned the yews had been there first. They were adamant that early Christians had built their churches on the sites of pagan sacred groves.

Whatever anyone said about why yew trees grew where they did, every website was keen to tell me how poisonous they are – wood, bark, needles and berries. I already knew that as well, thanks to my dad teaching me what was and wasn't safe to eat when I was out on my own in the woods. I didn't know that concoctions made from yew berries and a few other ingredients had been used for poisoning weapons and arrows in ancient Ireland. On the other hand, apparently, careful herbalists had made more positive uses of its berries for centuries.

Some websites were more sceptical about this than others. One listed these assorted alleged treatments alongside a supposed cure for 'water elf disease' which apparently involved yew berries, beer and singing. The website reckoned that just sounded like an excuse for a piss-up, and I couldn't really argue. Even so, I wondered what a water elf might be, and what diseases it might carry. Could those illnesses infect someone like me? I'd already encountered one vicious creature living in a lake. I might not have been so ready to fight that thing hand to hand if I'd known I might catch something nasty off it.

I told myself to ignore that distraction and carried on reading. I found myself going over more familiar ground. Whether or not those folk remedies might have been any good, I already knew that anti-cancer drugs had been developed from yew extracts. Now though, I wondered if these medicinal benefits were some modern-day manifestation of the tree's ancient reputation for warding off evil. Yew wood was also supposed to ward off damage from fire and lightning. Those ideas seemed to be widespread across a whole lot of mythologies and countries.

I wondered how far back those traditions went. As far back as some common knowledge or shared experience back in the days when giants had roamed the countryside? There had to be some chance, surely? One website reckoned the Celts had believed these trees linked them to their ancestors. They considered the yew was a bringer of dreams and played a role in otherworldly journeys. I was perfectly ready to believe that, given my own background. Especially after the things that had happened to me over the past couple of years.

Fine, but how were we supposed to find out what the yew trees knew? The closest I could find to an answer was a reference to resinous vapours coming off the trees in hot weather which shamans inhaled to be blessed with visions. That was no use to me. For a start, we weren't going to get tree-cracking hot weather in October. For a second thing, that sounded like a quick way to end up in A&E with a doctor ringing the local poisons unit. When I'd got those yew wood offcuts from the furniture maker, he'd warned me to avoid breathing in any sawdust while I worked. Like I say, every part of a yew tree is poisonous.

It would be best if the hamadryads decided to help us. We just had to wait for them to make up their minds. Meantime, I decided to see if I could find where the oldest yew trees near the Bockbourne valley might be. If the hamadryads wouldn't help, I was pretty sure Fin would agree to a trip to Brightwell, to try to enlist Sineya. She was the closest dryad I knew of, but I'd go and ask Mum if I had to, or even Asca and Frai. One way or another, I had to deal with this giant, and not just because the Green Man said so. Now I had seen the monster for myself, letting it rampage around the countryside eating people wasn't up for debate.

I started searching local tourist websites and North Wessex Downs walking guides. I didn't find anything useful. I started to think about knocking on the office door and asking if I should put the kettle on.

Then my mobile rang. It was Hazel. She didn't waste any time.

'Right. The police did indeed turn up at Sere Stock House after I called them the other day. When they took a crowbar to the lock on that shed, they found three men trapped in there. One was pretty much at death's door, so he's in intensive care. While the patients were hauled off to hospital, the police lay in wait for the swine running the operation. There were half a dozen, apparently, driving minibuses full of Eastern Europeans. When they turned up, all they were looking at was the damage, so they didn't notice they were being quietly surrounded by half the local police force. When they realised they were outnumbered, they gave up pretty easily.'

'Good to know.' I couldn't help asking, 'How do you know all this?'

Hazel answered readily enough. 'I've talked to a couple of journalists. You make some useful contacts when they know you're good for a quote about cheetahs being spotted on Salisbury Plain, or rumours of raccoons on Exmoor. Anyway, the reason there's nothing online is this seems to be part of a wider operation that the police are trying to unravel. Modern slavery. Recruiting people overseas for non-existent jobs, then forcing the men to work in hand car washes or on dodgy farms. Hanging on to their passports until they've paid back the costs of their travel and accommodation out of their alleged wages, which of course, they never do. Some of this lot were working in a cannabis operation set up in a vacant warehouse on an industrial park near Swindon. The police are very interested in that.'

'Have they spoken to you – the cops, I mean?' I still wondered if Fin would be getting a call. I still didn't like that idea.

'They have.' Hazel wasn't bothered. 'With organised crime involved, the official record says the police got an anonymous tip-off. No one but a very few top brass will ever know different. I said I was out there on my own and had borrowed a friend's phone to take with me, in case of emergencies as mine was playing up. I said Fin had absolutely nothing to do with this.'

'Right. Thanks.' We owed her for that. Then I wondered where this left us with the hamadryads.

Hazel answered before I had to ask. 'Apparently we did enough to convince our friends they owe us a favour. I've just had a hamadryad turn up in the garden again. They want to talk. How soon can you two get over here?'

'A couple of hours? Where shall we meet you?'

'Pick me up from the village green in Bockbourne Parva. Make sure Fin brings the largest-scale map that she can find.'

'Okay. I'll give you a call when we're about ten minutes out.'

'That'll be fine.' Hazel ended the call.

Now I had an excuse to go and knock on the office door.

'Come in.' Fin swivelled around on her chair.

I told her what Hazel had said.

'Right.' Fin turned back to her computer. 'Let me save this and we'll get going.'

'Okay.' I glanced at the back of Blanche's head. She had carried on typing while I was talking. She must have heard what I'd said, as well as Fin's answer, but she seemed to be ignoring us both. I backed out, shut the door and went to put the kettle on.

Fin soon came through to the kitchen. 'I know it's a bit early, but shall we have a quick sandwich? Who knows what we're going to end up doing for the rest of the day.'

'Fine by me.' I opened the fridge and looked at the packet of rashers. I reached for the cheese instead. If Blanche was already pissed off about something, I didn't want to make anything worse by filling the flat with the smell of frying bacon.

I put the cheese on the worktop and opened the cupboard where I knew I'd find the pickle. 'Is there some problem with Blanche – I mean, not *with* Blanche as such, but if she's bothered about something—'

'I know what you mean.' Fin began slicing bread as if the loaf had offended her. 'I don't know what's wrong with her. It's not as if we haven't got mixed up in things like this before.'

'Right.' Since I had no idea what to say next, I decided it was safest to say nothing at all. I got a knife out of the drawer and began buttering the uneven slices of bread. 'Decent boots and outdoor gear, do you reckon?'

'I think so,' Fin agreed.

We were soon out of the flat and back on the motorway. I would never have imagined I'd be getting so familiar with this stretch of the M4. When we took the turning with the signpost for Bockbourne Parva, I called Hazel to let her know we were close. She was waiting on the green, pretty much where we had dropped her off last night.

I resisted the temptation to look around at the scattered cottages. There was hardly going to be a sign to tell me that's where she was staying.

She got into the Toyota's back seat. 'Head for Feden Hanger.'

'Right.' Fin put the car into gear and drove on. 'Have you got any idea what the hamadryads want to talk about?'

'Not as such, but the one I saw this morning said they want to settle their debts.'

'Did she say anything about yew trees?' I persisted.

'Not as such. I asked, but I didn't get a straight answer.'

'At least you didn't get a no.' I hoped I was right about that.

'Fingers crossed,' Fin commented.

I wondered about telling Hazel I'd do the talking today, but decided against it. All the same, I'd be ready to interrupt her if she looked likely to get the hamadryads' backs up again.

Fin slowed for a bend and glanced at me. 'What did you find out about yew trees this morning?'

Telling both of them what I'd learned took us pretty much all the way to the steep hill crowned with that stand of beech trees. As we got close, I tried to emphasise what really mattered. 'There's a good chance the yew trees will hold the answers we want, but we won't have a chance of getting to them without the hamadryads' help.'

Hazel didn't say anything. Fin muttered under her breath, 'Where the hell am I going to park?'

Hazel leaned forward from the back, sticking her hand between the front seats as she pointed. 'Head down there and take the first left. Go on a bit further and there's a track that goes into the trees.'

There was, and no one else seemed to be using it at the moment. Fin drove a short distance off the road. She pulled up, and we got out of the car.

I looked around. 'What now?'

Fin pointed. 'Up there.'

She had seen a figure standing between the beeches further up the slope. As the hamadryad realised we had seen her, she nodded, turned and began walking up to the crest of the hill. We followed. At least it was an easier climb than last time.

In the daylight I could see how many hamadryads were waiting for us. There had to be more than twenty. Either I'd underestimated how many had been out there in the darkness at Wayland's Smithy, or a whole lot more had turned up to see what was going on today. There was no sign of the angry one, but I recognised the other three who had stood on the barrow's mound. I stopped what I hoped was a non-threatening distance from the spokeswoman.

'Thank you for agreeing to meet us,' I said politely. I hoped Hazel would take the hint that we had to play nice today.

The hamadryad kept us standing there for a long moment. Her face gave nothing away. If these spirits ever did start mixing with humans, she should take up poker. That would teach her a fair amount about human nature.

Then she smiled. As she gazed into my eyes, unblinking, I was relieved to discover my mother's blood meant I was immune to hamadryad charm. Well, nearly. I could certainly feel her allure. She was fucking beautiful. For an instant, I wondered what she looked like without those close-fitting clothes on. As soon as I realised what I was doing, I focused on the memory of Fin wearing nothing but her feathers. The moment passed.

'Very well.' Brisk, the hamadryad rubbed her hands together. 'Let us agree how things stand between us. Once we come to terms, we will see what the yew trees know that will help us all stay safe.'

I was listening carefully. She'd said 'will', not 'can'. Words matter in these conversations. So we were going to get what we wanted. We just had to agree the price. I tried not to look too relieved, in case that ended up being expensive. Then I realised the hamadryad was waiting for me to say something, Clearly, Hazel and Fin were okay with me taking the lead.

'The men who were making such a mess of your woods in the valley have gone.' That was my obvious opening bid.

The hamadryad nodded, but she looked regretful. 'Yet their filth remains.'

I looked at Hazel. 'Is anything being done to clean up the site?' She was the only one who could answer that.

'Not yet, and it'll be a while, if it happens at all.' Hazel sounded genuinely apologetic. 'Once the police have collected any useful evidence, the damage and everything else will be the owner's problem. At the moment, no one knows who that is. One of the journos I spoke to was trying to trace the last time the land changed hands through various shell companies and sovereign wealth funds. He's hoping to find a link with the slavery and drugs operation, but I think that's optimistic.'

It's hard to explain how someone's eyes can glaze over when they're a single colour without iris or pupil. That's what I was seeing on the hamadryad's face though, and honestly, I couldn't blame her. I understood what Hazel had said, but I had no idea what it meant.

Fin spoke up. 'I might be able to make a case that someone needs to take action and fast. There must be concerns about the groundwater there and possible contamination from raw sewage. I can't promise anything, but I will do my best.'

That didn't seem to make much more sense to the hamadryad, but at least she could see and hear Fin's sincerity. 'Thank you.'

'We cannot risk men going into those woods to clean up that mess if there's any danger they'll encounter the giant,' I said carefully. 'Such an encounter would be a disaster for us all.'

The hamadryad looked at her companions. Some of their faces were a lot easier to read. They might not necessarily like it, but these hamadryads had agreed that trying to solve their problems using the giant had been a mistake.

The leader looked back at me. 'We can keep the monster away from your father's kind, for a little while at least. Until we know what the ancient trees advise.'

I still wanted to know how they were influencing the giant, but this wasn't the time to ask. I nodded. 'Then I will do all I can, as fast as I can, to send the thing back to wherever it came from, as soon as I know how to do that.'

The hamadryad smiled. 'Then there is nothing to be gained by delay. Will you let me take you to the most ancient yew trees that our foremothers revered?' Now she looked at me with challenge in her eyes.

I didn't have any choice. I opened my mouth to agree, but Fin spoke first.

'You can take all three of us.'

'Or none,' Hazel added firmly.

I wished we'd discussed that beforehand. The head hamadryad was visibly startled, and a whisper of unease ran through the rest.

'Please.' I couldn't think what else to say.

'We all want to help you,' Fin added. 'I have my own debt to repay.'

'This giant is a threat to everyone here.' Hazel wouldn't accept any argument about that.

'Very well.' The spokeswoman ignored the stir behind her and held out both her hands. 'Let us go now.'

I walked forward. Then I realised Fin and Hazel weren't coming with me. I looked back and realised this was something else we should have discussed. I wasn't exactly used to being taken places by dryads, but I'd done it before. They hadn't realised this was going to happen.

I looked at them both. 'We can hardly give her a lift there in the car.'

That made some of the hamadryads laugh. They didn't sound particularly friendly.

Fin drew a deep breath and stepped forward. I took her left hand in my right and reached for the hamadryad's hand with my other. That left Hazel to complete the circle. She didn't move. For the first time since we'd met her, she looked uncertain, even nervous. I seriously thought she was going to back out. Then she squared her shoulders and joined us. I saw Fin give the older woman's hand a squeeze. I wondered who was reassuring—

Travelling by hamadryad turned out to be much the same as travelling by dryad. That's to say, there's nothing you can do about it. There's a faint sensation of movement, like feeling a breeze on your face, but you might as well be weightless. You're as helpless as a falling leaf, seeing and hearing nothing at all. Then your feet hit the ground and every sensation comes rushing back.

Fin's grip on my hand was as tight as a vice. I looked at her. It's hard for someone as fair-skinned as her to look even paler, but somehow she managed it. She gave me a shaky smile.

'That was... something.'

Hazel wasn't saying anything. Once, on a job in the Midlands, I'd been talked into going with a group to a theme park. We'd ridden a couple of roller coasters, which I hadn't particularly enjoyed. For one of the lads, though, once was enough. He'd looked as if he'd barely avoided throwing up, shitting himself or both. Hazel didn't look quite that bad, but she wasn't far off.

I looked away, to give her a moment to get herself together. That meant I met the hamadryad's gaze. She gestured at the trees surrounding us, but she didn't speak.

We were standing in an open space, maybe five metres across. We were surrounded by tall trees, and a lattice of yew branches met overhead to soften the daylight. The ground was springy underfoot thanks to a thick layer of brown fallen needles. Nothing else had seeded itself here. I didn't know if that was because of the yew trees' toxic properties or because other plants didn't dare intrude.

Each of the yew trees had its own distinctive character. I guessed their differences were some guide to their age. Some must be the youngest, most likely sprung from fallen berries. They had single trunks and were comparatively slender, standing upright with their neat green branches regularly spaced. Other, older trees looked as if four or five trunks had risen from a single root. These had grown twisted so close together it was impossible to tell them apart. These trees had far denser branches, thick with dark needles and dotted with bright red berries.

Other trees showed their greater age. The weight of their spreading branches had drawn those multiple trunks apart. Now they grew outwards at odd angles rather than straight up, while the bole of the tree thickened and swelled to support them. The year's new twigs and paler needles were at the very ends of their branches. That left the boughs bare as they spread out from the trunk, and their russet bark was deeply lined and grooved. Some branches rested on the younger, sturdier trees beside them.

I could see that a couple of trees must be even older. They had no central growth to speak of. Instead, a low tangle of thick, twisted timber that might have been trunks or branches sprawled outwards from their roots. Some boughs were about waist high to me, roughly horizontal. Others stretched across the ground, spiky with the dry ends of long-since snapped-off twigs. Here and there, they were half buried by the deep drifts of brown needles. Someone who didn't know better might have thought those trees were dead, unless they noticed the fringe of green at the furthest extent of their twiggy reach.

I could feel those most ancient yews' stubborn vitality from where I stood. I guessed that was thanks to my mother's blood. What I couldn't guess at was the age of any of these trees, even the youngest ones. I also couldn't tell how many yews were growing here. It was hard to see past the ones that surrounded us into the shadows of the wood beyond. Still, I could hear untroubled birdsong and catch glimpses of movement as the local wildlife went about its own business. There was power here, but I didn't feel any threat.

'Are you ready?' The hamadryad moved to stand by the closest tree. She laid a hand on a lower branch and stroked it like someone petting an animal.

I took a step and reached out towards the nearest yew's braided trunk. I looked at the hamadryad. When she nodded, I pressed my palm against the warm, flaking bark. I looked at Fin. Resolute, she took hold of a branch of the same tree. We all looked at Hazel. Her hand shook as she reached for a sturdy branch thrust out by one of the younger yews.

As soon as she did that, I couldn't see a thing. It was like having a bag dropped over my head. I could hear noises though. I recognised those grunts coming from deep in the gut, and the rasp of someone sucking down as much breath as they possibly could. There was heavy manual labour going on somewhere.

My sight came back. Now I could see what was happening. I also saw it wasn't happening here. Wherever these yew trees were growing, that ground was level. This long-ago work was happening on a dangerously steep grassy slope. I was looking at this scene as if I was standing there, but if I really had been present, I would have struggled to keep my balance.

The men and women doing the hard work of digging were mostly on their hands and knees. Barefoot, they wore rough tunics that might have been made from cloth or maybe animal skins. It was impossible to tell with so much chalk dust coating them. Their long hair and untidy beards were thick with the stuff, while sweat turned it to grey smears on their faces.

None of that slowed them down. They were digging like their lives depended on it, carving out a deep trench. A bit further along, other people had made more progress. Two men were lying with their chests flat on the turf as they reached down at full stretch to scoop up chalky rubble with rough wooden shovels. They dumped that onto what was definitely an animal hide. Two children dragged that away. I couldn't see where they went. My vision was limited to what I could see without turning my head. I couldn't even tell if Fin or Hazel was there with me.

There was nothing I could do about that, so I focused on learning everything I could. I couldn't see any sign of metal. These people were using tools made from deer antler, maybe bone, and from wood. There was no way I could tell what wood at this distance, and with the chalk dust coating everything. That didn't matter. Somehow I knew that at least some of those shovels and pick handles were made from yew. That made sense. Like I say, it's a dense, resilient wood.

My eyes were starting to make sense of the curves and circles these people were digging out of the hillside. My first thought had been that this must be a chalk horse. Now I saw that I was completely wrong. A face was being gouged out of the turf. It was crude but unmistakable, and definitely not my imagination seeing a pattern that wasn't there. It wasn't a human face though. In the same way that I knew these people were using yew tools, I knew they were creating an image of a giant. They were doing it in a hurry because they were terrified.

Maybe they were using yew for more reasons than its hardness. Two men crouched a short way up the hill. They might have had grey hair and beards, or that might just have been the chalk dust. What they did have was a yew wood stave as long as my arm, and they were expertly shaping it with what had to be flints in their hands. They paused for a moment and measured the stave's depth in the deep round pit they were squatting beside. I couldn't tell if they were satisfied with their progress or not. Regardless, they pulled the yew wood out again and carried on working it. As one of them shifted, I realised that the round pit was going to be one of the giant face's eyes.

I have no idea if me working that out was what ended the vision. I only know I found myself back in the yew grove. There was no sign of the hamadryad.

Chapter Eighteen

'She's left us here?' Hazel said, disbelieving. 'In the middle of bloody nowhere?'

Before Fin or I could say anything, she turned into a hare and dashed off into the woods.

I rubbed my eyes. 'I wish she'd warn me before doing that.'

Fin looked at the sky. 'I can try to get our bearings from up there, but I'm going to need space for a decent run up to get airborne.'

I tried to work out which was the best way to go to find open ground. Then I decided that could wait. 'Hang on a minute. What did the yew trees show you?'

'A dozen people cleaning up a chalk giant carved on a hillside. Three men were hammering a stake into one of its eyes.' Fin shivered, even though the afternoon wasn't particularly cold and she was wearing her weatherproof jacket.

'Cleaning it up? Like scouring an outline that was already there?'

'That's right.' Fin waited for me to explain.

I had another question first. 'What were they wearing? What sort of clothes?'

'Breeches, boots, long skirts. Regency costume drama stuff.' Fin raised her eyebrows. 'I take it you saw something else?'

'I saw it being made. Sometime in the Stone Age, I think.' I knew that covered a hell of a lot of ground, historically speaking, but I reckoned even an expert would have a hard time narrowing down a date from what I could tell them. Which I wouldn't be doing any time soon.

'I wonder what Hazel saw?' Fin looked around, but there was no sign of the hare.

'Unless it was something significantly different, I'm not sure that matters. You said they were driving a stake into the giant's eye? Did you get any sense that was yew wood?'

Fin nodded. 'Don't ask me— Shit!'

We both stepped back, startled, as a branch thudded onto the ground between us. We stared at each other. I looked up, in case anything else was about to land on our heads. I couldn't see anything that threatened to brain either of us. I couldn't even see where the fallen branch had come from.

A hare – the hare that had to be Hazel – darted back into the open space at the heart of the yew grove. I spoke quickly before she could shift back to human.

'Either warn me when you're about to change or do it behind me.'

The hare didn't give any sign that it understood me. It sat up on its hind legs to wash its face with its front paws, flipping down its long, black-tipped ears.

I looked at Fin, uncertain. She laughed. 'It's her.'

The hare bounded away. A moment later, Hazel stepped out from behind a yew tree.

'Did you find a road?' Fin asked. 'Anything to tell us where we are?'

Hazel shook her head. Her voice shook as well. 'It didn't matter which way I went, I ended up heading back here. Without turning around, I mean.'

'Oh.' Fin looked up at the sky.

'I wouldn't,' I said sharply. 'We don't know—'

'You have no need to find this place again.' The hamadryad was back. She gestured at the trees around us, and then at the fallen branch. 'The yews have given you that which you need.'

So that hadn't been an accident. I supposed I shouldn't be surprised.

The hamadryad nodded as if I had spoken. 'They agree that the giant must be sent back to slumber deep beneath the earth.'

'Where did you go?' Hazel demanded.

I hoped the hamadryad could see that this whole experience had unnerved her. That's why her voice was so harsh. As the spokeswoman smiled, I reckoned she understood, and seeing mortals knocked off balance was perfectly fine with her.

'I went to tell my sisters what the trees showed us. That was what we agreed among ourselves, if I was to bring you here.'

'That's reasonable, and thank you.' I spoke up before Hazel could say anything else and get the hamadryad's back up. We needed her help to get back. Even if the yew trees let us leave without her, we might be miles away from the beech hanger and the car.

The hamadryad's smile told me she knew that as well. She held out her hands. 'Shall we go?'

I glanced at the fallen yew branch. 'You're sure that's a gift we can take with us?'

'Of course.' The hamadryad seemed surprised I needed to ask.

'How—?' Fin looked at me, uncertain.

I realised what she meant. How would we join hands if I was holding that hefty length of wood? The thick end was as round as my bicep and the whole thing was longer than both my arms outstretched.

'All of you lay your hands on the yew grove's gift,' the hamadryad said impatiently.

223

I picked up the branch carefully. The broken end was ragged with vicious splinters. Most of this damage wasn't new, I realised. A storm or maybe another falling branch had almost snapped this one off some while ago. The tree was giving us something it could afford to lose. That suited me.

It was as heavy as I imagined, so I rested it across my elbows with my hands cupped in front of my chest. Fin walked around the waving twigs at the undamaged end to stand in front of me. She put one hand on the dark russet bark and laid the other on my right shoulder.

Hazel did the same on my left. She didn't say anything. She didn't have to. I could see she wanted to get out of here as fast as she possibly could.

The hamadryad obliged. I didn't feel her touch me, but we were back in the beech hanger in the blink of an eye. There was an expectant murmur. I saw the waiting hamadryads look at me with keen interest.

'So.' The spokeswoman was well satisfied about something. 'We will keep the giant from threatening mortals while you find the carving your ancestors made. Then you can bind the creature to the earth once again. That will settle all debts.'

Then she vanished. So did all the rest.

'Oh, for goodness' sake.' Hazel looked ready to say something a lot more forceful.

The branch was getting heavy. I lowered the end that didn't have twigs and needles to the ground. 'What did you see in the yew grove?'

'Medieval peasants clearing scrub to uncover a landscape figure.' She nodded at the branch I was holding. 'There was a priest waiting to stab it in the eye with a yew stave.'

A priest being involved surprised me, though I didn't doubt what she was saying. 'This makes a sort of sense, from something I was reading. Some legends say yew trees were planted in graveyards so their roots would grow through the eye holes of skulls and hold down the dead. One myth has two lovers' corpses being deliberately staked to make sure they stayed in separate graves and could never be reunited, even after death.'

Fin shuddered. 'Please don't tell me that zombies are real. I hate those movies.'

I wished I could reassure her. I realised I didn't actually know, one way or the other. That was an unnerving thought, after some of the things I'd seen in the past couple of years. I changed the subject.

'What have you got by way of saws and chisels?' I gestured at the branch. Turning that into a stake to get rid of a giant wasn't going to be an easy job, and my woodworking tools were back at Blithehurst.

She grimaced. 'The best I can offer is some screwdrivers, a hammer and a Stanley knife.'

That wasn't really a surprise. 'Okay.' I lifted the butt of the branch off the ground. 'Looks like I need to head home for a day or so.'

'How long are we talking about?' Hazel asked. 'When will you get back?'

I assessed the work I'd need to do on the branch. 'If we head off today? I can make a start on this first thing in the morning, and it'll be a pretty straightforward job. We should get back by tomorrow night. So we can be here as early as you like the day after tomorrow.'

While we were at Blithehurst, I could find out if the dry-ads had anything useful to tell us about any of this.

'Can you make a start on trying to find this carved giant in the meantime?' Fin asked Hazel.

'Wait a moment. Wait here.' Hazel walked off to the edge of the trees along the crest of the hill.

Fin and I looked at each other. I lowered the yew branch to the ground again. We both looked at Hazel. She was making a phone call.

'How can hamadryads take us places when we have things like phones and car keys on us?' Fin asked suddenly.

'No clue, sorry.' I supposed I could ask my mum, but there was every chance she wouldn't know, or be particularly curious.

Hazel was walking back towards us. We waited for her to speak.

'Right.' She didn't look particularly happy, but she had made up her mind about something. 'We're agreed that time is of the essence. I don't think we can afford to have you two spending hours on the motorway going back to wherever you're based, Dan. There are plenty of tools at the house where I'm staying, as well as a good collection of books. While you work on that branch, Fin and I can look for any local references or stories about this landscape figure, because finding that's going to be a job and a half.'

She paused, and now she did want a reply.

'Okay.' Fin nodded.

'That sounds like a plan,' I said cautiously.

'Okay then.' Hazel took another moment before she went on. 'The thing is, this isn't my house. I need your word that you won't look for anything that might tell you who lives there. She's tidying up and she'll be gone before we arrive, but still. It's not that we don't trust you, but—'

'You don't know us.' Fin interrupted her. 'And what we don't know, we can't let slip by accident. Believe me, we get it. I get it.'

You didn't need to be a dryad to see Fin was telling the truth. Hazel looked a whole lot happier.

'I'll promise whatever you want,' I assured her. 'I've spent my life keeping secrets anyway.'

Hazel nodded. 'Let's go then.'

We headed back to the Toyota. Hazel ended up sitting in the back with the thick, splintered stump of the yew branch on her lap. I had to tuck the twigs and needles on the other end up hard against the back window on the other side. I secured it with the seatbelt as best I could. If Fin had to brake suddenly because we met someone coming around a blind corner, I didn't want her getting that weight of wood in the back of her neck.

Thankfully, it wasn't a long drive back to Bockbourne Parva. Nothing happened on the way. Hazel gave Fin directions to a lane leading westwards off the top end of the green. When she told her to stop, we pulled up outside a white-painted cottage behind a privet hedge and a narrow strip of front garden. Small dormer windows poked through a thatched roof. From the car, it looked like the photo on the front of a box of tourist fudge. The sort of place where I'd have to be careful not to crack my head on low ceilings.

Fin and I got out, and I took the yew branch out of the back so that Hazel could get out and open the garden gate. Closer to, the cottage wasn't quite what it had first seemed. I saw the thatch was grey and ragged in places. The whole roof would need renewing sooner rather than later, and getting that done would cost an arm and a leg. Meantime, whoever lived here would be paying well over the odds for buildings and contents insurance on account of the additional fire risk. Picturesque can be very expensive.

However picturesque the village was, Bockbourne Parva wasn't an idyllic rural retreat where everyone left their doors unlocked. Fin and I waited while Hazel found her keys. I noticed a round wooden plaque on the wall by the front door. I'd been wrong when I'd assumed there'd be nothing to signpost who lived here. The carving on the plaque showed three hares, seen from the side and arranged in a circle, with their paws outermost. They were bounding along with their heads held high, and their long ears met in the centre of the plaque to make a triangle. I looked closer and saw there were only actually a total of three ears between them, but if you looked at any one hare, then each animal clearly had two.

That design was elegant and clever, and I suspected it held a deeper meaning for Hazel and her people than I was ever going to know. The plaque did tell me two things though. Whoever had carved it had been extremely skilled, and they had carved it a long time ago. The wood was well weathered despite the shelter from the thatched eaves jutting outwards overhead.

As I followed Hazel and Fin through the door, I hoped that unknown woodworker's tools had been looked after. If not, I'd have to head back to Blithehurst. Of course, if I'd had my Land Rover, I'd have had at least some tools in the back. Even if I needed something from my workshop, I could have driven myself back to Blithehurst and let Fin stay here to help Hazel search for any information on the lost carving of the giant. Then I realised I could do that anyway if I borrowed the Toyota. Why had we both assumed she would be coming with me?

Distracted by that thought, I nearly smacked my forehead on a low beam. I paid more attention to what was right in front of me. The front door opened into a wide kitchen with a quarry tiled floor and everything you'd expect to go with that, like a deep Belfast sink and a six-burner range cooker. There was plenty of space on the long worktops for a coffee maker, kettle and microwave, as well as a collection of cooking oils and vinegars and several stacks of well-used cookbooks. Windows with roller blinds front and back had herbs in pots on the sills and showed us the cottage was one room deep.

Hazel was unbolting a door straight ahead. That opened onto paving stones marking a path along a well-tended lawn. She took a key from a hook on the wall by the door and turned to offer it to me. 'The workshop's at the end of the garden.'

'Thanks.' I took the key from her and stopped myself looking at the thickly layered pinboard above the row of hooks. I'd promised I wouldn't look for hints about who lived here.

'I should have brought my tablet.' Fin put her backpack on the long pine table and got out her mobile. 'Never mind. May I use the Wi-Fi for my phone? I've got sod all data signal.'

The long table had eight pine chairs. There were three of one sort, four that were close but didn't quite match and one that wasn't like any of the others. The wall cupboards and units under the worktops were pine as well. Everything was clean and fairly tidy, but apart from that fancy range cooker, it was a long time since this place had had a makeover.

'You can use my laptop.' Hazel opened a door off to the right. 'I'll see if there's anything in any of – in any of the books in here.'

Just before I ducked my head to go out the back, I caught a glimpse of packed shelves from floor to ceiling through that door. Fin was heading in there to join Hazel, and I left them to it.

Outside, the long lawn sloped slightly uphill. It was flanked by a flowerbed on one side and a well-tended vegetable patch on the other. The cottage might be small, but the garden was big enough to have grown plenty of food to keep a family of farm labourers from going hungry in days gone by. Nowadays, high fences on either side kept the neighbours from looking in. At the far end of the lawn was what I'd call a shed rather than a workshop, and it had been there a good long time. Still, it was on a decent base of paving slabs laid level on a bed of gravel. It had been creosoted fairly recently, and the roof had been re-felted, probably at the same time.

The key turned smoothly in the lock. I propped the yew branch against the shed and opened the door.

Chapter Nineteen

The gardener who lived here kept her spades, forks and hoes neatly stored in the corner to the right of the shed door. Some were old enough to have been inherited from her parents or even grandparents. Others were newer and factory made. Everything was clean and well looked after. A set of metal shelves against the wall was equally well organised, with trowels and hand forks in empty seed trays, along with bottles and packets with names that meant nothing to me. Liz and Andy are in charge of the garden at Blithehurst, and I only get involved if they need a fence repaired or some hurdles making.

The woodworking tools were to the left of the door below the shed's single window in the side wall. A small, solid bench there had a vice positioned to get the best of the daylight. A stack of plastic cases must hold power tools, and a carrying tray with a central handle held chisels and planes that were the same mix of old and modern as the gardening stuff. Shelves on either side held more tools as well as jars of screws and nails and other fixings. A comprehensive collection of saws were hung on nails hammered into the walls. There was a pretty thick layer of dust over everything, and the spiders hadn't been disturbed any time recently.

I stepped inside and took a closer look. I saw a draw knife on a shelf and picked that up. It was an old tool with age-darkened wooden handles, but it had been oiled to ward off rust after the last time it had been used. I tested the edge of the blade with a cautious thumb. Not bad, though it could be better. I opened the workbench's single drawer and saw I'd guessed right. There was a whetstone there in a wooden case, as well as a battered squeezy tin of all-purpose oil.

I took my coat off and hung it on the hook on the back of the door. The dents in the whetstone's case matched the jaws of the vice, so I secured it in there. A few squirts of oil and strokes of the blade and I soon put a fresh edge on the draw knife. I found a rag in the drawer and used the cutting paste to polish the oil and dust off the old steel. Looking at the crosscut saws hanging on the wall, I found one that looked as if it had barely been used, which was good. Sharpening saws is an utter pain in the arse.

Seeing a wooden stool tucked under the work bench, I pulled that out and gave it a good look. There was no sign of woodworm or any other reason not to trust it, so I took that and the tools outside the shed. There was space out front on the paving slabs, and I wanted to work in the fresh air. I was remembering those warnings about the poisonous nature of yew trees. That wasn't necessarily a bad thing, if that made this stake effective against the giant. Add to that, working on a branch this big would be very awkward in that small shed for somebody my size.

Though feeling the fresh breeze brushing my face did give me another problem to think about. Back at Blithehurst, I have a wood-burning stove in the workshop where I get rid of wood shavings and the scraps that aren't worth saving because even my dad couldn't claim they might come in useful some day. I was going to end up with a fair amount of waste once I'd stripped the bark and twigs off this yew branch, even before I started to sharpen and shape it. I looked at the well-tended garden. Whoever lived here wouldn't thank me if I let the breeze scatter those bits and needles everywhere.

I went back inside the shed and hunkered down to look under the workbench. I'd heard something rustle when I pulled out the stool, and there was no sign of mice in there. I found a stack of battered plastic sacks that must have held compost or something like that folded up and shoved against the wall. One of those would do. I left it on the bench for the moment.

Going back outside, I rested the thick end of the branch on the stool and held it down as firmly as I could. Then I very carefully used the saw to cut off the split and splintered wood. That wasn't a quick job, and it wasn't easy. I had to put my weight into holding the branch steady, rather than into using the saw. It also reminded me just how hard yew wood is to work.

Still, I got it done without the saw sticking or slipping. That made the whole branch far safer and easier to handle. It also gave me a usefully heavy chunk of scrap wood to drop into the plastic sack when I fetched it. That would stop it blowing away. Now I could sit on the stool and rest the thick end of the branch on the ground as I trimmed off the twigs with the saw.

Once I'd done that, I put the branch down and gathered up the fallen twigs, shoving them in the plastic sack. While I did that, I considered how I was going to approach the next part of this job. A draw knife is a two-handed tool. I needed some way of holding the branch steady while I worked on it. There was the vice on the shed's workbench, but even if I cut the branch down a fair bit, I'd have sod all elbow room in there. Besides, I didn't want to make the stake any shorter than I absolutely had to. I wanted every possible inch of yew wood working against the giant.

A flash of movement in the corner of my eye made me look up. I saw a hare halfway down the lawn. I can't tell hares apart any more than I could tell one swan from another, but I was pretty sure that wasn't Hazel. I put down the sack and straightened up.

'Thank you for letting me use your tools.' Of course, if this was some random passing hare, it wouldn't understand a word I was saying, but the chances of that had to be slim.

The hare sat on the grass and studied me. I looked back at it – her? – for a moment, and then went back to sitting on the stool. If the hare wanted something from me, it would have to let me know. I wasn't willing to waste any time.

I sat looking at the yew branch from different angles. I still couldn't decide how to make a start. I was thinking I was going to have to ask Fin to come and be a spare pair of hands. I didn't think she would mind, but that would take her away from trying to find out where the giant's outline had been carved into some local hillside.

The hare lolloped past me and disappeared around the back of the shed. I didn't give it any more thought until I heard a frantic scrabbling noise. Shit. Maybe that hare was just some passing wildlife. It sounded as if it had got itself caught up in something. I put down the yew branch and went to see.

The hare was fine. It was standing up on its hind legs with its front paws resting on what looked like a wooden log box against the back wall of the shed, in the gap before the garden ended in a tall hedge. As I came around the corner, it – she – looked up at me and started scrabbling at the top of the box again. She stopped and looked at me with what had to be impatience. Definitely not passing wildlife. She hopped a few paces away to sit looking at me, her long ears pricked and expectant.

I lifted the log box lid. Whatever was in there was swathed in a bright blue plastic tarpaulin. I tugged at an edge and sent a collection of woodlice scurrying for cover. I pushed back another fold and saw what looked like a very odd collection of pieces of wood. Some of it was sawn and pressure-treated pine from a builders' merchant or a DIY store. Other lengths were oak, ash and holly from some local woodland, easily identified with the bark still on them.

I took hold of a piece of holly and pulled. Everything in the box moved as one piece. Unfolding the tarpaulin properly, I soon realised why. This wasn't some random collection of offcuts. I looked at the hare.

'It's a bodger's shave horse. Thank you. It's exactly what I need.'

The hare drummed on the ground with a long hind foot, then disappeared through the hedge. I lifted a selection of oak wedges, and then the shave horse itself, out of the box. Making a neat pile, I carried everything around to the front of the shed.

I'd never used a shave horse, though I'd seen them several times. Before I took the job as Blithehurst's resident woodworker, I'd spent Monday to Friday on building sites and about half my weekends from March to October paying for stalls at craft fairs, living history days and any other events where I could sell the carvings and wooden trinkets I made in my spare time. That earned me beer money when times were good, and rent when they weren't.

I'd got to know a few bodgers, which is to say, several highly skilled craftsmen who specialised in working with green, unseasoned wood using traditional methods and tools, as well as seeing the equipment they made for themselves, like a pole lathe and a shave horse.

I'd also got to know which of them really resented the way 'bodge job' was now taken to mean something half-arsed and inadequate. I learned to nod, agree and change the subject. They did have a point though. Working green wood is as skilled a trade as any other form of carpentry. It's not their fault the craft had almost died out and people forgot what the name had once meant.

I put the shave horse down on the paving slabs. First things first. I made sure it was up to my weight by leaning full on one hand halfway along the plank that made the seat.

There was no give in the pine that I could feel, or in the three ash legs that would hold it up, two under my backside and one at the other end. I sat cautiously astride the plank, which is of course why the thing's called a horse. Once I was satisfied nothing was going to break, I examined the clamp.

That looked sturdy enough, and like the horse itself, it had been made from a mix of sawn wood and foraged timber. Two-by-fours made the sides while the cross-pieces at the top and bottom of the rectangle were lengths of holly. I guessed that holly had also been used for the pegs about halfway down that went into sockets on either side of the plank. The clamp pivoted smoothly on those pegs when I tested it. When I pushed the bottom bar with my feet, the top bar would hold the yew branch firmly in place on the working surface. Good.

I got up and went to collect the oak wedges. These would go between the horse's back and the working surface, to raise that to different heights. The working surface was another length of pine plank not quite half the length of the seat. Holes had been drilled in it, and in the far end of the horse. The two lengths of wood were tied together with loops of orange binder twine and a couple of complicated knots which I wasn't going to touch. Once I found the wedge to raise the working surface to the angle I wanted, I fetched the draw knife and the yew branch. I rolled up my sweatshirt sleeves and set to work.

Laying the branch on the sloping work surface, I pushed the clamp's bottom bar with my feet, so the top bar held the yew wood in place. I had to shift my position a few times until I found the sweet spot for the length of my arms. Now I was settled, I soon got into the rhythm of pulling the draw knife blade towards me, to strip the bark from the branch. As I completed each section, I eased off the pressure on the clamp and rotated the branch to strip the next bit clean.

It felt good to be doing something with my hands again. I'd had enough of trying to think my way through the surprises and dangers of these past six days since the Green Man had startled me awake. I focused on the task and nothing else. The familiarity of working with wood eased tensions in my neck and shoulders that I hadn't even been aware of.

'Wow, you're really getting on with that.'

I looked down the garden to see Fin approaching with a mug of what I hoped was tea. I'd been so absorbed in what I was doing that I hadn't even heard the cottage door open. I also hadn't noticed how the light was fading.

I looked at the yew stake. She was right. After stripping and shaping the pointed end, I'd reversed the branch and was making good progress with the thick stump.

I grinned at her as I put down the draw knife and patted the shave horse's clamp. 'A hare showed me where to find this thing. It's just what I needed.'

'That was our hostess, I assume.' Fin looked around, but there was no sign of any animal. She came closer and offered me the tea.

'Thanks.' As I took a long swallow, Fin bent down and scooped up a handful of strips of bark. 'Careful with that,' I warned her. 'The sap brings some people out in a rash.'

'Oh, right.' She dropped the scraps into the plastic sack, but didn't pick up any more.

'How are you and Hazel getting on?'

Fin wrinkled her nose as she sat on the stool. 'Not great. There are only a couple of giants still visible on chalk hillsides anywhere in England. There's the one at Cerne Abbas, and another one near Wilmington in East Sussex. There are the same arguments about whether they're ancient or modern that we found about the chalk horses. One theory is they were both making fun of politicians in the English Civil War. Though apparently there used to be more giant figures, and some of those were definitely older. There were two fighting giants carved on Plymouth Hoe, until Charles the Second had a new fort built and they were lost.'

I thought about that while I finished drinking the tea. 'That's around the time people started telling the Jack the Giant Killer stories, isn't it? What would you have done if you knew giants were real, and they were stirring? When telling the truth would have got you locked up in a madhouse, or burned as a witch. Convincing everyone that carving a chalk figure is sticking two fingers up at the opposition sounds like a good cover story to me.'

'That's a fair point,' Fin said thoughtfully. 'But we still have no idea how carving a giant locks them down.'

'Do we have to know all the details?' I slapped the yew wood stake. 'If the trees reckon this will work, that's good enough for me. If we can ever find the right place to stick it.'

'Once we know where to look, we've found some stuff on techniques on pinpointing where there's something under the surface.' Fin looked happier. 'A couple of archaeologists went hunting for lost landscape figures back in the Sixties. They probed what they thought were likely locations with iron rods, and mapped the points where they found some give in the ground as opposed to hitting solid rock.'

'I can see how that could work.' I was glad we had the fencing stakes in the back of the car. 'Did they find anything?'

'That depends who you believe. Some people reckon they uncovered lost pagan gods carved into the landscape. Others say they found natural variations in the subsoil, then joined up the dots to show what they wanted to find.' Fin waved that away. 'None of that work was going on around here, so it's no help to us directly.'

'Has Hazel got any ideas where to look?' I wasn't hopeful.

Fin grinned. 'How about the pub? Those old news clippings and posters that are on the walls? Some of them are about archaeology and antiquarians. We can have dinner while we're there.'

'That sounds like a plan.' I wondered if she was going to ring Blanche to tell her not to expect us back to eat. Then I decided that was up to Fin. I looked at the shreds of yew bark scattered across the paving. 'I'll tidy up out here and then I'll be in. I've nearly finished this.'

'Really?' Fin was surprised.

I ran my hand down the yew wood. I was working with the grain, so there was no risk of splinters. The sap wasn't making my skin itch, and I guessed I had my mother's blood to thank for that. 'It's not as if it's going to be a display piece. No one's ever going to see it again, once we know where to stick it in the ground.'

I was oddly sorry about that. I would have liked to turn the branch into some sort of finished piece, sandpapered to silky smoothness and oiled to bring out the beauty of the wood.

Fin was still thinking about the task in front of us as she held out her hand to take the empty mug from me. 'Let's hope we find some clues at the pub.'

'Right.' As she headed back down the garden, I picked up the draw knife and got back to work.

Once I was satisfied I'd done enough, I cleaned up the scraps of wood and bark and shoved them into the plastic sack. I took that around to the back of the shed when I put the shave horse back in its box. Then I cleaned the draw knife with that rag I'd used earlier and put everything back in the shed as I'd found it. I locked the door and went down the garden, with the yew stake in one hand and my coat in the crook of my other elbow. Dusk was approaching now.

I went into the kitchen and propped the stake by the door. I drooped my coat on the closest chair. Fin was sitting at the far end of the long table, busy with a laptop. Hazel sat with her back to the front window, reading one of a stack of books. She looked up as I came in.

'I've put all the scrap wood in a sack behind the shed. It'll need to sit for a couple of months before it's composted or chipped to use for mulch.' There was every chance our gardening hostess already knew about the hazards of yew clippings, but it couldn't hurt to show I was being considerate. I held up the shed key. 'Does this have a particular hook?'

She shook her head. 'Any of them is fine.'

I hung the key up, ignoring the pin board since I was aware of Hazel watching me. I raised my hands. 'Where can I clean up?'

She nodded at the deep Belfast sink. 'In here is fine.'

I shoved the plug in, ran some water and found a no-nonsense chunk of dark green soap in a chipped floral saucer on the windowsill. I worked up a lather and washed my hands and forearms thoroughly.

Out of habit, I started silently singing inside my head, the way everyone had been told to do so often over this past six months. I'd opted for running through 'Twinkle Twinkle Little Star' a couple of times. I felt a bit stupid doing it, but not as much of a fool as I did wishing happy birthday to someone who wasn't even there, when it wasn't even their birthday.

Up above the world so high, like a diamond in the sky...

I remembered looking up at the starlit night. I wasn't thinking of our visit to Wayland's Smithy, but when Fin and I had been out on the downs, that very first evening we'd come here together. I stopped washing and rested my soapy arms on the edge of the sink as I twisted around to look at the table.

'Hazel. Is there any way the white horse could help us find where the giant was carved? The Bockbourne white horse, I mean.'

Hazel stared at me, wide-eyed. 'It's got to be worth a try.'

She wasn't saying that out of desperation. She clearly thought it was at least a possibility.

Fin looked at me with rising hope. I grinned at her.

Chapter Twenty

Hazel closed the book she'd been reading with a decisive slap. 'I need to talk to – to someone.'

Fin was already shutting down the laptop. She grabbed her jacket from the back of her chair and picked up her backpack. 'We'll wait outside in the car.'

I washed the soap off my arms as quickly as I could. Hazel was waiting at my side with a towel before I had finished.

'Thanks.' I dried off, grabbed my coat and the yew stake, and followed Fin out of the front door. She was already sitting in the Toyota.

I opened the front passenger door. 'Is there something you wanted to say to me that you don't want overheard?'

That's one advantage about cars. No invisible eavesdroppers can listen in on a conversation when you're sitting inside a steel box.

'What?' Fin looked at me, puzzled. Then she realised what I was asking. 'No, I just didn't want to stand out in the cold.'

I held up the yew stake. 'Can we see if there's room in the boot for this then?'

'Right.' Fin got out and went round to the back of the car.

I propped the stake against the door and put my coat on as she lifted the hatchback and looked inside. Now the sun was setting, the temperature was definitely starting to fall. I went to see what Fin was looking at. She handed me the three netting stakes.

I weighed one in my hand. 'These will come in useful if we need to try probing a likely site for the giant.'

Fin nodded. She was still looking thoughtfully into the cluttered car boot. I went to join her. There really wasn't much space. We certainly weren't going to get the yew stake in there at the moment.

'Do you really need all this stuff?'

She shot me a sideways look as she took the netting stakes back. 'You were going to say "crap", weren't you? And you're a fine one to talk. I've seen what you like to keep in the back of your Land Rover, just in case.'

I couldn't argue with that. I also wished we had my Landy here now.

'Fair comment, but do you think you could leave some of this back in Cainescombe? I don't just want to put the yew stake in there. We need to find a DIY store where I can buy a decent sledgehammer and maybe a few other things.'

'We can do all that first thing tomorrow morning.' Fin glanced at the cottage window. 'Assuming we get home to-night.'

'We can't go poking around on some hillside in the dark, even if the white horse can show us where to look.' I looked at the window as well.

Hazel had lowered the blind, so I couldn't see if there was anyone else in the kitchen. I'd bet there was, all the same. I reckoned the hare I'd seen in the garden had darted inside as soon as Hazel opened the back door. I went to put the yew stake on the back seat of the car. Hopefully no one would break a window to steal what looked like a fencepost. Fin closed the boot. We both got in the front. I went back to what we'd been talking about.

'If this giant's a creature of the shadows, I want to be hammering that stake into its eye at high noon, or as near as possible. We're going to need every advantage we can get.'

Fin shivered, and not because she was cold. 'Let's hope Hazel and her friends have some useful suggestions.'

I looked at the cottage again, where the lights in the kitchen outlined the dark fabric of the roller blind. 'I wonder if they've got any idea how the hamadryads reckon they can keep the giant away from us.'

I wanted to know what they were going to do so I could work out how many ways that could go wrong. I'd learned that the hard way. Hoping for the best and planning for the worst was the only way to go in these situations.

'Here she comes.' Fin turned the key in the ignition and switched on the headlights.

I looked at the cottage. The lights in the kitchen were still bright around the edge of the blind. As Hazel opened the gate, one of the dormer windows in the thatch lit up as a lamp was switched on in a bedroom.

Hazel got into the back seat. 'Right, let's go and get some dinner before we do anything else.'

'Anything such as what?' I didn't have room to turn and see her expression. She sounded keen though. That had to be a good sign.

'Some people need to get a few things together. You don't need to bother about the details. You just need to know you've had a very good idea.' Hazel tapped Fin on the shoulder. 'Let's get going. I rang and booked us a table.'

We went down to the White Hart. There weren't many cars in the car park, and the shadows were dark under the beech trees. I looked, but I couldn't see any sign of movement. I hoped that was a good thing.

This early in the week, only half the tables in the pub's dining room were occupied. That couldn't be good for their bottom line, since there were probably less than half the usual number of seats with everything well spaced out between plexiglass screens. No wonder the menu was still limited to one side of a sheet of A4 paper. The food was good though. I had a steak and chips, and a pint of stout from the same brewery as the Summer Lightning I'd had with lunch the other day. Fin and Hazel both had the mushroom risotto, which was the vegetarian option, and they shared a bottle of fizzy mineral water.

I guessed Hazel didn't eat meat either. I'd better remember not to call salad 'rabbit food' around her. That thought made me grin though.

'What's so funny?' Fin asked.

'What? Oh, nothing.' I concentrated on my steak, and wondered whose bright idea serving up pea shoots had been. They must be the most pointless things ever put on a plate.

We'd pretty much finished eating when Hazel's phone buzzed with a call. She'd put her mobile on the table by her plate, so it was clear she was expecting someone to get in touch. She answered it fast, before we could see who the caller was, though neither Fin or I was looking.

'Hi. Yes. Can you give me a minute?' She took her face mask out of her pocket, hooked it over her ears and headed out to the lobby by the toilets.

Fin watched her go, and then looked around the dining room. 'If there is anything useful in here, I've no idea how we're going to find it.'

I pushed my plate away. 'I know.'

It was obvious that a whole lot of local history was framed and hung on these walls, but the menu was headed with a firm request that customers stay at their own tables where they would be served, and wear a mask if they went to the loo. There was no way we would be allowed to wander around, however interested we said we were in local archaeology. We certainly couldn't explain what we were really looking for.

The waitress came over. She was the same woman who'd served us before. 'Was everything okay? Have you all finished?'

I looked over towards the lobby and saw Hazel beckoning to us through the glass-paned doors. That was my chance of a slice of cheesecake gone then.

I looked up at the waitress. 'Yes, thanks, we're done. And yes, my steak was very good.'

'The risotto was excellent.' Fin was finding her wallet in her backpack. She looked at me. 'I'll get this.'

'Fine by me.' I wondered what Fin and I were going to do about money if we were going to be spending a lot more time together. My last serious girlfriend had always insisted on settling debts down to the last penny. At times, that had been a real ball-ache. On the other hand, this wasn't going to be a good year financially for me or Fin. We were going to have to talk about it sometime.

Not now though. As soon as Fin paid the bill, we joined Hazel out in the lobby. She headed straight out to the car park. Fin looked at me. I shrugged. We followed. Fin unlocked the car with the button on the key fob, and we got in.

'Right.' Hazel leaned forward between the seats. 'Do you remember the field where you first saw the horse? Head back there.'

Fin started the engine and drove. We were soon heading back up the valley, passing through Bockbourne Parva and out to the lane that curved across the downs beyond. Fin parked the car in the field entrance where we had stopped that first time. The wind was more noticeable up here, and the night was cold and damp with the threat of rain. The sky wasn't nearly so clear, with clouds hiding the waning moon.

'Wait a minute,' I said as Hazel opened the rear passenger door. 'Will it cause any trouble – any offence – if I bring an iron rod with me? I don't want to piss anyone off, and I certainly don't want to get on the wrong side of the horse, but this is where Fin first saw that giant. I want something I can use as a weapon in case the bastard thing turns up. It knows I'm its enemy now.'

'We'll need something to test the ground,' Fin added, 'if the horse can show us where the giant was carved.'

Hazel considered that for a moment. 'If you really think you need it.'

She didn't sound particularly happy about the idea. That wasn't my problem.

'Thanks.' I got out and opened up the hatchback to take a netting stake from the boot. I glanced up and saw Fin was watching me. I raised my eyebrows and offered her the stake I was holding. She shook her head. That was fair enough, as long as she was ready to turn into a swan and fly out of any danger.

I closed the boot. 'Hazel—?'

'Give it a few minutes, then follow me.' She was standing behind me. A brief flash of golden light told me she'd shifted shapes. I saw a long-eared shadow squeeze under the wooden stile beside the metal gate and go running across the field. The sheep weren't remotely interested.

Fin pressed the fob to lock the car and dropped the keys in her backpack. She slid her arms around my waist, resting her cheek on my chest. I gave her a hug, careful not to hit her with the curled end of the fencing stake. She hugged me back. We stood like that for a little while, with the wind rustling the hedgerows. Then I felt Fin take a deep breath. As she stood up straight, I loosened my hold.

She turned for the stile. 'Let's make a move.'

I reached for the strap on her shoulder. 'Let me take this. Please.'

She paused for a moment, then nodded. 'Okay.'

She slipped the backpack off and quickly adjusted the straps to their maximum length. That meant I could actually wear it, keeping my hands free in case I needed to use the iron rod for anything.

By the time I got the backpack settled, Fin was over the stile. I followed her, and we walked across the field. The sheep were equally uninterested in us. We reached the next stile and climbed over it. More sheep ignored us.

But there weren't only sheep in this field. Dark shapes darted across the turf, criss-crossing the path ahead of us. They were hares, and there were three of them. A moment later and they raced around us in a circle, forcing us to stop. I remembered that carving of hares by the cottage door.

They moved so fast in the dim light it was hard to keep track of where they were. I wondered where the extra one had come from, and who she was in what other people would call real life. She couldn't have come far, even if she'd driven. We hadn't taken that long to eat our dinner. Was there a car tucked away by another field gate somewhere close?

Never mind that. Fin was pointing, intent on something far away in the distance. 'Look! Over there...'

I saw a pale glimmer in the darkness, well beyond the muted street lights of Bockbourne Magna, and beyond the beech wood there. Something was happening where the far side of this little valley swept up in a steep, grassy slope to join the great ridge of the downlands heading west.

I focused on the distant radiance. It was as pale as the moon, and as far as I was concerned, it might just as well have been that far away. If that's where the giant was to be found, we'd be driving there, not walking miles over danger-ously steep ground.

Then I blinked, and the light resolved itself into a grace-ful, shimmering shape. Not a man's shape, that much was clear. This was a horse. The design wasn't the same as at Uffington, but the resemblance was unmistakable. That hillside was where the Bockbourne valley's guardian had been carved aeons ago.

An unbroken line started as the tips of two pricked ears and swept down the horse's arched neck. The same line broadened along its backbone then narrowed again to flow away as a wind-blown tail. The equally fluid lines of the great beast's hind legs kicked out backwards. The front hooves reached forward beneath its questing head, as if it were speeding across the grass. For a carving as stationary as the chalk of these ancient hills, the horse was alive with movement.

I wondered who the last people to see it had been. Had they been standing where we were on this far side of the valley, to get the best possible view? I wondered how many centuries had passed since the graceful image was lost beneath the encroaching turf, until not even the locals remembered where it had been. Hazel had said that not even the hares had known where to find it.

Would they 'discover' it now? That would give Bockbourne, and whoever owned that land, their very own tourist attraction, when tourists could get out and about again. Or would the wise women reckon it was best left well alone? Either way, that was their business, not mine.

Then I realised the horse was actually moving. Those bright lines were rising into the air, leaving the grass beneath in darkness. The silver radiance swelled and shifted. From this distance it was impossible to see exactly what was happening, but everything became clear soon enough. High in the air above that distant hillside, the great horse we'd seen before was on the move again. It shone as bright as a full moon. Brighter than the actual moon above us, as that was waning and swathed in clouds.

The horse came galloping towards us. I don't mean that it headed down the hillside, to cross the valley bottom and make its way through Bockbourne Magna. It galloped through the air, straight across the valley, high above the village rooftops. We could hear it coming. Hoof beats echoed around us, battering the air. It sounded like an oncoming storm. I would have been running for cover if the wind in our faces hadn't stayed the same as it had been when we first arrived. Even so, I reached for Fin's hand and held on tight. She gripped my fingers just as hard. If we were swept away by some eerie force, we were determined to stay together.

As the horse and the noise grew closer, I realised I wasn't only hearing one set of hooves. There wasn't only one horse racing through the night sky, though I could only catch glimpses of the others. I saw white forelegs pawing the air, and an elegant head tossing a silver mane. A forceful shoulder came and went as the shadows shifted.

By now, the sound was so loud, it was hard to believe that no one else was hearing this. I expected to see lights coming on down in Bockbourne Magna. There should be doors opening as people came out of their houses to see what the hell was going on. Maybe there'd be car headlights as other people decided it didn't matter what was happening. The important thing would be getting away from the crashing plane or the landslide or the meteor storm or whatever this oncoming disaster might be.

The Bockbourne Horse and the half-hidden herd came galloping on towards us. The noise was deafening by now. My brain told me that the horses in the sky would pass over us by at least a hundred feet. My knees didn't care. I was crouching on the ground with my shoulders hunched and my chin pressed to my chest. I still had tight hold of Fin's hand as she huddled close beside me.

The bloody sheep didn't give a fuck. Half were casually tearing up mouthfuls of grass as if nothing was going on. The rest were standing around chewing with the concentration of someone trying to quit smoking with nicotine gum.

I saw that the three hares were cowering like me and Fin. They had their bellies pressed to the turf with their paws tucked up as tight as they could. Each one had its ears lying flat along its back, and their heads were so low it looked like none of them had a neck. That made me feel a bit better.

That stopped as soon as the lightning started. The Bockbourne Horse's hooves struck sparks from the sky up above us with an ear-splitting crack. Blinding white shafts speared the steep slope that fell away down the valley side ahead of us.

Fin flinched and turned her head away. I was as dazzled as she was by the searing light. My eyes watered as more lightning struck the ground. At least that got the sheep's attention. They went cantering away towards the uphill hedge, bleating in alarm.

I realised that with the sheep gone, I was the tallest thing on this exposed hillside. I might be crouching down, but I was holding an iron rod, for fuck's sake! I threw the netting stake away and tried to pull my hand free of Fin's. If I was struck, I didn't want the lightning to find its way to ground through her.

She clung on. I pulled harder, frantic. I tried to shout, to explain, but the horses were directly overhead. I couldn't make myself heard. The pounding was making my head spin. Lingering after-images of the lightning blurred my vision with yellow and purple smears. I've never had a migraine, but I wondered if I was about to find out what they're like.

Then it was over. The horses were gone. The only thing in the sky above us was a ragged cloud drifting across the misshapen moon. A couple of sheep were still complaining, but their bleats faded away. The night's stillness returned, as complete as if it had never been broken. The thumping in my head faded and I could see clearly again.

There was no chance of us thinking we'd imagined it all though. The unwavering wind was carrying the scent of scorched wood and burning leaves towards us. Smoke like shadows was rising from the steep slope where the lightning had struck. The darkness drifted away on the breeze. More smoke rose to replace it.

Fin let go of my hand and stood up. I looked around until I saw where the fencing stake had landed. I grabbed it and straightened up, showing her the iron rod. 'I was worried we'd both get hit if I was still holding this.'

'Oh, right.' She nodded, understanding. 'That was a hell of a thing, wasn't it?'

Before I could answer, the three hares sprang up. One raced away into the darkness to the east. Another headed westwards. The third disappeared somewhere behind us.

I glanced at Fin. 'Shall we see what we can see?'

I wanted to make sure no fires were about to take hold on that slope. I thought that was unlikely, given the time of year and the recent rain, but it never hurts to check. Truthfully though, that was a secondary consideration. The lightning had struck that hillside for a reason. I wanted to know exactly what the white horse was showing us. I guessed this was an answer to our question about the giant. That didn't mean it was necessarily the answer we needed.

We walked down to the hedge that ran along the edge of the field. After a bit of searching, we found a more open space between two untamed blackthorn saplings. Now we could see what lay beyond more clearly. The ground abruptly got a whole lot steeper here. It was no surprise that whoever owned this land had let the undergrowth and self-seeded young trees do whatever they wanted. There was no point in clearing pasture where sheep would just fall over and roll all the way down to the bottom of the hill.

I understood that, but it was still bloody inconvenient for me as I tried to see what was down there. I could make out pulsing streaks of sickly pale light cutting across the ground. The lingering lines were bright enough to be seen through the tangles of brambles and thorn bushes. At least, they were at the moment. As we watched, the radiance was already fading.

On the other hand, there was no sign of flames or anything smouldering. The last of the smoke had disappeared into the night. That was a relief. I didn't fancy the idea of fire-fighting just at the moment.

Fin looked up at the dark sky. 'We need to get a better idea of exactly what that's showing us.'

Before I could say anything, she took a few long strides and broke into a run. I turned away just in time to avoid being dazzled. As I looked back, the swan that she had become soared away on great white wings. She headed out into the darkness. I did my best to follow her path through the sky as she flew across the face of the hill.

Then I sensed rather than heard movement behind me. I spun around, gripping the netting stake and ready to use it as a weapon.

'Whoa!' Hazel took a hasty step back with her hands raised.

'I thought you were the giant.' I searched the night for any hint of a threat in the shadows. 'I can't imagine it hasn't felt whatever the white horse just did to reveal it.'

'That was pretty spectacular, wasn't it?' Hazel's voice betrayed her. Those lightning strikes had come as just as much of a surprise to the wise women.

'Come and take a look.' I moved aside so she could step up to the gap between the blackthorns.

Hazel's eyes shifted as she followed the pulses running along the streaks of light. They were the colour of a torch with a dying battery now. 'That has to be the chalk carving of the giant, surely?'

'Fin's gone up to take a look.' Turning around meant I'd lost track of her in the night sky though.

Hazel brushed a stray wisp of hair out of her eyes. 'So what are we going to do now?'

'We leave before the giant turns up. We come back to hammer that yew stake through its eye here as soon as we can in the morning.' I looked up. I wanted Fin back on the ground. Then we could get out of here.

Since there was still no sign of her, I looked at Hazel. 'We need some sort of cover story. The last thing we need tomorrow is someone ringing up whoever owns those sheep to tell him he's got trespassers or rustlers or something. If the giant turns up to try and stop us, I don't want it biting the head off some poor bastard farmer. That'll leave us with a hell of a mess to clean up.'

I've read enough whodunnits to know a dead body is hellish hard to get rid of.

Chapter Twenty–One

Blanche had gone to bed by the time we got back to Cain-escombe. Fin and I were up and out before she got up. That wasn't particularly early since we had to wait for the nearest DIY store to open. I wondered if Blanche was staying in her room to avoid talking to us. Unless she was avoiding the smell of bacon. If I was going to be putting in a long day working outside, I was going to start it with a full English breakfast. Fin had a mushroom omelette, and we both had plenty of toast.

I didn't know how to ask Fin if what we were doing was causing friction with her sister. I didn't want to find out that me simply being in their flat was the problem. So I didn't say anything. I just carried boxes of maps and the other stuff we got out of the Toyota up the stairs and put them in the office. Once we'd emptied the car's boot, Fin started filling it up again. She started with a roll of black-and-yellow plastic tape as well as all the netting stakes we could find.

'I think we'll need these.' She took a couple of billhooks out of a cheap chest of drawers that they were using for storage in the garage.

I guessed some of her site visits must involve hacking away vegetation to see what was going on with a drain or a culvert. I took one out of its leather case and tested the edge out of habit.

'We do keep them sharp,' Fin said, amused.

'So I see. Have you got any rope in here?' I was thinking how steep that hillside was as I had another look around the garage.

'Good idea.' Fin took two neat coils from a hook on the back wall.

'Work gloves?' Probing rough ground with the netting stakes wasn't going to be a task for bare hands.

'I've got mine, but none of ours will fit you.'

'Something else for the list then.'

We added the billhooks, the rope and Fin's gloves to the stuff in the boot. I locked the yew stake safely in there as well. It just fit, which was more luck than judgement, I have to admit.

There was a builders' merchant in the same retail park as the supermarket where I'd done the grocery shopping. Better yet, it was one that dealt with the trade as well as home improvers. It didn't take me long to find a decent six-kilo sledgehammer with a carbon steel head.

That wasn't too expensive either, unlike the fence post drivers, which were three times the price. Add to that, I can do a whole lot of things with a sledgehammer, so I didn't mind adding another one to my collection of tools. A fence post driver's only good for one job, and it wasn't as if I was going to be hammering a whole line of yew stakes into that hillside. I thought about doing that for a moment, and left that aisle of the store. Now I looked for the one with unbreakable plates, catering-sized tins of instant coffee and jumbo packs of teabags.

Fin had been waiting for me to choose the sledgehammer I wanted, and watching as I examined the post drivers and decided against buying any of them. She didn't ask what I was doing. That was obvious. Me picking up the biggest enamelled mug I could find did need explaining.

'Are you planning ahead for a tea break?' she asked with a smile.

I grinned back. 'That's not a bad idea, but no. I want something to protect the top of the stake, so the yew doesn't split when I hit it.'

'That'll fit?' She wasn't at all sure about that.

I hefted the sledgehammer in my other hand. 'It will once I hit it with this. It'll be wrecked by the time we're done, but it's a cheap, quick fix for the job.'

'Okay.'

We headed for the check-outs and I remembered to grab some work gloves on the way. Those were something else I'd always have a use for once we were done here. Thinking along those lines, I picked up a roll of gaffer tape as well. It never hurts to have that handy.

While we were waiting to pay, my mobile chimed with a text. Fin got one as well. We both checked our phones.

Fin looked up. 'Hazel's got us permission to survey the hillside. If anyone asks, we're looking for a chalk horse carving.'

I nodded. My text said the same. 'That's a good idea. Always keep as close to the truth as possible.'

We'd discussed the practicalities of today's job as we drove back to Bockbourne Parva to drop Hazel off at the cottage. She'd said that she'd make some calls and get back to us first thing. I reckoned whoever she was staying with would know who to contact in the village. As long as we got what we needed, I didn't care how that happened.

'Do you suppose they'll tell the farmer there's a chalk figure on his land?' Fin wondered quietly. 'I wonder if actually uncovering it and scouring it will help keep the giant bound. Or do we say we didn't find anything, to make sure the yew stake is left alone?'

I had no idea. I looked to see there was no one close enough to overhear us. Thankfully, the few other customers were keeping their distance.

'That's something we'll need to talk to Hazel about, and she'll need to ask her contacts. It would be good if we could get some clue from the dryads or the hamadryads about the best thing to do. I'm not holding my breath though. Either way, we need to agree what we're saying to the landowner. All of us, Hazel and her friends, we have to tell the same story.'

We paid for everything we'd picked up and added the stuff to the boot of the car. I looked over the Toyota's roof at the supermarket.

'Getting some water and a few other supplies wouldn't be a bad idea.'

Fin wrinkled her nose. 'As long as we're quick. Time is getting on.'

She had a point. We hit the meal-deal display close to the door and bought sandwiches, crisps and a few bottles of soft drinks. Then we headed for the motorway. There was the new-normal level of not much traffic, and while the sky was overcast, the road was dry. We made good time.

I texted Hazel to let her know we were nearly there when we were about ten minutes out from Bockbourne Parva. I was getting to know these lanes as well as I knew the motor-way.

There was no reply. I looked at Fin as we passed the 'Please drive carefully' sign on the edge of the village. 'I've got nothing back from Hazel yet. Are we going to go straight to the field?'

'Let's swing by the cottage.' She checked her mirrors before she made the turn.

There was no sign of anyone in the kitchen or the living room when we pulled up on the lane outside. There weren't any lights on, and I reckoned there would have to be on a gloomy day like this. Old houses have small windows, built when keeping heat in was more important than getting day-light or admiring the view.

Fin drummed her fingers on the steering wheel. 'I wonder if we should knock on the door.'

'You said we needed to get on. If there's anyone in there, they'll have seen or heard us by now. If they're busy with something else, they won't want to be disturbed.'

I still couldn't decide if I wanted to know how the wise women had summoned the Bockbourne Horse. I couldn't forget that another name for wise women was witches.

Fin switched on the engine and turned the car around in the narrow lane. It was more of a seven-point turn than three, but I couldn't have done any better.

'I hope everything's okay.' She straightened up the Toyota's wheels.

'It was when she texted us. That was only a couple of hours ago,' I pointed out.

'A lot can happen in a couple of *minutes*,' she retorted, 'especially for people like us.'

'That's fair,' I acknowledged, 'but we could waste half an hour waiting here, and they could have gone to the shops. Hazel could have forgotten her phone or left it on charge.'

'True.' But Fin's sigh told me she wasn't happy as we drove away.

I was more focused on the task ahead. When we parked in the field gateway, I was trying to work out the best way to carry everything over two stiles and across two fields.

'Can you take this, please?' I dropped the roll of plastic tape, the gaffer tape, the enamel mug, both billhooks and both pairs of gloves into the hessian shopping bag Fin had used for the food and drink. Luckily it was a big bag. I handed that to her, along with one of the ropes. She put her arm though the coil to sling the weight up on her shoulder.

I used the other rope to lash the netting stakes and the yew wood into a bundle. I could carry that balanced on one shoulder, if I was careful, and hold the sledgehammer in my other hand. I passed everything over the gate first, climbed over the stile and loaded up. We started walking.

'I suppose this explains why there's a footpath here,' Fin said suddenly. 'A right of way, I mean. This must be how people got to the carving, when they still remembered where it was, and when they used to clean it, even if they didn't know what they were doing that for.'

'It's not as if there's anywhere else to go.' I wondered how many hill walkers had come up here, only to find the route dead-ended at that ankle-breaking slope.

'We should have looked here first,' Fin remarked. 'It's where I saw the giant, after all.'

I shrugged. 'We didn't know what we were looking for back then, or why.' That seemed ages ago. It was hard to believe it had been only a week since the Green Man had sent me here.

We reached the second stile. Fin put her load down and climbed over. I passed everything across the hedge and she stacked it neatly. I climbed over and we loaded up. A few of the sheep watched what we were doing. Most of them didn't give a toss.

Something occurred to me when we were about halfway across the field. 'If this giant needs to eat meat to get a solid foothold in this time, why hasn't it been snacking on these woolly idiots?'

Fin was a few paces ahead. She glanced back over her shoulder. 'All the stories say they're man-eaters, don't they? Maybe it has to be something…' She searched for the right word. 'Sentient? Self-aware? With a soul, or a spirit, or whatever you want to call it?'

'Could be.' There was still so much we didn't know. Too much, and we had no way of finding out. I swallowed my frustration. We had to work with what we'd got, and that was that. 'Promise me you'll get out of here at once if the bastard thing turns up?'

Fin stopped walking. I spoke before she could argue.

'You can go for help, as quick and as straight as the crow or anything else can fly. Tell the hamadryads. Tell Hazel. Tell her to get her friends involved.' I waved the sledgehammer and shrugged the opposite shoulder where I was carrying the netting stakes. 'These should help me hold it off until you get back.'

'I suppose so,' Fin said reluctantly.

That was good enough. We walked on to reach the untidy hedge where the pasture gave way to the scrub-covered slope. I put everything down. That was a relief. A six-kilo sledgehammer gets heavy after a while, never mind a dozen or more metre-long iron rods. The yew wood wasn't exactly light either. We were both wearing our weatherproof coats as well as the boots and clothes we'd worn yesterday, thinking the hamadryads would be taking us on a woodland hike. When we'd got out of the car, we were comfortably dressed for the autumn weather. Now I had worked up quite a sweat. I unzipped my coat.

Fin put her loaded bag and the coiled rope down next to the bundle of stakes. 'So where's the best place to get over, do you reckon? I can't see a stile.'

This was the first time we'd seen the edge of this field in the daylight. A three-strand wire fence ran along the boundary, threaded through old angle-iron uprights. That must be there to stop the sheep achieving their life's ambition of dying in the most inconvenient way possible. At the moment, it was bloody inconvenient for us.

'How good a look did you get at the giant last night?' I asked Fin. 'From up above.'

She was confused by the question. 'I told you. It's an outline with outstretched arms, like the Cerne giant, and the Wilmington one. It doesn't seem to be holding anything though. There are circles for eyes and a line for a mouth, like at Cerne, but no eyebrows or any detail on the body. No giant cock that I could see.'

I realised I wasn't clear. 'Sorry, what I mean is, can you say where its head is, roughly? That's as much as we need to find if we're going to skewer its eye. We might as well get over this fence as close to that as possible, if we can.'

'Oh, right.' Fin looked around to get her bearings. 'It's a bit further along, I think.'

We picked everything up and walked eastwards. Fin kept stopping to assess our position. Everything I was carrying felt heavier and heavier. I kept my mouth shut. Bitching about things wouldn't help anyone.

Fin stopped again. 'I think if we cross here—' She broke off. 'What was that?'

I wasn't sure what she'd heard. The wind wasn't as strong as last night, but there was the rustle of a breeze in the thorn trees and through the undergrowth. There was birdsong, and the intermittent flutter of little wings.

Then I heard something panting. A dog? If that's what it was, it was a bloody big one. Maybe it was more than a dog, I thought uneasily. We reckoned Will Darrell had been hounded to his death by black shucks.

Then I heard another sound. A very human, very male sound. Someone was having a very good time on the other side of the red-berried hawthorn thicket flourishing just over the fence. A female voice murmured wordless encouragement.

Fin looked at me with astonishment. I stared at her, equally taken aback.

Seriously? We were going to stumble over fucking ramblers? Or should I say, ramblers fucking? At this time of year? Don't get me wrong. I've enjoyed outdoor sex with keen girlfriends, when we both found ourselves in the mood, in a secluded spot on a nice sunny day, on soft dry grass. On a bed of leaf mould and brambles, on a forty-five-degree slope, on a chilly grey day like this? Seriously?

'What are we going to do?' Fin was trying not to giggle.

'We've got permission to start an archaeological survey.' I spoke deliberately loudly. 'Whoever that is will just have to go on their way.'

We waited for some response. The sounds of shagging went on without a pause for breath. We were going to have to get a lot closer to interrupt whoever was on the other side of those hawthorns.

What were we going to do if embarrassment at being caught didn't have them pulling up their pants and sodding off? Outdoor sex isn't against the law, as long as you're somewhere you're unlikely to be seen. I know, I've checked. People get into trouble for shagging in lay-bys and car parks, but this hillside had to qualify as away from public view. We were in the middle of bloody nowhere.

Well, we had to do something. We'd start with telling them we had permission to be here and they had to leave. I'd tell them, not Fin. I do my best not to intimidate people by accident, but I can look pretty unfriendly when I put my mind to it. All the same, I put everything I was carrying down first. I didn't want whoever this was getting their own back by telling the coppers I'd threatened them with a sledgehammer.

I assessed the best way to get past the fence. It was an awkward height, and the ground on the far side was a good bit lower, and slippery with long grass and dead leaves. I decided against trying to force the top strand of wire down to swing a leg over it and risk knackering myself if I lost my balance.

I pulled the top and middle strands apart and bent down, twisting to step through. It wasn't easy, but it was definitely safer. Once I was sure of my footing, I held the wires apart so Fin could get through as well. We went in search of the hardy shaggers. They were just on the other side of the hawthorn thicket, where tussocks of grass flourished on a stretch of flat ground.

A blonde woman lay on her back, eyes closed as she moaned in ecstasy. She had her coat and shirt wide open. Her arms were outspread and her back was arched. I could see one of her pale breasts exposed, but a man's head hid the other as he sucked on her tit. I guessed her trousers or whatever were down around her ankles. His certainly were, but his flapping coat hid his bare arse as he pumped away. That was a relief.

'Excuse me!' Fin's voice was high and tight with embarrassment, and she was blushing scarlet.

The woman opened her eyes. For an instant her gaze flashed steely grey. She was a hamadryad.

Fin and I stood there, startled.

The hamadryad shed her illusion of a human woman and rolled the poor bastard she'd lured here onto his back. Don't ask me how she did that in one swift movement. He was a good three inches taller and must have outweighed her by thirty pounds.

She didn't do that to get away. Straddling him, naked and golden-skinned, she clamped her hands on his throat. He bucked under her hold, but his flailing hands were groping for her tits, not her wrists. He wasn't trying to break her grip. He was still trying to fuck her. His eyes were glazed and his face was slack, like someone stoned out of his mind.

He might as well have been drugged. I'm immune to any dryad's charms, but a naiad had once proved she could send the blood rushing from my brain to my cock any time she liked. A fully human man wouldn't have a chance of resisting. You couldn't even call it seduction.

Realising that took me a couple of seconds. That was long enough for the poor bastard's face to darken with blood. His unseeing eyes bulged, and he looked like a hooked fish gasping as he tried to speak. The hamadryad wasn't interested. He could forget safe words or begging for mercy. She was going to kill him unless we stopped her.

Fin vanished back up the slope. I got behind the hamadryad and planted my feet on either side of her victim's feet. He was starting to struggle now, as survival instinct won over lust. His trainers knocked my boots, but there wasn't a lot he could do with his feet tangled in his jeans and boxers.

I grabbed the hamadryad's shoulders and pulled. I couldn't shift her. She twisted her body and my hands slipped loose. She ignored me, intent on killing her prey. I couldn't see his face past her golden head, but I could feel his kicking feet getting weaker.

I grabbed her again, digging in my fingers as hard as I could. My work's given me a hell of a grip. Anyone who's tried that macho knuckle-crushing handshake game has always regretted it. That didn't help a bit. The hamadryad shook me off, like a deer twitching to get rid of a fly.

The only good thing was that she momentarily slackened her hold. I heard a hoarse rasp as her victim sucked in a deep, desperate breath. That was better than nothing, so I tried again, and again. Each time, she shook me off. I hoped I was stopping her killing him, but I needed to do better than this.

A memory surfaced. I recalled a wet afternoon in a Portakabin when a day's work on a site was held up by torrential rain. I've come across plenty of blokes who talk bullshit about martial arts. They mostly do that downing a pint and don't look as if they could fight off someone armed with a kebab. Every so often though, you come across someone different.

One lean electrician there was well into his sixties. He wasn't tall or heavily muscled, but he put a brickie who tried the knuckle-crushing handshake on his knees with some sort of twist of his wrist. That wet afternoon, he'd talked about various techniques, and explained what he called a naked strangle. I tried to remember what he'd done when the roofers had volunteered their apprentice to be his crash-test dummy.

I hooked my right arm around the hamadryad's neck, getting my elbow under her chin. I rested my left forearm along the back of her neck. That meant I could grip my own right shoulder with my left hand, while I hooked my right-hand fingers into the crook of my left elbow.

The electrician had barely moved once he'd done that, and we'd all seen the apprentice panic as he felt the blood to his brain cut off. The electrician released him at once, and bought the boy a pie and a pint that night. He told everyone else it was so dangerous that he would have words with anyone he saw experimenting. No one decided to risk it and get on his bad side.

I didn't let go of the hamadryad. I had no idea if I could cut off the flow of ichor to her brain, but I did know she couldn't get her head free of my hold. I bent my knees as low as I could go and straightened up again. However supernaturally strong she might be, she couldn't make herself any heavier. That said, she was a hell of a lot heavier than I expected.

Even so, I lifted her up and off her victim. Taken by surprise, she let go of his neck. He began coughing and spluttering. A moment later, he yelped in pain as she kicked him, trying to find her footing.

When she got a foot to the ground, the weight I was holding eased. A moment later, I yelped as well. I couldn't see what she'd done, but something stabbed me in my forearm.

JULIET E. MCKENNA

I couldn't help it. I loosened my grip just a fraction. That was enough. She got both feet solidly planted and twisted free of my grip. I grabbed for her long blonde hair. I got hold of a good handful and wrapped it around my fingers. At least that stopped her dropping to her knees to strangle her victim again.

'Dan!'

Fin was back, with a netting post in both hands held like a baseball bat. The hamadryad tried to back away, but I was right behind her. Fin belted her across the midriff with the iron bar. There was a sound like a hammer hitting wood. The hamadryad screamed, doubling up so hard and so fast that she tore her hair out of my hand. Well, most of it. She left a fair amount of bright blonde behind as she vanished. That wasn't her only injury. The iron rod glistened, wet with ichor. That's what tree spirits have flowing through their veins instead of blood.

As for me, I was bleeding badly. 'Fuck!'

Now I could see what she'd done to my forearm. I looked like I'd been clawed by the Beast of Bodmin or some other big cat. Four parallel gashes ripped right through my coat and sweatshirt, as well as deep into the skin under that.

'Shit.' I held my right arm up in front of my face and clapped my left hand over the wounds. That hurt, but I didn't care. I backed off, careful not to trip over the unconscious man's feet. I did my best to look at him as I moved. That wasn't easy as I was still trying to hold my injured forearm up above shoulder level to slow the blood flow. That's what they tell you to do in site safety videos. Fuck, that hurt.

'Can you see any blood?' I asked Fin. 'Is there any of my blood on him? Anywhere at all?'

A few years back, when I'd been a suspect in that vicious murder, the police had lost interest once my DNA sample cleared me. In theory, that sample should have been destroyed. I wasn't relying on that. Accidents happen and things get overlooked, especially if a copper decides you might not have done it this time but he's convinced you're a wrong'un who'll do something, given half a chance. I didn't want my blood turning up on this poor bastard and giving some forensics tech an exciting result that would have the cops asking awkward questions at Blithehurst.

Fin was still holding the netting stake, ready to use it as a weapon again. She was looking in all directions, alert for any sign of movement. Deciding there was no immediate threat, she looked down at the hamadryad's victim.

'I don't think there's any blood on him,' she said with a grimace. 'Is he dead?'

Now I was well clear of the poor bastard, I took a better look. To my relief, I reckoned Fin was right. He was lying flat on his back, essentially naked from the ankles up. I couldn't see any red splashes on his pasty-white thighs, belly or chest.

What I could see was the faint rise and fall of his hairy chest, as well as vicious bruises already turning purple on his neck. I realised I'd been wrong earlier. There was something more inconvenient than a dead body to deal with. What the hell were we going to do with the unconscious victim of a savage assault in the middle of nowhere?

Chapter Twenty-Two

'What the hell was she doing?' Fin looked at me.

'Leaving a gift for the giant. Fresh meat to make it stronger.' I had a horrible feeling I had given the hostile hamadryads that idea. 'Some of them must still think the sodding thing is the answer to their problems.'

'I suppose that explains how he got here. We didn't see another car anywhere.' Fin looked around. 'I'll fly over to the beech hanger and get one of the hamadryads there to take him off our hands.'

'Hang on,' I said, alarmed. 'I don't think that's a good idea. We have no idea which ones we can trust, and even the ones who aren't working against us don't really trust us. We still don't know any of their names. I didn't recognise this one. Did you? I wouldn't know her again either.'

To be fair, I hadn't got much of a look at the hamadryad's face. I'd been too busy grabbing her from behind.

But Fin was shaking her head. 'No, I couldn't pick her out of the crowd of them. So what are we going to do?'

'We have to get him back to the road. Then we call Hazel and see if she has any bright ideas about where we can dump him without being caught.'

Fin looked down. I could see concern as well as distaste on her face. 'Shouldn't he be waking up by now?'

'I think he's away with the fairies.' I really hoped so.

'Ha ha.' Fin thought I was making a joke, and she didn't think it was funny.

I realised she had no idea what I was talking about. 'I'm not taking the piss. You know those old stories about some- one going away with the fae folk for a night and coming back to find they've missed a year? Dryads can do that. Take people out of time, I mean. My dad lost a whole week once, before he realised what my mum had done.'

Fin was startled. 'Hamadryads can do that too?'

'I have no idea, but I know the wood wose could.' I'd told Fin about my first run-in with a scary thing that prowled the woods, but apparently I hadn't told her everything.

I was starting to think that hamadryads had more in common with wood woses than they had with my mum and the other dryads, even Frai. She could be unpleasantly prickly, but I didn't think she'd pull a stunt like this.

Of course, the poor bastard at our feet might be so oxygen-deprived he was already brain-dead, but I decided not to mention that possibility. 'Either way, let's get him moved before he wakes up or that hamadryad comes back.'

'Or the giant turns up,' Fin said grimly. She drove the iron netting stake into the ground beside me. 'Just in case.'

Before I could ask what she was doing, she disappeared behind the red-berried hawthorns. To my relief, she soon came back. She was carrying the heavy hessian bag in her arms. Putting it down, she took out her work gloves and tossed mine over to land by my boots.

'Can you lift his feet? Then I should be able to pull his trousers up.' She glared at the hamadryad's oblivious victim, as if this was all his fault.

'Can you gaffer tape my sleeve up first, please?' I was still holding my wounded forearm. It hurt like a son of a bitch, but doing anything more than first aid to stop me bleeding over everything was going to have to wait.

I wasn't only worried about leaving traces on the unconscious man. We needed to find the carved giant fast, if a faction of hamadryads was actively working against us. I hated to think what might happen if my blood dripped onto one of those lines we'd seen pulsing with eerie light in the darkness. Fee fi fo fum...

Fin didn't say anything, so I didn't know if she was thinking the same. She came over and wound several lengths of tape tight around my arm. That made the pain different, not less. I didn't care as long as the gashes in my clothes were sealed up.

'Okay, thanks.' I snapped the plastic tie holding the work gloves together and put them on. At least that covered the blood on my hands.

I squatted down and lifted the victim's heels to raise his trainers off the ground. Fin put on her own gloves. I didn't know if she was thinking about leaving her own DNA traces, or if she just didn't want to risk touching this stranger's sticky, sweaty naked skin. I didn't ask.

She managed to get his jeans and boxers untangled and started dragging the clothes up his legs. A wallet fell out of his pocket. Fin picked it up. 'Do we want to know who he is?'

'No. I don't want to be lying if we ever have to say we've got no idea who he might be.' I was avoiding looking at the stupid sod's face, to give me some chance of sounding convincing if I ever had to say I didn't recognise him either.

Fin shoved the wallet back in his pocket. 'There's a phone in his coat as well. If he hasn't been robbed, maybe he won't go to the cops.'

'Hopefully he won't have a clue what to tell them, even if he does.' I wondered if he'd think he'd been slipped a date-rape drug somehow.

It wasn't easy to get him dressed, even when I lifted his feet up so far that his arse was off the ground. Finally, Fin managed to pull his clothes back up to his waist. She buttoned his jeans and zipped him up. It took her several attempts, thanks to the work gloves, but at last we were spared the sight of his wrinkled cock and the condom half slipping off it.

I didn't suppose he'd be comfortable when he woke up, with his underwear twisted around his bollocks and probably full of dead leaves, but that was the least of my worries. If he ever woke up...

Fin didn't bother with his shirt buttons. She zipped up his coat and left it at that. 'How are we going to carry him?'

'If we can get him to the field, I can give him a fireman's lift.' I zipped up my coat, walked around to his head and hooked my hands under his armpits. 'Get his feet.'

Between us, we got him to the fence. Then we turned around and Fin lifted his feet up onto the middle strand of wire. Then she went through herself, a bit further down the fence line. With her on the other side and me lifting his shoulders, we managed to post him through the gap. He hit the ground harder than I intended when I reached through to lower his shoulders, but there was no helping that. I went to get through the fence at the same place that Fin had.

When I rejoined her, she was staring down with disbelief. 'Is he snoring?'

'Sounds like it.' I hoped that was a good sign. 'Help me get him up.'

Dead weight is sodding hard to handle, even when someone's unconscious, not an actual corpse. Hell, a corpse would have been easier to deal with. We could have dragged that along by its feet, instead of worrying about dropping this randy bastard on his head. Eventually, we got him vaguely upright, and I was able to bend down and hoist him onto my shoulder. We started walking.

Heavy as he was, this was easier on my back. I knew that was an illusion though. I'd be knackered by the time we reached the car. I also knew we'd be leaving all sorts of evidence on him, even without drops of blood. Every contact leaves a trace. I'd read that in plenty of crime thrillers. I only had to hope no senior copper would authorise the budget for testing for anything less obvious than an actual bloodstain.

'Have you got a phone signal?' I asked Fin. 'If you have, try Hazel.'

She got out her mobile. Seeing her find Hazel's number answered my first question. Now I prayed she'd get an answer. She did. Thank fuck for that.

Fin started explaining what had happened. We reached the stile in the hedge between the fields, and I carefully lowered my burden down so he was sitting on the step, eyes closed and still oblivious. Keeping him upright with a hand on his forehead, I caught my breath while Fin finished her call.

I kept an eye out for random ramblers. There was no way we could explain what we were doing. We'd found this stranger collapsed on the path? Then why were we lugging him around like a sack of potatoes instead of calling an ambulance? We couldn't claim there was no phone signal.

Fin put her mobile away. 'Hazel will meet us at the car. She said—'

'Don't tell me.' I took a deep breath. 'What I don't know, I won't have to lie about.'

'Right. Let's get on then.' She managed to get over the stile, even with our unwelcome friend in the way.

I lifted him up. Fin grabbed his shoulders. She dragged, I shoved, and between us we got him over the wooden bar. His coat got ripped on something, but that served him right. Hopefully he'd think twice the next time, if some inexplicably attractive woman he didn't even know invited him to go for a country walk and suggested impromptu open-air sex. Stupid prick.

Okay, I knew that wasn't fair. He couldn't have resisted the hamadryad. At the moment though, I didn't care. I got him up onto my shoulder again, and now my back was aching. It was also hard to look down to see where I was putting my feet. I trod in sheep shit and slipped a couple of times, nearly losing my balance.

By the time we reached the field entrance where the Toyota was parked, I was sweating like a pig. My sleeve under the gaffer tape was sodden, and I couldn't tell if that was sweat or blood. I did know my forearm felt like I had burned it, and badly.

Thankfully, Hazel was waiting for us. She'd even got the gate open. Fin fished in her coat pocket for her car keys and pressed the button on the fob. As the lights flashed, Hazel opened the rear door. When I lowered him down to the edge of the seat, she grabbed the man's head just in time to stop his ear smacking into the edge of the roof. He flopped forward, with his chest hitting his knees.

Fin was already around on the driver's side. 'We can't leave him hunched up like that. He could suffocate.'

She opened the rear door and reached in. With some more pulling and pushing, we got Sleeping Beauty bundled into the back seat. Even with his knees bent, he was lying flat enough for us to hear him snoring again.

Hazel looked at me, concerned. 'We can't get you in there as well. Are you okay to walk back to the village?'

I shook my head. 'I'm not coming back with you. I've got to start searching for the giant's head. We need to get that thing's eye staked with the yew branch as soon as possible. If there are hamadryads working against us, there's no telling what they'll try next.'

Hazel looked as if she'd like to argue. Thankfully she realised she couldn't. Besides, Fin was already in the driving seat and turning the key in the ignition.

She ducked her head so she could see me through the open passenger door. 'I'll be back as soon as I can.'

'Watch your back.' I closed the rear door as Hazel got into the front, and watched them drive away.

Part of me wanted to know exactly where they were headed, to check that I agreed with whatever the wise women were planning. Part of me was relieved that particular problem was out of my hands. It wasn't as if I didn't have plenty of other things to do.

I unzipped my coat to cool down again. It was tempting to stand there a while longer, telling myself I'd earned this breather. I knew that would be a mistake. I'm fit, but there are limits. I can do a fireman's lift, but I'm no firefighter. I could already feel the muscles in my back and legs stiffening up after carrying that weight. I would really feel this tomorrow.

Better to keep moving. I took a deep breath and started back across the fields. A few sheep watched me pass by, then got back to their grazing. I reached the fence line at the edge of the slope and picked up the bundle of netting stakes tied up with the yew wood. I was a lot happier once I got that through the fence and down on the other side of the hawthorns. Now there was nothing for anyone to see and get curious about.

If someone followed the footpath right across the field now, there was every chance they wouldn't realise I was here. Even if someone walked along the fence line, I should be out of sight down on the slope. As long as I kept quiet, no one would have any idea what I was doing.

I'd be even happier if I could take my coat off, but I reluctantly decided that would be a bad idea. Probing the ground was bound to start my arm bleeding again. I needed those taped-up sleeves to keep soaking up any gore. I settled for rummaging in the hessian bag and finding the bottles of lemon iced tea Fin had bought in the supermarket. I drank one and then the other. That helped, and so did tipping a packet of crisps into my mouth, to avoid touching what I was eating with my blood-stained fingers.

I tucked the rubbish into the hessian bag and put my gloves back on. Pulling up the iron stake Fin had stuck in the ground, I started to prod the earth around my feet. I tried shallow thrusts at first, then used my weight to drive the iron rod deeper. That was hard enough work to make me glad I was wearing gloves, even if my hands were soon sticky with blood and sweat inside them.

I started walking, and tested different spots. I soon realised this sort of search would be a lot easier out on the hillside where the bedrock was only covered with a layer of sheep-nibbled turf. That soil would be a lot thinner. Here, the earth was thick enough to support these thorn trees. I was soon glad I was still wearing my coat as I brushed against their spikes.

I persevered. Gradually, I began to get a feel for what I was finding with the iron rod. I started to recognise solid chalk when I hit it the first time, instead of trying a few more thrusts until I'd convinced myself. I worked my way along the strip of flat ground and found the same chalk ran underneath it. I went far enough in each direction to have left the giant behind, as long as Fin was right about its rough location. I hoped she was right about that.

I came back to the bag and the other stuff we'd brought with us and wondered where to look next. I didn't want to risk overshooting the buried chalk figure. I went about a metre down the slope below the level stretch and started working my way along. There was a carpet of tangled brambles, but I could trample them under my boots.

Taking a stride, I forced the iron rod down though the undergrowth and into the soil beneath. I hit unyielding chalk. I took another pace and tried again. Same result.

About halfway across the hillside though, I felt something different. There was some give down there.

I pulled the rod back a little bit and tested the ground again. It took a fair bit of effort, but this definitely didn't feel the same as pushing the metal through soil. I twisted the coiled metal end that I held in my hand, trying to wriggle the blunt spike that I couldn't see.

Something shifted, and the rod sank down a good ten centimetres. I leaned my weight on the netting stake again. Now there was more resistance, but it wasn't the same as striking chalk. I tried a third time, and I was certain. I had to have hit a trench that had been dug out to be packed with pale rubble. I'd found the carved giant.

Hallebloodylujah. I left that stake where it was and hurried back to our heap of stuff. I took the black-and-yellow tape out of the bag and picked up another netting stake. Walking carefully back down over the low-lying brambles, I tied one end of the tape to the stake I'd left sticking in the ground.

Now I had to work out where I needed to go next. A single point's no guide to anything. I stood there and thought this through. I had to believe I'd hit a point somewhere on the carved giant's head. I was searching the area where Fin had said it would be. Looking at the lay of the land, I reckoned that first stake had to be marking a point somewhere on the top of its head. I'd worked my way all along that stretch of flatter ground higher up without finding anything. Add to that, as far as I could remember from what the yew trees had shown me, the carving had been cut into a long, unbroken sweep of hillside. This all fitted.

So far, so logical, but I had no idea exactly where I'd hit the carved circle that was the giant's head. If I was right over to one side or the other, the trench would soon turn sharply downhill. If I was somewhere around the centre on the top, the curve would be a lot shallower, but that could still go slightly uphill or down below the point I'd just marked.

I had to probe the ground in a tight circle around that first stake where I'd tied the tape. Once I had some idea where the line was going, I could try spots further apart. For now, I had to take this slowly or I risked wasting time we didn't have to spare.

So I'd better get on with it. Thankfully, I soon found a soft spot to the right-hand side of the first stake. I marked that with the stake I was holding and unrolled the black-and-yellow tape to join it to the first one. Fetching another stake, I started searching to the left of my first point, on the same line and about the same distance away. No luck. I probed the ground a bit above that new spot. Still no result. I tried again, going slightly further down the hill. The third time was the charm. I felt the now familiar sensation of broken stone shifting under the ground.

I rammed the stake solidly home and went to fetch the roll of tape. Retracing my steps, I threaded it through the curled iron at the top of the stake I'd just planted. As I went to get another one, I realised I was going to have to use some different markers soon. I wouldn't have nearly enough netting stakes to mark out the giant's entire head. Okay, I might not need to do the whole circle, but I'd have to outline at least half of it, maybe more, before I could try to guess where to find its eye. Well, I could use one of Fin's billhooks to cut some blackthorn—

Something grabbed the back of my collar. It dragged me backwards, hard and fast. Standing facing up that steep slope, I didn't have a hope of staying on my feet. I fell hard to land flat on my back, and the only thing that saved me from being winded was the springiness of the brambles under me. Even so, my boots were higher than my head. Getting up was going to be impossible unless I was able to right myself. That wasn't going to happen while I was still sliding down the hill.

A blackthorn thicket stopped me going any further. I grabbed at a tangle of long grass, trying to haul myself around so my head was uphill, twisting to get onto my front. A fist hit my wrist, as heavy and hard as a mallet. A hamadryad was crouching in front of me, unbothered by the crazy angle of the ground. She grinned with vicious glee and aimed a punch at my face.

I rolled away just in time to avoid it. That didn't help. Another hamadryad kicked me in the gut. I was barely able to tense my stomach muscles as I curled up around her foot. She wasn't expecting that. Good. I grabbed her leg with both hands and rolled back over, dragging her with me. As her arms flailed, I threw her at my first attacker. They collided with a sound like someone dropping an armful of firewood. Then they both vanished.

I didn't bother trying to stand up. Scrabbling with hands and feet, I managed to get myself facing uphill again. Staying on my hands and knees, I began to climb back up. I wasn't sure how far I'd fallen, and I didn't waste time looking up to work that out. I had to get back to our stuff as fast as I possibly could. An iron rod had driven off the first hamadryad we'd seen here. I would do a lot more damage with a steel-headed sledgehammer.

I saw movement in the corner of my eye. I dodged, and a hamadryad's thrusting fingers slid through my hair instead of stabbing my eye. She still drew blood. The side of my head was stinging and I felt wetness trickle behind my ear. Knocked off balance, I sprawled on my back. She sprang forward to land on my thighs. That bloody hurt. Kneeling there, she hammered my chest and shoulders with her fists. All I could do was shield my face with my forearms to stop her trying to blind me.

As soon as I got a chance, I punched her in the face. I'll be honest. Doing that was a lot easier because she wasn't pretending to be human. She didn't even look like the hamadryads we'd met in the beech hanger, smooth-skinned and alluring in their leggings and tunics. This one wasn't pretending to wear clothes. She could have been an athlete or a gymnast in a bodysuit of mottled grey and gold. Blonde hair flared outwards from her head like a mane.

My fist hit her jaw. She didn't flinch, and I thought I'd broken my hand. It was like hitting a wall. A brick wall, not wood and plasterboard. She grabbed my arm, quick as a striking snake. Not the arm I'd punched her with, but where I was already injured. She tightened her grip and her fingertips went through the gaffer tape as if it was tissue paper. When her fingers dug into the gashes already torn through my skin, the agony was indescribable.

My knees came up as every instinct screamed at me. I had to get away from the pain, but I couldn't think how. The agony was short-circuiting my brain. All I could do was yell so hard my throat hurt.

The hamadryad got to her feet, laughing. She stood astride my waist. She still had hold of my arm, digging her fingers in even harder. By now, though, the pain couldn't get any worse. I was able to string two thoughts together. I let her feel my whole weight. Going limp, I closed my eyes and pressed my chin to my chest. That didn't bother her in the slightest.

I bent my knees and dragged my feet up under my backside. I still had one hand free, so I braced that on the ground. I forced myself up with a bellow, trying to hit the hamadryad with the arm she was still holding. My fist didn't reach her face, but my unexpected attack was enough to knock her off balance.

She was stronger than me, but I was heavier, and now I had gravity on my side. As I crashed into her, I wrapped my free arm around her, to stop her ripping my injured arm out of its socket. We tumbled down the hill together. At some point, she must have let go of me as the pain in my forearm went from unbearable to only excruciating. Then we hit a bramble patch and stopped rolling.

She tried to headbutt me. I saw that coming. Her forehead hit my cheekbone. I didn't have time to feel how bad that hurt. Turning my head meant I'd seen her open hand coming to slap my face. She had bramble stems as thick as my thumb draped across her palm. Those thorns were as big and as vicious as the spikes on barbed wire. I planted my hands on her chest and shoved her away as hard as I could.

As soon as we broke apart, she vanished. I lay there for a moment, panting. Once I got my breath back, I forced myself to assess my situation. Good news, there wasn't a hamadryad trying to rip my face off. Bad news, I had fallen a whole lot further down this fucking hill. That meant anything I could use as a weapon, or even just to defend myself, was that much further away. Worse news, I'd bet everything I owned these hamadryads would be coming back, and soon.

I began fighting to get free of the brambles. Thorns like cats' claws caught on my clothes and stabbed right through the cloth to prick my skin. Not because any spiteful woodland spirit wanted them to, but because brambles are bastards like that. I was grateful I had the thick work gloves on, and decent boots, as well as my combat trousers and what was left of my coat.

I managed to get to my hands and knees and began climbing up the slope again. Keeping my face away from waving bramble sprays meant straining my neck, but that was better than getting clawed by thorns. I kept a look out as best I could, to left and right at least. I couldn't see much further up the hill.

I'd hit the hamadryad with my right hand. That ached like I'd dropped a breeze block on it. My left forearm was burning worse than ever. My face felt bruised where the hamadryad had butted me, and I could still feel the tickle of ooz-ing blood by my ear. Despite my best efforts, several thorn sprays caught my chin and my cheek, and those scratches itched as well as stinging.

I ignored everything and struggled on up the hill. I reached the blackthorn and used that to keep my balance as I hauled myself to my feet. I stood as straight as I could on the precarious slope and took a good look around. There was no sign of hamadryads, or of anyone else, come to that.

My blood ran cold as I thought of a new danger. How soon would Fin be coming back? I didn't want her walking into a murderous attack. I had to warn her. I held on to the blackthorn and tugged the glove off my right hand with my teeth. I checked my coat pocket for my phone. For a won-der, it wasn't broken. That was as far as the good news went. There wasn't a trace of a signal.

I shoved the mobile into my pocket and dragged my glove back on over an ugly bruise. Dropping onto my hands and feet, I started climbing the slope again. Every bit of me ached. Never mind that. I didn't have any option. I had to get back up the hill to meet Fin. Then we still had a job to do. Everything we needed to stop the giant was up there as well. I kicked the soft earth hard to get decent toeholds, and wished there weren't so many sodding brambles in my way.

I'd just got clear of another matted tangle when some-thing landed on my back. My hands and feet slipped. I landed flat on the rough grass, barely twisting my head to one side in time to avoid breaking my nose. Brutal fingers gripped my shoulders. I drew the deepest breath that I could with this attacker weighing me down. I dragged my hands close, trying to get them under my chest, as if I was going to start doing a few press-ups.

That's what the hamadryad had been waiting for. As soon as I levered myself up off the grass, a grey-gold arm snaked around my neck. I could feel her knees in the small of my back as she leaned forward to press her cheek to the bleeding scrapes on my scalp.

'Your mother and her sisters did always breed stubborn sons. I wonder who will tell her how you died? I wonder if the giant will find your flesh all the sweeter for your greenwood blood?'

I recognised that voice. This was the angry hamadryad who'd taken a stand against the others when we'd met them all at Wayland's Smithy.

She chuckled in my ear. 'I saw what you did to my sister who was trying to leave our offering for the giant. Never mind. You will do instead.'

Her arm tightened around my neck. Hamadryads were clearly quick learners. She didn't know exactly what she was doing though. She was choking me, crushing my windpipe, instead of cutting off the blood to my brain. She wasn't doing that as effectively as she hoped, either. She was scarily strong, but she was slender and not that tall. I take a size eighteen in shirt collars. That's a pain when I'm shopping for clothes, but it was making it harder for her to kill me now.

I clawed at her arm, but my hands slipped inside my thick gloves. Not that it mattered. I had as much chance of scratching her skin as I did of cutting down a tree with my fingernails.

I was getting dizzy. My vision blurred. I could feel myself getting weaker. As I struggled to breathe, the hamadryad's scent surrounded me, as fragrant as spring blossom. That confused me even more. Then everything went black.

Chapter Twenty-Three

'**D**an! Daniel!'

I heard somebody calling my name. Was that my mum?

'Is he still breathing?'

That was someone else. I wanted to tell her that of course the man we'd saved from the hamadryad was still breathing. How else could he be snoring? For some reason though, I couldn't speak.

'I think so. Yes. Yes, he is.' The first voice suddenly got a lot louder.

Fin was here. I recognised the scent of her shampoo. I felt her breath on my face. A strand of her hair brushed my cheek.

Why couldn't I see her? Why couldn't I see?

'Try this,' the other voice said.

I smelled something indescribable. Whatever it was, it startled my lungs into a sudden, deep breath. That cleared the fog from my brain. I coughed and opened my eyes to see Fin bending over me as I lay on my back. She was kneeling at my side on the rough grass.

'Oh, thank heavens.' She screwed her own eyes tight shut for a moment. 'Are you okay?' she demanded.

I wanted to ask what that brutal smell was, and found that I still couldn't speak. Telling myself not to panic, I swallowed hard. The bruises on my neck ached like a bastard, but I got some saliva into my mouth.

'I'll live.' That hoarse whisper startled both of us. I cleared my throat and tried again. 'I'll be okay.'

That sounded better, and it was true, even if it wasn't the whole truth. It would be a while before I stopped feeling the after-effects of today's encounters. But that would have to wait. I braced my hands on the ground by my sides and tried to sit up. Fin's hand on my chest stopped me moving.

'Wait a moment. Let's take this slowly.' She was worried.

I realised she was peering at the blood on the side of my head. 'That's nowhere as bad as it looks.'

I forced myself to a sitting position and wondered how I'd ended up on my back when I'd collapsed face down. Not that it mattered.

'Have you got a first aid kit in the car?' Hazel asked from somewhere behind me. 'There's everything else we might need at the cottage, if we can get him back there.'

'He can hear you, you know.' I twisted around to squint at her.

'Sorry.' She didn't sound remotely convinced that I was okay.

'Let's get you up the hill for a start.' Fin reached up to hand something to Hazel.

I caught a whiff of whatever had startled me awake. 'What is that?'

'Smelling salts.' Hazel showed me a small brown bottle before she slipped it into one of her waxed-cotton coat's many pockets.

I didn't think those existed outside Agatha Christie-type novels. You learn something new every day. As I thought that, I realised I was still a bit light-headed.

'Can you stand up?' Fin tucked her hand under my elbow.

'Careful,' I warned. 'If I slip, I don't want to take you down with me.'

'No danger of that.' She stood up and showed me she had one of the ropes we'd brought with us tied around her waist.

'Good thinking.' Moving slowly and carefully, I got onto my hands and knees. Fuck me, I ached.

'Do you want a hand?' Hazel approached on my other side. She had a rope on her as well.

'Give me a minute.' I made sure my feet weren't going to slip and slowly straightened up.

Fin and Hazel both offered me a hand, but I waved them away. I took hold of the ropes instead. Cautiously, I tested them, to make sure they were up to my weight. They were solid.

'We're tied to the fence posts,' Hazel told me. 'Don't worry.'

That was a relief. I got a firm grip and started hauling myself up the slope, hand over hand. Hazel and Fin let me set my own pace. Each of them gathered up the slack in the ropes as we made our way slowly and awkwardly up the hill.

As we got closer to the top, I saw that the line of black-and-yellow tape was a short way away to my right. The fencing stakes I'd stuck in the ground were still where I'd put them. Of course they would be. Hamadryads couldn't handle the iron. Thinking how that must frustrate the head trouble-maker made me feel better. A bit better, anyway.

I paused for a breather. 'I made a start. You can see where. We need to mark out more of the arc to know exactly where the giant's head is. Then we can work out how to find its eye.'

The two of them exchanged a glance that I really didn't like.

'What?' I demanded.

'Let's get you to the top of the slope first,' Hazel said, soothing.

I ignored her, because the alternative was telling her not to talk to me like a sodding six-year-old. I looked at Fin. 'What is it?'

She didn't mess me around. 'We can't find the yew stake anywhere.'

'What the fuck?'

I didn't wait for an answer. I grabbed the ropes and started climbing again, as fast as I could. I was out of breath by the time I reached the level ground below the hawthorns, but that didn't matter. There was sod all for me to do except stand there and look at the mess.

Fin untied the rope around her waist and handed the coil she was holding to Hazel. As the wise woman headed past the hawthorns, Fin started clearing up. The hessian bag had been ripped into rags. The plastic bottles and cellophane-wrapped sandwiches had been crushed flat. That looked like pointless spite. I hoped that one of the hamadryads had got a nasty shock when she'd stamped on a bag of crisps and it went bang. There was no sign of the roll of gaffer tape. Wherever that had been thrown, we had no hope of finding it. That pissed me off to a ridiculous extent.

Fin picked the billhooks out of the long grass. Those had been left where they fell, I guessed, even though they had wooden handles and leather sleeves over the metal blades. I walked over to where I'd left the netting stakes. They were still there, along with the sledgehammer.

But Fin was right, not that I'd doubted her. There was absolutely no sign of the branch I'd so carefully shaped with the draw knife and the shave horse.

I looked around, but that was pointless. 'They'd have no problem carrying yew wood away with them, would they?'

Fin bent down to pick up the enamel mug. 'And they'd be fools to leave it anywhere near here, where we might find it again.'

'Right. Fuck!' I said with feeling.

Hazel came back around the hawthorns, carrying both ropes neatly coiled. 'Now you've got that out of your system, shall we discuss what to do next?'

'I don't think there's a lot of point carrying on with the search here.' Fin raised a hand to silence my protest. 'Not yet. Not until we've got another yew stake to use. As soon as we start again, the hamadryads are sure to try to stop us. We'll need to work fast, and have everything ready to go as soon as we find the giant.'

'And we can't risk any of us being caught on our own again,' Hazel added.

'You two had better each carry one of those billhooks.' I'd like to see a hamadryad try attacking me now I had that steel-headed sledgehammer in my hands. But I still needed something to hit with it, and I didn't only mean an attacker. 'So where do we get another yew stake?'

Fin shrugged. 'We had better ask the hamadryads. The good—' She corrected herself. 'The hamadryads on our side. If that's what we can call the ones who aren't trying to kill us.'

'It'll do for now.' It wasn't a warm day, but I felt colder than I should have done as something occurred to me. Why wasn't I dead? I'd been completely at that hostile hamadryad's mercy. Why hadn't she finished the job?

'Perhaps they can talk some sense into their sisters,' Hazel said waspishly. 'But you need to get cleaned up first, Dan.'

I was too battered and bruised to argue. 'I could certainly do with a cup of tea.'

I picked up the remaining iron stakes. Hazel stuck one of the billhooks in the poacher's pocket of her green waxed-cotton coat and carried the ropes. Fin bundled everything else up in the largest piece that was left of the hessian bag. We climbed through the wire fence, walked through the fields, and the sheep didn't give us a second glance.

The afternoon was turning to dusk. We dumped everything in the Toyota's boot and drove back to Bockbourne Parva in silence. The lights were on when we got to the cottage, and the door was unlocked, but there was no sign of anyone when we followed Hazel inside.

She glanced at Fin as she hung her coat on a hook. 'Would you get some coffee on, please? And boil the kettle. You, sit down,' she ordered me.

'Boots?' Fin hesitated on the mat.

'Keep them on. We'll be going out soon enough, and the floor will wash.' Hazel opened a door at the end of the room. That turned out to be a cupboard under the stairs which I realised must be behind the identical door next to it. Hazel took a big tin of all-butter cookies off a shelf.

That was a lie. When she put it down on the table and took the lid off, it was full of cotton wool, boxes of sticking plasters and assorted bottles and tubes. She fetched a newspaper from a cardboard box under the pinboard and looked at me as she spread it open on the table. I was still standing beside a chair.

'I can't clean that blood off your head unless you sit down,' she said briskly.

'Let me take this off.' I unzipped my coat reluctantly.

'Do you want a hand?' Fin had hung up her own coat and filled the kettle at the sink. Now that she'd switched that on, she was taking mugs and a storage jar out of the wall cupboard above the coffee maker.

'Let's see.' I got myself out of most of the coat with a bit of effort. Then I tugged on the cuff of the gaffer-taped sleeve to ease that over my hand. Dried blood stuck everything to my forearm. I gritted my teeth and pulled harder. I wanted to swear, for a whole lot of reasons, but Hazel was watching me and she clearly didn't like bad language.

I bit my lip and thought 'fuck' repeatedly and extremely loudly inside my own head.

The sleeve came free and I dropped the coat on the floor. I sat down fast on the closest chair. My forearm was bleeding again, and the wounds were painful enough to make me dizzy.

Hazel took my hand and laid my arm on the open newspaper. She didn't ask as she started cutting my sweatshirt sleeve with a pair of scissors I hadn't even seen her find in the tin. She started at the cuff and cut the seam as far as my elbow. Then she cut off the torn and bloody cloth completely. There was no point in me protesting. The sweatshirt was only fit for the bin now, along with my new coat. This trip was going to be sodding expensive in clothes. I decided I would stick to army surplus in future.

She studied the oozing gashes in my forearm as she pulled on some blue vinyl gloves. 'I suppose there's no point in me saying you need to take this to A&E?'

'None,' I said shortly.

'Where is that? Swindon?' Fin came over to see how badly my arm was hurt. She shook her head reluctantly. 'We could be waiting there half the night.'

'Catching who knows what from other people in the waiting room.' I could also see me facing awkward questions about how exactly I had ended up in a knife fight. The four parallel cuts were as clean as if they'd been done with a blade, or one of those martial arts tiger claws, maybe.

'Fin, can I have a bowl of water from the kettle, please?' Hazel was already finding a packet of butterfly strips. 'Any of the glass ones out of the dishwasher will do.'

Fin did as she was asked. She stood and watched as Hazel carefully cleaned the blood off my arm, dipping each piece of cotton wool in the hot water and discarding it once it was used. 'Are you a first aider?'

'Technically my certificate's lapsed.' Hazel's smile surprised me as she wiped my arm dry. 'You have to be prepared to look after yourself if you're searching for signs of orang pendek in Sumatra's forests. That's a hominid who's supposed to live in the remote mountains. This is going to sting.'

She wasn't wrong. I guessed she was swabbing the wounds with some sort of antiseptic, but I was too busy blinking away tears to see the name on the bottle. I felt a chill on my skin as it dried, and silently swore a bit more to myself.

Hazel opened up the butterfly strips and drew the edges of the first gash together with a strip across the middle. 'How's that coffee coming along? And there's a fruit cake in the Tupperware by the bread crock. I think we could all do with a slice of that.'

'Thanks.' Fin went back to the counter. 'Dan, would you prefer tea?'

'Coffee's fine, thanks. Milk and two sugars.' I had a feeling this was going to be a long night.

The coffee maker soon finished burbling and Fin brought two mugs over, followed by generous lumps of cake. Then she fetched her own drink and plate and joined us at the table.

Hazel, wise woman, first aider and who knew what else, finished closing up my cuts and sat back. 'I'll dress that in a minute. Coffee first, and some painkillers for you.' She tossed me a packet of paracetamol and codeine tablets out of the tin, stripped off her gloves and started eating her cake.

'Fine by me.' I reached for my own mug. It was a relief to shift my position. Holding still had been getting painful, never mind the way my arm was throbbing now, and itching. I needed some sort of distraction. 'What did you do with that bloke from this afternoon?'

'We found out where he'd met the hamadryad, so we took him back and left him.' Hazel drank some coffee.

'How did you do that?' I couldn't begin to imagine.

'Using a pendulum and a map.' Hazel looked at me, unblinking.

I realised she was daring me to ask her to explain. What I couldn't work out was whether that was a good idea or not. I glanced at Fin. She was eating cake. Her face promised she'd tell me about it once we were on our own.

For now, she just went on telling me what they had done. 'It was down in those woods by the eel house. He was starting to come round when we left him, thanks to a jolt from Hazel's smelling salts. I watched from the water until he woke up. He phoned a friend to pick him up. As far as I could tell from what he was saying, he has absolutely no idea what happened.'

'Let's hope it stays that way.' With luck, that would be one less headache for us to deal with. We still had plenty of other problems. I got up to wash my filthy hands at the sink, and a thought occurred to me. I looked back at Hazel. 'Could you find out where that yew grove is? Maybe if we went there ourselves, and told the trees—?'

'Sorry.' She shook her head, exasperated. 'I can't locate it. Believe me, I've tried. Those trees don't want to be found.'

'Oh well. It was just an idea.' I came back to sit down and finish my coffee. Now that I had clean hands, I took a couple of tablets and ate my slice of cake. It was the sort of rich fruit cake that you get at Christmas, and at the moment it was everything I needed. Apart from anything else, my various aches and pains were killing my appetite. 'Then we'll have to go and see the hamadryads in the beech hanger.'

'And soon. Time's getting on.' Hazel reached for the first aid tin again.

I sat still while she taped a cushioned dressing pad over the butterfly strips on my arm and covered that with an expertly wound gauze bandage. A casualty nurse couldn't have done a better job.

'Thanks.' I went to stand up.

'Not so fast.' Hazel put on a fresh pair of gloves and reached for the bowl of water and the cotton wool. 'Let me take a look at your head.'

She swabbed at the dried blood above my ear while Fin put the mugs and plates on the counter above the dishwasher. I struggled not to pull away. The scrapes along my scalp didn't hurt any more, not much anyway, but the trickles of water down my neck tickled horribly.

'I think we can leave this as it is.' Hazel sounded relieved. 'How about your other hand?'

I laid it flat on the table and flexed my fingers. We could all see the ugly discolouration spreading across the back from my wrist to my knuckles.

'I'm pretty sure this is only bruised.' If I had fractured any of the bones, that could only be a hairline crack, and there was nothing anyone could do about it. Making a fist hurt, but the painkillers were taking the edge off.

'Let's go then.' Hazel bundled up the newspaper with the used gloves, the bloody cotton wool and the end of my sweatshirt sleeve inside it. She left that on the table and went to get her coat.

I looked at Fin. She shrugged. If Hazel wanted us to bin the rubbish, she could ask us. We weren't going to be nosy and ask if someone else was going to come in and clear up. Whoever had baked that cake, presumably.

We both put our own coats back on. I started with my arm that had the dressing on it. That wasn't easy with those rips in my sleeve still taped up, but without the roll of gaffer tape, we couldn't strip that off and redo it. I eased my forearm through the narrow band little by little. That started the cuts throbbing, but I didn't feel any hint of the bandage coming loose, never mind any of the butterfly strips beneath it.

By the time I was doing up my zip, Hazel and Fin were ready to go. Fin had her car keys in her hand. As we went out, Hazel came after us. She didn't switch the lights off or lock the door. Fin didn't say anything and nor did I. These wise women seemed to know what they were doing.

Fin drove us to the beech hanger and parked on the same track as before. As we got out of the car, I glanced at the boot and hesitated.

'Do we want anything out of there?'

Hazel shook her head. 'We want them to help us. They won't do that if they think we're a threat.'

She was right, though I didn't have to like it. She also still had that billhook in her pocket. I was about to point that out when Fin opened the car boot and took out the other one. She pulled up her coat and stuck it in the waistband of her jeans, then closed and locked the car. Hazel didn't say anything, so neither did I.

We headed for the trees. This slope was nowhere near as steep as the hillside where the giant was carved, but it was still a painful climb after the beating I'd taken today. I decided that when all this was over, when everything was over and we could visit people and places again, I'd suggest Fin and I had a holiday in the Fens. That would be nice and flat.

We reached the trees. The wood was dark and deserted. Moonrise was still some way off. I looked at Fin and Hazel and they looked at me. Then I noticed a burr on one of the beeches at the very edge of the hanger. If it had been there before, I hadn't seen it. It caught my attention now. Like the swollen lump on that tree by the river, it looked just like a face.

I walked over. 'We need to speak to—'

I didn't know what to say. Did the trees consider the hamadryads were their owners? Their guardians? Did these tree spirits even call themselves hamadryads? That was a name from human myth. Dryads and naiads have accepted such names, but they have a lot more to do with people.

I settled for repeating myself. 'We need to speak.'

The beech tree got the message. A steely flash lit what looked exactly like eyes in the twisted folds of bark. Inside a minute, a hamadryad stood facing me with one hand resting on the tree. To my intense relief, I recognised her. She had taken us to the hidden yew grove.

I didn't waste any time. 'Your sister who stood against you at Wayland's Smithy, she or someone who follows her has stolen the gift the ancient trees gave us. We cannot subdue the giant without the yew stake.'

The hamadryad vanished.

'What the—?'

Before I learned if Hazel was going to swear, the hamadryad was back. She wasn't alone. Two of her allies had firm hold of the leader of the hostile faction. They stood on either side of her, gripping her arms. As soon as she saw me, she started to struggle. I was extremely pleased to see she hadn't got a cat in hell's chance of breaking free.

Chapter Twenty–Four

More hamadryads were appearing. I could see some of them clearly, while others were hiding in the shadows cast by the trees. There were shadows because some sort of eerie radiance was glowing on the ground here and there. That gave enough soft golden light for me to see the hamadryads weren't interested in me, Hazel or Fin. They were looking at each other. Recognising their allies, they moved around until they stood in two distinct groups. I wondered which ones were on our side, or at least, which ones weren't actively working against us. Working to let the giant loose, to wreak all the mayhem it could.

The hamadryad we'd managed to summon raised her voice to speak to her sisters. 'The yew trees agree that the giant must return to his sleep under the hills. This is not the time for him to rise. The Green Man sent this mortal here to subdue him. The yew trees gave him the means.'

She rounded on the captive so quickly that a shiver ran through the others. The leaves on the beech trees rustled. 'Who are you to say different? To attack this man? When the ancients tell us his mother is our distant kin.'

The hostile hamadryad didn't answer. She had stopped struggling though. She stood tall and defiant as she looked around the wood. I was relieved to see the two who'd brought her here were holding her arms just as tight as before. Everyone waited. She still didn't speak.

Well, I had something to say. Let's see what they made of that. 'She's done more than try to stop us doing what the Green Man wants. She left me for dead, so the giant would eat me. After we rescued the first man she'd left unconscious for the monster to find.'

'So you say.' A sceptical voice said from the shadows. 'Yet here you stand.'

Another hamadryad spoke up. 'No mortal has died at our hands.' Everyone could hear she was telling the truth. 'And we all know your kind lie as easily as you draw breath.'

So that's why I was still alive. Hamadryads might not know the expression 'plausible deniability', but they clearly understood the concept.

'I said I was left for dead—' I began.

'That is done with.' The spokeswoman waved an impatient hand. She took a pace to stand toe to toe with the hamadryad who'd choked me. 'What have you done with the branch that the ancient trees gave to these mortals?'

The captive looked towards us and sneered. Well, that was one way to avoid saying something that everyone would know was a lie. Everyone except Hazel and Fin. She looked back at the hamadryad who was confronting her. She still didn't say a word, but she looked spitefully triumphant. The spokeswoman glared at her prisoner, frustrated.

'Have you destroyed it?' Hazel demanded. 'Do we need to ask the yew trees for another gift? Shall we tell them what you have done?'

A loud murmur that was half shock and half fear drowned out the wise woman's questions. Even in this dim light, I could see the other hamadryads looking at the captive. All the hamadryads were staring at her, whichever side they were on. They were equally appalled at the thought of the yew stake being – what?

Hang on. How would a hamadryad make something like that solid wooden stake unusable? They couldn't handle the metal tools needed to hack it to bits. I couldn't believe they had any way of lighting a fire to burn it. More than that, I didn't believe this hamadryad would do something that would surely turn her followers against her. Clearly, as far as they were concerned, that offence against the ancient yews would be a far greater crime than leaving me as a snack for the giant.

She was looking around the gathering now. I could see the urgency in her eyes, the unspoken plea. They mustn't believe she would do such a dreadful thing. Every so often, she gazed more intently at one or another of her sisters, presumably reminding them of some earlier conversation.

'No,' I said slowly. 'She hasn't destroyed it. She can't. She's hidden it. It's in a place where she thinks we can't find it.'

The hostile hamadryad couldn't help looking at me as I spoke. Realising she'd given herself away, she forced a mocking smile, as if she'd intended to taunt me all along. I did my best not to react.

Knowing what she'd done, or hadn't done, didn't get us any closer to finding the stake. The damn thing could be in any one of a hundred thickets or hollows along the downs. She could have thrown it into the river, or into any one of several rivers within easy reach. If she'd done that, I had no idea how we'd get it back. I didn't think we had time to find a naiad we could persuade to go searching.

'It has to be in a place where the giant can't find it either,' Fin said thoughtfully.

Hazel saw what she meant. 'If she thinks she can force the giant to do what she wants, she has to have something to hold over it. Some threat that it will truly fear.'

Fin and I realised the answer within a second of each other.

'Wayland's Smithy.'

The hamadryad couldn't hide her fury. If she had, it wouldn't have mattered. The expressions on her followers' faces would have given the game away.

Now it was my turn to grin at the vicious bitch with an unspoken 'fuck you'. The Smithy site wasn't that big. With three of us looking, we should soon find something the size of the stake. I turned to Fin and Hazel. 'Let's go and get it.'

The spokeswoman raised a hand. 'Let us—'

One of the hamadryads exploded. There's no other way to describe what happened. The shock was as loud and as brutal as a shotgun blast. One minute, she was standing there, as intent as the rest on this confrontation. The next second, she was a shower of splinters, and I don't mean the sort you tease out of a finger with a sewing needle.

Watch some historical documentary about the days of Nelson's navy. The chances are you'll see a reconstruction to demonstrate the lethal impact of a cannon ball hitting a wooden ship. Flying pieces of wood the size of daggers and just as sharp killed sailors as they came scything across the decks. This was as bad, or worse.

Hamadryads who had been standing close by staggered backwards or dropped to their knees. Ichor glistened in the golden light as they clutched at ragged wounds on their arms and legs. Fragments of their dead sister had ripped into them. One collapsed with her hands pressed to her face. She writhed on the ground, screaming like an animal in a snare. In the next instant, she vanished.

More hamadryads disappeared. Cries of pain and fear from the ones who stayed echoed around the beech hanger. Above our heads, the trees creaked and thrashed their branches in distress. The pools of glowing gold flared as bright as lightning. More than half of them faded and died though. The darkness that the light had been holding at bay surged back under the trees.

Fin and Hazel stared at me, horrified. I looked around and braced myself for trouble.

'Car keys.' I held out my hand to Fin.

As soon as I knew where the attack was coming from, I'd head for the Toyota as fast as I could. I'd need some weapon to fight whatever it was, and the sledgehammer seemed a good bet. I could only hope the danger didn't turn up between me and the car.

As Fin shoved a hand into her pocket, a hamadryad appeared out of nowhere, right in front of the spokeswoman.

Her voice was tight with terror. 'He has realised what we are. He knows he has been deceived.'

I stepped forward. 'You mean the giant? Where is it? What have you been doing?'

The spokeswoman rounded on me as if this was somehow my fault. 'You wanted him kept away as you worked.'

'You said you could do that,' I reminded her. 'You never told us how.'

The hamadryad who'd just arrived answered. 'Giants are as lustful as they are greedy for mortal blood and bone. We lured him away, pretending to be mortal women. He thought he could seize one of us to dominate and brutalise as he slaked his desire. But he caught one of my sisters unawares and discovered her nature. Now he swears he will kill us all. He's tearing down our trees.'

That provoked even more outcry from the others. The beeches swayed and creaked as if a winter storm raged overhead. Somewhere in the darkness, I heard sobbing. A moment later, another hamadryad died with a deafening crack. Anguished screams from the injured around her tore through the night. The remaining golden radiance dimmed further.

'We did this for you.' The spokeswoman had to shout above the noise to accuse me. 'You must find him and fight him, to settle that debt.'

'No,' Fin shouted back instantly.

'How?' demanded Hazel.

'I can't,' I bellowed.

That shut them all up. I paused to make sure I had everyone's attention. Hazel and Fin looked at me, as tense as the hamadryads, as they waited to hear what I had to say.

'I can't fight that giant and win.' I was looking at the spokeswoman, but I was speaking to everyone. 'I could barely slow it down last time, and that's when there was a building to drop on its head. The only way to stop it once and for all is to use that stake and do what the yew trees showed me.'

I looked around at the hamadryads. The only one I ignored was the troublemaker still being held captive.

'Who knows where she put the yew branch?' I challenged the others. 'The sooner I can do this, the fewer of you will die.'

'I know.' One of them stepped forward from the shadows. 'I will show you.'

'No!' The hostile hamadryad started fighting to free herself. The other two struggled to hold her.

'Bind her!' The spokeswoman gestured. 'Now!'

Hamadryads clustered around the captive and the two who were trying to restrain her. Hazel, Fin and I got out of their way as quick as we could. The hamadryads packed together, closer and closer. None of them spoke, but I heard an ominous murmur. A second later, I realised I was feeling it as much as hearing it. I couldn't tell if it was coming from the hamadryads, from the trees or up from the ground through the soles of my boots. I did know I felt sick with apprehension and my skin was crawling.

They vanished. All of them. The last of the eerie lights blinked out. We stood there in the darkness. A faint, cold breeze whispered through the trees.

'Are you ready?' a voice asked.

My eyes adjusted to the night. There was one hamadryad still here with us. The one who knew where the yew stake was hidden. I didn't think I'd seen her when I'd been attacked earlier. I hoped that meant we could trust her.

Fin held out her hand. 'Let's go.'

'No.' Seeing Fin was about to object, I explained quickly. 'We need to do this job as fast as possible, and that means splitting up. I'll go and get the yew stake. You won't be able to take me there if I'm carrying a whole load of iron tools, will you?'

I was asking the hamadryad, but I didn't wait for her to reply before I turned back to Hazel and Fin.

'You two take the car to the field above the chalk slope. Park up and wait for me there. Then everything I need will be ready as soon as our friend here brings me and the yew branch back from the Smithy.' I looked at the hamadryad again. 'You can do that? You know where I mean? Where the giant was carved into the hill?'

She nodded. 'I can.'

'Okay.' Fin didn't sound thrilled, but she didn't argue.

'Let's go.' Hazel was already walking away.

The hamadryad took my hand, catching me by surprise. I could hardly complain. I was the one who'd said we needed to go at once. The darkness around me became emptiness. I couldn't feel the cold breeze. I couldn't even feel the dull ache of my injured arm. A moment later, my feet touched solid ground, and I could count each and every one of my cuts and bruises.

Never mind any of that. I was standing in front of the barrow, pretty much where we'd stood to meet the hamadryads. The sky above us was vast and full of stars just as it had been before, and the beeches that ringed the site cast the same shadows over the long swell of turf. They whispered to each

302

other on the very edge of hearing. At least, I really hoped that was the trees whispering.

I looked at the hamadryad. 'Where is it?'

She pointed to the entrance to the barrow, between the two looming sarsen stones. 'We threw it in there.'

Shit. I supposed I should have expected that. Hell, who was I trying to fool? It was the first possibility that had occurred to me when Fin and I realised the yew stake must be here. I'd shoved that thought away fast. I didn't even want to remember the feeling of looking into that unknowable void.

'Fetch it for me, please.' I meant to sound calm and commanding. Instead I heard myself begging for help.

The hamadryad looked at me. 'No.'

I really wanted to argue with her. I wanted to say that she owed me this, for being part of stealing the branch in the first place. I should insist she do me this favour, to win back some goodwill from the ancient yew trees. I should remind her I was here on the Green Man's orders, and she really didn't want to get on his bad side. Give me a minute and I could probably come up with something else.

It would make no difference. I could see that as clear as day. I might not be lying exactly, but trying to bullshit or guilt-trip her would be a complete waste of breath. Her 'no' had been final, and I wasn't going to change her mind. I might learn more about her reasons for siding with her hostile sister, but I was pretty certain she wasn't going to apologise for anything she had done.

I'd only be wasting time we didn't have to spare. Fuck.

'Will you wait here for me?' I sounded like a kid who was afraid of the dark. That's because I was scared shitless by whatever was beyond those age-old stone uprights.

The hamadryad answered calmly. 'Yes.'

That was good to know, but it didn't solve my fundamental problem. The thought of ducking beneath that low lintel still paralysed me. This wouldn't be stepping into some ordinary night-time shadow that my mother's blood would help me see through. It wasn't even the impenetrable blackness of the underground caverns cut by the rivers that flowed under the Derbyshire Peaks. That had been scary enough, when the naiad Kalei had taken me underground when we set out to destroy the wood wose. This was something else entirely. I knew that much, even if I didn't know what lay ahead.

I could think of plenty of possibilities and none of them were good. Folk tales don't only talk about men seduced by faerie women who lost years of their lives. There are plenty of stories about people stupid enough to go through doorways into hillsides. Best case, they came back to find the world had gone on for decades quite happily without them. Worst case, those idiots were never seen again.

Right, and while I was standing here being such a useless chicken shit, Fin was driving back to that hillside where the giant's image was carved into the chalk. What was going to happen when she got there if I was still standing here with my dick in my hand?

'Does the giant know what we're trying to do?' I asked the hamadryad.

'Yes.'

I could have asked her for more. I could have asked if the hostile hamadryad betrayed us, or if the giant had worked out what was happening for itself. Had it felt some distant pain when I started sticking iron spikes into that chalk outline like some sort of giant voodoo doll? There was still so much we didn't bloody know.

I could ask, but there was no guarantee that the hamadryad would have any answers. Meantime, Fin could be driving back to find the giant was already lying in wait. I'd told her to stay in the car though. She would be safe if she stayed in the Toyota with Hazel.

Right, and how likely was that? They both knew there was still a load of work to be done to pinpoint the giant's eye. They had the gear they needed in the back of the car. There was no way they would sit and wait for me to turn up and take charge.

Come to that, there was no guarantee they would be safe in the car. Ripping the roof off would hurt the giant, but the monster might think that was a price worth paying to get its hands on two human women. Two more than ordinarily human women. Women who would know exactly what was threatening them, making their terror all the sweeter...

The toes of my boots knocked against something. Looking down, I saw the low stone that blocked the entrance to the barrow. I'd been edging forward without even realising it. Okay then. Since I was here, I might as well go on.

I took a deep breath and stepped over the barrier. My boots were loud on the flat stones underfoot. The trees stopped whispering. I really wished they hadn't done that. I went onwards anyway. A couple of paces brought me to the uprights that held up the capstones. I pictured the plan of the barrow that I'd seen on the website. There was a shallow chamber straight ahead, and one on the right and another to my left. All I had to do was reach in to find the yew branch. At most, that would take me three tries. The woodcutter's son always gets three goes in fairy tales, doesn't he?

Right, and what was squatting there in the darkness unseen, waiting to grab my wrist as soon as it got the chance? Waiting to pull me through this portal. I was sure I could hear something breathing in the shadows. Was it to my right, to the left or straight ahead?

Unless I was hearing my own breathing echoing back from the stones. My chest was tight with stress, and I could hear a rasp in my nose and throat. My mouth was as dry as dust. I forced myself to hold my next breath, listening as intently as I could.

I couldn't hear anything at all now, but I could feel a chill coming from the hollow darkness beyond the door stones. It wasn't a breeze, exactly, but it raised the hairs on the back of my neck. I realised I was shivering, and I couldn't say if that was from cold or fear.

That didn't matter. Fin was relying on me to do this. It was time to shit or get off the pot. I crouched down to avoid braining myself on the capstone and stepped over the threshold.

Have you ever gone down a staircase without switching on the light and miscounted? You take a step into thin air instead of reaching the ground. There's that lurch in the pit of your stomach. It sets your heart racing. There's an instant of panic when you think you've lost your balance, even when your foot finds the floor. I felt all that as I stepped into the void, and I had bigger things to worry about too.

I was standing in pitch darkness, and I wasn't alone. Somewhere way out ahead of me, something snickered with evil glee. There was a moment's silence, and whatever it was laughed again. The sound was louder now. Whatever might be out there, it was heading my way.

That stopped me looking back over my shoulder to see if the doorway was still there. I'd worry about escaping once I'd got the yew stake back. If nothing else, I wanted to have the heavy, pointed wood that I'd so carefully shaped as a weapon. Let's see whatever bastard thing was out there try and grab me if I smacked it with that.

I dropped to my hands and knees. I could feel cool stone under my fingertips as well as fine grit and a few dead leaves as I swept my hands around. It wasn't cut and laid stone though. This wasn't a man-made floor, but something more like a cave.

What I couldn't feel anywhere was that bloody yew branch. How far could the hamadryads have thrown it? I didn't want to go crawling any deeper into the darkness. If I left this spot, I had no idea how I would find my way back. I had no idea what I might bump into. I could hear that horrid giggle getting closer, as well as the scrape of something else. Claws?

I dropped down onto my belly, spreading my arms out to either side at full stretch. I ignored the painful tug of the butterfly strips holding my gashed arm together, and the sharp ache in my bruised belly where the hamadryad had kicked me. There wasn't anything on the floor to my left or my right. I brought my hands forward, reaching straight out as far as I could. My fingertips brushed something directly ahead. I risked inching forward on my elbows and toes, even though that took me closer to that awful laughter. If I was quick, I should be okay, as long as I went straight backwards.

My fingers found something long and smooth. It wasn't cold like stone or warm like a living creature. I ran my hands along it and recognised the feel of wood. Wood that was thicker at one end and tapered to a point at the other. Thank fuck for that. Breathless with relief, I grabbed it and retreated as fast as I could, shuffling on my knees.

As soon as I had the yew stake in my hands, everything changed. I was still in darkness, but this was a normal night. That ominous sense of emptiness around me shrank as my eyes adjusted. Now I was kneeling in the cramped entrance to the empty burial chambers. I could make out the solid wall of ancient stones ahead of me. This was no more than the well-known archaeological site that visitors came to look at and take their photos. All I could hear was the idle rustle of beech leaves in the night breeze.

Don't ask me how, but I knew it was safe to turn my back on the barrow's burial chambers now. I got to my feet and went out through the great sarsens, stepping over the low stone between them. The hamadryad was waiting. Her face was as unreadable as it had been before. I cupped my hand around the thick end of the yew stake and rested the length of wood against my shoulder. I held out my free hand to her. 'Let's go.'

Chapter Twenty-Five

I was right about Fin and Hazel. They hadn't stayed in the car. When the hamadryad landed me on the hillside by the hawthorns, I could see Fin was hard at work. Further down the slope, the black-and-yellow tape stretched out a lot further on both sides of the line that I'd started. At least five more netting stakes had been driven into the ground.

How fast had she driven to get here so quickly? How soon had she got the hang of probing the ground? How long had it taken me to retrieve the yew branch? It hadn't occurred to me to check the time on my phone before we left the beech hanger. Looking up, I saw the moon riding high in the sky. It hadn't even risen above the horizon when I'd arrived at the Smithy. Had it been visible when I'd left the barrow? I couldn't remember. I looked around to ask the hamadryad what was going on, but she had vanished.

I didn't bother seeing what time it was now. 'Fin!' I started walking down the hill.

She looked up, startled. She dropped the iron stake she'd been holding and scrambled up the slope to meet me.

'Oh, thank goodness.' She hugged me hard enough to hurt.

I didn't care. I was more concerned with not accidentally knocking her senseless if the heavy yew wood slipped off my shoulder. As I managed to lower the shaped branch to the ground, I realised we were alone. 'Where's Hazel?'

Fin let go of me and turned to look across the valley. 'We did wait, but when you didn't turn up, we realised we had no way to know how long you might be.'

The catch in her voice told me what she wasn't saying. She'd had no idea if they'd ever see me again.

'So Hazel took the car,' she went on determinedly, 'to see if she and her friends could rouse the Bockbourne Horse, to ward off the giant if it comes here to stop us.'

'Have you seen it? Either of them? The horse or the giant?'

'No.' Fin shook her head.

That was good news as far as it went, but there was no way of knowing what the giant had been doing while I was losing time under Wayland's Smithy. 'Have you seen any of the hamadryads?'

'No.' Fin looked down the slope to the line she'd been marking. 'We really should get on.'

'Right.' Picking up the yew wood, I followed her very carefully down the hill. We had the moonlight now, but the ground was still steep and uneven and the thorn bushes cast awkward shadows. I was especially wary of brambles lurking like trip wires. I'd had absolutely enough of falling down this bloody hillside today.

We reached the line of stakes. Fin picked up the one she had just dropped and handed it to me. She found another one for herself.

'I got a feel for what we're looking for from the ones you'd already done. I'm pretty sure this line is the top of the giant's head. If it came to it—' She walked away and began probing the ground a few metres beyond the end stake. She wasn't looking at me. 'We were going to see if driving one of these spikes into its eye would at least hold the giant temporarily.'

'Good thinking.' That was true. It was a good idea. I still felt sick at the thought of Fin desperately trying to force the iron into the ground, not knowing if that would keep the giant at bay or if it was going to turn up and grab her.

I gripped the metal rod in my hand. I hated the thought of Fin being out here alone. About as much as Fin had hated not knowing what had happened to me, I guessed, from the strain I could hear in her voice. She'd still got on with the job though, and she wasn't wasting time now.

I needed to do the same. There would be time to tell her what had happened to me later on. I headed for the other end of the line of tape, passing the first stake that I'd used to mark the hidden carving. It was hard to believe I'd only done that this afternoon.

Moonlight gleamed on steel as my boot knocked something hidden in the rough grass. I looked down and saw the sledgehammer laid across Fin's backpack that would be holding her phone, wallet and keys. I put the yew branch down beside it and saw that Fin had remembered to bring the enamel mug as well. She'd had no way to know if I would be coming back, but she'd made sure everything would be ready if I did.

Reaching the end of the tape, I resisted the temptation to pull up the newest stake, to test what was under the brambles, just enough to satisfy myself that Fin had really found the rubble-filled trench. We didn't have time to waste, and either I trusted her or I didn't. If I didn't, I was the one who deserved a smack around the head with a yew branch.

I began testing the next stretch of ground. All I could feel was solid chalk. Looking back down the tape, I tried to assess how much the line was curving. That was no use. The netting stakes were leaning at different angles and the tape zig-zagged from side to side.

It wasn't going to be long before we ran out of metal stakes. I wondered how much of the giant's carved head we would find by then. Did we dare risk doing any more, cutting extra markers like I'd planned to this afternoon? I wished I knew where the giant was. I wished I knew how much time we might have before something else dire happened. I really wished those sodding hamadryads hadn't fucked everything up in the first place.

I vented my frustration by slamming the iron rod into the ground. I didn't have any gloves on and the rough metal was harsh against my palm. Every impact jarred my cut arm as well as my other bruises, but I didn't care. I was so busy being pissed off with everything that I nearly missed the telltale shifting sensation as the metal slid through the soil and hit broken chalk underneath.

I told myself to stop being a wanker and concentrate on the job in hand. Making sure the stake was firmly planted, I hurried back to the middle of the line to fetch another length of iron. I met Fin coming back with the roll of black-and-yellow tape. She'd looped it around another point that she'd just marked. I saw that was quite a way further down the hill.

'Do you think you've found the side of its head?' I took the roll of tape as she offered it to me.

'I hope so.' She bent to pick up another netting stake. 'Have you—?'

She broke off and stood up, looking out across the valley again. 'What was that?'

'What was what?' I'd been looking down at my hands, untwisting the tape.

'I saw something – there!' Fin pointed.

This time I'd seen it too. The burst of light was painfully bright, even at this distance. 'That's where we saw the Bockbourne Horse carving, isn't it?'

'Yes,' Fin said after a moment. 'Above the beech woods on the far side of the village.'

She jumped as we saw another flash. 'Do you think that's something to do with Hazel?'

I didn't have an answer.

There was another flare of white light. This time we heard a distant crack. It echoed across the valley like the sound of a lightning strike, but there were no clouds overhead, or anything else that could explain it. We stood and waited, tense, but nothing else happened that we could see or hear.

'The hamadryad said the giant was tearing down their trees.' Fin bit her lip. 'It must be able to tell which beeches they're bonded to. Do you think that's what's happening over there?'

I reached down to pick up another netting stake. 'If they're in trouble or Hazel is, the only thing we can do to help them is getting this done as fast as we can.'

'Here, take this.' Fin unzipped her coat and reached around to the small of her back. She handed me the billhook she'd had shoved into the waistband of her jeans. 'I need to get a better idea of what we've found so far.'

'Wait a minute.' I closed my eyes and pictured the scene that the ancient yew trees had shown me. I did my best to work out where the bearded men had been digging out the pit when the carving had first stared out across the valley. I opened my eyes again. 'I'm pretty sure we need to find the giant's left eye. That's where the people who made this planned to bury their yew stake.'

'I think that's what I saw the people later on doing as well.' She looked around, scowling. 'I'm going to have to go up to the field.'

She didn't wait for me to agree that this hillside was lousy terrain for a swan wanting to get into the air. As she hurried away, I put the billhook into my own coat pocket. It wasn't very secure, so I kept a hand on it as I headed for the point Fin had just marked. I started probing the ground. If that was on the left side of the giant's head, then the more of that line we could find, the more that would help us pinpoint the monster's eye. A few minutes later, I heard the rhythmic rattle of a swan's wings above me. I looked up to see Fin flying over the hawthorns.

Her feathers were brilliant white in the moonlight. Turning in a wide arc, she flew across the hillside. As she drew level with me, she swooped low. A moment later, she made that fearsome hissing sound that tells anyone with half a brain to give swans all the space they want. I watched as she flew away. She flapped her wings and soared higher, before coming back around to make another pass. She wasn't fast. Swans can do a lot of things, but a swift one-eighty in mid-air isn't one of them. She hissed again just before she reached me.

Okay, I got the message. She was trying to tell me where to look. That still covered a fair amount of ground. Something else swans can't do is hover. She disappeared back over the hawthorns, and I went to see what I could find where I thought I was supposed to be looking.

As I tested the ground with the end of the rod, I heard a crash of something heavy hitting leafy branches further up the hill. Before I could go and see if some hamadryad had turned up to cause more trouble or to give us bad news, Fin reappeared.

'Where's a bloody pond when you need one?' She was rubbing her shoulder and scowling. 'I think you need to be a metre or so further down. A bit further in from the side of its head.'

I was glad she said that because I wasn't finding any hint of give in the ground where I was. I moved and tried again. I still didn't have any luck. Fin picked up a stake and joined me. We worked methodically across the slope, step by cautious step, and almost shoulder to shoulder.

A few minutes later I felt something shift as I shoved the iron rod through the undergrowth. At the same moment, Fin looked over at me.

'I've got it.'

'Same here.'

I forced the netting stake in deeper to make sure we wouldn't lose the spot and dropped to my knees. Taking the billhook out of my pocket and out of its leather sleeve, I used the sharp, curved blade to clear away tangled grass and brambles. Thorny tendrils snared my hand, drawing blood, but I didn't care. Once I could see the soil, I began digging with the broad tool. That was no way to treat the billhook, but we didn't have any other option. I was seriously annoyed with myself. I should have realised we'd need to dig.

Fin knelt down. 'We should have brought a trowel.'

'Or a shovel.' I thought of the entrenching tool I used to keep in my Land Rover. That would have been ideal.

Fin started scooping up loose earth and clumps of roots with her gloved hands. She tossed everything away into the shadows. 'How deep do we have to go?'

'Until we're sure.' I kept digging, careful not to smack Fin's knuckles as she carried on clearing away the debris. To my relief, the hooked tip of the blade soon dragged up lumps of broken chalk.

'Is this it, do you reckon?' I asked.

She brushed earth off her gloves. 'Should we try to find the edge? If it's curving in a circle, then we know we've got it.'

'Right.' I shuffled backwards on my knees, digging like some demented dog who'd forgotten where he'd buried a really good bone.

Fin shifted around so she could work at right angles to me. Now we could both see what I was uncovering in the moonlight. Just as I thought this job would be a hell of a lot easier if the chalk wasn't so dirty, Fin started picking out the loose pieces. That uncovered the cleaner layer below. It was nowhere near as bright as a properly tended and scoured chalk outline, but it was a whole lot better than nothing. We worked as quickly as we could. I soon felt a difference under the billhook's blade. Now the chalk stayed solidly obstinate when I scraped the layer of soil away.

'Hang on. Mind your hands.' I put the billhook down and got to my feet. I pulled up the iron stake and started smacking the pointed end down as hard as I could, hitting points a few inches apart. 'Can you hear that?'

I honestly wasn't sure if I was imagining the faint change in the sound as the metal struck the ground, but Fin nodded.

'Give me a minute.' Still on her knees, she picked up the billhook and began scraping the soil away.

I used the iron stake to help as best as I could. A few minutes later, Fin reached forward and grabbed the end. 'No, don't let go,' she said quickly.

I wasn't sure what she was doing, but I held on to the metal rod. Then I realised she was using it to gouge a line through the mess of soil and chalk we'd dug up.

'That's it. That's the edge of the eye.' She sat back on her heels. 'Near enough, anyway.'

I assessed the curve, estimating the eye's diameter. 'Then the centre's going to be about here.' I stabbed the iron stake in hard.

Fin scrambled to her feet. 'Let's get the yew wood.'

'Shit.' I'd just looked back across the valley.

'What is it?' Fin followed my gaze.

'Nothing good.' That was as much as I could say.

A shadow was moving through Bockbourne Magna. There was nothing to cast it though. No fearsome giant was stalking the streets. I guessed we should be thankful for that. Even so, there was plenty to worry about. The smear of darkness slid steadily across roofs and gardens, and it was snuffing lights as it went. Windows and street lamps went dark, and I couldn't see any sign of them coming back on. As the shadow crossed a road, it brushed against a passing car. The vehicle stopped dead. There was no sign of anyone opening a door. I hoped the engine and the electrics were all that had died.

The shadow was getting faster. Soon it would reach the edge of the village. We would have no way of knowing where it went after that. Not that we needed to see, given the unerring line it was following. It was heading straight for us. Fear chilled me to the bone.

Fuck that. If I'm on a site in the depths of winter, work's the best way to warm up. 'Come on!'

Fin didn't move. She was still staring at the streak of darkness cutting across Bockbourne Magna. She looked like a rabbit mesmerised by a weasel. I shook her shoulder. She jumped like someone startled awake and stared at me, wide-eyed.

'Come on!'

'Right.' Her voice cracked.

I grabbed her hand to reassure her, and we scrambled up the hill together. Fin found the enamel mug and the sledge-hammer. I picked up the yew stake. We half walked, half slid back down to the shallow pit that marked the carved giant's eye.

'Give me a minute.' Fin pulled up the iron stake and dropped to her knees. She snatched up the billhook and gouged out a small hollow where the metal rod had been.

I looked back across the valley. The shadow had left the village. It was hidden somewhere in the night, down where the curve of the hill meant we couldn't see the woods and fields. Over in Bockbourne Magna, there was no sign of the lights it had touched coming back on. I wondered if they ever would...

'Dan!' Fin's sharp voice snapped me out of – I could hardly call it a daydream. This was more like a waking nightmare.

'Give me the pointed end.' Fin reached up for the yew wood.

'Mind out of the way.' I resolutely turned my back on the valley and dropped the shaped branch into the little hollow she'd made. The weight did a bit of the work for us, burying the spike in the chalk rubble.

It didn't go very far. In the uncounted centuries since this carving had been made, soil and rain must have seeped between the lumps of soft stone. The infill might not be as solid as the untouched rock on either side, but it was pretty well glued together. Driving the yew wood through it was going to be a pig of a job...

'Dan! Get on with it!' Fin was kneeling, holding the stake upright, ready for me to hit it.

I hadn't seen her move. That couldn't be good. I really couldn't afford to let my thoughts wander. I took a deep breath and reached for the sledgehammer. I didn't just take hold of its handle. I gripped the steel head, and I instantly felt my own head clear. Now I saw that Fin had tucked the billhook under one knee, so she didn't lose it in the shadows. That touch of metal was obviously enough to keep her focused.

I grabbed the enamel mug and rammed it on the blunt end of the yew stake. I made sure my feet were solidly planted and tested the weight and balance of the sledgehammer. I focused on the white mug capping the yew branch. I couldn't afford to make a mistake. If I missed, the best we could hope for was Fin's arm or wrist getting broken. The worst didn't bear thinking about.

I swung the hammer. I hit the mug on the end of the stake square on. The wood sank into the ground a few centimetres. I didn't look at Fin. I couldn't risk any distractions. I swung again, putting all my weight and strength behind the blow. The stake sank a bit deeper. I hit it again, and this time the stake really moved. I couldn't tell if that was thanks to my skill at hammering fence posts or because something uncanny in the yew wood was forcing the chalk rubble apart.

A cold breeze brushed the back of my neck. Unease crawled down my spine. That breeze was coming up from the valley bottom. That wasn't right. Cold air rolls downhill. It didn't smell right either. At this time of year a gust of wind out here in the countryside should carry scents of leaf mould and recent rain, maybe the richness of freshly turned earth. This was a dry, dusty breath from some cavern deep underground.

I tried to ignore it. I went to make another swing with the sledgehammer. I pulled up short. I didn't trust myself.

'Back off,' I ordered Fin. 'Let go of it and move away. Let's see if it stays upright.'

To my relief, she did as I said. The yew wood wavered, but I slammed the capped end with the sledgehammer as fast as I could, now I didn't have to worry about hitting Fin. It wasn't the hardest strike I'd made, but it was enough to wedge the stake firmly in the ground. I hit it again, and again.

'Dan.' Fin sounded apprehensive. 'There's something...'

She was right. There was something coming up from the shadows at the bottom of the hill. I could hear feet crushing the undergrowth. Big feet, with a long stride. Fee fi fo fum... The giant wasn't coming up the hill fast, but it was definitely coming towards us.

I paused before taking another swing. 'Get the billhook, quick. Keep watch for me. As soon as it gets close, get the hell out of here. Before it gets close enough to grab you. To force me to stop.'

Hopefully, the monster would think twice about attacking her if it saw the gleam of the broad steel in her hand.

Fin didn't argue. She ducked quickly down to scoop up the billhook and stood up again. Looking down the hillside, she gripped the blade's handle. 'What are you going to do?'

'Get this done as fast as I can.' I focused all my attention on the yew wood. I concentrated on the feel of the hammer in my hands. I brought all my experience to the front of my mind.

Swing and hit. Swing and hit.

I timed my breathing to maximise each blow.

Swing and hit. Swing and hit.

The yew wood sank deeper into the ground.

Swing and hit. Swing and hit.

My shoulders were aching, along with my back and my thighs.

Swing and hit. Swing and hit.

I was having to bend my knees now, to follow every strike all the way through.

Swing and hit. Swing and hit.

Fin turned and ran. She scrambled up the slope on hands and knees, getting away as fast as she possibly could.

Swing and hit. Swing and hit.

I lost sight of her as I focused on the stake. Darkness and cold closed around me. The sound of harsh breathing filled my ears. Something stank like the world's worst bad breath.

Swing and hit. Swing and hit.

I could still see the yew wood. It was a pillar, golden as sunlight in these threatening shadows.

Swing and hit. Swing and hit.

The darkness was hiding the moon, but the sledgehammer's steel head shone bright silver.

Swing and hit. Swing and hit.

I had a job to do. I would do this until I couldn't do any more.

Swing and hit.

The rasp of labouring breath somewhere behind me stopped. The foul smell that surrounded me drifted away. The shadows thinned to leave only the faint shapes cast by the thorn bushes. Moonlight shone untroubled again.

I was standing alone on the hillside. There was a stub of yew wood sticking up from the ground. I tried to hit it with the sledgehammer again and missed completely. I fell to my knees and was barely able to stop myself falling face first into the dirt. My injured arm was agony.

'Dan?'

Fin was somewhere at the top of the slope. I took a deep breath. The shakes faded, though the pain in my arm didn't. I coughed and shouted back as loudly as I could.

'Yes?'

'Are you okay?'

'I will be when I finish this.' Still on my knees, I forced myself upright and swung the sledgehammer again. It only took a few strikes to drive the yew wood right down into the ground. By then, Fin was back at my side.

I dropped the hammer and began dragging bits of chalk and clods of earth back into the hollow. 'We need to cover this up. Hazel needs to tell whoever she spoke to there's nothing to find anywhere on this hill. The last thing we want is some nosy bastard having a dig around.'

'I'll get everything else together.' Fin went to collect the rest of the iron stakes and the tatters of black-and-yellow plastic hanging from them.

I wondered what had shredded the tape. I wondered how close it had come to shredding me. I decided it didn't matter.

We'd done what the Green Man had sent me here to do. Now we could go home.

Though that wasn't going to be the end of it. Not this time. I'd already decided that.

Chapter Twenty–Six

Fin's phone rang when we were halfway across the field, heading back to the gate where we'd parked the car. Not that the car was there.

'Is that Hazel?' I took the armful of iron stakes off Fin so she could slip her backpack off her shoulder.

'It's Eleanor.' Fin was surprised as she looked at the screen. She answered the call. 'Hi. Let me put you on speaker.'

'Is Dan there too? He's not picking up.' Eleanor didn't wait for an answer. Her voice was taut with urgency. 'I've just talked to Kalei. She says you won't be able to kill the giant in a fight, not with ordinary steel. But if the Green Man says it was bound before, Kalei says it can be bound again. You can do that with a yew stave. You need to look for a carving. That might be stone, or maybe it's wood—'

'We found it,' Fin interrupted. 'We've done it. We've bound it, or subdued it. Whatever, it's gone.'

'About ten minutes ago.' And hopefully that particular giant wouldn't be seen again for another few thousand years. I rested the heavy things I was carrying on the ground. It was that or drop everything.

'Oh.' Eleanor's surprise was loud enough to make the closest sheep look up. Surprise, and something else. Irritation?

'Thanks anyway,' I told her. 'Seriously, I mean it. We were having no luck here at all until a few hours ago. That could have literally been a life-saver. Tell Kalei I'm grateful regardless.'

'Okay.' Eleanor sounded a bit happier. 'If you're sure you want to owe her one. You know she'll turn up to collect.'

I nodded, even though she couldn't see me. 'I'll risk it.'

'Fair enough. You sound shattered,' Eleanor commented.

'You have no idea. I'm definitely having a lie-in tomorrow. How are things at your end?' I felt guilty as I realised I hadn't given Blithehurst's problems a thought for days.

'That's a tale and a half. Short version? I think we're going to be okay.'

I was relieved as well as surprised to hear the amusement in Eleanor's voice. But I wasn't up to standing here in the cold listening to some convoluted story.

'Can I call you tomorrow?'

'Of course. Whenever you're ready.' Eleanor ended the call.

Fin looked at me. 'Why do you want the naiad to think you're in her debt?'

Before I could reply, her phone rang again.

Fin looked at the screen. 'This is Hazel.' She answered it.

'Are you okay?' Hazel's voice was hoarse and anxious.

'We are, both of us. We're pretty sure we've bound the giant. How about you?'

We waited for Hazel to speak. That was a long moment of silence broken only by murmuring sheep.

'We're fine.' Hazel sounded a bit steadier.

We waited for her to say something else. When she didn't, Fin shrugged.

'Are you coming to get us?'

'Right, yes, of course,' Hazel said hastily.

'We'll be waiting by the field gate.' This time Fin ended the call. 'Do you suppose she's going to tell us what happened?'

'She will if I've got anything to say about it.' I gathered up the sledgehammer and the netting stakes.

'Let me have those back.' Fin put her phone away and slung her backpack onto her shoulder.

We split everything we had to carry between us and walked the rest of the way to the gate. Thankfully, we didn't have long to wait before Hazel arrived in the Toyota. She got out and offered Fin the keys. 'Can you take me back to the village?'

'Of course.' Fin opened the hatchback and we dropped everything into the boot.

No one spoke as we drove back to Bockbourne Parva. I waited until Fin pulled up outside the thatched cottage in the lane.

'We need to talk.' I twisted around in the front seat to look at Hazel.

She had already unclipped her seat belt. To my relief, she leaned back instead of reaching for the door release.

'There's not a lot to tell,' she said. 'The giant was in the beech woods on the other side of the river. It was killing the hamadryads by smashing down their trees. Crude but effective. We were able to summon the horse to drive it off. That was quite some fight. Then we saw the shadow was heading for you.' Weary, she rubbed a hand across her face. 'I'm really sorry we weren't able to keep it away, but there was nothing we could do.'

'Thanks, but that's not what I meant.' Though I wished I'd seen the horse fight the giant. 'We need to talk about a whole lot more than just what's happened tonight.'

I waved a hand at the cottage. The lights were on inside, upstairs and down. We could all see the flicker of movement behind the blinds at the windows.

'We don't necessarily need to meet your people – I understand everyone needs their privacy if we're going to stay safe – but we need to know what you know. You need to know what we can tell you. We all need to know a whole lot more about whatever we might find ourselves facing. That means getting the dryads and naiads, and whoever else any of us can make contact with, to tell us what they know before the shit hits the fan.'

Hazel looked dubious. 'I think—'

I spoke over her. I could see she didn't like it, but I was too knackered to be polite.

'We just had a phone call from Eleanor Beauchene. This evening a naiad told her what we needed to know about fighting that sodding giant. If we'd known any of it a week ago, think what we could have done different. How many hamadryads would still be alive, for a start?'

I nodded at Fin. 'Her family have their own contacts. You don't need to meet them either, but I'll bet they know things that could explain some of the sightings that people ask about on your website. Come to that, you could well be getting early warnings of trouble that we could put the brakes on, if you gave us a heads up and we asked around. We need to start working together, or at the very least, keeping in touch. Then we might be able to deal with threats like this giant before the Green Man or anyone else has to get involved.'

Hazel wasn't looking irritated now. 'That's certainly worth considering.'

'Talk to your friends.' I gestured towards the cottage. 'Please.'

'We can set up a group video call online,' Fin suggested. 'In a few days' time?'

Hazel had opened the car door, but she paused before getting out. 'That sounds like a good idea.'

I wondered if she was talking to me or to Fin. We watched her go through the cottage garden gate. Fin turned the key in the ignition.

'What do you think Eleanor Beauchene will say about this new idea of yours?'

'I've no idea,' I admitted. 'I hope she'll be okay with it.'

I waited for Fin to tell me what she thought. Perhaps I should have talked it through with her first.

'I wonder what's happened to help the situation at Blithehurst.' She leaned forward to get the best possible view at the junction.

'I'll need you to drive me back. If you can stay overnight, I'm sure you'll hear all about it. Unless you're too busy,' I added hastily. 'There must be trains.'

'I think I can find the time.' Fin took the quickest route around the village green. 'Do you want to make a stop on the way, and talk to Sineya at Brightwell? See what she reckons to your new network?'

That hadn't occurred to me. 'I don't know. It might be best to talk to Frai first. Dryads can be touchy.'

Fin nodded. 'Fair enough.'

Speaking of touchy, I wondered how Blanche would react to this proposal. 'Do you think your mum will agree to get involved?' I asked instead.

Fin's sideways glance told me she knew exactly what I wasn't saying. 'Not unless everyone else in the family does. Don't say anything when we get in. I'll need to pick the right moment, and work out the best way to approach it.'

I nodded. 'I won't say a word.'

At least I knew Fin was on my side.

We drove back to Cainescombe without saying much else. We left everything in the back of the car and went into the flat to shower as quietly as we possibly could. A couple of the butterfly strips on my arm had given way, but the injury didn't look as bad as I'd expected when we swapped the bloody dressing for a fresh one. It was still hellishly sore, and every inch of me ached.

Fin found a couple of pairs of tweezers, and we helped each other pick the broken tips of bramble thorns out of our assorted scrapes and grazes. After that, neither of us was in the mood for anything more energetic or erotic than cuddling up together. I was just about falling asleep when Fin got up to turn her alarm off. We were both spark out within minutes after that.

Fin set up that video call she'd suggested a couple of weeks later. She was over in the Fens by then. She'd gone to talk to her mother, aunts and cousins in person, to convince them this plan for sharing what we knew was a good idea. It had taken her a lot of country walks and conversations, but she managed it. Once everyone else had agreed to it, Blanche had no choice but to go along with the plan.

I was back at Blithehurst, sitting on the sofa with my laptop in the manor house library. Eleanor was back in Durham in the house she shared up there. Before she'd gone, when Fin had taken me back and stayed for the weekend, the three of us had discussed my idea. Eleanor was all in favour, and pointed out she had access to obscure books in libraries that might well help people like Hazel.

She had also told us what had happened while I was away fighting the giant. An unexpected treasure hunt had turned up some family silver that could be sold off to save the business if the worse came to the worst. She was right. It was a hell of a story.

I finished telling Fin about the estimate from the auction house while we waited for Eleanor and Hazel to join the call.

'That must be a relief,' Fin said. 'So anyway, what have the dryads said about sharing what they know?'

'After a lot of arguing, they agreed it was probably in their own interests to find out what other people know about things that might be a threat to them.' I grinned. 'Asca told me I should visit Brightwell and tell Sineya what was going on. I didn't even have to suggest it. Well, I say "told". She as good as ordered me to go down there as soon as I can.'

'Stop off on your way, next time you're able to head here for visit.' Fin smiled. 'How about your mum?'

'Convincing her was a piece of piss. If anything, she seemed surprised that I hadn't thought of this before.' I wasn't smiling any more though. 'My dad's the one who really isn't happy. He says he's just about okay with the Green Man sending me places to do things. After all, it's not as if I can avoid that. The Green Man doesn't exactly give me a choice. What Dad doesn't like is the idea of me looking for trouble. That's what he thinks this is.'

I wished I'd been able to talk to him in person, instead of over the phone. 'I'm trying to convince him I'll be safer if we can get in as early as possible, when we see there's going to be trouble whether we like it or not. That's got to be better than playing catch-up, like we were doing with the giant.'

I thought I was making progress, but I wasn't sure.

'I'll try to think how to make him feel happier about it. I'll talk to my mum. She might have some ideas.' Fin's hand came towards the camera as she gestured. 'Is your arm still bothering you? You keep rubbing it.'

'What?' I hadn't even realised I was doing that. 'No, it just itches a bit.'

I was more bothered by the realisation that I was going to be left with some nasty scars where the hamadryad had clawed me. That had never happened to me before. I normally healed fast, and none of my other cuts or bruises had ever left a mark. I didn't want to talk about it though. That could wait until we saw each other again.

Thankfully Fin had moved on. 'Have you seen Kalei?'

'Not yet. Soon, hopefully. She has a debt to collect, after all.'

I'd told Asca and Frai I needed the naiad to share whatever her people knew if I was going to put an end to trouble as soon as some menacing creature tried to start it.

I hadn't told the dryads everything I was thinking. Eleanor had said Kalei told her that ordinary steel couldn't kill a giant. I remembered those folk tales where there were definitely weapons that could. I'd been asking myself how both those things could be true, and something interesting had occurred to me.

According to Monty Python, strange women in ponds distributing swords might be no basis for a system of government, but I reckoned one of those blades might come in handy if I ever faced a giant or a wyrm again. I wanted to ask Kalei if she knew a naiad who was looking after anything like that. If I could get hold of it without getting arrested for looting some historic artefact, or possessing an offensive weapon.

I was trying to work out how to explain what I was thinking to Fin when the laptop's speakers chimed. Eleanor and Hazel were ready to join the call.

Hazel appeared sitting at a table. She wasn't alone. Two women flanked her. One looked at me and grinned.

Hazel had a gleam in her eye. 'We're in, along with at least six more of us. The others will need a bit of persuading, but I reckon they'll come around.'

Eleanor had heard what she'd said. 'Then let's start making plans.'

We talked for over an hour. When we finally logged off, I looked up at the library's ancient, ornate ceiling, decorated with leaves, fruit and flowers, and creatures that most people would call imaginary.

Those medieval craftsmen had carved a Green Man's face made out of oak leaves for each corner of the room. I looked at them in turn. In the south-west corner, I saw an emerald gleam of approval shining bright in the Green Man's eyes. He was smiling at me. I guessed I'd done what he wanted.

Luck Is Where You Find It

Daniel Mackmain is a man of few words. If you're using one of those American dictionaries that insist on pictures, he'd make a very good illustration for 'strong and silent type'. So when I saw that he was ringing me, even at the end of a very long day when I was debating with myself whether to have a cup of tea or a glass of wine, I was happy to take his call.

Well, not happy, exactly. Who could say that, with autumn deepening in this strange and unpleasant year, with a frightening virus loose and the way ahead still so uncertain? But I knew Dan must have a good reason for ringing, and equally important, he would get straight to the point.

That said, I really hoped there wasn't some crisis at Blithehurst. I didn't need any more headaches thinking about the old house just at the moment. But no, I decided. If anything was seriously wrong, Dan would have texted the details, or left a voicemail, in case I was still working with my mobile switched off. He'd want to make sure I'd get the news, along with an update on whatever he was already doing about it, as soon as I turned my phone back on.

As a caretaker for the Tudor manor house that's at the heart of my family's history and property, we couldn't ask for a better man. My father has often said so, adding how incredibly lucky we had been. Dan is certainly better suited to working on the Blithehurst estate than Dad could possibly know, and luck's had very little to do with that.

I tapped the phone's screen to answer Dan's call. 'Hello. How's things with you?'

'Are you on your own at the moment?'

'Yes, and there's no one else in the house.' I normally share my home in Durham with a couple of other postgraduates, but Emma had moved in with her boyfriend for the first lockdown and stayed on, while Amy had gone back to stay with her parents. I didn't bother explaining any of that. Dan doesn't really go in for small talk.

But him asking that question told me something odd was happening. One of the things that makes Dan so well suited to life at Blithehurst is he can see the dryads who've tended the trees there for centuries, as well as the boggarts and sprites and other uncanny things that turn up from time to time. I can see them as well, thanks to a dryad who gave one of my ancestors a son, though at the moment, I'm the only one of my family who has that dubious gift. As you can imagine, this can lead to conversations you don't really want anyone else overhearing, because people will think you're nuts.

Even so, even knowing there's a whole world of mythical beings living unseen alongside us, I wasn't expecting Dan to tell me his girlfriend had seen a giant down in Wiltshire. More than that, apparently the Green Man expected Dan to sort it out.

'The thing is,' he said finally, 'at the very least I need to go and see what's down there. That means being away for a night, maybe longer.'

I needed a moment to think this through. 'Well, that's not what I expected to be talking to you about today.'

'What's the matter?'

I could hear Dan's concern. Well, he had to find out sooner or later.

'I was going to give you a ring this evening,' I admitted. 'I need to call a family meeting. The Blithehurst Trust needs to make some decisions.'

That's what I'd been putting off, standing in the kitchen, looking at the kettle and the bottle of red wine that still held a glass and a half. Now I had no excuses.

'I'll make a few calls to set things up this evening, and then I'll come down tomorrow,' I said briskly. 'You can set off any time you like.'

'Thanks. I'll let you know how we get on.'

'Good luck. Be careful.' One thing I'd learned since Dan came to Blithehurst was the unseen world can be lethally dangerous. We'd buried my brother Robbie the year before last, after what everyone else thought was a freak accident. Dan and I knew better.

'I will be,' he assured me.

'I'll talk to you soon.' I ended the call, put down my phone and opened the wine.

After taking a long swallow of red, I rang my sister Sophie in Manchester, and then my brother Ben in London. I kept the calls short as I explained the accountants had been in touch first thing this morning. The end of September just gone was the end of the financial year's second quarter and Blithehurst's numbers weren't looking good, even with everything we'd done to furlough staff and access other government support. That hardly came as any surprise. They both knew that although the garden centre and cafe had reopened over the summer, the manor house itself was still closed to visitors, and that was what brought in most of the revenue.

We agreed we'd set up a Skype call on Saturday afternoon. I rang Mum and Dad and told them I'd be driving down tomorrow and I'd come to see them the day after, so we could talk to Sophie and Ben online. They didn't need me to explain the details when I said I'd heard from the accountants. My parents might be retired, but they'd run Blithehurst and the other family businesses for long enough between them.

I resisted the temptation to open another bottle of wine, and had an early night.

I had a few things to sort out the next morning, and then I got on the road. There wasn't too much traffic, even on the stretches around Leeds and Manchester which can so often be a pain, especially on a Friday. All the same, I was glad when I was finally able to get off the motorways and take the country roads to Blithehurst. Staffordshire was looking lovely as the trees turned to copper, gold and bronze.

I headed for the back gate to the estate, which I found Dan had left securely padlocked. Going in that way and parking in the old dairy yard meant I could avoid a conversation with Janice, who manages the cafe. She had taken to ringing me up at least once a week to discuss the most trivial things. She never quite got up the courage to ask what we both knew she really wanted to know. How secure was her job? What were the prospects for the rest of the staff, whether they were on short time at the moment or out on furlough? She might as well have tried asking me how long was the proverbial piece of string. Well, with luck I'd have some interim answers for her after Saturday. I'd try to avoid her until then.

I carried my overnight bag down to the manor house and went in through the side door. We'd always used that instead of the grand entrance when this had been our family home instead of a tourist attraction. As I'd expected, Dan had set the alarm before he left, and the beep warned me to enter the code.

As I did that and walked through the ground floor and up to my room, the usual mix of emotions I felt every time I came back here swirled around me. Whenever I was alone in the house, it felt familiar and safe, the way it had when I was a kid, and I liked that. On the other hand, even under dust sheets, the furniture was in stiff, formal arrangements with selected antiques on display when the house was open. It had never been like that when we lived here. Other, far more important things would never be the same. There's one reason in particular – okay, it's the main reason – why I spend so much of my time in Durham.

I opened the door to the upstairs sitting room with bedroom and bathroom attached. This had been my private retreat when I'd lived and worked here full time. I looked out through the window towards the wooded pasture on the other side of the river. That's where the dryads live. I still wondered if Robbie would be alive if they'd told me more about the threat Dan Mackmain and I had defeated here. If they had warned us sooner. There's no way to know. Much as I'd loved Robbie, sometimes my brother could be his own worst enemy. Even so, I'm not sure if I can ever forgive the dryads.

I dropped my overnight bag on the floor by the table and went back downstairs to make myself a coffee. In the small, modern kitchen off the manor's historical showpiece, I found Dan had left me with an unopened pint of milk, eggs and bacon in the fridge and a new loaf in the bread crock. I swear that man lives on fry-ups. It's a good thing his work as the estate's resident carpenter and woodsman keeps him so active.

That reminded me of something else as I sipped my coffee. Dan's been living here in the main house since the manor was closed to visitors, to reassure the insurance company and deter anyone thinking of robbing the place. We'd agreed he'd make regular patrols. If he wasn't here, making those evening checks was down to me. Since I have nowhere near Dan's height and heft, I decided I'd do that before the day got much darker. I'd also leave some lights on, so anyone watching wouldn't think I was here on my own.

I finished my coffee and left my mug in the sink. There was an old pair of my boots and a spare fleece with the

Blithehurst logo in the staff coat room. As I got ready to go out, I wondered if I would ever see this room bustling again, with our friendly employees and lovely volunteers getting ready for a day's work.

I took a deep breath and told myself not to be a silly cow. It was my responsibility to make sure that Blithehurst reopened. There were ways to address the accountants' concerns. As a family, we Beauchenes would discuss the options, and I'd abide by the family's decision, even if it wasn't the solution I would choose. Meantime, I needed to walk around the house and make sure everything was secure. I opened the cupboard in the old, battered dresser and took out the biggest, heaviest torch I could find.

Once I got outside, I found the sky was still lighter than I'd realised. I was able to do a full circuit of the house and outbuildings without needing to switch on the torch. When I turned the final corner, though, I saw someone standing by the side of the house. The dusk was dark enough that I couldn't quite make out who was there on the gravel by the door.

'Hello?' I called out, not hostile but certainly not welcoming. 'Excuse me, but this is private property and the house is closed to visitors.'

Dan had told me he'd had problems with customers for the garden centre assuming they could wander around the grounds as well, despite the signs clearly saying 'No Admittance Beyond This Point'. Well, not problems exactly. When someone six foot four and muscled like Dan tells you to leave, people get the message pretty quickly.

I walked a bit closer, with the torch in one hand and my phone in the other, inside the pocket of my fleece. Whoever it was heard my boots on the gravel and turned around. I saw that it was Frai.

'Hello.' I couldn't hide my surprise. I couldn't recall ever seeing the old dryad this close to the house. I'd only seen her on this side of the river a handful of times. Though that didn't mean she hadn't been over here more often than that. Dryads can stay invisible even from the likes of me and Dan when they want to.

'Eleanor.' Frai nodded. That was as much of a greeting as I was going to get. 'Is he here?'

She doesn't go in for small talk either, and she sees no need to appear as a human when there's no one else around to see. Swathed in a flowing wrap, she looked as if she'd just strolled off a Greek vase in some museum. If she'd been human, you might have thought she was in her eighties. She's more than ten times as old as that.

'No. He's gone to look for a giant.' I looked at her warily.

Frai's the oldest of the dryads, and while I don't know exactly how old she is, she was here when my ancestor Sir Graelent de Beauchene was granted this manor and its lands by William the Conqueror. She's also the hardest to deal with, as far as I am concerned. Not only as far as I am concerned. Two dryads have left these ancient woods to live elsewhere that I know of. I don't know exactly why they went away, but my guess is Frai tried to run their lives as mercilessly as she tries to run mine.

It was hard to tell what she was thinking. A dryad's eyes are a single colour without white or pupil. People like me and Dan can see that even when they're masquerading as human. That doesn't make their expressions any easier to read.

She shrugged. 'Tell him I have asked Kalei if she knows how to defeat such an enemy. She does not, but she will try to find out.'

'I'll let him know.' I wondered when the naiad had passed through, and why. That seemed an unlikely coincidence, given how rarely we saw the river spirit here.

Frai nodded and turned to leave. Then she turned back. 'Why have you come home?'

One of the most inconvenient things about dryads is they can always tell if you're lying. At the moment, though, I had no problem telling Frai the truth. Let her worry about the future as much as me for a change. How would she like it if we ended up with no other option but handing the manor over to the National Trust?

'We're not sure how we'll find the money we'll need to keep the house and the grounds in the family. You must know it's been a very bad year for us.'

I half expected her to say something about enjoying the peace and quiet. Frai's always been quick enough to complain about anything and everything that we've done to keep Blithehurst up to date, to maintain footfall and visitor numbers.

Instead, she looked at me thoughtfully. 'A bad year for all mortals, I would say.'

Before I could ask what she meant by that, she vanished into thin air. Bloody typical.

I went into the house, locked up and closed the ground-floor shutters on all the windows. I had bacon sandwiches for supper. Sometimes comfort food is just what you need. I texted Dan to say thanks for stocking the fridge and told him what Frai had said.

Then I had the worst night's sleep I could remember for years.

I spent Saturday morning in the library with my laptop, going over everything the accountants had sent. It's my favourite room in the house, and the one that's still the same as it was when I was a kid. There are two deep bay windows facing south and looking out over the gardens. Each one has a vast antique writing desk that's surprisingly comfortable to work at, with high-backed leather chairs. For more relaxed reading, there are sofas and armchairs around a low table that's just right for keeping coffee within easy reach.

The walls are lined with bookshelves, and yes, I have probably read – or at least looked at – all of the books. I bought a fair few of them myself, to add to the collection of folklore started by my several-greats uncle Harold. As far as I can work out from his diaries, he was one of the few in the family before me who could see the dryads. Since he came back from the Western Front with PTSD, that really didn't help him regain his mental equilibrium. He drowned himself in 1918.

When I was satisfied with my summary of what we needed to discuss, I emailed that to Soph, Ben, Mum and Dad. Then I leaned back in the leather desk chair and looked up at the library ceiling. I'd spent hours gazing up at the carved panels as a child, identifying the flowers, fruit and leaves, and picking out the artfully hidden faces of woodland and fairy tale creatures.

These panels are even older than the rest of the house. Sir Graelent built himself a fortified Norman manor down in the valley, complete with a moat and a turreted gatehouse. That's where the family lived until the Beauchenes, who got rich from the dissolution of the monasteries, decided to build themselves this smart new residence further up the slope. They salvaged these carved panels from the original medieval chapel though, and family records make it clear this new library was used for Catholic services when such worship wasn't officially allowed elsewhere.

I looked at the corners of the room. There's a Green Man's face made from carved oak leaves up in each one. Dan says he's seen emerald light flicker in their eyes, to let him know when the Green Man's around. I couldn't see anything today. I hoped that meant the Green Man was busy keeping an eye on Dan down in Wiltshire.

After lunch, I headed over to the Dower House, where Mum and Dad live now, though the land between there and the manor doesn't all belong to the family trust these days. Beauchene fortunes have risen and fallen over the centuries and decades, and thinking about that as I drove was grimly reassuring. Somehow or other, we've always found a way to survive, even if that's meant selling off land in the bad times and setting up new ventures once things improve. Ventures like opening up the house to visitors when Grandpa handed the reins over to Dad.

Mum had her laptop set up in the drawing room, where we could all comfortably see the screen. Dad sorted out a pot of tea while Ben and Soph were dialling in, and then we got down to work. It was a long afternoon, but by the end of it, we were all clear on the situation, and everyone had agreed to their income from the trust being cut back. Mostly, we were just relieved that things weren't as bad as they could be.

Dire as the overall economic situation might be, people still need to eat, so the various farming enterprises were doing okay. Not great, but okay. With everything we had already done, and a few new measures I proposed, the cafe and garden centre should just about cling on, as long as life returned to something like normal by next summer. Janice would be glad to hear that, though I didn't think that would stop her worrying, and I could hardly blame her.

The big question was the manor house, where money would keep going out and nothing was coming in. The Christmas Markets before the bloody virus first appeared had been very profitable, so we had started out with a decent contingency fund in the bank, but that wouldn't last forever. Daniel had done a lot of work turning the estate woodlands into a resource that would contribute to the bottom line, from setting up Christmas tree plantations to coppicing hazels and using estate timber to supply the garden centre, and more besides. The thing was, though, nothing that involves trees happens fast. Dan's projects were well on track, but it would be at least a couple of years before we saw a decent level of return.

In normal times, that wouldn't be an issue, but there was nothing normal about this year. We had no idea when anything like normal would return, or what it would look like when it did. In all likelihood, we would have to find a sizeable sum of money from somewhere when the contingency fund ran out.

I suggested the obvious solution, to save anyone else from having to bring it up. 'We need to consider selling the Durham house. That'll give us a useful lump sum to use wherever it's needed. I'll have finished my PhD in a year or so, and I can always rent somewhere up there instead.'

'It's an idea.' Ben looked so guilty I could tell he'd definitely already thought of that option.

'Let's see where things stand at the end of next quarter, maybe even wait out the full year. Heading into winter is hardly the best time to put a house on the market,' Sophie pointed out.

'True, but it'll take time to sell, whenever we decide,' Ben countered.

I let them debate the pros and cons. Sophie's a solicitor and Ben's an architect, so they both know more about this stuff than me. At least their jobs are as secure as anyone's might be these days. However bad the economy gets, death, debt and divorce will keep solicitors in work, and Ben had mentioned earlier that his firm were taking the initiative by designing projects to repurpose office blocks that weren't going to be needed.

Mum got up and fetched a ginger cake from the kitchen. It was Grandma's recipe, and my particular favourite. So she and Dad had seen this coming too. That was hardly a surprise, and I could hardly complain. Not many students have families who are able to buy a house for them to live in instead of spending a fortune renting somewhere. Then they'd agreed that the family trust would keep the house and rent it out after I graduated, while in theory I was debating whether or not to do a doctorate, spending a few years managing Blithehurst in the meantime.

Of course, what none of my family knew was that the dryads had threatened to make my life hell if I left again, and believe me, Frai can and will inflict serious bad luck on anyone who gets on her wrong side. But then Dan turned up, and as long as the dryads had someone to boss about who was able see them, they had agreed to let me go back to my studies.

The family meeting wrapped up with us agreeing to review the situation in three months. So all told, it was a productive afternoon. Then Mum suggested I stayed for some supper, and the three of us caught up on the rest of the family's news and talked about good books we'd read and TV that we'd seen.

That didn't mean I wasn't thoroughly fed up by the time I got back to Blithehurst. I like my little house in Durham, and I like the life I have there, researching the English Civil War for my thesis. I didn't want to give any of that up.

Not for the first time, I asked myself why I hadn't struck out on my own like Sophie and Ben, making a life away from Blithehurst. Of course, the answer to that was obvious. The dryads would never have let me do it. But that had never seemed so much of a burden when Robbie had still been alive and he and I had run the family businesses between us.

I made myself some cheese on toast, opened a bottle of wine and took everything into the library to curl up on a sofa and sulk while I half-watched some forgettable thriller on Netflix. I had finished eating and was on my second glass of red when I realised that someone was watching me.

This is going to sound odd, when you know I can see dryads, naiads and boggarts, but I've never believed in ghosts. Oh, there are ghost stories at Blithehurst. How could there not be? A weeping Elizabethan lady is supposed to walk in the long gallery of the Tudor house, while a stalwart medieval man at arms allegedly stands watch on the gatehouse's tower down in the valley.

Right, and there's no mention of either spook in any of the family diaries or papers before the mid-1850s. Instead, I found clear hints in a couple of letters that one of my more creative ancestors invented them both to liven up a rather dull house party. Of course, we don't tell the visitors that when they turn to their guide, wide-eyed, saying a place this old must surely be haunted? When I'm leading a tour I tell those stories like the other guides, though I won't tell lies. I always say I've never seen a hint of an apparition.

I was seeing one now. He was leaning against the wall by the door, and he was translucent enough for me to see the spines of the books on the shelves behind him. He was no medieval man at arms, but his clothes could be Elizabethan, or certainly Tudor. I'm not one of those TV drama historians who can instantly identify and explain an artefact from any era, but you don't grow up in a house with a collection of old portraits without getting a reasonable grasp of period costume.

He wasn't wearing the smart and expensive clothes that my ancestors had chosen to make a statement when they were painted. 'Workmanlike' was the word that came to mind. His shirt cuffs were rolled up to his elbows, under a dark sleeveless tunic that buttoned down the front. Dark blue? Dark brown? I couldn't say. I realised I couldn't see any distinct colour, just lighter and darker shades. His loose breeches were tied at the knee to hold his stockings up and his leather shoes were laced rather than fastened with fancy buckles. His receding hair was tied back, and his greyish beard was as neat and tidy as the rest of his appearance. His smile as he looked at me was reassuring. That was nice of him, but I still found seeing an honest-to-goodness ghost extremely unnerving.

Before I could decide what to do or say, a whole load of other ghosts appeared. Though maybe 'ghosts' isn't the right word. Figures came and went, but they were no more than glimpses and shadows of men and women hurrying to and fro. That was still enough to show me there was some commotion as they walked through the modern furniture as though it wasn't even there – which, of course, it hadn't been.

As far as I could tell, as far as they were concerned, there had only been a table in the library, draped with an embroidered cloth. In the instant I thought that, it became much clearer. For a moment, the table almost looked solid. Solid enough for me to see a silver crucifix flanked by two candlesticks, together with a chalice, a paten and a ciborium – which is to say, for non-churchgoers, the cup and plate used for Holy Communion and the silver box for holding consecrated wafers. So these flickering figures must be my defiantly Catholic ancestors, and by the look of things, they'd been warned that someone was coming to catch them holding Mass. We had records of several such pursuivant raids.

A tall young man solidified like a blur through binoculars coming into focus as he snuffed the candles between finger and thumb. Tossing the candles to a nearby shadow, he wrapped the silver from the altar up in the embroidered cloth. Then he put everything in a wooden box and clutched that to his chest as he hurried out of the library. I put down my wine and hurried after him.

He was heading for the stairs. He passed straight through the wooden partition that had separated the later dining room and sitting room when the original Great Hall was divided. I followed through the closest arch. I had an idea where he was going now.

Other indistinct figures were milling around. The whole household must have been attending Mass, and perhaps a few other rebellious locals. Then everyone stopped and stood still. Shadowy heads turned towards the front door. There wasn't a sound, but the rhythmic shock that rippled through the gathering told me someone was hammering on the iron-studded oak. Even though I knew this was all an illusion, a shiver of fear ran down my spine.

The young man thrust the wooden box into a maidservant's arms. As soon as he did that, she solidified while he started fading from view. The last I saw of him, he was heading for the fireplace. I turned to go after the maid.

She ran past the kitchen door and took the servants' stairs down to the cellars. I opened the modern door that was in my way and followed, switching on the light as I went so I wouldn't trip and break my neck in the darkness. The electric bulbs made the girl much harder to see, so I didn't hit the switch at the bottom. There was just enough light from the stairwell for me to see her running away down the cellar corridor that's flanked by the cluttered rooms we use for storage these days. She ran to the far wall, paused to do something I couldn't make out. Then she walked straight through the bricks.

Well, that answered one long-standing question about Blithehurst. Family lore has always said there was a secret escape route out of these cellars, most likely built at the same time as the priest hole accessed by the door concealed in the panelling by the fireplace. That's where the tall young priest must be hiding now – or rather, had been hidden back then. That sanctuary had done its job. There were no records of priests being caught here, despite those raids.

Whatever. What had happened to the maidservant? We had never known where this tunnel was exactly, though it supposedly led all the way down to the medieval manor, or so a couple of stories claimed. I walked slowly back up the stairs and wondered if this had been the raid that persuaded my ancestors that using the library could be too dangerous. At some point, they had built a secret chapel upstairs, with its own tightly twisted staircase leading down to the cellars and that underground escape route that someone had evidently bricked up later.

As I reached the house's ground floor, I found the ghost standing by the library doorway. The first ghost, the one who had been watching me. All the other apparitions had vanished. The workmanlike ghost smiled at me again.

'Did you make the priest hole?' I asked him. 'And the hidden stair?'

I knew there had been at least one famous carpenter and joiner who had travelled between Catholic households doing that kind of work. He was famous because unfortunately he had been caught, and since under Elizabeth Tudor and James I and VI helping to hide Catholic priests was high treason, Nicholas Owen had been tortured and executed, or martyred and sainted if you prefer.

This ghost looked far too cheerful to have suffered such a fate. He was also looking at me expectantly. I wished I knew what he wanted from me.

I shook my head. 'I'm sorry. I don't understand.'

He turned and walked through the library door. I opened it and followed him. Ignoring the modern furniture, he went over to the windows. As he passed the spot where the table had stood, the phantom of the silver-laden altar briefly reappeared. The ghost gestured towards the glittering array and turned to point an emphatic finger towards the valley bottom. He did all that again, not just once but twice. I remembered the old saying: three times is the charm. Then he looked at me expectantly.

'Are you telling me,' I said carefully, 'that the altar silver is still hidden somewhere in the medieval manor?'

His smile widened to a triumphant grin, and then he vanished.

I sat down on the closest sofa. What on earth was I supposed to do with this information? Why on earth had the ghost turned up just now to let me know where to find some hidden treasure? I looked at my laptop. I'd been in here working on those figures from the accountants, making notes and rough calculations on a pad of paper to get my thoughts in order. And yes, I had vented my exasperation aloud a couple of times.

If dryads could observe us mortals unseen, could ghosts do the same? That was a creepy thought. I forced myself to set that aside and focus on the issue at hand.

If the ghost had been watching me, and as a carpenter, he could presumably do maths, perhaps he thought selling off some family silver might be the only way to save Blithehurst. If he had been hanging around since the sixteenth century, he must know there wasn't much of that left, after a couple of my more dissolute ancestors had been forced to give up such assets to settle their debts. We still had some nice Georgian pieces, but the choicest items recorded in wills and inventories were long gone.

I reached for my laptop and went online. I had absolutely no idea what Elizabethan church silverware might be worth. Dad still takes charge of getting the updated valuations for the house's various antiques and paintings. Thankfully we don't have anything that's simply too valuable for us to insure. I ran a search and clicked on a few links.

How much?!

I stared at the screen. That couldn't possibly be right. I ran a different search and looked at some other specialist websites. By the time I was finished doing that, my hands were shaking. It looked as if the candlesticks and chalice on their own could be worth at least half the current price of my house in Durham. Who knew what the whole matching altar set might fetch at auction?

Seriously?

I took a deep breath and closed my laptop. I absolutely needed to take this seriously. For a start, I needed to go down to the ruins and have a good look around. Though if the silverware really was hidden there, that box would only be the start of what I needed to find.

It was too late and too dark to do anything tonight. I finished my wine and went to bed.

I was up at first light, though thankfully that's not brutally early in October. After thinking about what I might need while I drank my tea and ate my toast, I headed for the dairy yard first and got a crowbar from Daniel's workshop. Those medieval buildings had been stripped back to the stonework centuries ago, so anything hidden there was going to take some retrieving.

I walked down through the ornamental gardens that stretch along the valley side. The medieval manor had been built right by the river, to be defended by a loop of moat that could be refreshed from the flowing waters. The plan of the original building had been simple enough. A gatehouse flanked by two towers overlooked the drawbridge on one side of the hollow square. The Great Hall had been built opposite that, and two ranges of buildings had joined them.

Even after the new house had been built, the old manor had been maintained as extra accommodation and servants' quarters. My family had been thankful for that when the English Civil War made having a moat and battlements to hide behind worth putting up with some damp. It wasn't until the early 1800s that the Great Hall's roof had been stripped off and the accommodation ranges were demolished to make a 'romantick ruin', according to my idiot ancestor responsible. Only the gatehouse was left sufficiently intact to be of any use, and when we'd opened up the house for visitors, we'd turned that into a second cafe.

As I approached the moat, a handful of ducks came waddling up to see if I had any food for them. I'd found the tail-end of some very out-of-date porridge oats in the kitchen, so I emptied the packet and left them quacking happily over the treat as I unlocked the small wicket gate in the sturdy iron-studded gatehouse door. Walking through the arched entrance, I went to stand in the middle of the cobbled courtyard and wondered where on earth to start this search.

Then something occurred to me that made me frown. If the mysterious tunnel led all the way down here from the newer house, how did it get under the moat and inside the battlements without getting flooded? I wondered if the exit was somewhere else, perhaps in the rocky hollow left when stone for the new house had been quarried. That would make more sense. I turned around to take a look.

'Good morning.' Asca smiled at me.

The middle of the three dryads I had known growing up, she looked ten or fifteen years younger than my mum. She'd looked the same for as long as I'd known her, and she'd looked the same when my six-or-so-greats-grandfather had fallen in love with her and filled sketchbooks with her portraits. According to Dan, she must have loved him as well, to bear him a son to continue the Beauchene male bloodline when his sickly wife died not long after her sixth and still-born daughter. As far as I'm concerned, the jury's still out on that. I know what the dryads are capable of when they're determined to safeguard their trees.

350

Unlike her mother, Asca appeared dressed much the same as me, in jeans and a Blithehurst staff fleece. If anyone did wander down here from the garden centre, they wouldn't give her a second glance. Not unless they had greenwood blood themselves. Then they'd see her eyes were solid leaf green, where her mother's are autumnal copper.

She looked around. 'What are you doing in here?' She raised her eyebrows as she pointed at the crowbar in my hand. 'What are you going to do with that?'

In for a penny, in for a pound. I told her about the ghost, and the possibility of a stash of silver hidden somewhere in these ruins. I told her why we needed the money. I had the rare satisfaction of seeing her utterly astonished. Unfortunately, that was all I got from her. Asca knew absolutely nothing about any secret tunnel, or the trials and tribulations of sixteenth-century recusants.

I sighed. 'Then I need to get on. If I can find the box—' I waved helplessly with the crowbar '—that silver could solve a whole lot of problems.'

'Quite so.' Asca disappeared.

And thank you for nothing, I didn't say out loud. I headed for the remains of the Great Hall instead. I didn't bother unlocking the undercroft door. We'd had metal detectorists searching the earthen floor down there a year or so ago. They thought they were looking for historical trinkets, and happily for all concerned, buckles and buttons and spoons and the like were all that they had found. Dan and I had been very relieved, even though we'd been ninety-nine per cent sure there wouldn't be any more nasty surprises buried there.

I climbed the steps up to the Great Hall's floor level and decided to approach this methodically. Any hidey-hole would have to be within easy reach, so I only needed to check the lower courses of stonework. I couldn't imagine a loose flagstone over a hollow would be where anyone might step on it, so I only needed to check the floor right by the wall. I gave the stone that was closest at hand an experimental tap with the end of the crowbar. That sounded solid enough to me. I moved on and tried again. Then I tapped the flagstones at the base of the wall.

By the time I had made a complete and careful circuit of the entire hall, I had come to a couple of conclusions. For a start, if there really are people outside the movies who can tell if a stone hides a hollow by tapping it, I definitely wasn't one of them. That meant I was wasting my time, whether the silver was hidden in here or in some other room. I was never going to find it this way.

I sat on the low remnants of the inner wall and pondered other options. Would Dan have a better ear for the different notes that the crowbar could strike from the stones? I wasn't convinced. He's a carpenter, not a stone mason. I supposed I could ask him, but I'd left my phone up in the house, so that would have to wait.

Perhaps Kalei, the naiad, would know something about the tunnel. She had taken Dan through hidden underground passageways in the Peak District, after all. Perhaps, but she turned up here as and when it suited her, and there was no telling when we might see her next.

I looked around the hall again and wondered what new archaeological equipment there might be that could find hidden hollows in walls. Perhaps I could find out and offer some keen department head a chance for a test run. Then there would be witnesses to me finding the silver, at least. That could be very useful. But how would I explain my reasons for thinking there might be something there? What would be more believable? A ghost told me or I saw it in a dream?

I decided I had better go back to the house and try to get the ghost's attention again. If I explained the problem, perhaps he could come down here and show me where to look. As long as he was able to leave the house. I realised I knew next to nothing about ghosts. How far would stories be an accurate guide?

I was heading across the cobbled courtyard when I saw the shadows in the gatehouse archway thicken and darken. I stopped walking. The shadows got blacker, and a nightmare shape emerged. Imagine the Hound of the Baskervilles having an aggressively bad day, and twice as big as the biggest dog you've ever seen. It stalked towards me, growling, with its head held low and the hackles on its massive neck bristling. Its eyes glowed red, even in the daylight, and eerie phosphorescence dripped from its jaws to vanish in mid-air.

Hell hounds, devil dogs, black shucks; there are a lot of names for huge spectral canids in folklore, and I'd assumed they were probably real. Since there had never been one seen at Blithehurst, I hadn't thought much more about them. Then this one had turned up not long after Dan first arrived. We weren't sure if it had followed him here or whether his presence had somehow roused it. Whatever the case, it clearly preferred his company, so I did my best to stay out of its way.

Then I saw Asca walking behind the beast, and I breathed a little easier.

'I don't think he likes the crowbar,' she called out. 'Can you put it down?'

I compromised by holding the tool behind my back. 'I don't want to leave it somewhere by mistake. It belongs to Daniel.' That and holding on to the solid metal was helping convince my subconscious not to run away as fast as my feet could carry me, even if that meant swimming the moat.

At least the shuck stopped growling when Asca caught up with it.

'You're going to need some help.' From her nod she clearly meant the beast. Thankfully, she explained. 'He is of the shadows. He will sense the fear and distress that will surely be bound up with the box that you seek.'

If she said so. I wasn't about to argue. It wasn't as if I had any better ideas. 'Thank you.'

I waited for Asca to tell me what she wanted in return for this massive favour. Dryads never do anything for nothing. Instead, she just snapped her fingers. As the shuck looked around, she waved her hand, and the creature went bounding past me. I turned to see it take the steps to the Great Hall in a few loping strides. It began to quarter the room in search of a scent.

It didn't find anything of interest, so it moved on to search the demolished ranges on either side. It didn't find anything there either. I wondered if some psychic residue of ancient fears could really linger this long. I was starting to doubt it. I didn't say anything though. There's never anything to be gained by antagonising a dryad.

The shuck headed for the gatehouse. I expected it to baulk at the narrow, iron-studded doorway, but it wasn't trying to leave. It stopped by the substantial kennel that had been standing just inside the courtyard for as long as I could remember. We have ancient black-and-white photographs of a rather blurred dog sitting in it, from Victorian days when the estate's head gardener and his family had made their home in the gatehouse.

Dan had said it was made of oak, and as that had weathered, the timber had become harder and harder. He reckoned the kennel could easily be a couple of centuries old. Regardless, it was certainly robust, and large enough to offer roomy accommodation for a sizeable dog. These days, small children found it irresistible, and there must be hundreds of three-year-olds who'd been photographed crouching in the doorway.

The shuck butted the steel-grey wood so hard the whole thing shifted on its plinth. That neat rectangle of stonework raised the kennel a foot or so above the courtyard. I'd never thought anything of that. It simply seemed sensible to lift the watchdog's retreat out of the way of anyone sweeping up muck left by horses or sloshing water across the cobbles. Now, though, I was seeing something very different. Even if someone was prepared to risk searching a big, unfriendly dog's kennel, who on earth would think of looking underneath?

The shuck pawed at the stones, then threw back its head and howled. The deafening noise was so bone-chilling that I clapped my hands over my ears. My keys and the crowbar both hit the cobbles with a crash. The shuck spun around to stare at me with a head-splitting snarl. For a heart-stopping moment, I thought it was going to spring.

'No!' Asca clapped her hands, and the shuck disappeared, leaving only a faint, dank smell like the bottom of a scuttle that's been emptied of wet coal.

I waited a moment for my heart to stop racing, then bent down to retrieve what I'd just dropped. 'Can you—?'

But Asca was gone as well. I was alone with the kennel knocked askew on its plinth, where the last luminous traces of the shuck's drool were slowly fading on stones that hadn't seen the light of day for generations. I went over and got down on my hands and knees to study the exposed masonry as closely as I could. I found a slightly wider gap where one side of one stone had an uneven edge. I would never have seen it if I hadn't been looking. Even so, I could easily have convinced myself that shaping this block had been some Friday afternoon work by an inexperienced stone mason's apprentice, used where it wasn't going to be seen.

But the shuck reckoned there was something there. Of course, the beast hadn't moved the kennel nearly far enough to uncover all of this particular stone. That would have been too easy. I was going to have to manhandle the kennel out of the way on my own.

Or I could wait for Dan to get back. I discarded that thought in the next breath. There was no knowing how long he would be in Wiltshire, and I didn't fancy nightly ghostly visitations in the meantime. Oh, who was I kidding? I was far too curious to wait.

Even so, I nearly changed my mind several times as I heaved and shoved and moved the kennel, which was far heavier than I expected. My heart was in my mouth when I finally got it teetering on the edge of the stonework, and then I had to lower the door end down onto the cobbles as carefully as I could. The last thing I wanted was some weakness in the wood to crack or splinter under this stress. I'd have some very awkward questions to answer if that happened.

Breathing heavily and sweating despite the cold day, I got it done. I satisfied myself that the kennel was resting solidly on the cobbles and wasn't about to slip. I reached for the crowbar. Easing the pointed end into the crack was unexpectedly easy. I pushed cautiously and wondered if something had moved, or if that was my imagination. I pushed again, and this time I heard a faint grating sound.

Levering the stone up wasn't easy. Working out how to lift it out and lay it safely down again took me several attempts. I was terrified of dropping the heavy slab and seeing it break. I still had no idea how I was going to explain finding the silver, but I wanted to keep my options open, and any signs of damage would make that difficult. Eventually, I fetched several packets of paper napkins from the cafe kitchen, to cushion the stone as I lowered it down.

All that effort was worth it. The maidservant and whoever had helped her, because she certainly hadn't done this on her own, had stowed the box here with what I guessed had once been handfuls of straw but were now little more than dust. The wood was a little discoloured, but a master mason had made this hiding place, fitting the stones together so tightly that the hollow was proof against vermin or damp.

I lifted the box out and found it wasn't locked, just secured with a hook to catch on a metal stud. I opened the lid and carefully unfolded the creased, embroidered velvet. That would be valuable in its own right, at least as far as textile historians were concerned.

The silver was tarnished, but the ornate altar cross that I uncovered was still strikingly beautiful. Feeling the other shapes through the cloth, I was pretty sure everything else I'd seen was in there as well. I didn't take anything out, tucking the dark blue cloth back down instead. I closed the lid again and put the box back. The treasure had been safe here for centuries, so I reckoned it could stay hidden for a bit longer.

I replaced the flagstone that covered the hollow with agonising care. When that was done, I was surprised and relieved to see how little sign there was to show that it had been lifted.

That was the easy bit. Lifting the kennel back up and shoving it into place was nearly as much hard work as moving it out of the way had been in the first place. Eventually, I got it done. Then I fetched the stiff broom from the kitchen cupboard and went over the marks I could see on the plinth a couple of times. After a shower or two of rain, I hoped there'd be no trace at all.

So far, so good. If only the other problems that lay ahead of me could be solved so easily. I recalled another old saying. Be careful what you wish for: you may just get it.

Back up at the house, I made myself some coffee, and seeing the time, I ate a sandwich as well. I hoped some food and caffeine might give my brain a nudge towards the answers I needed now.

This silver had to have a solid provenance before any reputable auction house would touch it. Obviously, the altar set wasn't going to turn up on any police database of stolen antiquities, but I still had to prove it belonged to my family. Then I had to come up with a convincing story to explain how the box had only just come to light, right at the time when Blithehurst needed a massive injection of cash. A story to convince the authorities that successive generations of Beauchenes hadn't squirrelled this treasure away to avoid paying death duties on something clearly so valuable.

I decided that whatever the legal situation might be, that could be Sophie's headache. There would almost certainly be taxes to pay, because there always are, but that would be the case if we sold my home in Durham, so that wasn't worth worrying about either. The trust's accountants could deal with the sums.

Though none of them would be troubled by any of that if I couldn't find some documentation to show that the silver was really ours. I headed for the attics, where we keep the family archives and other stuff that's not suitable for putting on display but is too good to join the junk in the cellars. And by attics, I mean the topmost floor right under the roof, with a proper stair and floorboards as well as decent lights. That's another advantage of living in a big old house.

One way and another, I've spent a lot of time up there, sorting out the family papers. I'd been determined to make some use of my historian skills while I tried to work out a way of getting out from under the dryads' control. That meant I could go straight to the old-fashioned deed boxes that held the Elizabethan-era paperwork. There are only a couple of boxes though, and as I dragged them under the lightbulb and started sorting through the ledgers and letters, I found I was remembering right. Pretty much everything in there was household accounts, along with some correspondence over boundaries or rights of way, and notes swapping mundane gossip with relatives.

I went through everything twice, checking every line. I wasn't expecting helpful receipts from ecclesiastical silversmiths, or detailed descriptions of the altar set in copies of household inventories, which would of course have been evidence the authorities could use to convict my ancestors of treasonous Catholicism, but I really hoped I'd find something. Finally, though, I was forced to admit defeat.

What now? I racked my brains as I put the papers back in order in the boxes. As I put the boxes back on their shelves, I caught a flicker of movement in the corner my eye. I stopped dead, my heart pounding. Had I forgotten to lock the side door? I certainly hadn't set the alarm.

I turned, ready to use the deed box as a weapon if I had to. Then I realised the shadowy figure wasn't the world's worst-timed burglar. The ghost who had led me to the treasure in the first place was standing by the storage rack that held pictures not wanted downstairs. He gestured at the painting at the front.

After a moment's thought, I recognised one of Francis Beauchene's sisters, or strictly speaking, one of his half-sisters, since Francis had been Asca's son. Since we have more family portraits than we can comfortably hang in the long gallery, Grandad picked the best and the most interesting for tour guides to talk about for the permanent display. Dingy depictions of maiden aunts by indifferent artists had been permanently exiled up here.

I looked at the ghost, puzzled. 'She was long after your day, surely?'

He looked at me, frowning, exasperated. He gestured at the collection of portraits again.

'Okay.'

I went over to the rack and began looking through the pictures of more maiden aunts. What did that remind me of? I was on the edge of remembering something important, but I couldn't quite...

Elizabeth Beauchene stared back at me. She'd been a maiden aunt by vocation rather than because she'd been left on the shelf. The Beauchenes had carried on being defiantly Catholic for centuries after the Reformation, and Blithehurst has the priest hole and secret chapel to prove it. She didn't look much fun, but I don't suppose there had been many laughs in going to France to be a nun after Charles I had been executed. I looked at her unsmiling face, framed by a white wimple. It was hard to tell where her black habit ended and the background began. The picture really did need cleaning.

I suddenly realised I'd been a complete fool. I looked at the ghost, who was standing a few paces away. 'There's no way the silver has been in that hiding place ever since the raid you showed me. The cross and the chalice and everything else needed for Mass would have been brought back to the house once the immediate danger had passed.'

The ghost nodded vigorously and gestured towards Elizabeth's portrait.

'Did she have something to do with hiding the silver?'

He shook his head.

'Then what are you trying to tell me?'

He pointed at the portrait again.

'I'm sorry, I don't understand.'

This was like the world's most exasperating game of Charades. Though I don't suppose that would have been much of a hit in Tudor times, when only the rich had leisure for reading. For everyone else, the game would have been short and repetitive. It's a book? The Bible? Correct!

I shoved that thought aside and stared unseeing into the attic's shadows, trying to work out how to solve this puzzle. A few moments later, I looked back at the ghost.

'I need to know when the box was finally hidden. There must be some reason why it was forgotten.'

He nodded vigorously. So we were getting somewhere, and I realised this must have happened amid enough turmoil to leave whatever lingering traces had drawn the shuck to the hidey-hole. I looked at the portrait of the humourless nun and painstakingly recalled some more family history. I glanced at the ghost again.

'Elizabeth wasn't the last Beauchene daughter to head for France and the religious life. Does this have anything to do with Anne?'

The ghost nodded again, and this time he smiled. So I was getting warmer. Then the ghost stepped forward and reached for my hand. As his fingers touched mine, I gasped. I felt so cold I could barely catch my breath.

'For pity's sake, Robert, let me fetch the priest!'

For a moment of utter confusion, I thought someone was talking to my dead brother. Then I realised I was standing in the corner of the King Charles bedroom on the floor below. At least, that's what the guidebook calls it for the tourists these days. When I was a kid, it was just Granny and Grandpa's suite. Don't ask me how we had got down there from the attic.

I wasn't alone, and I don't only mean that the ghost was with me. He was still holding my hand, and as I looked down, I saw that my arm was as insubstantial and transparent as his own. The people gathered here, however, looked as solid as the house itself. There were three men, one standing on each

361

side of the canopied bed and the third at the foot. A woman in a black dress knelt with her back to me. Her clasped hands rested on the edge of the counterpane and her head was bowed. The room was lit with a few candlesticks, and I thought I could smell a faint trace of lavender.

An elderly man lay in the bed, unmoving and with his eyes closed. His mouth was open just a little, and I thought I heard him give a faint moan.

'Didn't you hear that?' the man at the foot of the bed cried out. 'He wants a priest!'

'He's beyond such concerns,' the man on the far side said stubbornly. 'If we send for anyone, we send for the vicar.'

The young woman raised her head. 'May God forgive you, Robert. I can only pray that I might one day do the same.' Her voice was shaking with anger.

Okay, I could put these clues together. At least Elizabeth had taken the veil with her family's blessing. A century or so later, Anne Beauchene had been disowned when she found the Protestant rule of George II more than her pious sensibilities could bear.

'I will not have my loyalties to the Crown questioned,' Robert said vehemently. 'I will not have my sons' prospects blighted. As for your prayers—'

He took a pace backwards with a startled expression. Since she had her back to me, I couldn't see the look Anne had given him, but it must have been pretty deadly. He rallied swiftly all the same.

'If you are determined to go to France,' he said spitefully, 'you will go with only the clothes on your back and a single change of linen. If you are determined to live a life of poverty, that can start as soon as you set foot outside my gates.'

'Robert.' The man who hadn't yet spoken, the one standing closest to us, reproached him. 'You heard our father, not two days ago, give Anne his blessing, when she told him she wishes to dedicate her life to Christ. Will you ignore his dying wish?' he asked with disbelief.

Robert had the grace to look embarrassed. Once again, that didn't last long. He avoided his brother's eye, looking at his sister. 'If you are still set on this foolishness, once your mourning for our father is over, you may have sufficient money to cover your travel on the common stage coach and by the cheapest possible sea crossing. You will not see another penny piece from me,' he added savagely.

Anne ignored him. She produced a rosary from somewhere and began saying her prayers. The man at the foot of the bed looked at Robert with undisguised contempt. Then he turned and strode from the room. After a moment, the man closest to us hurried after him. I recalled this had been an era when the Beauchenes had successfully raised too many sons instead of too few. If the pigheaded one was Robert, I guessed the man at the foot of the bed was the youngest brother, John. That meant the poor devil trying to keep the peace was one of the middle sons.

Before I could remember their names, the ghost tugged at my hand, and I found myself following the two brothers without any apparent choice in the matter. I also realised my fingers were aching as badly as if I'd slammed them in a door. Overall, I was chilled to the bone.

We followed the two of them down the stairs into the Great Hall. By the time his brother caught up with him, John already had the secret door in the panelling by the fireplace open. We – by which I mean me, the ghost and his exasperated brother – followed him up the cramped stair to the hidden chapel. The tiny room looked much the same as it did in the present day, barely large enough for half a dozen people to kneel beneath the curved wooden ceiling painted with roses and lilies.

'Don't try to stop me, Dickon,' John warned. 'I leave tonight. The prince's army has nearly reached Derby. I will join the fight to see England's rightful Catholic king restored, and Robert can beg my forgiveness on bended knee when he needs someone to speak on his behalf, when he's called to account for his treason!'

'You think the prince will welcome a thief into his service?' Dickon – the nickname told me he must be Richard Beauchene, the second-oldest – leaned against the closed door to stop his brother leaving.

John was kneeling in front of the tiny, ornately carved altar. He had thrown back the cloth embroidered with the Lamb of God and pulled out a familiar-looking wooden box. He looked up, shocked. 'You think – you think—?'

He opened the lid to reveal the priceless altar silver and ran a finger over the crucifix. 'You think that Robert will honour our father's bequest?' His earlier anger had faded as fast as it had flared up. Now he simply sounded sad. 'You heard what he said. He will never allow Anne to take this to the convent as her dowry, no matter what our father wished. That's why he promised this treasure to her. He knows Robert will sell it to pay for his political ambitions or to see his sons mix in the most extravagant circles at Oxford.'

Richard didn't move. 'You will see our family heirlooms sold to fund the Jacobite cause instead?'

John shook his head, closing the box. 'No, but I will not let Robert seize these holy things along with everything else in this house. When I return, I will take Anne to France myself, and her dowry will go with us. In the meantime, I will put this somewhere safe, in a place where Robert won't find it.'

'Where?' Richard demanded.

John looked up at him. 'Do you really want to know? Or would you prefer to swear to Robert that you have no idea what I have done, without a shadow on your conscience?'

They stared at each other. Richard was the first to look away. He stepped away from the door as John got to his feet and picked up the box.

In the next breath, the ghost and I were back in the attic under the unshaded lightbulb. I snatched my hand out of his grasp and shook it hard, to try and get some feeling back into my fingers. My nails looked positively blue in the electric light. I tried to speak, but I was shivering too violently. I dragged a deep breath into my lungs and waited for the worst to subside.

At least my wits weren't frozen. I could recall the rest of this particular family story. A lot of people forget that Bonnie Prince Charlie's army advanced as far south into England as Derby. That's where John had enlisted, only to see the 1745 rising falter. Family legend said he had been killed at Culloden, though there was no official record of his death. So he had never come home to take Anne to her convent with her precious dowry.

'Thank you,' I said to the ghost when I felt reasonably sure my chattering teeth weren't going to bite my tongue.

The ghost smiled and offered me a courtly bow, incongruous in his craftsman's clothes.

So far, so good, but I still needed proof of what I'd just seen. I headed for the shelves where that generation's correspondence, diaries, commonplace books and ledgers were stored. The ghost came with me, looking expectant.

The good news was that far more family papers had survived from the eighteenth century. The bad news was that far more family papers had survived from the eighteenth century. It took me quite literally hours to find what I was looking for. More than once, I was on the verge of giving up, half convincing myself that I must be imagining what I thought I remembered seeing here before.

Finally, I found the diary entries and letters that I had once read with no idea of their significance. The ghost was still by my side, still keenly interested. Well, I don't suppose he knew what had happened, if he was tied to the house. If that much is true about ghosts.

I explained as I leafed through the letters to find the one that I wanted. 'When John ran off to join the Jacobites, Robert accused him of stealing "sundry silver heirlooms of our house", to sell to finance the revolt. He threatened to send thief-takers after him, brother or not.'

I found Richard's reply. 'Dickon persuaded Robert to let him go and negotiate with John. He finally caught up with him somewhere near Glasgow.'

Richard's exhaustion and exasperation with both his brothers was vivid in his letters. He couldn't talk John out of his folly, and he had absolutely no sympathy with the Jacobite cause. On the other hand, he wasn't going to let Robert condemn their brother as a thief. I read a bit of his last letter out loud.

'I believe John when he insists that he has taken nothing from Blithehurst. Our brother may be misguided, but you cannot deny he is devout. He swears his innocence with his hand on the Bible our father gave him. Though I do not expect you to take our brother's word. Accordingly, I have made enquiries among the silversmiths in the towns wherever the Jacobite army has halted. I have found no evidence whatsoever that John has sold the articles he has supposedly stolen. The candlesticks might have gone unremarked, but the rest would not be so easily bought and sold without someone taking note.'

I shuffled the pages to find Robert's reply, blotted with fury. 'Robert said that silver can be melted down to be bought and sold with no one the wiser about its origins. I guess Richard must have passed that on, because John's last letter vehemently denies doing any such thing.'

I read a few lines aloud to the ghost.

'I would never so callously deprive Anne of her dowry. This is a vile accusation, and all the more repugnant when Robert himself intends to deprive our saintly sister of the inheritance which our father of blessed memory promised her on his deathbed. Tell her I will resolve this matter on my return home. Tell Robert to consider the fate of his immortal soul, since he has decreed the holy Mass will no longer be celebrated at Blithehurst.'

I put the letters together and made sure I would know where to find them again when I needed them to make a plausible argument to explain the mysterious origin of the box. I turned to the ghost.

'I wonder how hard Richard tried to find where John had hidden the silver, when he finally gave up hope of seeing him again. And why was John the only one who knew about the hidey-hole down in the old manor's courtyard?'

The ghost reached for my hand. I recoiled before I could stop myself. 'No! Sorry—'

But the ghost was gone. I felt oddly bereft. Then I yawned so hard my jaw clicked. It was well after midnight by now. I decided to go to bed. There were still plenty of questions that needed answers, and there might be hints in some of these other letters, but that would have to wait. I went downstairs to the family bathroom to wash my very dusty hands. Then I headed for my bedroom.

As I undressed and cleaned my teeth in my en-suite, I couldn't help wondering what else the ghost might have wanted to show me. There can't be a historian alive who hasn't daydreamed about what they might learn through time travel or some other kind of window into the past. I didn't think they'd be quite so keen if the price of seeing more than fleeting shadows and hearing what they said was losing a few fingers to frostbite. Even hours later, I could still feel the lingering ache in my hand. On balance, I didn't regret declining the ghost's offer, though hoped I hadn't hurt his feelings. Do ghosts have feelings?

As my head hit my pillow, I wondered if I would ever find out the ghost's name. Could he have been another dryad's son? If he had built the priest hole and the secret chapel, he had clearly been a skilled woodworker. There must be some reason why he had stirred himself after all these centuries, especially now when Blithehurst's future was threatened.

I would have to find a way to ask Asca and Frai when I talked to them tomorrow to see if they had found out anything that could help Dan with the challenge he was facing in Wiltshire.

JULIET E. MCKENNA

Acknowledgements

In normal times, I would be listing the interesting places and local museums I visited as I researched the background for this story. Since these are far from normal times, other than visiting Uffington, I've had to do most of my research from my desk. My sincere thanks go to the local history and folklore enthusiasts whose websites and podcasts have been invaluable. I'm also indebted to the ramblers and walkers whose online photos offered further inspiration. My mum and Hampshire resident, Susan told me about eel houses, and the threats to the chalk streams of southern England.

Books that supplied more of the threads woven into this particular yarn include 'Wiltshire Folk Tales' by Kirsty Hartsiotis, 'Wiltshire Folklore and Legends' by Ralph Whitlock, 'White Horses of Wiltshire and Uffington' by Esther Smith, 'Trees in Anglo-Saxon England' by Della Hooke, and 'Lost Gods of Albion' by Paul Newman.

Once again, I am profoundly grateful for the technical and production support I have had from the established team. Cheryl Morgan of Wizard's Tower Press sets a high bar for other publishers to equal. Toby Selwyn holds himself to the highest standards as an editor, which means I can do no less as a writer. Ben Baldwin continues to create stunning artwork to delight us all.

Finally, I would like to thank the readers of this ongoing series. Your enthusiasm continues to spread far and wide. This creates the eagerness for more stories that keeps me writing in times of unprecedented challenges for authors. I am also grateful for your companionship online through these strange and stressful months. Here's looking forward to better days for us all.

About the Author

Juliet E McKenna is a British fantasy author living in the Cotswolds, UK. Loving history, myth and other worlds since she first learned to read, she has written fifteen epic fantasy novels so far. Her debut, *The Thief's Gamble*, began The Tales of Einarinn in 1999, followed by The Aldabreshin Compass sequence, The Chronicles of the Lescari Revolution, and The Hadrumal Crisis trilogy. *The Green Man's Heir* was her first modern fantasy inspired by British folklore, followed by *The Green Man's Foe* and *The Green Man's Silence*. She also writes diverse shorter stories that include forays into dark fantasy, steampunk and science fiction. She promotes SF&Fantasy by reviewing, by blogging on book trade issues, attending conventions and teaching creative writing. She has also written historical murder mysteries set in ancient Greece as J M Alvey.

www.julietemckenna.com

@JulietEMcKenna

The Tales of Einarinn

1. The Thief's Gamble (1999)
2. The Swordsman's Oath (1999)
3. The Gambler's Fortune (2000)
4. The Warrior's Bond (2001)
5. The Assassin's Edge (2002)

JULIET E. MCKENNA

The Aldabreshin Compass

> 1. The Southern Fire (2003)
> 2. Northern Storm (2004)
> 3. Western Shore (2005)
> 4. Eastern Tide (2006)

Turns & Chances (2004)

The Chronicles of the Lescari Revolution

> 1. Irons in the Fire (2009)
> 2. Blood in the Water (2010)
> 3. Banners in The Wind (2010)

The Wizard's Coming (2011)

The Hadrumal Crisis

> 1. Dangerous Waters (2011)
> 2. Darkening Skies (2012)
> 3. Defiant Peaks (2012)

A Few Further Tales of Einarinn (2012) (ebook from Wizards Tower Press)

Challoner, Murray & Balfour: Monster Hunters at Law (2014) (ebook from Wizards Tower Press)

Shadow Histories of the River Kingdom (2016) (Wizards Tower Press)

The Green Man (Wizards Tower Press)

1. The Green Mans Heir (2018)
2. The Green Man's Foe (2019)
3. The Green Man's Silence (2020)

The Philocles series (as J M Alvey)

1. Shadows of Athens (2019)
2. Scorpions in Corinth (2019)
3. Justice for Athena (2020)